The Stolen Voice

Also by Pat McIntosh

The Stolen Voice

A Gil Cunningham Murder Mystery

Pat McIntosh

Constable • London

Constable & Robinson Ltd
3 The Lanchesters
162 Fulham Palace Road
London W6 9ER
www.constablerobinson.com

First published in the UK by Constable,
an imprint of Constable & Robinson Ltd, 2009

This paperback edition published by Robinson,
an imprint of Constable & Robinson Ltd, 2010

First US edition published by Soho Constable,
an imprint of Soho Press Inc., 2009.

This paperback edition published by Soho Constable,
an imprint of Soho Press Ltd, 2010

Soho Press, Inc. 853 Broadway
New York, NY 10003
www.sohopress.com

A copy of the British Library Cataloguing in Publication
Data is available from the British Library

UK ISBN: 978-1-8490-1313-0
US ISBN: 978-1-5694-7651-2

US Library of Congress number: 2009005431

Printed and bound in the EU

1 3 5 7 9 10 8 6 4 2

May the blessing of Angus, of Mary mild and Michael
be upon all who read this book

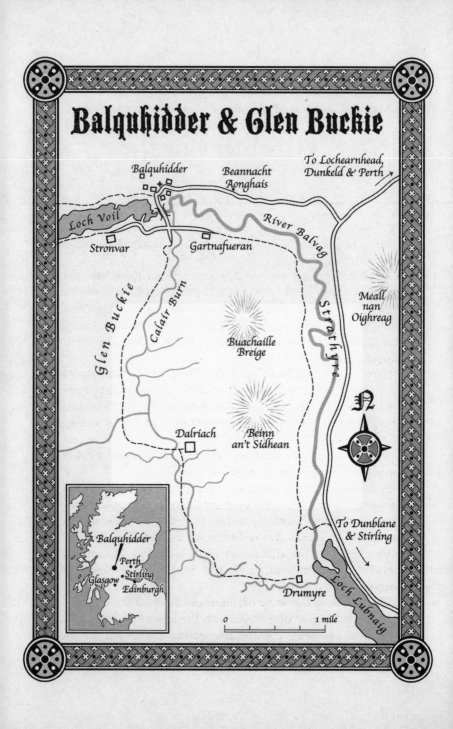

Chapter One

'And you are telling me,' said Gil Cunningham, 'that this David Drummond vanished away forty year since, and is now returned seemingly not a day older?'

'That's about the sum of it,' agreed Sir William Stewart. He cut a substantial portion off the haunch of venison on the platter before him, looked round the supper table, and conveyed the slice to his own pewter trencher. Satisfied that all four present were served, he addressed himself to his supper.

'Not quite,' qualified his lady. She accepted the sauce dish from Gil's wife Alys and went on, 'It was thirty year, for one thing, not forty, and for another I'd aye heard he was eleven or twelve when he vanished, and he's at least sixteen now by the look of him.'

'It still seems very strange,' said Alys, 'but this is a country where strange things happen, I think.'

She turned to the window, and Sir William's steward, bare-legged and bearded and swathed in a vast checked plaid, looked enquiringly at her from where he stood by the sideboard. She shook her head and smiled, looking beyond him at the distant view of loch and mountains, woods and farmland, and the long narrow glen of Balquhidder.

They were in the solar on an upper floor of the impressive fortified house of Stronvar, on the shores of Loch Voil. It was a pleasant, comfortable room, furnished in the modern style with light linen hangings and pale carved oak, the open windows bringing in evening air and late

1

sunshine. A pot of herbs smouldered on the sill. Beside Gil's feet, Socrates the wolfhound sprawled full length, snoring faintly.

'It's more than strange,' said Gil, 'it's unbelievable. What do you think, sir?'

'I don't credit it either,' Sir William assured him, and bit a lump off the piece of meat impaled on his knife. Bailie of Balquhidder and second cousin to the young King James, he was a stout, long-nosed man, with the dark red Stewart hair now turning grey and thinning somewhat, and even here in this remote place he was clad in taffeta and velvet to receive guests. His big-boned Campbell wife was equally finely dressed; Gil found himself comparing her unfavourably with his own slender, elegant Alys, glowing opposite him in dark blue silk faced with apricot, her rope of pearls pinned to the bodice with the sapphire jewel he had given her on her birthday, her honey-coloured hair hidden under black velvet. He and Alys had arrived at Stronvar that afternoon, after two days' journey from Glasgow, and had been made lavishly welcome, but he was still not completely certain why they were here.

He ate for a while in silence, while Sir William expounded on the other unlikely things which were claimed for the neighbourhood, until Marion Campbell, Lady Stewart said, 'Aye, very true, Will, but the lad is there at Dalriach, there's no getting round it.'

'You have seen him, then, madam?' said Alys.

'I have,' agreed their hostess. 'They hold the tack direct from us, so I rode up the glen to Dalriach a month ago as soon as the word reached me, to congratulate Mistress Drummond.' Gil appreciated this turn of phrase. 'The lad is certainly a Drummond, you've only to look at him, and the old woman claims she knew him for her son as soon as he came over the hill.'

'It sounds like one of my nurse's tales,' said Gil. 'How old is Mistress Drummond? Is her eyesight that good?'

'Oh, a good age. Near seventy, I'd think. Caterin Campbell, poor woman, that's wedded to her son Patrick,

2

tells me she has eyes like a hawk at a distance, can tell you how many stooks of barley are on the top rig, but can scarce see to eat her dinner.' Lady Stewart mopped green sauce with a piece of wheaten bannock. 'So young Davie is welcomed home and established in the midst of the township, and if you set him in a row with the other youngsters – they'll be his nephew and nieces, I suppose – there's not a hair of difference between them all, except the changeling.'

Changeling? thought Gil. What does she mean?

'What about the rest of the family?' Alys asked. 'Patrick must be his brother. What do he and his wife think? Are they pleased to see him returned?'

Gil shot her a quick look, but her face was as innocent as her voice. Lady Stewart shook her head.

'No knowing,' she said. 'They would never say to me, of course, if the old woman went against them.'

'And does he himself claim to be David Drummond?' Gil asked, staying with the point. 'Where has he been these thirty years, if so?'

'I got no word wi him on his own. Aye, take it, Murdo, it will do another meal.' Lady Stewart leaned back to allow her steward to lift away the platter of meat. 'He said almost nothing in front of the old lady, I would say out of shyness rather than anything else, and she gave me a great rigmarole about the *sidhean* on their land, and how the ones who dwell there were envious of the boy's voice. He was a singer at the Cathedral down in Dunblane when he vanished, you ken.'

'Sheean?' Gil picked out the unfamiliar word.

'*Sidhean*,' she repeated. 'It's an Ersche word. It means a hill where the Good Neighbours dwell. The Fair Folk – the People of Peace,' she amplified. 'The one on Dalriach land, away at the head of Glen Buckie, is a great fearsome stony mound wi tall pine trees growing over it.' Gil recalled more of his nurse's tales, and nodded, getting a glimpse as he did so of the steward Murdo crossing himself and mouthing something.

3

'So we're to believe young Drummond has been all this time in this sheean?' he asked.

'So it seems. Murdo? What do they say in the glen?'

'Indeed,' agreed Murdo solemnly. 'That is what they are saying. He has been thirty years under the earth, and the time passing as if it was no more than a day or two.'

'Then how's he got six years older, then, Murdo?' demanded his master. 'Tell me that?'

'I would not be knowing,' said Murdo, offended. 'I have not the learning Sir William has.'

'When did he vanish?' Gil asked. 'How long ago was it?'

'It would be the year of the long drought,' supplied Murdo, 'just before St Angus' fair.'

'Long afore my time. Sixty-three, according to old Sir Duncan,' said Sir William. Gil raised his eyebrows, and the other man gestured at the window with his knife. 'Priest yonder in the Kirkton. He's been priest here man and boy since James Fiery-Face's day and longer. They say he recalls the eclipse in thirty-three, though I'm no certain he was here then.'

'Poor old soul,' said Lady Stewart thoughtfully. 'Robert gives me a sad report of him.'

'Aye, well,' said her lord. 'He may not be able to tell his hat from a jordan but he minds the history of the place like no other.'

'He's getting childish,' Lady Stewart explained to Alys. 'His clerk's near as old as he is, but we've got a laddie to look after him, this past year. It's made quite a difference.' She wrinkled her nose. 'The kirk smells better, for one thing. But the old man is sinking now, just this last week or two. He may not have much longer, so Robert says.'

Alys tut-tutted in sympathy, and Gil said, pursuing his own train of thought:

'So the boy's been gone thirty years, as you said, madam. How did he disappear?'

'Set out from the house after a few days' leave of absence,' offered Sir William, 'to walk back to Dunblane, and never was seen again.'

4

'It's a long walk for a boy that age,' observed Gil. 'Was he alone? Was it winter?'

'No, no, St Angus' fair's in August. Next week, indeed. He was to meet a friend in Strathyre, another singer, but he never came to the tryst.'

'He was sought by all the paths out of Glenbuckie,' said Murdo, setting clean small glasses on the table. 'My own father was among those that would be searching. But by then it was over a month since he had left his home, the time it took to be knowing he was not at Dunblane nor at Dalriach neither. You would be grieved to see how my mother wept when he was not to be found. They were thinking he must have fallen into a drowning pool or the like, for all Euan nan Tobar said he had seen him lifted up and borne off, but now it seems they were wrong and Euan was right.'

'Did you know him, Murdo?' asked Lady Stewart. He straightened up and looked at her, dignified in his velvet doublet and colourful plaid.

'I did. We were playing at the shinty together.'

'Have you spoken to him,' said Gil carefully, 'since he came back?'

'I have,' said Murdo. 'I was getting a word with him only on Sunday there, when all of Dalriach was coming down to the kirk, except for Mistress Campbell who could not be leaving the changeling.' There it is again, thought Gil. Are they serious?

'Did he mind you?' asked Sir William abruptly.

'Oh, he did.' Murdo laid a dish of what looked like cream before his mistress, and a jug by Sir William's hand. 'I had to tell him who I was, but then I was a beardless laddie when he saw me last, Sir William would be thinking, and it was him recalled what we were doing at that time.'

'And what was that?' asked Sir William. Murdo looked sideways at him, and he snorted. 'Some mischief, I suppose. Who else would have known of it?'

'Just the two of us,' averred Murdo. 'And maybe the two MacLarens from Auchtoo,' he added thoughtfully, 'and Angus MacGregor at the Kirkton that were there with us.'

'Small proof in that, then,' said Sir William irritably, 'if half the glen was in it.'

Alys, seeing how Sir William's colour rose, turned to Murdo and said what sounded to Gil like, 'Jay sho, lair toll?' Both Lady Stewart and her servant looked sharply at her.

'*Cranachan*, it is, mistress,' said Murdo, distracted. 'Cream, and burnt oatmeal, and new raspberries that Seonaid gathered this day morn. And there is the good Malvoisie to go with it.'

'Ha ma,' she said, smiling. The hint of an answering smile twitched at his beard and Lady Stewart, lifting the chased silver serving-spoon, said:

'You never said you spoke Gaelic, my dear. As well as French and Scots?'

'Murdo, man,' said Sir William, recovering his countenance, 'see us anither glass. You'd best ha some of this Malvoisie, and tak a seat and tell us what you know of the matter.'

To Gil's amusement, the steward accepted the glass of wine with alacrity, but had to be persuaded to sit down in the presence of his lord. At length, formal and upright on a stool by the sideboard, he sipped the golden wine and reluctantly answered questions.

It began, naturally, with a genealogy. Old Mistress Drummond, 'that is Bessie MacLaren,' amplified Murdo, 'a MacLaren of Auchtoo she is,' and her late husband James Drummond, had had four sons and one daughter who was married to Angus MacLaren and dwelling away along the glen – here Sir William cut off the steward's intention to detail all their offspring – and one son was now working the farm.

'Aye, and a good farmer he is,' confirmed Sir William. 'Mind you, it's sound land up Glenbuckie, but Patrick Drummond makes the most o't, him and his nephew.

They pay a good tack, in cheese and flax and two kids every spring.'

'And the cloth,' said Lady Stewart. 'The daughters-in-law,' she explained. 'Caterin spins and dyes, she has the best dye-pot in Balquhidder, and Mòr weaves. Lovely stuff they turn out, them and their lassies.'

'I thought you said there were four sons,' said Gil. 'This Patrick, and the one that disappeared and has turned up again – what happened to the other two?'

'There was James,' agreed Murdo, counting on his fingers, 'and Patrick, and Andrew, and Davie. James is dead ten year since, and left Patrick with all the work of the farm, seeing the bairns were young, and Andrew is away at Dunblane.'

'Canon in residence,' said Lady Stewart. 'He's sub-Treasurer, doing well.'

Gil glanced at her and nodded.

'What does he make of it?' he asked. 'I'd ha thought a churchman would have strong views on the matter.'

'Och, I could not be saying,' said Murdo.

'Patrick could do with another pair of hands about the farm,' said Sir William, 'and he and Jamie Beag can as well share the tack with one more. But what Andrew makes of it there's no knowing, seeing he's not shown face yet. Carry on, Murdo, man.'

The steward set his empty glass on the sideboard.

'They are saying along the glen that old James Drummond must have offended the Good Neighbours in some way,' he paused to cross himself, muttering something in Ersche, 'for though the farm is doing well the family has no fortune.'

'They've no worse fortune than any other in Balquhidder!' expostulated Sir William. Murdo shook his head.

'Sir William would be knowing better than I,' he said, sounding unconvinced. 'Davie vanished away, and then his father, James Mor Drummond, was dead in a night, in his full strength, after a day at the reaping, and then

Patrick's first son James Breac was taken of a fever. And after that James, that would be Mistress Drummond's eldest son, fell in the stackyard, and was taken up for dead, and buried a week after and left three bairns –'

'I mind that,' said Sir William, 'it was a year or two after we came here. Murdo, you ken as well as I do, in thirty years on a farm, these things happen! No need to talk of offending the – the Good Neighbours. You'd as well say they had a dislike of the name James Drummond!'

'It could be so,' agreed Murdo politely. 'It could be so, indeed, but it would not be the only name they were disliking, for they stole away John the other son of Patrick Drummond and left a changeling.'

'You mentioned that before,' said Gil. 'What makes you say he's a changeling?'

'It's a terrible thing,' said Lady Stewart. 'He's eight, of an age wi my own John. He was the bonniest bairn, bright and forward and talking already at two year old, I mind it well, and then he was changed to this shrivelled creature they have wi them now, willny walk, screaming all the time and eating enough for four.'

Gil thought of the sturdy eight-year-old Stewart who had brought them the welcoming cup of mead, handing the beakers with a solemn greeting in Ersche. It must be painful to compare the two children, particularly for the Drummonds.

'The bairn was sick,' pronounced Sir William. 'They sicken like flies at that age. That's all it was.'

'Caterin his mother,' said Murdo solemnly, 'that is the wife of Patrick Drummond, was leaving him asleep in his cradle, and she was outside, no further than the spinning wheel at the end of the house, working away, when there was a – a whirl of wind, *oiteag sluaigh*, travelling on the tall grass stems, went by the house door. And the bairn burst out in screaming, from his cradle where he was, and would never be stopped since that time.'

'Caterin should have thrown her shoe at them,' said Lady Stewart, and the steward nodded agreement.

'Aye, well,' said Sir William. 'We get a lot of these whirl-winds in the summer,' he informed Gil. 'You'll be out in the open, not a puff of air stirring, and all of a sudden here's this eddy crossing in front of you, lifting the straws and the dust. The Ersche says it's a party o the Good Folk on the way past.'

'Indeed I think there are many of the Good People dwelling in these parts,' said Alys seriously. Gil met her gaze across the table, startled, and she smiled quickly at him.

'Get on wi your tale, Murdo, man,' commanded Sir William.

'There is little more to tell, Sir William kens. Thirty year ago, that was the year of the great drought, like I was say-ing, Davie and Andrew was away singers at Dunblane, for they were singing like linties the both of them. Davie came home to Dalriach at Lammastide, and he went away scarce a week later before St Angus' fair, though his mother wished him to be staying to sing at the great service in the kirk here. He was going away up the glen by the track that goes over into Strathyre, and past the *sidhean*, and was never seen more in this world for thirty years, until a month since he came walking down the glen and his mother spied him coming a great way off and knew him for her son.'

'It's quite a surprise, your wife speaking Ersche,' said Sir William.

'She's a surprising creature,' said Gil. 'A *periwinkle of prowess*.'

'Aye, and a bonnie one.' Sir William, ignoring the quotation, strolled along his gravel path towards the last of the sunshine. Gil followed, Socrates at his knee. 'How long since you were wed? Eight month? Aye, too soon, too soon. I don't wonder you wanted her wi you.'

Gil repressed comment, and looked about him in the evening light. They were in the garden, a hard-won patch of small flower beds defined by low aromatic hedges, with a sturdy fence round it against the goats. Below them lay the house of Stronvar, from where Sir William was expected to keep order and the law of Scotland in a sprawling, unruly stretch of the Highlands. Below it again hills and sky were reflected in Loch Voil as in a mirror, and across the narrow water smoke rose from the group of houses around the little kirk, the great bare rock above them catching fire from the westering sun. Apart from the clouds of biting insects, kept at bay by the herbs burning pungently in a little pot which Lady Stewart had given them, it was very pleasant out here, but Gil thought he could imagine it in winter. He had never expected to feel so much of a foreigner in his own country.

'How much did Robert Blacader tell you?' said Sir William abruptly.

'Very little,' said Gil. There had been one hurried interview with his master when the Archbishop halted in Glasgow two days since, on his way to Dumbarton with the King and half the Council. 'Something about vanishing singers, and now that this one has reappeared his mother wants him back in his place at Dunblane. The Chapter at Dunblane were in disagreement about it, and Bishop Chisholm referred it to the Archbishop. My lord seemed to feel the two matters were connected, and directed me here.'

'Aye,' said Sir William, sitting down on the bench at the top of the little enclosure and placing the smoking pot beside him.

'They've moved gey fast at Dunblane,' Gil commented, and hitched the knee of his best hose to seat himself beside his host. The dog, who had trotted ahead, returned and settled on his feet. 'In general sic a thing would take months to be resolved even that far.'

'Aye, well. It's a Drummond,' said Sir William, as if that explained all.

'Does your steward genuinely believe it's his playmate come back, do you think?'

'Murdo?' Sir William looked about him, as if to make certain they were not overheard. 'No telling, to be truthful. I like these wild Ersche,' he said, in the tone of one admitting to liking squirrels, or hares, or some such unchancy creature, 'but there's no denying they go their own way. If the old woman accepts the laddie, the rest of the Drummonds will, as my lady was saying, and if the Drummonds accept him Balquhidder folk would never tell me if they'd any doubts.'

He was silent for a little, then went on, 'So Blacader never tellt you the full tale?' Gil made a small negative noise. 'Aye, well.' He stared out across the loch, apparently seeking inspiration. 'These singers,' he said at length. 'The great kirks aye hunt about for good singers, you'll ken that, but in general they arrange matters atween themselves, maybe a donation of money or the gift of a benefice in exchange for a good high tenor. Good tenors are like hen's teeth, so they tell me.'

'I've heard that.' Gil rubbed Socrates' ears and grinned, thinking of his friend Habbie Sim's strictures on the high tenors in the choir of Glasgow Cathedral.

'But now there's been three or four songmen left their posts in Perthshire alone in the last year, and no sign of where they've gone to. It's almost as if they're no still in Scotland.'

'No trace of them anywhere?'

'None. Spirited away like the Drummond lad.'

'These are grown men?' said Gil. 'Priested?'

'As it happens, no. In minor orders, naturally, but none of them priests.'

'So none of them has broken any vow of obedience. Where have they vanished from? When? Do you have the details? And are they all tenors, indeed?'

'One Dunkeld man,' said Sir William, 'one from Dunblane, two from Perth.' He paused. 'One less than two weeks since, the two Perth fellows in May, one in March. Not all tenors. I think they're different voices. One was an alto, I recall.'

'This is hardly the best place to start from, if I'm to ask questions in Dunkeld or Perth,' said Gil. 'Hidden away in the mountains like this.'

'It's closer to either than Glasgow is,' said Sir William unanswerably. 'Forbye you'll find George Brown spends the most of his time in Perth. It's safer than Dunkeld.'

'And what else has gone missing?'

The older man turned sharply to look at Gil. After a moment he said, 'Aye, I see why Robert Blacader speaks well of you. That's the nub of the matter,' he acknowledged. 'No so much what's missing as what he took wi him in his head, so to speak. The last one that's vanished, the Dunkeld man, that went in July there just ten days since, is no singer. He's secretary to Georgie Brown.'

'The Bishop of Dunkeld.' Gil stared into the gathering evening. The fire had fallen away from the rock above the little church, and the sky was darkening above it. 'Who assisted William Elphinstone when he received the ambassadors from England in June.'

'Aye,' agreed Sir William.

'But why should that be a problem?' asked Alys. 'The truce was signed six weeks since. Surely the terms are common knowledge across Europe by now.'

'I assume,' said Gil cautiously in French, 'there must be more to learn than that, since the Council is concerned about it.'

They were alone. The dog and the two grooms they had brought with them were snug above the stables with the other outdoor servants, but Gil and Alys had been lodged in a guest apartment on the principal floor of the house. Its two chambers were furnished with ostentation, and the images and crowned IS monograms on the painted linen bed-hangings suggested that it had housed one King James or the other, presumably on a hunting expedition, in the time since Sir William was put in place here. Two candle-stands and another pot of burning herbs made it a

12

little stuffy, but it was both comfortable and private, and the girl whom Lady Stewart had supplied to be Alys's tire-woman had left giggling, after unlacing the blue silk gown and hanging it reverently on a peg.

Now Gil shut the door behind her, and sat down on the faded embroidery of one of the folding chairs by the bed. 'They would hardly tell me what it is, I suppose, but they are clearly anxious about where the information has gone,' he added.

'They must be,' said Alys, closing her jewel-box. She drew off her linen undercap, shook out her hair and took up her comb. 'So where must we begin?'

'I wish you had not come with me, now,' said Gil, watching the light sliding down the long honey-coloured locks. He began to pull his boots off. 'This is a different matter from –'

'I'm your wife,' she said. 'Where else should I be but at your side? But why did the Archbishop send you here? Surely we should start by searching in Perth or Dunkeld.'

'Aye, for the missing singers. There is this other one who is not missing – who has reappeared. By what Blacader said, the Chapter at Dunblane has no wish to have him, and I imagine they hope I can prove him to be an impostor. I think he's crossed the main trail, but it seems as if I'm expected to follow both.'

'It would be a great attraction for pilgrims,' said Alys, pausing with the carved bone comb in mid-stroke, 'to have such singer in their choir I mean, but I suppose it would be very awkward for the Chapter, since Holy Church teaches us that fairies are sent by the Devil.' She ran the comb to the end of the lock she held, and gathered up another. 'How does my lord think they are linked? The missing ones and the returned one, I mean.'

'He hasn't said he does think it,' said Gil, unlacing his doublet.

'But he has sent you here to investigate both matters.'

'So it seems.'

13

She continued combing in silence for a little, then said, 'I could speak to the family here, while you go to those other places.'

'Yes.' Gil hung the doublet on a nail considerately placed in the panelling beside him. 'That's why I wish you hadn't come with me, sweetheart. If we aren't to be together, I'd sooner you were safe in Glasgow than stranded alone here while I ride all over Perthshire.'

'Do you wish to send me home, Gil?' she asked, looking straightly at him.

'No,' he admitted. Then, 'Besides, if you speak Ersche, how can I waste your talents?'

'It was fortunate that Murdo answered me in Scots,' she confessed. 'I have only a few words that I have learned from Ealasaidh McIan, and at times I confuse those with Breton.'

'Breton?' he repeated in surprise.

'When we lived in Nantes,' she smiled reminiscently, 'until I was nine, all our servants were *bretons bretonnants*, they spoke Breton rather than French. My nurse Annec used it all the time. Many of the words are the same, which I find astonishing. *Ty* is a house, for instance.'

'That is extraordinary,' he said, digesting *all our servants*. He knew her father was a wealthy man, wealthy enough to have fostered Ealasaidh McIan's motherless nephew without a second thought, and now it seemed he had been well-to-do for most of Alys's life.

She set her comb down on the little table beside her, and began to braid her hair for the night.

'So I can speak to the family,' she said again, 'and find out what I can.'

'That would be –' he began. There was a tapping at the chamber door.

'*Mo leisgeul*,' said a male voice. They stared at each other, and Gil snatched up his whinger and drew the blade.

'Och, the gentleman has no need of his weapon,' said another voice.

'Seonaid?' said Alys.

14

'It is Seonaid, mistress, and Murdo Dubh MacGregor, that would be wishing a word?'

Gil gestured, and Alys nodded, lifted her linen cap and moved to the far side of the bed. Whinger in hand, he padded to the door and opened it cautiously. The girl Seonaid was revealed in the lamplight, a plaid drawn over her hair. The man beyond her, far enough away to be half-shadowed, wore doublet and great belted plaid like Murdo, but was dark-haired and beardless.

'You aren't Murdo,' Gil said.

'The gentleman will pardon me, maybe,' said the young man. He stepped into the light and drew off his feathered bonnet in a graceful bow. 'Murdo Dubh mac Murdo mac Iain MacGregor, to serve you,' he said. His face was lean and handsome and he had an amazing wealth of long dark eyelash.

'So you're Murdo's son,' said Gil in puzzlement. 'Is that a reason for lurking in our chambers after the rest of the household's abed?'

'He is to wait on you,' said Seonaid, bobbing a curtsy, 'and it's myself is telling you, mistress,' she craned her neck, searching for Alys within the chamber, 'he is a good servant, if maybe he is talking too much.'

Alys came quietly forward from her concealment, her hair covered once more, and the young man's glance flicked to her and back to Gil.

'I am to wait on you, as this – as Seonaid says,' he said, and bowed again, with a glowing smile. 'My father was giving me the instruction just now, and I thought I would be coming to make myself known.'

'And?' said Gil.

'Och, nothing more,' Murdo mac Murdo assured him. 'Nothing more. Excepting only –'

'Yes?' said Gil unhelpfully.

'Would there be orders for the morning, maybe?'

'Not yet,' said Gil. 'I've made no decisions.'

'I have,' said Alys. 'I would like to meet this David

Drummond who has returned – who has been away for thirty years. Can you arrange that, Murdo?'

'Och, he's just a laddie,' said Seonaid. 'Hair like bog-cotton, he has, like all his kin, and never looking at the lassies in the Kirkton at all when he comes down on a Sunday.'

Murdo spoke sharply to her in Ersche, and she giggled, pushed him playfully, bobbed another curtsy to Alys, and departed. As soon as the outer door closed behind her Murdo said, 'That can be easy arranged.' Had he relaxed a little? Gil wondered. 'Indeed I can be taking the lady to Dalriach myself. If you were to ride up Glen Buckie to see the *sidhean*, what more natural than to call at the house? The more so since I am well acquainted with the family.'

'Are you, then?' said Gil.

'I know everyone in this country,' said Murdo Dubh modestly. Allowing for the common use of *country* to mean the stretch of land bounded by the mountains one could see, Gil felt he could believe this.

'Mistress Drummond has granddaughters living with her at – at Dalriach, I suppose,' said Alys.

'She has indeed,' agreed Murdo, with that brilliant smile. 'There is Elizabeth nic Padraig, and Agnes nic Seumas,' he enumerated, the Lowland and Highland names mixing oddly, 'and Ailidh nic Seumas. That is all her granddaughters that lives up the glen.'

'Two daughters of James's and one of Patrick's,' Gil elucidated, as much for his own understanding as Alys's. Murdo nodded. 'And there are two grandsons, I think.' Another nod. 'Quite a household. Now if that was all you wanted, Murdo –'

'Is it?' said Alys. She glanced at Gil, and looked back at their visitor. 'I think Murdo wanted a longer word, not?'

'*Bha*,' he agreed, a little reluctantly. There was a pause. 'It was just,' he said, and swallowed. The eyelashes swept his cheek as he looked down, then up again, and then he went on hurriedly, 'Just there is a – there is need of taking care if you are going about the country.'

'Why?' asked Gil. 'Are you warning us? What danger d'you mean?'

The dark gaze slid sideways away from his.

'There has been a *bodach* seen hereabouts,' he said. 'In Glen Buckie, and here by the side of the loch.'

'A *bodach*?' said Gil. He had heard the word before. 'An old man?'

'Not just an old man,' said Murdo, again with that reluctance. 'He is not – he is being –'

'Is it a spirit of some sort?' Alys asked. 'A wicked spirit?'

'Not wicked,' prevaricated Murdo. 'Not friendly, just. That would be it,' he nodded in satisfaction. 'Not very friendly at all, at all. So you will take care going about the place? Go nowhere by night, and never by your lone?'

'Not very friendly,' Gil repeated. He had met this feeling when trying to talk to other speakers of Ersche. It was like wrestling with fish, or fighting with a featherbed; no sooner was one aspect of the conversation under control than another surged up from nowhere to overwhelm him. 'What do you mean by that?'

'Maister Cunningham,' said Alys, at her most formal, 'might we ask Murdo to enter, so we can be seated and hear him in comfort?'

'I was about to be leaving you,' said Murdo Dubh hastily, half turning away. 'No need to be putting you out.'

'Come in,' said Gil, recognizing that Alys was right. The young man had all the appearance of an Erscheman with something to impart, but it would have to be coaxed from him.

Like his father Murdo was unwilling to accept a seat, but stood, lean and upright in his swathing of checked wool, looking from one to the other of them as they asked questions. Alys was more successful at getting answers; gradually they pieced together a tale of a small misshapen figure seen at a distance by twilight, where nobody was absent from the township or shieling. Murdo himself had not seen it, but Ailidh nic Seumas of Dalriach and three others together had watched it from the high shieling the same day that Davie Drummond came home. It certainly brought ill luck, Murdo stated simply, for now things were happening at the farm.

'What sort of things?' asked Gil resignedly. It had been a long day, and a long ride from Stirling; he was deeply aware of the bed behind him, with its embroidered counterpane and pile of pillows.

Murdo looked down and sideways again, then said slowly, 'There is all the wee things that happens. The hens got into the garden, the cat was at the cream. Some of them is blaming the *bodach* for that, but they are things that can happen any time. But –' He hesitated. 'There was a ladder that broke, before Jamie Beag could climb it. There was a rope gave way, and Davie fell. There was a pitchfork dropped out of nowhere when the barn door was opened, and tore Davie's shirt from neck to hem. There has been other things the like of those.'

'I see what you mean,' said Gil.

'Does it all threaten David Drummond?' Alys asked. The dark lashes rose like a curtain as Murdo looked at her.

'Not all,' he admitted. 'But many does.'

'And Ailidh likes her new uncle,' said Alys.

'I believe she likes him well,' agreed Murdo, his face impassive.

'You'll be careful, sweetheart,' said Gil into the darkness.

'I will,' said Alys.

Finally, finally, they were alone and curled together in the great bed. Murdo Dubh had eventually left them with promises of horses and an escort for Alys in the morning, and they had made haste to prepare themselves for sleep. But there was too much to talk through first.

'This David could be the boy returned from wherever he has been, I suppose,' said Alys thoughtfully, 'all things are possible under God, but it does seem unlikely.'

'Quite so,' agreed Gil. 'And yet Lady Stewart said he looks like a Drummond. We need to find out who else he might be, and where he could have come from, and who sent him, and if the family have accepted him that won't be easy.'

'And who is trying to kill him,' said Alys. 'Some of those things Murdo described sound to me like a woman's actions. I wonder how the sisters-in-law feel about the boy's return?'

'No, I don't like the sound of that.' Gil clasped her closer. 'Maybe I should come too.'

'No, no, that makes it too formal. I think you should pursue these missing songmen. Is it far to Perth from here?'

'A day's ride, Sir William said, and another one back again.'

'Oh!' she said in dismay. 'I hadn't realized – so you'll be gone for several days.'

'That's why I wish you'd stayed in Glasgow. Will you mind being left here?'

'You have your duty to see to.' She clung to him. 'Tell me again what my lord said.'

Gil was silent for a moment, calling up the scene. Blacader, blue-jowled and expensively clad, had been seated at one end of a carpeted table, his rat-faced secretary William Dunbar making notes at the other end while several clerks shuffled papers for the Archbishop to sign, but he had swung away from this scene of industry when Gil entered the chamber.

'Ah, Gilbert,' he said. Maister Dunbar had risen to fetch a sealed packet from a rack of shelves, and brought it to his master's hand. 'Aye, thank you, William, I mind it. What d'ye ken of Perthshire, Gilbert? No a lot? Well, now's your chance to learn more.' He drew out his tablets, and peered at one leaf. 'There's singers disappearing all across the shire, which is bad enough and you need to take a look at it for me. But now Jimmy Chisholm's got a wheen trouble at Dunblane wi a singer reappearing, saying he's been in Elfhame these forty year.' He laughed sourly. 'Singers is aye a trouble, whatever they're doing, but that's a new excuse. I want you to visit Will Stewart at Balquhidder and talk to the fellow.'

'Reappearing?' Gil questioned, disbelieving. 'From Elfhame?'

'Maister Secretary will gie you the story.' Blacader waved a hand. 'Jimmy Chisholm's Chapter couldny agree, so if you can find me a sound reason why this lad shouldny go back to his place at Dunblane, I'll be pleased and so will he. This ought to cover you to begin wi,' he thrust the sealed package at Gil, 'and you'll report all to me. William! Take him off and gie him the tale, will you?'

'He never directed you,' said Alys now, 'to find the missing singers, only to talk to this one.'

'I've to look at the matter,' Gil said. 'Dunbar mentioned them too, though not this matter of the Bishop of Dunkeld's secretary. It was Sir William gave me that part of the story.' He rubbed his cheek against her hair. 'But I think I'll begin in Dunblane, where the two trails seem to cross.'

'Yes,' she said thoughtfully. 'And it's closer.'

'It's closer,' he agreed.

Chapter Two

'You must know this country well,' said Alys. She relaxed in the saddle, gazing out over the expanse of loch and hills. 'It seems very wild to me.'

'I was growing up here,' said Murdo Dubh.

They had climbed up the south wall of the long glen, beside a tumbling river, and paused at the mouth of another, higher valley to breathe their small shaggy ponies. Even Socrates seemed glad of the halt. Below them Alys could see the rooftops of Stronvar and its outbuildings on the shores of the loch, half a mile to the west, and another group of houses to the east which Murdo said was Gartnafueran.

'That is where Sir William's brother Andrew Stewart dwells,' he explained.

'Gartnafueran,' repeated Alys's groom Steenie. 'They were telling me last night in the stables, they've seen this Bawcan or *bodach* or whatever they cry it there and all.'

'At Gartnafueran?' said Murdo, turning to look at him. 'When? Who was saying that?'

'One of the men. I never catched his name. I think by what he said it was just a day or two since.' Steenie laughed. 'Seems a lassie saw this wee dark shape in the field across the river in the gloaming. I said it sounded more like a bairn going home late for his supper, and he wasny best pleased.'

'No, he would not be,' said Murdo. He gathered up the reins of his own steed and the extra beast with the two barrels loaded on its back, a contribution from Lady

Stewart for the forthcoming harvest celebration. 'Will you ride on, mistress?'

They rode on, into a narrow valley between steep, lumpy green slopes, at whose tops were small dots which Alys took to be boulders, until some moved, there was a distant bleating, and she realized that they were sheep and the hills were higher than she had first thought.

'You'd think these mountains was going to fall on you,' said Steenie uneasily.

'That is not often happening,' said Murdo in a reassuring tone. Alys looked at him, recognized a joke, and thought that, though these people were different in build and habit from the taciturn Bretons of her childhood, they had a lot in common.

'They are so tall,' she said. 'Have you climbed all the way to the top of them? One might almost be able to reach up and touch Heaven from there.'

'These are not so high,' said Murdo. 'That one is Buachaille Breige, which is the Shepherd, and behind him is Beinn an't Sidhean. And on that side it is Clach Mhor which is just meaning –'

'The Big Stone!' said Alys in triumph. He nodded, with that brilliant smile again.

'The Big Rock, maybe. There is higher ones across Loch Voil. But it is a strange thing, when you are on the top of them it is still as far up to Heaven as when you are standing by the side of the loch, though sometimes there is clouds below you.'

'Why would you want to do that?' asked Steenie. 'Stand on the top, I mean. The whole thing might fall down, and you wi it.'

Murdo shrugged. 'The hunting is good,' he said.

They followed the narrow glen, beside the same tumbling river, with oak woods on either hand and wild flowers growing down the riverbanks. Socrates ranged round them, checking the scents of the place. Overhead the sky was blue, with fluffy clouds sailing in it, and a small wind kept the insects at bay. Alys thought of one of the

22

poems in Gil's commonplace-book. *Dayseyes in the dales, notes swete of nightingales, each fowl song singeth.* If Gil had been with her she would never have been happier. She wondered how far he had got.

'Did Tam say him and the maister was going back to Dunblane?' asked Steenie. 'What are they doing there, mem? He'd as well ha stopped there on the way up from Stirling.'

'The maister needs to talk to someone,' said Alys. And so do I, she thought. What do I say to these people? What must I find out? That depends on what there is to find out, I suppose.

About them, the signs were growing that this was not the green desert it appeared at first sight. Some of the trees were coppiced, a dry stone wall scrambled up the hillside, a small burn gurgling down to the river spread out over a well-maintained ford where the track crossed it. Someone was about; she heard a snatch of singing on the light wind. Then abruptly the glen widened into a broad green hollow, and Murdo halted his pony.

'Glen Buckie,' he said, gesturing widely.

'Good land,' said Steenie approvingly. 'If we were in Lanarkshire I'd almost say you were on lime here,' he added, 'it's that green.'

'Lime?' said Murdo. 'I would not be knowing.'

Alys looked about her. The hay crop on the flat ground near the river had been cut and turned; nearer them stooks of barley-straw marched up a slope in the sunshine. Across the river more tiny white dots bleated on the steep hillside.

'Is that the – the *sidhean*?' she asked, pointing to a rocky knoll bristling with tall trees, the hay crop washing its margins in a green-gold tide.

Murdo crossed himself and said hastily, 'Wiser not to be naming it, mistress, here in the open. That is Tom an Eisg, just. The – the place you named is being a lot bigger, and it is away far up the glen, beyond Dalriach, beyond the low shielings.'

'So when the boy left home,' said Alys, looking about her, 'he went that way, up the glen and not down it.' Murdo nodded. 'I had thought of him coming down past Stronvar and the kirk, but I see that was wrong.'

'By far shorter the road he was taking,' said Murdo. 'Over the high pass into Strathyre and down the burn at the other side. It would be a scramble, but a fit laddie would have no trouble. He has told us he had got that far before he was lifted away.'

'Told you? You mean he has spoken of it? Did he describe what happened to him?' Alys asked, trying to conceal her surprise.

'Only that much. He saw nothing when he was lifted up, it seems.'

'And where was he to meet his friend?'

Murdo shrugged. 'That he never said exactly. Somewhere on the Strathyre side of the hills, I have no doubt. If my father ever heard it in his time, he has not told me.'

'Your father says he has recognized the young man,' said Alys carefully. Murdo looked at her, the dark lashes shading his eyes. 'Is that right, do you think?'

'Who am I to say?' said Murdo, in faint surprise. 'Davie vanished away long before I was born. The family has recognized him, and he is dwelling with the old woman in Tigh-an-Teine, and that will do for me.'

'Tigh-an-Teine,' Alys repeated. 'The house of – of fire?'

He nodded awkwardly. 'It's the name they give the chief house of the clachan. Just a name, it is.'

'But is the fire particular in any way?'

'No, no. But a woman from further up the glen, one with the two sights, was making a great outcry one time, and saying that she had seen flames leaping from the thatch. Before I was born, too, that was,' said Murdo dismissively, 'and it has never burned yet.'

'And David dwells there with the old lady, and she is certain he is her son.'

'Indeed, yes.'

'It's a daft tale,' said Steenie roundly. 'Who ever heard the like, except in the ballads or the old tales? Folk doesny get carried away wi the fairies nowadays.'

'What do you think, Murdo?' asked Alys.

'I think your man should not be mentioning those people aloud,' said Murdo. He gathered up his reins. 'It will be another mile or so to Dalriach, past Ballimore. Will you ride on, mistress, and meet the Dalriach folk?' He smiled, those dark lashes sweeping his cheekbones. 'They will be ready for us by now. The hills has eyes, we have been counted already.'

'I was never at Glasgow myself,' said Mistress Drummond, 'but my son Andrew was there in the year of eighty-seven.'

Whatever Alys had expected, it was not quite this.

The farm at Dalriach was clearly prosperous, despite the bad luck Murdo Dubh and his father had detailed. The main steading, beside the track which separated infield and outfield, contained three substantial longhouses, built of partly dressed field stones, ranged round a cobbled yard. The cattle-fold at the byre end of one of them stood empty at this hour of the day, and hens crooned to one another among mysterious pieces of farm gear. Gardens, a barn, a stackyard, several smaller cottages down the slope nearer the river, made it almost a village.

A dozen people, men and young women, were visible shearing the barley at the top of the outfield as they approached the farm. Their work-song floated on the breeze, one voice with a line, the other voices with a rhythmic echo, keeping the swing of the sickles. The song never faltered, but the shearers paused, one by one, to straighten up and stare at the approaching riders. An old woman working with a hoe in one of the small kale-yards called to Murdo in cheerful Ersche, and he waved in answer.

They were met in front of the biggest of the houses by two lean black dogs who glared at Socrates, and a sturdy young man of twenty or so, with fair skin burned pink by the sun and a shock of light frizzy hair above a high forehead. Alys thought at first this was the returned singer, but Murdo had addressed him as James and introduced her in Ersche; she had caught Blacader's name and title and then Gil's, despite the strange twist the language gave them. James had ordered the dogs off in Ersche, then saluted her gravely in good Scots with a heavy Highland accent, and led her within to meet his grandmother, before excusing himself to return to the field. The harvest would not wait.

Now she was seated in the shadowed interior of the house, answering the inevitable civil inquisition about her background, origins and status and accepting oatcakes and buttermilk from one of the granddaughters, a plain girl of about twelve with a strong resemblance to the young man who had met them. Socrates lay at her feet; Murdo Dubh had vanished, taking Steenie with him. A surprising number of people had passed the doorway, peering casually through it with a greeting in Ersche for the old woman or the girl. Hens wandered in and out, a loom clacked somewhere, and from time to time, echoing across the yard, there was a piercing scream like a peacock's. Through the open door Alys could see a woman spinning on a great wheel slung on the side of one of the other houses, padding back and forward on bare feet, her slender ankles and calves visible below her short checked skirts. She was singing like the reapers; there seemed to be music everywhere. A long cradle near her rocked erratically and seemed to be the source of the screams.

'But you came there from France, mistress?' went on Mistress Drummond. 'There's a thing, now. And what brought you into Scotland?'

'My father is a master-mason,' she answered. 'He is building for Archbishop Blacader at the Cathedral.'

'That would explain it,' said the old woman, nodding. She wore a dark red gown of ancient cut, laced over a checked kirtle which was probably her everyday dress about the place, and the linen on her head and neck was crisp. She herself was bent and shrunken, so that the wide wool skirts had to be kilted up over a man's worn leather belt; her face was a veil of wrinkles, her hands crabbed, but her voice was sweet and clear. 'And what is Robert Blacader building?' she asked, with interest.

Alys opened her mouth to answer, and there was another of those peacock screams. Mistress Drummond peered round. 'Agnes, *mo chridh*, go and see what ails Iain, will you?' The girl slipped out, and her grandmother turned her smile at Alys, awaiting her answer as if nothing had happened.

This was difficult, she thought, explaining the Fergus Aisle. 'And yourself, Mistress Drummond,' she said, finally turning the questioning. 'Are you from these parts?'

'Oh aye, indeed. A MacLaren of Auchtoo, I am. My father was the chief man of this country, and my brother after him, until the king put his kinsman William Stewart into Balquhidder as his bailie.'

'Kings do what they must,' said Alys.

'Aye,' said Mistress Drummond darkly. 'But I wedded James Drummond,' she added, 'and St Angus blessed the marriage, and we dwell here in Glen Buckie now.'

'Does your man live?' Alys asked.

'James?' she said, suddenly vague. 'And we have four sons,' she added, 'and also a daughter, and all well and doing well.'

'My!' said Alys in admiration, comparing this with what the elder Murdo had told them last night and finding it incompatible. 'Are they all wedded?'

'Not all,' the old woman said in that musical voice. 'For Andrew is a Canon at Dunblane, and my son David is by far too young to be wed.'

Alys caught her breath, trying to work out how to answer that, but was forestalled. There was a shrill babble of Ersche in the yard; Socrates raised his head to stare, and the spinner and another woman came in at the open door, scolding like rival blackbirds and followed by the eerie peacock wail.

'Caterin! Mòr!' said Mistress Drummond, and the argument broke off. 'Not before our guest, lassies,' she said, though neither woman was young. Alys rose and curtsied. 'This is my good-daughters, the wife of Patrick and the wife of James.'

'Indeed I am pleased to meet you both,' said Alys. 'Murdo Dubh MacGregor was telling me as we rode up Glen Buckie, that you make the best cloth in Perthshire for colour and web.'

The two looked sideways at one another in the dim light, and curtsied simultaneously in acknowledgement of this, setting their bare feet as precisely as any lady at court.

'It is my good-sister's weaving that does it,' said the spinner, a small woman, her body still curved and sweet under her checked kirtle, her face an extraordinary little triangle within the folds of her linen headdress. 'She can weave like no other in Balquhidder.'

'Och, no, Caterin, it will be the colours you put in the thread,' said the taller woman. Another scream resounded from the other side of the yard, and Caterin jerked like a child's toy.

'He's wanting his uncle,' she said to her mother-in-law, still speaking Scots. 'You know how Davie can soothe him. I wished Agnes to go up the field and fetch him, and *she* will not be permitting it –' She tossed her head at the weaver.

'Agnes has enough to do –'

'But Agnes was about her duties under my roof,' said the old woman. Alys watched, fascinated by the contradictions in the scene. 'Will you go, Mòr, and fetch the boy in?'

This had not been the answer Mòr hoped for or expected. She recoiled, drew breath on a retort of some sort, then turned on her heel and walked out of the house with uneven steps.

'Is that the laddie that's returned to you?' Alys asked, snatching her chance.

'That it is,' said Caterin. 'You would think we were in one of the old tales, for such a thing to happen here at Dalriach.'

'I could hardly believe what Murdo Dubh was telling us,' Alys confessed. 'Does he have the right of it?'

'Murdo? Likely he does. He's hardly off Dalriach land long enough to sleep, the notion he has to Mòr's Ailidh,' pronounced Caterin, confirming Alys's deduction. 'He is knowing more of our business than we are ourselves.'

'It was a wonderful thing, and Our Lady be praised for the moment it happened. My laddie came walking down the glen,' said Mistress Drummond, 'and I caught sight of him from where I sat at the end of the house there.' She had clearly been waiting to recite her tale again. 'I thought to myself, *There is Davie coming now,* and then I minded that Davie was gone for thirty year, and then I looked again and I saw it was Davie right enough. Is that not a strange thing?'

'It must have given you a great shock,' said Alys.

'Och, indeed yes, such a turn it gave me, I thought the heart would fly away out of my breast. I hurried to meet him, and he saw me coming and he said, do you know what he said to me? He said, *Is it my grandmother?* Did you ever hear the like? And I said, *Heart of my heart, it is your own mother.* And he said, *Do you know me, then?* As if I would not know my own bairn!'

Alys glanced at Caterin, who still stood near the open house door, and caught a strange, wry expression crossing her tiny face. Sensing Alys's gaze, she looked round and gave her a smile which seemed to convey sympathy for Mistress Drummond and something else besides. There was another scream from outside.

'But how did you know him at such a distance?' Alys asked carefully. 'Was it his bearing, or the way he walked, or what he wore?'

'All of those,' said the old woman, nodding. 'And the great shock of hair, white as flax, like a coltsfoot gone to seed. All my bairns have that hair, you see, lassie. Mistress

Mason,' she corrected herself. 'They take it from their father, and he took it from his mother, *an Beurlanaich*, that was English.'

'English?' repeated Alys in astonishment. 'How ever did that come about?' The two countries have been at war for centuries, she thought, how would a man living in this remote place find an English wife?

'My good-father met her at Stirling when he was there selling beasts, and her a sewing-woman in Queen Joan's household. My man was the only child they reared, all the others was carried off with the Good People. But there is nobody else in the whole of Balquhidder that has such hair.' She chuckled. 'I was always saying to my man, he would never stray from me, for I would be knowing his get wherever I saw it, and my sons' the same.'

That Alys could well believe, recalling the young man who had met them. 'And what clothes was your son wearing? Surely not the same clothes that he went away in,' she suggested. 'They must have worn out, in the time.'

'Och, they would so,' agreed Mistress Drummond, 'and it was *sasainneach* dress he went away in, seeing he was walking back to the kirk at Dunblane. Those clothes would not be fitting him any more at all, the way he is grown, so he was not wearing them, but only the plaid on his back. His plaid I knew at once, for it was my own dyeing and weaving. He was clad in what they had given him to wear under the hill,' she added something quick in Ersche, and Caterin echoed it, 'fine strange clothing, every bit as fine as Sir William is wearing.'

'I should like to see what the – those people wear,' said Alys, with perfect truth.

'That I can show you, easy,' said Mistress Drummond triumphantly, 'for I put it by. Too good to be wearing about the farm, it is. Jamie Beag's old doublet and sark fits him fine, and does him for ordinary.'

'So many of your men are called James,' said Alys, as the old woman rose and made her way cautiously across the chamber. The boy outside screamed again.

'A true word, lassie,' agreed Mistress Drummond. A small sound by the door, a change of the light, made Alys turn her head just in time to see Caterin slipping out of the house, her head bent. Mistress Drummond, ignoring this, knelt stiffly before a painted kist by the far wall, felt for and removed the stack of turned wooden platters which lay on it. 'There was my man's father,' she enumerated in that musical voice, 'that was James *an-t bean Beurlain*, James with the English wife you would say, and there is my man himself, that is James Mor, and my son James, and there was Patrick's son James, that was James Breac, since he was freckled like a troutie, and died before he was seven year old, poor laddie,' she paused to cross herself, 'and Mòr's James, that is Jamie Beag.' She counted again on her twisted fingers, and nodded.

Alys, trying to recall what Murdo had said, reckoned that three at least of these were dead. Had he mentioned another James still about the place? And was Mor the same word as Mòr? The woman's name had a different twist from the man's by-name.

'And of course there is Seumas MacGregor that dwells at the foot of the clachan, but he is not kin, though he is our tenant,' added Mistress Drummond, lifting a bundle of linen out of the kist. She laid it on the flagged floor before her and unwrapped it. 'There now. Is that not fine? And there is his boots as well, in the other kist.'

Alys came to kneel beside her, touching the garments she unrolled. The outermost layer was a shirt of fine soft linen, well made, cut and stitched in a subtly different way from the shirts she made for Gil, or the other women of Glasgow made for their men. It was much less full and long than the great belted sarks Murdo and his father wore, and she could imagine that it would seem quite strange to someone used to those. The dog leaned against her shoulder, sniffing at the folded cloth.

'And see this,' prompted Mistress Drummond, groping for the sleeve of the garment and holding it out to Alys. Her thick, twisted fingers felt at the cuff, and Alys duly admired the little knots of needle-lace worked along its edge.

The garments wrapped in the shirt were also of good quality, though travel-stained. There was a pair of joined hose, of grey worsted cloth, a blue velvet doublet trimmed with fathoms of bright red cord, two pairs of drawers, and a thigh-length gown of dark blue broadcloth. Alys turned them, half-listening to Mistress Drummond exclaiming over the thickness and quality of the cloth, the strangeness of the cut. The doublet was lined with red linen, and inter-lined with something which crackled faintly in her hands; the gown was made to fasten on the breast, and was sim-ilarly lined, with several pockets cunningly worked into the lining to hold coin or papers. All seemed to be empty.

She realized that she was picking over someone else's clothes without their owner's knowledge. Suddenly over-whelmed by embarrassment, she folded the gown neatly and put it down on top of the other garments.

'We soaked the linen and washed it,' said Mistress Drummond, 'but not the others, of course.' She wrapped the bundle together again and returned it to the kist. 'I never thought to see my laddie again in this life,' she con-fessed, accepting Alys's help to rise. 'Such a blessing it is, I have lit candles to Our Lady and to St Angus every Sunday since he came back to me, and so I will be doing the rest of my days, whether there is Mass being said at the Kirkton or no.'

'And this was all he had with him?' Alys asked. 'Had he no scrip, no coin? Surely he must have had something when he left here.'

'No, no. What would a laddie that age be wanting with coin? He had a roasted collop and a good oatmeal bannock in his pouch, to stay him on his travel, and a spare shirt, and another I was sending to his brother Andrew. And we sang the blessing to him for the road, and he set off up the glen,' this was also, clearly, a familiar recitation, 'all in the morning sunshine, and the birds calling, and I stood at the roadside here and watched him out of sight, and I never saw him no more till four weeks since.'

'It's a great wonder that he is returned,' said Alys. 'You must be thankful indeed.'

'Thankful indeed,' agreed Mistress Drummond. She put a hand on Alys's arm. 'And also I was blaming St Angus,' she admitted, 'for I had wished my laddie to sing here at his feast day, down in the Kirkton, but he was saying he must get back to Dunblane for St Blane's great feast, that's the same day. So I was blaming St Angus for not keeping him safe, and it will surely be taking my own weight in candles to put that right.'

'Has he spoken about his time with – with those people?' Alys asked. 'Why did they carry him off?'

'Och, for his singing.' The old woman made her way stiffly to her chair by the low peat fire in the centre of the floor. 'It would be his singing. Him and Andrew both, they had voices like angels, though Andrew lost his afterwards. David has been singing for them under the hill,' again that muttered phrase in Ersche, 'since ever he was stolen away.'

Across the yard the loom began clacking again, and then, right on cue, a new voice lifted in a lilting, floating melody. The words seemed to be Ersche, the voice was a clear rich alto, and with the singing came bursts of braying laughter.

'It is only David can make Iain laugh, the poor soul,' said Mistress Drummond, settling herself comfortably. 'If you wait a little, lassie, Mistress Mason I mean, he will come in to speak to his mammy, and you will be meeting him.'

'He has a fine voice,' agreed Alys, listening to the singer. It seemed to her to be a trained voice, such as one might encounter in the choir of a great church; the strength and delivery were professional, the tone was true. The tune changed, and changed again. Suddenly she realized that she had sat listening for a long time, and turned quickly to apologize.

'Och, there is no offence, lassie,' said the old woman seriously. 'One could listen for a day and a night and never move. Do you wonder that those others took him away to sing for them?' She tilted her head. 'Ah, there it is. He is always singing our own song last of all, as the poor soul falls asleep.'

The tune had changed again, to a slow rocking song, a lullaby. Mistress Drummond sang softly along with the words, *Dalriach alainn, Dalriach math, ho ro, ho ruath*. Alys's limited vocabulary covered that: *fair Dalriach, fine Dalriach*. A song for the farm where they sat.

'What a bonnie tune. Who made it?' she asked as it ended.

'It was my man made it for James our firstborn, and we both sang it to all our bairns.' The old woman smiled. 'Do you ken, David was singing it to Iain when he first set eyes on him, the day he came home, I think that would be how Iain was taking to him immediate.'

'He –' Alys paused, and revised what she was about to say. 'He remembered it, then?'

'Och, yes, he was remembering it, and just the way his father was singing it. My son Patrick has the tune a wee bit different, you understand, but David minds it his father's way.'

'And has he learned other songs while he was away? Do they have other music in the – in the *sidhean*?'

The quick, averting phrase in Ersche, and then the answer.

'Fine music indeed, though David tells me none of it they make themselves, all is from singers they've carried off from one place or another.' There was a movement in the yard, and a shadow fell on the doorway. 'This will be him now. David, *mo chridh*, come within.'

'I think it must be the bonniest place in the realm of Scotland,' said Davie Drummond, gazing round the bowl of the hills in which the farm lay cradled. To Alys's ear his

Scots was not quite like the way Murdo Dubh or Mistress Drummond used the language. 'My –' He checked, and continued. 'My father aye said it was a place where you are near to the kingdom of the angels.'

'Bonnier than where you have been?' she prompted.

He looked quickly at her, and half-smiled.

'Wherever I was, I think it is not in Scotland,' he said.

'And where were you?' she asked directly.

Her first response to Davie Drummond was liking. He was taller than she was but seemed a year or two younger, perhaps sixteen. Clad in another of those huge sarks belted about him, with a leather doublet over it, he bore a powerful resemblance to the young man who had welcomed them, and to the girl Agnes. A strong-featured, pink-skinned face burnt by the sun, wide open blue eyes, their lashes and brows so fair as to be invisible, and that extraordinary halo of lint-white, frizzy hair, all marked him as their close kin, as Lady Stewart had said. Stepping barefoot into old Mistress Drummond's house, his great plaid bundled over his arm, he had bowed to Alys, but said gently to the old woman:

'No need, surely, to be sending Mòr up the field for me when her hip is as sore? One of the lassies could have fetched me.'

'Och, so it is, *mo chridh*, but they were arguing again,' she said, smiling up at him.

'Just the same, Mammy, there is enough pain in her life without adding more to it.'

'Well, and that is a true word. David, here is a lassie – here is Mistress Mason come all the way from Glasgow to hear about how you came home to me.'

His back to the door, his face in shadow, he seemed to stiffen slightly, but he said with grave courtesy, 'I will gladly to talk to the lady. Are you tired, Mammy? Will I take our guest to see the farm?'

'Yes, indeed,' said Alys hastily. 'Have I tired you with talking, mistress? I'm sorry for it if I have.'

Now she stood at the side of the bridle-road along the glen, which ran here between outfield and steading, while Davie Drummond named the hills for her, pointed out the path to the summer grazing, named the families in the other steadings of the valley. The reapers were still working along the rigs of barley; in the shade of the barn Steenie was minding the ponies and talking to the old woman with the hoe, who seemed to be called Mairead and who was getting a lot of amusement from the conversation. Socrates was exploring the yard.

At Alys's blunt question Davie looked away, staring northward at a ridge he had just identified. After a moment he said, 'You know where they are saying I have been.'

'Is it the truth?'

He turned his head and met her eye.

'Wherever I have been,' he said carefully, 'I am back.'

'You are,' said Alys after a moment. 'You are home, I think.'

A flicker of something like surprise behind the blue eyes, but no answer. After a moment she went on, 'What was it like there? How do they live, the – those people?'

'Not so different from us,' he said. 'Their houses are fine, their clothes are bonnie. There is more colour in them, perhaps. The old woman would show you the clothes I came home in?' Alys nodded, and he smiled fondly. 'She is showing them to everyone. And there is feasting and fasting, the same as here, and music all the time.'

'What kind of music?'

'Voice and harp,' he answered readily, 'and playing on all kinds of pipes, and fiddle and bells and drums. Much the same as here, indeed.'

'I heard you singing to the boy John,' said Alys. He looked away, screwing up his face in compassion.

'Aye,' he said, 'the poor soul.'

'What ails him?'

'The hand of God, I suppose. I've seen the like in – He will not be touched, he will not be dirty. He won't walk, though he can crawl. If he is crossed he screams. Likely you heard him.' He shrugged. 'If I can help him, I'm glad of it. His mother has a deal to bear. Both the old woman's good-daughters has a hard life.'

'I can see that,' Alys answered seriously.

When they first stepped into the yard, it was occupied by the girl Agnes, seated at a winding-wheel filling a bobbin with blue yarn, and Caterin the spinner, who was once more padding barefoot back and forth over the cobbles while the broad wheel fixed on the house wall turned the dark iron spindle, twisting locks of fleece into thread for the dyeing. Beside her the long cradle was still. The child sleeping in it was small for seven or eight, his face pinched and cream-coloured, the hand which lay outside the covers long-fingered and twisted. Caterin had paused in her work as they approached, turning her head under its heaped and folded linen, with that wry smile for Alys and an ambiguous look at her guide.

'He is asleep,' she said in Scots. 'There is none but you can soothe him now, it seems.'

Davie shook his head.

'I'm still a new thing to him,' he said. 'If Elizabeth had some of my tunes she could be singing him to sleep as well.'

'I must be glad you are come home, then,' said Caterin. 'We are all glad he is come home,' she said slyly to Alys. 'The songs and the tales he has to tell, you would not believe. You would almost be wishing to visit the – the place he has been, to see the marvels for yourself.'

'Och, not so much,' said Davie, colouring up. 'And I think not all are so pleased to see me.'

'She will become used to it,' said Caterin, as the door of the other longhouse swung wider. 'Och, Mòr, we were just speaking of you. Have you finished that shuttle of thread, then?'

'I have.' Mòr added two empty bobbins to the heap beside Agnes and crossed the yard towards them in uneven steps, bending her head to Alys. She was a tall lean

woman, clad in a kirtle of checked cloth which looked like
her own weaving, in the natural browns of the yarn; the
sleeves were rolled up, baring muscular forearms, and
the skirt was as short as Caterin's. The linen on her head
was much plainer than the other woman's. 'And is that
you at the crack with our good-brother, then, when he
should rather be at shearing the barley?'

'No, no,' said Caterin. 'Davie is showing Mistress Mason
the land his brother and his nephew works, are you no,
Davie mhic Seumas? Better that than the shearing, when
your hands are still soft.'

'I'll go back to work in good time,' Davie assured them,
his colour rising further. 'Will you be showing Mistress
Mason some of your weaving, then, Mòr, while Agnes
winds the next shuttle?'

'The shuttle is wound,' said Mòr, shaking her head, 'and
the lady is not wanting to be bored with a heap of cloth.'

Alys, recognizing her cue, had protested firmly, and
found herself at Mòr's door being shown folded lengths
of cloth fresh from the loom, in colours and patterns such
as she had not seen in Glasgow. She said so, and admired
the work with truth, setting off another competition in
modesty between the two women which lasted until
Caterin said, with a sidelong look at Davie:

'And then the cloth must be fulled, of course. You will
not have seen that since you came home, Davie.'

'No, he has not,' agreed Mòr, like a fish rising to a piece
of bread. 'You will not be knowing our waulking song,
Davie.'

'Why, has it changed?' asked Davie, and began a lilting
tune with a regular beat. Both women joined in, smiling,
and Mòr's hands moved in time with the music as if she
was shifting and beating a length of cloth.

'And what do they use for waulking songs under the
hill?' asked Mòr. Davie shrugged.

'That and others,' he said. 'I had little to do with the
weavers, you understand, for all they were near as good
as – as someone standing near me.'

Mòr looked modest, and Caterin nodded approval at the ellipsis.

'They admired my plaid, often,' he continued, 'if they could see this work they would admire it even more. I hope you are keeping it safe, good-sister.'

'Rowan twigs in all the folds,' said Mòr succinctly.

'Patrick's plaid is just like it,' said Caterin, looking at the bundle of cloth on Davie's arm. 'The colours would be the same, if they were not faded.'

'The *cailleach* was weaving that and all,' said Davie. 'She was weaving for all her bairns.'

Agnes said something in Ersche; Mòr inclined her head briefly to Alys, took the handful of bobbins her daughter held out, and vanished into her house again.

'This will not get the yarn spun for the tribute-cloth,' pronounced Caterin, and turned towards her wheel. 'We must all of us be working longer, if what we get is to be split three ways, rather than two. You will be showing Mistress Mason the stackyard and the barns, Davie.'

And now they stood by the track, and Davie Drummond said, 'Here is Ailidh nic Seumas and Murdo Dubh coming down from the shearing.'

The two figures making their way down the field were quite separate, but somehow might as well have been entwined. Watching them approach, Alys said, 'And what did you eat, under the hill?'

'The food is good enough. Less meat than here, maybe. Bread of wheat and rye, eggs and cream, butter and nuts and fruit.'

'Kale,' said Alys wryly. It was one thing she had not yet become used to in her years in Scotland, the relentless serving of the dark green, nourishing stewed leaves, so ubiquitous that *kale* simply meant *food* on many tables. Davie Drummond gave a small spurt of laughter.

'They've no great love for it either, mistress.'

'A good life, then,' she prompted, aware of that liking again. He nodded. 'Were you not sorry to leave it?'

'I wanted to know how they did here,' he said earnestly. 'I wanted word of – of my brothers, and the old woman. And of the man of the house too, but it was too late for that.' He crossed himself and muttered another phrase Alys did not catch, though it did not sound like Ersche.

'Davie,' said Murdo Dubh, handing his companion across the turf dyke, and contriving to bend his head in a brief bow to Alys as well. Socrates, recognizing an acquaintance, beat his tail in the dust a couple of times. 'I saw Mòr nic Laran call you down from your rig. You'll not reach the end of it before Jamie finishes his, I would say.'

'Good day to you, Murdo,' responded Davie Drummond. *'Ciamar a tha sibh?'*

'The better for seeing you hale,' said Murdo Dubh enigmatically. 'Ailidh nic Seumas was wishing a word with the guest.'

The oldest granddaughter was clearly a Drummond too, though her hair was a darker shade, nearer to gold, and clung to her brow under her straw hat in sweaty curls rather than a flyaway frizz; her high forehead and blue eyes made her kinship to Davie very clear. The sleeves of her checked kirtle and her shift were rolled well up past her elbows, displaying sturdy forearms scratched by her work among the harvest. Her skirt, like the girl Agnes's, was barely knee length. She bobbed a curtsy in answer to Alys's greeting, and smiled shyly, but whispered something in Ersche to Davie.

'Mistress Mason is speaking Gaelic,' said Murdo hastily.

'Only a very little,' said Alys equally quickly, as Ailidh Drummond blushed crimson.

'I have not told her yet,' said Davie. The girl glanced at him, her colour still high.

'If you will not say it, then I will,' she urged in a half-voice. 'Go on, Davie. It must be said.'

'What must be said?' Alys asked. 'What do you wish me to hear?'

'I was telling them some of it last night,' said Murdo.

40

'Go on, Davie,' said Ailidh again. He was silent for a moment. Then he turned to face Alys, meeting her eye.

'Mistress Mason,' he said, his accent suddenly more Scots than Ersche, 'I ken fine, for the word came up the glen yestreen, that you and your man are here from the Archbishop to speir at whether I'm who I say.' She stared at him, open-mouthed, aware of her face burning like Ailidh's. 'But it seems to me there is a more important thing to be speiring at. Since ever I cam hame, someone is trying to kill me, and whoever it is they've been near killing the old woman more than once. I'm feart they'll get her.'

Chapter Three

'It's a by-ordinar thing indeed,' said Maister James Belchis, shuffling papers on his desk. 'I never encountered sic a tale, never in all my time in the Law.'

'Nor I,' agreed Gil. 'Nor anyone else that's heard it.'

The road to Dunblane, back through Strathyre, was the same as the one they had taken into Balquhidder, and led past a long and winding loch and through a narrow pass which Sir William's men had taken with their hands on their sword-hilts. Nevertheless, with only three men and no baggage-animals, Gil had made better speed than yesterday, reaching the little town a couple of hours after noon. Enquiry in the cathedral precinct had led him to the chambers of Maister Belchis, who as well as practising as a notary held the office of sub-Dean.

'What's more, I'll be glad, we'll all be glad, if you can get at the truth of the matter,' went on Maister Belchis. He was a small man with a strong Perthshire accent, clad in an old-fashioned belted gown of black worsted, his tonsure hidden by a frivolous red felt hat. He put another sheaf of papers on top of the stack he had made, and left the desk. 'You'll take a drop of refreshment, Maister Cunningham? It's a long ride from Balquhidder.'

'How did the word reach Chapter?' Gil asked, as his colleague poured the wine the servant had fetched in earlier.

'Well.' Maister Belchis passed Gil a beaker, offered him the platter of small cakes, and sat down again with a handful of the sweetmeats for himself. 'The first we heard of it was a message to Canon Andrew Drummond, about four week since.'

'That's the brother?'

'It is. A letter to Andrew from his mother. Andrew being,' a pause while Maister Belchis sought for a word, 'a wee thing taigled at the time, paid no mind to it, but another letter came maybe the fortnight after it, and that he had to bring to Chapter.'

'Have you read either letter?' Gil asked. And what might *taigled* refer to in this context? What distractions was a Canon of the Cathedral liable to encounter?

'Only the second one.' Gil waited, and the other man ate two little cakes one after the other while he thought. 'I suppose Andrew might tell you himself, if you talk wi him, and you need to hear the content to make sense o it all. Aye. It was writ by the parish priest's servant, who writes a good clear hand, on behalf of Andrew Drummond's mother. In it she declares in so many words that Andrew's brother David has returned from Elfhame and that she wishes him to have his place in the choir again, since he still has a boy's voice, and to attend the sang-schule. And,' continued Maister Belchis, raising one eyebrow at Gil, 'to this end, she promises that if Chapter accepts the laddie back, she'll grant land with an income of twelve merks per annum, to be succentor's mensal.'

'A handsome bribe,' said Gil. 'Twelve merks a year to provide food to one man's table is worth having. Does she have the means to do that?'

'Oh, never a bribe, maister,' said Belchis with irony. 'A gift, surely. And Dougie Cossar would be glad of it, his table being ill-furnished the now. As to the means, I'd say –' he paused, and then continued with careful discretion, 'I had the impression Andrew thinks she can do it.'

'The diocese is still short of money, then?' said Gil. 'I'd heard Bishop Chisholm had improved matters a bit.'

'Oh, aye, he's improved things, but we're still a bit tight.' Belchis sipped his wine. Gil did likewise, appreciating the light sharp flavour.

'And how did Chapter react to this letter?' he asked after a moment.

'Chapter couldny agree,' said the other man. He laughed, without humour. 'It's been tabled for three, no, four meetings now, and every time we end up arguing about whether it's possible the laddie really has come back from Elfhame, or whether he still has a voice fit for the sang-schule after thirty year, or whether he was stolen or ran away, and in the second case whether we'd be within rights no to accept him back. We've said all that's to be said on it, more than once, and we're no nearer a decision.'

Gil nodded in sympathy, and looked at the tablets on his knee. It would probably be tactless to make a note of this right now.

'Where would the original records be, from when the boy first vanished?' he asked.

'Likely wi the other sang-schule records. There's one or two of the Canons mind the matter well enough, we've never needed to look it up for the meetings.'

'It's the Abbot of Inchaffray is your Precentor, am I right? He'll not be in residence. So I suppose I should talk to the succentor about that.'

'Dougie Cossar.' Belchis glanced at the sun pouring in the window beside him. 'He keeps the sang-schule in his own manse, but the boys have a holiday the now. I couldny just say where he'd be, for he might ha one choir or another to rehearse, but you could start at the manse.'

'A hardworking man,' Gil commented, and went on, 'And can you tell me anything about the other singer, maister? I'm told one of the quiremen vanished from here earlier in the year,' he lifted the tablets and referred to a leaf, though he had no need to, 'a man called John Rattray.'

'Aye, that's right. Sometime in Lent, it was, and it's still a speak for the whole countryside.'

Gil nodded; his note said *Eve of St Patrick*. Five months ago, he reflected. The trail was long since cold. Aloud he said, 'Mid-March. Hardly the best season to go off travelling. What happened?'

'The Deil kens,' said Maister Belchis, and popped another cake into his mouth. 'Indeed, his man tried to say,' he went on through it, 'it was the Deil himself had carried him off, but I put a stop to that. A good singer and a good-living man, John Rattray, and the two are no often to be found in the ane person, I've no doubt you'll agree, maister.'

'Very true,' Gil said. 'What, was there no sign at all of where he'd gone to?'

'None.' Belchis reflected briefly. 'You'll want to speak to the servant, I've no doubt, but best if I gie you the rights of it first. We've no enclosed street for the singers here the way you have in Glasgow, you'll understand, they all dwell in rented chambers here and there about the town, and Rattray was lodged behind Muthill the soutar's shop.' He leaned towards the window and pointed. 'That's it yonder. His man is Muthill's young brother and dwells wi him and his wife, two doors along from the shop.'

'That's clear enough,' said Gil. 'Convenient for all, I suppose.'

'Aye. And one morning in Lent the brothers Muthill went down to the shop to open up, and found it lying open. Street door unlocked, though the latch was still drawn, the soutar's shop closed up as he'd left it but the door to John's chamber along the passage standing wide. No sign of an inbreak or any ill-doing, the laddie's wages left on the table, John's clothes and valuables gone but his household gear left –'

'Valuables?' Gil questioned. 'Did he have much?'

'This and that. A couple of books, a bonnie wee carved Annunciation which I'd envied him myself a time or two, a painted Baptism of Christ,' Belchis enumerated, 'a seal-ring, two-three jewels for a hat so his man said. That kind o thing.'

'Nothing of any size,' said Gil thoughtfully. 'And I think he's in minor orders only?' His colleague nodded, his mouth full of cake again. 'So it looks as if he went deliberately enough, with what he could carry easily, rather than being carried off unwillingly.'

'It never occurred to me to think he was carried off,' said Belchis in surprise, swallowing. 'No, no, the soutar came straight to me the first thing, seeing I'm so close. I saw the chamber mysel afore the laddie had a chance to redd it up, and all was in good order. Andrew Drummond,' he paused, pulled a face, and nodded. 'Aye, Andrew Drummond came wi me the second time, and neither of us saw anything untoward. There was never a struggle or fight in it. I'd say you're right there, the man took time to pack what he wanted and then just rose and went out.'

'And there's nothing to show why he went?'

'Nothing. His friends, the other quiremen ye ken, were as amazed as the soutar.'

Gil nodded, and drank down the last of his wine.

'I'll get off and speak to the succentor,' he said. 'Thanks for this, maister. And I can speak to the soutar and his brother, I should be able to catch the quiremen after Vespers, and then I'll need to see when Canon Drummond can speak to me.'

'Aye, well, I wish you luck at that,' said Belchis obscurely.

There were two or three boys of the choir-school playing football in the street as Gil approached the succentor's manse. It was a well-built two-storey house of stone, thatched with reeds from the low-lying valley of the Forth above Stirling, but the lower part of the walls and the stair to the battered side door bore scrawls and scribbled drawings in chalk or charcoal, interspersed with the characteristic round muddy prints of the ball. Enquiring for the succentor, Gil found he was at home; he came out on to his fore-stair to greet the guest and waved at the boys, who ran off laughing and shouting fragments of Latin parody.

'They mostly behave well enough while they're in school,' said Maister Cossar tolerantly. 'They have to kick

46

their heels up when they're free. And how can I help you, maister?'

He had been rearranging the benches in the empty schoolroom, and still had a sheaf of crumpled music under his arm. He was not a lot older than his charges, certainly younger than Gil, with a lean face and dark eyebrows, and the powerful fists and distant, listening look of an organ-player; he saw the purpose of Gil's enquiry immediately, but shook his head.

'It would be in the old records. My predecessors' papers are mostly in the kirk, I would think, in one great kist or another.'

'Nothing here?' asked Gil hopefully.

'There might be. Oh, not in here,' he added, grinning, as Gil looked about the room. 'The boys would have the o's and a's inked in and faces or worse drawn in all the white space if I left anything in reach.' He exhibited the battered music with its crop of marginalia, and set the bundle down on his tall desk. 'Come away ben, and we'll take a look in the register cupboard. You never ken when you'll be lucky.'

The registers of the sang-schule, like any other records Gil had ever dealt with, had been kept up very unevenly by different succentors, some with meticulous accounts of each singer's attendance and standard, some merely noting lists of names not even divided into different voices. It must be difficult, he reflected as he sorted through the dusty volumes, to hold a post where the superior was always absent and the man who did all the work got little of the credit for it. Maister Cossar was obviously one of the more careful record-keepers; he was exclaiming in disapproval as he worked backwards through the sequence.

'What year did you say?' he asked suddenly. 'Sixty-three, was it? *Register of yhe sangschuil at Dunblain yeirs 1458 to 1466*. This should be it.' He set the volume down before Gil at the window.

'We're getting dust on your table-carpet,' Gil said.

'No matter.' Cossar flicked at the fragments of leather which fell from the edges of the binding. 'My man Gregor will sort it. Is there anything there? It's no a bad record,' he added critically as Gil turned up the year he wanted. 'There's the laddie there, wi the trebles.'

'There he is,' agreed Gil, running a finger down the page. 'And his brother wi the altos.'

'I never knew Andrew Drummond was a singer,' said Cossar. 'He's no voice to speak of now, a course.' He tilted his head to read the column of names. 'Aye, no a bad record. See, he's keeping a note of which boy sang in which of the great services, so as not to strain their wee voices by making them do too much. This David Drummond sang first treble at Easter, along wi James Stirling and William, William Murray is it? I wonder if that's any kin of old Canon Murray? And Andrew Drummond wi a big part, he must ha been good to sing Judas.' Gil turned a page, and they both read on. 'There's your laddie again, first treble at Pentecost, wi the same boys, William Murray and James Stirling. You know, the succentor at Dunkeld is a William Murray,' he said thoughtfully, 'he'll be about forty I'd say. I wonder could it be the same man?'

'At Dunkeld,' Gil repeated.

'And the boys that sing together regularly tend to make friends wi one another. Thirty year ago I suppose a Drummond and a Murray could well ha been friends, though it's different now since Monzievaird a course. Did this William and David sing at Yule?'

Gil turned back the pages. Outside, across the square, a bell rang five times somewhere.

'Yes, here they are,' he said. 'And the Stirling boy too. The Vigil of Yule. Then on St Stephen's day, and the morrow of Holy Innocents. Alternate days, in effect.'

'Good practice,' said Cossar approvingly. 'Lets the voices rest. Mind you, it looks,' he ran his finger down another column, 'as if your David was the Boy Bishop that year.'

'And William Murray was his Archdeacon,' Gil agreed. 'I think you're right, maister, they've been friends. What happened in August, I wonder?' He leafed forward through the book. 'Here we are. The two of them sang at Lammas, with the Stirling boy again. Then none of the trebles is present the next week – did they all go home for the harvest?'

'We give them a holiday after Lammas,' agreed Cossar. 'Just the week, seeing St Blane's feast falls on August tenth. They come back fresh in time for the patronal feast. And the succentor gets a holiday and all,' he added, smiling wryly. 'You're about ready for it, by then.'

'I can believe that. And here in the middle of August we have your patronal feast, *Vigil of Sanct Blain, Fest of Sanct Blain*, and here's the boy Murray, and James Stirling, and there's Andrew Drummond again, but no mention of David.'

'So that's when he vanished away,' said Cossar. He turned his attention to the other names on the page. 'Is any more of these fellows still about the place, I wonder? Is that John Kilgour? He's one of the quiremen yet, and chaplain of St Stephen's altar.' He glanced at the window. 'Here, that was five o'clock sounded from the kirk. I must away, maister – I've the blowers waiting for me, I need to play through the organ part for the morn's office hymn. Maister Belchis needs a sure lead, so I'd not want to make mistakes.'

The shoemaker Muthill was a square, dark-haired man, who wore a pair of brassbound spectacles fastened on with a green cord round his head. The heavy hinged frames perched over the bridge of his nose gave him a strange predatory look, like a crow. He peered at Gil through them, listening to his cautious introduction, then removed them and rubbed at the marks they had left on his nose.

'Aye,' he said.

Since this was not a wholly adequate response, Gil waited. After a moment the soutar rose from his last, set down his needles and reel of waxed thread, and put his head out at the open window beside him. 'Walter! Wal*terr!*' he shouted, then sat down without looking at his visitor, replaced the spectacles and took up his work again.

Gil continued to wait. In a few moments, the sound of running feet heralded a much younger man, very like the soutar in appearance though without the spectacles.

'Is it my maister?' he demanded as he burst into the shop. Seeing Gil he stopped abruptly, and his shoulders sagged. 'No,' he answered himself, and then warily, ducking his head in a rudimentary bow, 'You haveny brought news of him, have you?'

'No,' said Gil. 'I'm trying to find out what might have happened to him. Can you help?'

The brothers looked at one another, and the soutar nodded.

'You help the man, Walter,' he directed.

'Can I see his chamber,' Gil asked, 'or is it let again?'

'Oh, aye, it's let,' said Walter with a resentful look at his brother. '*He*'d no see it lie beyond the month.'

'He's out,' said the soutar, biting his thread with notched teeth. 'No harm in looking, if you don't go poking about. Show the man, Walter.'

Walter obediently led Gil into the flagged passage which led from street to yard, and along to the next door. This he opened cautiously, peered round it, then flung it wide and stood back for Gil to look. The chamber within was much the size of the workshop, furnished with a low bed, a kist, a bench and table and a couple of stools. Its present occupant's plaid was flung over the bed, some worn liturgical garments were heaped on the bench, and there was music, a pen-case and some ruled sheets of paper on the table.

'It's let to another quireman,' Gil said. The boy looked at him in amazement.

'Aye, it is,' he agreed. 'How did you ken that?'

'Tell me what you saw when you came in here the morning your maister vanished,' Gil prompted. 'Was it like this?'

'No, no, it was quite different,' said Walter earnestly, 'for my maister's gear was all here, and none of Maister Allan's.'

Careful questioning got Gil a clearer description. The bed had not been slept in, for Walter's brother had checked and it was cold. The two wee pictures, which were right bonnie things, had gone, and so had Maister Rattray's two books, that lived on that shelf there. Walter's wages were set on the table, on a piece of paper with his name writ on it clear so he could read it, and beside them was Maister Rattray's own key to the front door.

'And there was no smell of burning nor sulphur,' added Walter, 'for all it was the Deil himsel carried him off.'

'Why do you say that, Walter?' Gil asked, looking at him curiously.

'Is that you at that nonsense again?' demanded Walter's brother loudly from his shop. 'Pay him no mind, maister, he's been on about that since ever Rattray gaed off, for all we've had half the Chapter in telling him it was no sic a thing.'

'Where does the window of this chamber look on?' Gil asked.

'Out in the yard.' Walter closed the chamber door and led him to the end of the passage, where another door revealed a small yard, with two ramshackle sheds and several tubs of daisies. A gate in the fence seemed to lead out on to the cattle track. 'Maister Allan grows these flowers. They're bonnie, aren't they?'

'Why do you say it was the Deil carried your maister away?' Gil asked again. The young man glanced over his shoulder, and moved further into the yard.

'Acos I saw him mysel,' he said earnestly. 'That's how I'm certain.'

'You saw him?' Gil also moved away from the door, out

of earshot of the soutar. 'When was that, Walter? What did you see?'

Walter's face split in a gratified smile, and he crossed himself energetically.

'It was just two days afore my maister was taen away,' he said in a hushed voice. 'I came by wi his supper, which our Mirren sends from our own table, I mean she aye sent it, and cam in by the back gate here, and my maister was looking out at his window –'

'In March?' said Gil, surprised.

'Aye, in March, and he was talking to the Deil that was standing here in the yard.' He pointed to a spot under the window. 'Just there, he was stood.'

'What time was it?' Walter looked blank. 'Was it dark?'

'Aye, just getting dark, I seen the first star as I came by the wynd and wished on it,' said Walter, nodding, 'and then I came in at the yett and seen the Deil.'

'And what did he look like?' asked Gil with care.

'No bigger than a bairn, for he didny come up to the window-sole,' said Walter, his voice hushed again, 'and he had great wings like leather all down his back, and a big hat on to hide his horns, and he'd a great deep voice like a big man's.'

'What was he saying?'

The young man licked his lips.

'I heard him threaten that he'd come for him on St Patrick's Eve, and that good singers was needed in Hell, and then I ran away, for I was feart, maister,' he confessed, and crossed himself. 'And I canny rid mysel of the thought of my maister, that was aye good to me and left me my wages at the last, burning in flames and tormented by imps wi great pincers, all acos he's got a bonnie voice.'

'Was there snow on the ground,' Gil asked, 'or was it muddy? Did he leave any tracks?'

Walter shook his head.

'He must have flew away,' he said, 'on his great wings. There was no sign that any of us saw.'

'I thought as much!' said the soutar angrily in the doorway. 'Is that you annoying the man wi your tales, Walter Muthill? Pay him no mind, maister, and I'll thank you no to encourage him, for he's naught but a daft laddie.'

'He must have seen something,' Gil said. 'Did you come to look, maister?'

'I did not,' said the soutar, pulling off his brass spectacles again, 'for I'd my boots off, and no notion to go tramping round the cow-wynd in the dark. When this bawheid cam in crying out that he'd seen the Deil in our yard my wife made him go round by the street, for Maister Rattray paid us good rent to get his supper brought him, as well as the chamber, and he never saw any sign by the front way, and his maister tellt him the Deil had never been here.'

'Aye, but he'd have to say that,' muttered Walter. Gil put one foot on the edge of a tub of daisies and leaned forward, meeting the young man's eyes.

'Walter, you said your maister's pictures had been taken as well?' Walter nodded. 'What were they, can you tell me?'

'One was the angel's salutation,' Walter raised one hand in the conventional pose of Gabriel in an Annunciation, 'and the other was St John Baptist baptising Our Lord, wi the water all up round his waist, paintit on a wee board.'

'So one showed Our Lady and the other showed Our Lord.' Walter nodded. 'Do you really think the Deil could carry away somebody wi those images in his pack?' Is that a syllogism? he wondered. Something is defective in the logic, but this laddie won't notice.

'You see?' said the soutar triumphantly. 'I tellt you it was nonsense.'

'You mean he's no in Hell?' Walter stared at Gil, a huge relieved grin spreading across his face. 'Oh, thanks be to Our Lady! She must ha saved him! Oh, wait till I tell our Mirren.'

Gil exchanged a glance with the soutar, and decided to leave well alone.

'Afore you do that, Walter,' he said, 'had Maister Rattray taken all his gear wi him?' The young man shook his head, still grinning. 'Can you tell me where the rest is? What happened to it?'

'It's a' packed up and lying in the corner o my shop,' said the soutar, turning to go back in. 'You can tak a look if you want.'

Rattray's discarded gear was not copious. Emptying the canvas sack on to the floor, Gil turned over the contents and identified a shirt, a pair of worn hose, one ancient house-shoe, some mismatched table-linen. There was a platter and wooden bowl but no beaker, several spoons of wood or horn, a couple of blackened cooking-crocks which had rubbed soot on everything round them, and two worn blankets padding the bundle.

'He had very little,' he commented, comparing this collection with the well-appointed houses of his friends among the songmen at Glasgow.

'He's took the best wi him,' said Walter eagerly. He had cheered up enormously with Gil's reassurance, and was almost bouncing beside the heap of goods. 'See,' he went on, 'he had a new blanket, and other four sarks besides that one that was in the wash, and some linen besides, and four bonnie wee metal cups and a wooden one, and a pair o good boots my brither made to him –'

'Boots,' repeated Gil.

'Stout sewn boots, oxhide wi a double boar's-hide sole,' itemized the soutar.

'Aye, and the great socks to go in them that our Mirren knittet,' contributed Walter. 'My good-sister's a fearsome knitter,' he informed Gil. 'I'm right glad my maister had a pair of her socks wi him. That'll keep his feet warm.'

'He's set off on a journey, hasn't he, maister?' said the older Muthill. Gil sat back on his heels and nodded.

'I'd say so,' he agreed. 'A long journey, at that. I wonder where he's gone?'

* * *

The Bishop was absent from his Cathedral at present, but being on official business Gil had been able to claim lodging for himself and his escort at the Palace. Strolling back across the precinct, he considered what he had learned so far. It hardly seemed to lead him anywhere, other than to more witnesses. The Drummond boy might have confided in his friend, or the fellow Kilgour might know something useful, Rattray appeared to have left willingly for a long journey, and that was the sum of it. Perhaps Canon Drummond could help him, he thought doubtfully, and wondered why he was putting off speaking to the Canon. Was it the fact that, a month after being told his brother had reappeared, Andrew Drummond had still neither visited nor written to his family? Or was it the slight wariness of sub-Dean Belchis's reference to the man?

He glanced at the sky. Most of Dunblane would be sitting down to its dinner shortly, and then the quireman and his fellows would be singing Vespers. Best to go and see what was to be had from the Palace buttery, and consider what to do next.

'No, you don't want to talk to Andrew Drummond,' said John Kilgour. 'Even if he wasny –'

'We never do, if we can avoid it,' said one of the other quiremen. 'He doesny like singers. Mind the way he got across John Rat, all last winter? All because John got before him in the procession at Candlemas.'

'No, he really hates singers,' agreed another voice.

'Why's that, then?' asked Gil innocently, and reached for the nearest jug of ale.

He had heard Vespers in the Cathedral, standing in the nave while the familiar chants floated through the choir-screen, and then had made himself known to one or two of the choir as they left the vestry. As he had hoped, a friend of Habbie Sim of Glasgow was welcome, the more so when he stopped by the Tower tavern on the way back to Kilgour's lodging and paid for enough ale for most of the choir for the evening.

'You'll mind it better than me, Jockie,' said Kilgour's neighbour. 'You were at the sang-schule wi him, were you no?'

'I was, Adam,' agreed Kilgour. He was a balding, fairish man in his forties, with a light, breathy speaking voice, though when he had joined in the snatches of chant in the street his deep tones had astonished Gil. 'I was. It was a bad business.'

'What happened?' Gil asked.

'He was never much liked, save by the adults,' said Kilgour, with what seemed to be reluctance, 'but he'd a good voice, maybe the best mean, the best alto, I ever heard in my life, pure and clear wi a compass to astonish you, so a course he sang in the Play of the Resurrection. In the nave at Pace-tide, you ken.'

Gil nodded. He knew the kind of thing Kilgour meant, more of a dramatized service than a play as such. The Resurrection would mean at the least three women's parts, two or three disciples, perhaps an angel, and Christ. Not all the parts would be for boys' voices.

'Who did he sing?' he prompted.

'Judas,' said Kilgour. 'A big part, and the second year he'd sung it.'

'But the rope slipped,' said someone else. Gil looked from one face to another in dismay.

'What, you mean he was hanged in earnest? But he's –'

'No, no,' said the man called Adam. 'No that bad. But he fell off the stool, and his throat was hurt bad wi the rope.'

'How did it happen?' Gil asked. 'Was anyone to blame, or was it an accident?'

'My brother aye said he'd seen a cord,' remarked someone in the corner. 'But he never jaloused who had pulled on it. To upset the stool, you ken,' he expanded. Gil nodded, taking this in. 'He said the enquiry was something fierce, but nobody ever owned up nor clyped, the more so as the mannie that was to fix the rope – one of the cathedral servants, you ken – dee'd not long after.'

'What happened to him?' asked his neighbour. The narrator shook his head.

'My brother never said. I think it was some kind o accident round the building. Fell off the window walk, or the like.'

'And nobody admitted to causing Andrew's accident,' said Gil, digesting this.

'Andrew was never well liked,' said Kilgour.

'Why not?' Gil asked.

'Boys can take a dislike to someone,' said Adam. 'Often enough there's no accounting for it.'

'The way my brother tellt me,' protested the man in the corner, 'there was plenty reasons to dislike Andrew. The football, for one.'

'I'd forgot that,' said Kilgour. Gil raised his eyebrows. 'A sorry thing that was, too. One of the fellows had a football, a rare good one, for a yuletide gift. We'd several games wi it, and the boy it belonged to thought he was in Heaven, for everyone would be his friend, you ken.' Gil nodded, recalling the muddy prints on the wall of Cossar's manse. 'Then one day at the noon break it was found under his bench flat as a bannock, knifed beyond mending.'

'Sweet St Giles!' said Gil, and several people exclaimed with him, obviously hearing the tale for the first time. 'And Andrew Drummond was blamed for it?'

'It was never proved,' said Kilgour quickly. 'Several folk had had the chance. But you ken what boys are. Andrew got the blame among his fellows, for none of the others seemed like to have done such a thing.' He grinned wryly. 'Our maisters paid no mind. All that happened was the lad that belonged to the ball got beaten for bringing it into the school.'

'I see,' said Gil. 'And then at Easter the rope slipped.'

'And he never got his voice back,' agreed Adam. 'That's how he hates singers.'

'There's plenty folk sing well as boys and lose it once the voice changes,' said Kilgour, 'but this was different, you see, Andrew's voice was stolen from him, and he's got no love for those that can still hold a tune. He speaks well enough,' he added, 'but kind o hoarse, and he sings when he has to like a heron croaking.'

'Was that before his brother vanished away, or after it?' Gil asked.

'It must ha been after it,' said Kilgour, considering, 'for he was singing well at the time his brother was stolen. It was the two of them sang the great hymn at Lammastide, just the two voices. I mind them practising it, and old Rob Clark that was our succentor shouting at them for not holding the tone.'

'It was just after that David Drummond disappeared, was it no?' said the man in the corner. 'Do you mind of that and all, Jockie?'

'No much,' said Kilgour. 'You ken what it's like when you come back, you're straight into the rehearsals for St Blane's feast, working all the hours of daylight to get the music by heart. It was a wonder for a few weeks that David hadny come back like the rest of us, but he wasny the only one, there were other folk went on to the college at St Andrew's or Glasgow, or maybe the Grammar School at Perth. Then we forgot about it, except maybe for Billy – aye, Billy Murray that's at Dunkeld now, and the Stirling boy, that was his bedfellows.'

'Where do the boys lodge?' Gil asked. Kilgour paused in reaching for the ale-jug.

'At the time,' he said, 'we dwelt in the succentor's attics, and studied in the chapter-house. Some of the younger ones found it hard. These days they're lodged about the town, in one household or another, which is fine if they get on wi the wife.'

'How did his brother no disappear wi him?' asked another voice.

'Geordie, it was thirty year since. I canny mind,' said Kilgour, and took a pull at the ale-jug. After a moment he offered, 'Likely Andrew never went home wi him, went to a friend's or stayed here in the town. There's some of them do that,' he added to Gil. 'If they've no notion to the walk home and back.'

'Maybe if Andrew had gone home and all, the wee one would never ha vanished,' said someone. 'He'll ha fallen into some crack in those hills, or been lost in a drowning-pool, or the like.'

'It's strange he was never found then,' objected Kilgour.

'If you can lose a beast and never find it, you can lose a laddie. Eleven, was he? That's no a big corp to be seeking.'

'How far do the boys come to sing here?' Gil wondered. This gave rise to a long discussion, which concluded that the furthest anyone had ever come was one Duncan McIan from some place Gil had never heard of, five days' walk to the west.

'Most of them's from Stirling or hereabouts,' said Adam. 'But there's aye a few from further away.'

'How do you find them?' Gil asked. It was not a problem he had ever heard the Glasgow songmen discuss; there was a sufficient crop of youngsters in the burgh and its immediate surroundings to keep the choir, and the sang-schule in St Mary's Kirk, well supplied.

'Word gets about,' said the man in the corner. 'The most of us has kin that can sing, and we pass names to the succentor. You hear of a laddie wi a good voice in another parish, or the Archdeacon when he visits takes note of a soloist's name –'

'That's if the Archdeacon can tell *In nomine* from *In taverna*,' said someone else sourly, and they all laughed again.

'And is that how the men move about and all? Would that be how John Rattray went?'

There was an awkward silence.

'It's a strange thing, that,' said Adam at last.

'How so?' asked Gil.

'The Ratton just vanished. Like the Drummond laddie –'

'No, no, Adam, the Drummond boy was on his way back, by what we hear.'

'There's no knowing that,' argued Adam. 'He'd maybe not have told his kin if he was planning to go a long journey.'

'Aye, but he'd a gied his bedfellows some notion, surely!'

'The Drummond boy met wi some accident, how could he warn his bedfellows?'

'So you'd no inkling Rattray was going away?' Gil put in, before this could build into an argument. 'You don't think his servant was right and he's been taen off by the Deil?'

'Ha!' said Kilgour.

'Walter Muthill's a daft laddie,' said someone else. 'The Deil kens what he saw, but it wasny the Deil.' This got a laugh, but the speaker protested, 'Aye, fine, but you ken what I mean. There's plenty folk in Dunblane I'd sooner believe had been borne off by the Deil than John Rattray. He's aye been a good-living kind o fellow.'

'It's a funny thing just the same, he'd got across Andrew Drummond,' said the man called Adam, 'and then vanished the same as Drummond's brother.'

'Adam, I tellt you, it was nothing like the same,' said Kilgour. 'Besides, the way Andrew Drummond came speiring about it, he knew no more than any of us.'

'He was interested, was he?' asked Gil.

'Oh, aye, asking all around.'

'What about Rattray's kin? Has he nobody else that might hear from him?'

A short debate turned up the fact that John Rattray was the last of his house, save for a brother teaching, or perhaps studying, the Laws in some university in Germany. That would account for the length of time it took before anyone was concerned, Gil thought.

'I mind he did say his parents were carried off in the pestilence,' said someone.

'And when he left, he never said anything, or gave any sign? What generally happens?'

'Not a word,' said the man called Geordie.

'It's usual for one Precentor to write the other,' said Kilgour. 'Dougie Cossar had a message only last month, to ask if we'd a tenor we could spare to Stirling.'

'So it's arranged between the Precentors?' Gil prompted.

'Aye, in general. Wi maybe an offering to sweeten the exchange. But Dougie had no notion John Ratton was off either.'

'He did buy the ale that night,' said another voice.

'Aye, that's right, Simon, he did,' agreed Kilgour. 'We take it in turn,' he explained to Gil. 'It wasny John's turn, but he bought the ale, and bannocks too.'

'But he never said a thing about going away,' said Geordie, shaking his head.

'You never found anything in his chamber when you took it on, did you, Nick?' asked Kilgour. A man perched on the end of the bench shook his head.

'Nothing at all, save a couple o Flemish placks away under the bed where Muthill's wife hadny swept far enough. I found them when I shifted it round – I canny abide to sleep wi my head to the window.'

'He'd never been to the Low Countries, had he?' said Geordie.

'No, but we all get enough o those, this close to a market the size o Stirling,' said Nick Allen. 'I'd another three in my purse only last month.'

'And you've never heard where he went to? Where do you suppose he's gone?'

'Somewhere they pay their singers better,' said the man in the corner.

'Near anywhere in Scotland, you mean?' said Adam, and got a general sour laugh.

'Aye, but Maister Belchis writ every other diocese,' objected Kilgour, 'asking was he in their pay now, and they all said he wasny.'

Gil privately doubted this. If Rattray owed nobody money there was no motive to hunt for him, and there was by far too much work to do in any diocese to pursue a single missing singer for no reason.

'How good is his voice?' he asked. 'What does he sing?'

'He's countertenor,' said Kilgour. 'A high tenor, ye ken. And he's no bad, no bad at all. In fact he'd come on a lot last winter, you'd think he'd been practising or something.' This raised another laugh; it seemed to be a joke. 'It was the kind of voice we don't get to keep very long, it's no surprise he's left us. The only by-ordinar thing about the business, Maister Cunningham, is the way he slipped off wi never a word to say he was away or where he was going. And that nonsense of his laddie's about seeing the Deil at his window,' he added.

'That's two things,' said Adam.

Kilgour swung a friendly fist at him, but said to Gil, 'So if you find him, maister, we'd be glad to hear it.'

'If I find him,' said Gil, 'I'll send you word.'

Chapter Four

In the morning, nursing a headache, Gil asked the Bishop's steward how to find Canon Drummond. This got him a close look, and a dubious,

'Aye, m'hm. You'll need to speak to him, right enough, though I've no notion what good it might do.' The steward, a lean-faced individual with straggling grey hair, looked down at the towel and bread-knife he carried, and absently wiped the knife with the towel. 'He's had his troubles to bear, Maister Cunningham, and he's badly afflicted by them.'

'Troubles,' repeated Gil, lifting an eyebrow.

'His, er – his, er – a woman dear to him,' said the steward euphemistically, 'dwelling outside the town, dee'd a month since, and the bairn wi her. It seemed as if he'd ha been right enough, what wi his faith in God and His saints, and the comfort o his brothers in the Chapter, but then he'd the letter telling o his brother David's return, and then ten days syne another, and since that time he's fell straight into a great melancholy. His folk say he neither moves nor speaks the most o the time.'

'Why should that have sent him melancholy?' Gil asked in surprise. 'I'd ha thought it would help him.'

'Aye, well.' The steward looked uncomfortable. 'I'm no one to gossip, maister, you'll understand –'

'Of course not,' said Gil reassuringly, 'but anything you can tell me that helps –'

'Aye. His man tellt me. The bairn lived a few hours, see,

but it was never like to do well, and they gied it baptism in the name o David for his brother. And then it dee'd.'

'And then his brother came back from wherever he's been,' said Gil. 'I see.'

'Aye. The way I heard it, it's as if he's thinking, if they'd gied the bairn some other name, it might no ha been taken.'

'Hardly the way for a clerk to be thinking,' observed Gil.

'A man canny aye school his own thoughts,' returned the steward sagely. 'So you can call at Andrew Drummond's manse, maister, but you might no get much good o't.'

Thus warned, Gil was almost prepared for the sight of Canon Andrew Drummond, seated in the arbour at the far end of his little pleasure-garden, hands dangling between his knees, his felt hat on the bench beside him and the sun beating down on his tonsured head while he stared blankly at a knot of clipped box-hedge.

'Here, Canon, you'll get stricken by the sun,' said the servant who had led Gil out from the well-appointed house. 'Put your hat on, now,' he instructed, lifting it. He placed it over the tonsure as if his master was a child, turning it so the single silver badge on the brim showed to advantage. 'Here's a man to speak to you, sent by Robert Blacader, so you'll need to gie him an answer.'

There was a pause.

'Blacader,' repeated the Canon dully, and turned his gaze on Gil. 'Aye, I feared he'd send someone. You can tell him I'm full aware o my guilt, maister. Or am I summoned to make a confession?'

'No, sir,' said Gil, bowing politely and trying to conceal his dismay. 'I'm right sorry for your loss. But I'm here about another matter entirely. May I sit and talk wi you?'

'I kent it,' stated Drummond, his speech slow and hoarse. He was a big-boned man in his forties, in clothes which hung on him as if he had lost weight lately. Pink cheeks slumped over a square jaw, blue eyes ringed with dark shadows stared guiltily at his audience. Below the brim of the hat fair frizzy hair, clipped short, exposed his bare neck and showed a long shiny mark like an old burn scar. Sweet St Giles, thought Gil, if that was the mark of the rope, he was lucky to lose no more than his voice. 'I kent she would dee, right from the moment she said she was howding again. And the bairn and all.'

'It's a great grief,' said Gil awkwardly, and sat down uninvited so that he could put a hand on the man's arm in sympathy. 'Death comes to us all, soon or late, but it's a sad thing for those left living.' Hoccleve, he thought. *That chaunge sank into myn herte-roote.* Poor devil, and he has no means of mourning his mistress officially, either.

'Now, Canon,' said his man in bracing tones, 'you've two bonnie bairns yet. Think on them, and take heart, maister.'

'They've gone from me and all,' said the Canon in his croaking voice, and sighed again. 'A' that's close to me, wede awa.'

'There's no telling what's God's will,' said Gil. 'No sense in going to meet grief.'

'Come away, now, maister, Mistress Nan was shriven in childbed,' the servant pointed out, 'and the bairn baptised all in his innocence. They'd be taen straight to Paradise, borne up by holy angels, the both o them. You've no call to grieve on their account, maister. And yir ither bairns are only the length o Perth wi their grandam, you can see them any time you've a mind to it.' He made sympathetic faces at Gil over the Canon's felt hat, and said in what was obviously intended as an aside, 'It was just after we'd took the bairns to Perth, when the second letter came from Balquhidder, that he fell into this state, and I've no notion what to do for him.' He bent to the Canon's ear and went on encouragingly, 'Brace up, now, sit nice and talk wi Blacader's man, and I'll bring you a wee drink and some o the honey cakes, will I?'

He departed without waiting for an answer. Drummond looked briefly at his retreating back and then at the gravel beneath his feet. Gil cleared his throat, wondering whether he should remain. The Canon's condition answered his major question; it was hardly surprising that a man in this state had not ridden out to Balquhidder to greet his returned brother.

'She must ha been very dear to you,' he said. 'Had you kent her long?'

The shadowed blue eyes flickered in his direction, and the man nodded.

'Ten year,' said the hoarse voice.

'Long enough. What drew you to her? Was she bonnie?'

Another blue glance, another nod. 'A bonnie, loving lass wi no tocher,' pronounced Drummond in that harsh voice.

A strange epitaph, thought Gil, though he knew the kind of arrangement a cleric would offer. For a girl with no dowry like Mistress Nan, it was often an attractive alternative to a life as a poor relation in another household. What did a churchman's mistress do to please him, apart from the obvious?

'Did she sing for you? Play the harp?'

The Canon's broad shoulders straightened a little, and he said more attentively, 'What way would she be singing? I've to listen to the choir all day, I'll hear no singers in my own home. She would harp for me, maister. She harpit as good as any woman in the realm o Scotland. She could ha played for the King, my poor lassie.' Another of those huge sighs.

'*God hath her tane, I trowe, for her good fame,*' Gil quoted, '*the more to plese and comfort his seintis.*'

'That's bonnie,' said Drummond after a moment. 'Aye, that's bonnie. My poor lass. *To plese and comfort his seintis,*' he repeated, on a bitter note.

The servant returned, crunching down the gravel path with a wooden tray. The drink he had brought tasted of fruit and honey, and the little cakes were sweet and spicy.

Gil was not hungry, but nibbled one to encourage Drummond, and said:

'Canon Drummond, I'm sorry to break in on your grief –'

'No matter, for I've no right to mourn her,' said Drummond harshly, 'I'm guilty o her death.'

'I wanted to ask you,' persisted Gil, 'about your brother David.'

'I've no brother David. He's been gone these thirty year, whatever my mother's writ me.'

'What do you recall of the time he vanished?'

'Nothing.'

'Where were you when he disappeared?'

Another shadowed glance.

'I was here. I never left the town.'

'Why did you not go home with him?' Gil wondered. 'Did you not want to see your family too?'

'Hah.' Drummond shook his head with a bitter laugh. 'Walk that distance to help wi the reaping, when I could stay here and –' He broke off the sentence.

'What about St Angus' fair?' Gil asked. 'That would be worth the journey, surely?'

Drummond put up a hand to straighten his hat, though it had not moved.

'Another ancient saint out of Ireland,' he said, rather bitterly. 'Not to me, maister.'

'Had you any reason to think your brother might not come back to Dunblane?'

'No!' said Drummond sharply.

'So he'd never said anything to suggest he might go away from here, like John Rattray?'

The Canon's blue stare settled on Gil's face, unreadable.

'Like Rattray?' he said. 'How do you think it's alike? The two cases are no the same.'

'They've both vanished,' Gil said, grateful for this show of alertness.

'Aye, but Rattray was –' Drummond turned his gaze on the knot of trimmed box. 'Rattray left all in good order, he'd clearly planned to go, as you'd find out if you questioned the soutar that rented his room to him, maister, whereas my brother was borne up and taken away unexpected.'

'By the fairy-folk,' said Gil. Drummond gave another of those small bitter laughs.

'So my mither aye said. It contented her.'

'And now he's returned,' said Gil deliberately.

'Aye. I should never ha baptised the bairn in his name. It's fetched him back, hasn't it?'

'I'd have thought his friends would be glad to hear he's home,' Gil offered. 'Has William Murray at Dunkeld heard, do you know?'

Drummond was still for a moment, then raised his head.

'His friends,' he said. 'Aye. He'd more than one. I'd forgot Billy Murray.'

'And you? Were you glad to hear it?'

A sour smile spread across Drummond's face.

'That depends,' he said. 'That depends on how well he can sing now.'

Riding back past the winding loch, with the men joking at his back, Gil tried to fit the new information into the picture he held already. It seemed to do little to clarify matters. The songman did appear to have left peacefully and of his own accord, but what was one to make of Walter Muthill's account of the figure at the window in the twilight? The boy was very clear about what he had seen and heard, but in the absence of a smell of sulphur or scorch marks on the windowsill, Gil was not inclined to believe the interpretation Walter had supplied. There seemed no obvious reason why the Devil should carry away a decent man. And why had the decent man given his friends no sign that he was leaving? He must have had at least a day in which he could have said his farewells, and yet he seemed to have gone to some lengths to leave in secret.

As for the older matter, the only gain there was another tangle of questions, and some new names to ask them of. If David Drummond had really fallen into some crevice in the hills, thirty years since on his way back from Dalriach, then the young man using that name now was not the same person. If he had not – if he had vanished in the same way as John Rattray and the other adults this year – then he still seemed unlikely to be the same person, but in that case who was he? His brother Andrew would make little sense any time soon, Gil judged, and Kilgour's account suggested there was not much more information to be got in Dunblane. More useful to ask around Balquhidder, and perhaps in Dunkeld.

'Haw, Maister Gil,' said Tam from behind him, and urged his horse forward alongside Gil's. 'See yon farm?' He pointed across the loch, where a burn tumbled down a narrow glen from a saddle-like pass between a vast rugged shape and a smaller one. A huddle of low buildings lay near the foot of the glen, where the slope eased before it met the loch shore. 'They're saying that's where the laddie's friend dwelt.'

'What, there?' Gil looked about, surveying the landscape. They were near the head of the loch; there would certainly be a track to that side of the glen. 'How did you learn that, Tam?'

His servant shrugged eloquently.

'Lachie, him that's head o the stables at Stronvar, minds when the laddie vanished, and he tellt me and Steenie all about it, and how he was to meet Billy Murray o Drumyre at the foot o the pass and never came there. And now these fellows,' he jerked his head at the two sturdy men of the escort, 'are saying yon's the pass, and yon's Drumyre, and still a Murray holding it.'

'Well, I think we'll go and call on them,' said Gil, looking over his shoulder, 'see if anyone minds the day. Can you guide me there? It's no so far off our road, after all.'

The senior of the two men nodded.

'Aye, I can take you there. But you'll need to watch, maister,' he cautioned, 'it's a Drummond you're asking after, and these are Murrays. Gang warily, won't ye no?'

'I will,' promised Gil. And don't mention Monzievaird, he thought. How long is it – five years? No, it's no more than three. He recalled news of the atrocity reaching Glasgow in the autumn of 1490. A scion of the house of Drummond had burned Monzievaird church, together with all the Murrays who had taken refuge inside it, shocking even his wild contemporaries. It had shocked the King and his Council too, and young Drummond had paid with his head despite the pleading of his mother and sister. This was barely sufficient for the Murrays, who still hoped to see the Drummonds wiped out in retaliation, and it seemed likely that tact would be needed.

Most of the folk of the steading were occupied with the barley. Three lean tawny dogs barked at their approach, and some of the shearers paused to watch them, gauging whether their intent was peaceful, and then whistled the animals in. The younger man-at-arms, Donal, dismounted and tramped up the long ridged field to account for their presence, returning with a laughing remark in Ersche and saying to Gil:

'They'll not stop the work to speak wi you, maister, but they tell me Andrew Murray's Sìle is keeping the house, since the babe is too young to be leaving.'

The group of houses seemed to have been abandoned to the hens, but eventually they located Sìle by the gentle singing drifting from her door. She proved to be a pretty young woman with her baby at her breast, and assured them in vehement Ersche which needed no translation that she knew nothing about the tale of David Drummond. Questioned further, she pointed to a barn at the top of the settlement, dislodging the suckling baby, which began to wail angrily.

'Euan Beag nan Tobar,' she said firmly through the noise, and ducked back into her house. They turned to lead the horses up between the low buildings, the baby falling silent behind them as its mouth was stopped.

'Euan'll no be much use,' objected the older man, whose name, Gil had established, was Ned.

'Who is he?' Gil asked.

'He's had an eye to the barn and the stackyard here, for ever so it seems.' The man guided his horse round a discarded plough. 'He's wanting four of his five wits. Fell down a well at the market in Callander when he was a bairn, they say,' he explained to Gil, 'and was lacking in his head afore ever that happened. He's harmless, is the best you can say o him.'

'He's no that bad,' said the younger one. 'He's a Christian soul. He speaks Scots, a bittie.' He tethered his own beast in the shade of the barn and stepped into the shadowy interior. 'Euan? Euan Beag? There's a man here wants a word wi you.'

There was silence.

'Come out, you daft loon,' ordered Ned from the doorway.

The silence continued, but Gil had the feeling of someone keeping silence rather than that of an empty space. Behind him Tam swallowed, and said quietly, 'Could it be a trap, maister?'

'No, it's no trap,' said Gil, and moved to the door in his turn. 'Euan Beag, are you within? Might I have a word?' Inside the barn, straw rustled. 'I was told you might know something.'

The straw rustled again.

'They'll be pointing their big knives at him, and cutting his good ropes,' said a quavering voice. It sounded very old.

'No, for I'll not allow it,' said Gil.

It took a little more coaxing, and Ned and Donal had to be persuaded to move away from the barn door, before the owner of the voice would come out from the shadows. When he finally emerged, he hardly seemed human, a crouching figure with crooked limbs and big hands, his

71

neck twisted so that his face turned sideways and up. He was clad in a filthy shirt and doublet, yellowish-white hair hung round the back of his head, clumps of darker beard sprouted along his jaw and a brown hen was perched comfortably on his shoulder. His eyes were large, dark and very lovely. Advancing crabwise across the packed earth floor, a hank of heather rope dragging behind him, he said in that cracked, quavering voice:

'Who wants Euan Beag, then? What is it you would be asking him?'

Gil, aware of Tam beside him making the horns against the Evil Eye, raised his round felt bonnet to the extraordinary figure and said, 'Good day to you, Euan Beag. How are you?'

A smile spread over the tilted face, exposing three yellow teeth and a quantity of gum.

'Good day to you, maister. Euan's well, and yoursel?'

'I'm well, thanks,' returned Gil. Was this conversation really happening? 'Might I have a word?' he asked again, and wished he had a pomander, or one of Lady Stewart's pots of burning herbs. The creature had probably never been washed since he was pulled out of the well.

'Aye, but no a long one,' said Euan warily. 'He's got things he needs to get done. The ropes is all to be checked, and the barn swept and the stackyard make ready, afore the hairst comes hame, and all's for Euan to do.'

'And right well you'll do it, I can be sure,' said Gil. 'I'll not keep you long, I hope. Someone was telling me you'd mind when David Drummond vanished away.'

'David Drummond,' said the twisted man thoughtfully, scraping with bare, powerful toes at the dusty ground. The hen stretched out her head, tilting it to peer down at the movement.

'Wee Davie from Dalriach,' prompted Donal. Euan turned to bring the young man into his view. 'Thirty year since, it was.'

'Aye, it was,' agreed Euan. He turned to face Gil again. 'Aye, Euan can mind o't.' He waited, apparently for the

72

next question. Gil, resisting the urge to twist his own neck so that his head was tilted like the one before him, said:

'Can you tell me about it? What do you mind?'

'Why, he was lifted up.' Euan waved his free hand in the air, describing an airy flight. The hen scrabbled with her yellow feet, finding her balance. 'They lifted him from the path, wi ropes.'

'Wi ropes?' repeated Ned. Euan gave Gil a sly smile full of purple gums, and nodded.

'Aye, wi ropes. Many ropes, and made o hemp, better than Euan's. That's how he would ken them for the Good Neighbours, you ken.'

'You saw them?' Gil asked, startled. 'What happened?'

The creature nodded again, a strange movement of his head on the wry neck, parallel to the ground.

'That's right, maister, Euan saw them. It was a great party o folk on fine horsies, as fine as your big horsie there, and they lifted wee Davie Drummond wi their ropes, and bore him away,' again the airy gesture with the free hand, 'and Euan fell down wi fright and never saw Davie again. Billy grat for him,' he confided. 'And Euan grat and all.'

'Where was this?' Gil asked. Euan turned to look up the glen, where small trees bent over the burn's rocky descent.

'Yonder,' he said. 'Euan was gathering heather for rope, you ken, maister, and he seen it all.'

'Euan makes the ropes for the whole of Drumyre,' supplied Donal, 'and further afield and all, don't you, Euan.'

'On the open hillside,' said Gil thoughtfully. 'What like were the people?'

'Oh, fair folk, fair folk. Dressed as fine as fine, in silk-satin-velvet, all bright colours, all in green, all wi their bonnie ropes, and the *bodach* in a red doublet in their midst. Euan never saw them.'

Now was that complete nonsense, or was there a grain of truth? Gil wondered.

'And what way did they carry him off?'

Another sly smile.

'Och, is the maister saying he believes Euan?'

'I do,' said Gil. At least, he prevaricated, I believe he thought he saw something strange, probably involving ropes.

The bent figure before him struck its grimy hands together and said joyfully, 'It's a many year since anyone was believing Euan! Och, he'll be lighting a candle for the gentleman, so he will! Away south they took him, in a great whirl and noise, maister.'

'South,' repeated Gil, glancing at the sky. 'Not westwards? Not up to the pass?'

'South, they were going, maister,' Euan reiterated. 'And he was coming back from the south when he came home. Just last month, that would be, maister, and he's in his own place over the hill now.'

'How would you ken what way he came, you daft body?' demanded Ned, from where he stood by the corner of the barn. 'He cam down Glenbuckie, no Strathyre.'

Euan turned his misshapen back on the man, and gave Gil a significant look.

'He was in Strathyre afore he was in Glenbuckie, for Euan seen him.'

'You saw him come back?' said Gil. 'When was that?'

'Euan was watching when they set him down,' Euan agreed in his creaking voice.

'Tell me about that,' said Gil, trying to conceal amazement. 'What did you see?'

'Och, little to tell. A great whirling and sound of horses, like the first time, and they set him down on the track yonder,' he waved a hand southward, 'and then they were off and left him standing there. There was no ropes, not a single one. But Euan saw the *bodach*, aye,' he added, 'all in his red velvet again.'

'What way did the horses come?' Gil asked.

'There's a track up this side o the loch,' said Ned.

'Why would those ones be using a track?' objected Donal.

'Euan never saw,' said Euan sulkily. 'Just they were there, and set the laddie down, and bade him Godspeed and gie's your scrip, and send word if you want us, and then they went away. They went south,' he added, turning again in order to glower at Donal.

Gil held his breath, setting this story against his own speculations.

'Did you speak to David?' he asked gently. Euan turned back to consider him.

'Aye,' he said after a moment. 'Euan was speaking to the laddie.'

'What did you say to him?' Gil prompted, and got another display of the purple gums.

'Euan said, Billy's no here, he couldny wait.'

'Daft,' muttered Tam at Gil's elbow.

'And what did David say to that?' Gil asked.

Careful questioning got him the substance of the exchange. David Drummond had known Euan, had addressed him by his name, and then said that thirty years was a long time for Billy to wait and enquired if his friend was well. Euan had given him the news of Drumyre and its folk, which Gil suspected would have taken some time, and then David, asking if the way over the pass was still fit to use, had extracted himself with what was obviously tact and charm and set off up the side of the burn. Euan seemed in no doubt that he had been speaking to Billy Murray's friend.

'How easy is the way over to Glenbuckie?' Gil asked. 'Could I find it?'

Euan emitted a wheezing noise which seemed to be a laugh.

'No, no, maister could never take it,' he said kindly, 'no wi a great horsie to drag along the path. The horsie would fall down and be hurtit,' he explained.

'He's right at that,' commented Ned. 'It's a track for a man afoot, no for a powny. But it's no so difficult to make out, and it's an easy enough walk down to Dalriach from the crown o the way. If you knew it was there, you'd find it no bother.'

Euan laid a huge, filthy hand on Gil's arm, peering up at him with those beautiful eyes. The hen tipped her head and eyed him with a very similar expression.

'Was that all the word you was wanting?' he asked. 'For Euan has to sweep the stackyard afore the hairst comes home, you ken.'

'Aye, you get on wi your work.' Gil patted the hand and stepped away. 'That was a good word, Euan. My thanks, and God's blessing on you.' He raised his hat again, and watched as the crouched figure made its crabbed way back into the barn, the hen spreading her wings to keep her balance.

'Daft thing,' said Ned, leading Gil's horse forward.

'Waste o time that was, maister,' said Tam.

'On the contrary,' said Gil. 'It was well worth it. I'm glad you pointed the place out, Tam.' He glanced at the sky. 'Now, have we time to call at the Kirkton afore we get back to Stronvar, do you think, Ned?'

The Kirkton of Balquhidder hardly seemed a larger settlement than the group of buildings which made up Drumyre. Having sent Ned and Tam onwards from Gartnafueran with the weary horses, Gil followed Donal on foot across the flat valley floor, and paused at the end of the resonant wooden bridge to study the clachan. There was the little kirk itself, perched on a natural platform some way back from the river. Perhaps half a dozen houses lay around it, a ring of tall grey stones stood on a grassy slope below, and there was enough farmed land round about to make it clear that more than the old priest's glebe was being worked, although the harvest was not quite ready. Several small black cows were making their slow way home from the water-meadows, with a herd laddie singing among them. Above the kirk, on the steep, imposing bare rock he had seen from the garden at Stronvar, two goats were perched casually nibbling tussocks of grass.

'No, no, Sir Duncan is not dwelling in the kirk any longer,' said Donal when asked. 'He would be falling off the loft ladder, you understand, the age he is. Sir William got him a fine house built on the glebe land, with a good stout door and a latch, and even a tirling-pin as if you were in Callander.'

'He'll be there now, I suppose,' said Gil, looking about. 'It's a wide parish for an old man to take care of. Who has the living? Can Sir William not get a younger man put in?'

'The way I was hearing it,' said Donal, 'Sir William was asking them at Dunblane to name a new priest for the parish, last year it would be, and one of the Canons came himself to see.' He grinned. 'It was maybe one of Sir Duncan's good days. He was having more of those, you will understand, maister, what with young Rob Ruaidh that is keeping him washed and fed now, even if the laddie can't be making a peat fire stay alight. Whatever, Canon Fresall went home saying it was all as it should be and no need to put the old man out of his living. We were thinking,' he said with an innocent expression, 'he'd maybe have to pay a new man more to dwell here, so of course he would be pleased to think all was well.'

'I've no doubt of it.' Gil paused beside the ring of stones. Several children playing in its heart scattered to peer shyly at the stranger from under a group of hawthorn trees. 'Which is Sir Duncan's house?'

Donal pointed to the nearest of the long, low buildings. This one was stouter than some, with good stone gables and a sound layer of bracken thatch held down by a new rope net. Peat smoke filtered up through the mesh; it looked as if Rob Ruaidh was in control of the fire for the moment. Gil picked his way along the path, avoiding more hens and an inquisitive sheep, pausing at the open door to savour the smell of cooking which met him before he reached out to rattle at the tirling-pin Donal had mentioned.

'Sir Duncan?' he called. 'Are you within? May I enter?'

There was a clatter in the shadows inside, and something hissed on the fire.

'Christ and his saints preserve us!' said a voice. A young voice, a lowland voice. A hostile voice. 'What in the Deil's name are you doing here, Cunningham?'

'Christ aid!' said Gil, equally startled. 'Who – Robert Montgomery?'

'The same.' Another clatter as something was set down, movement in the shadows, and a tall young man came to the doorway, chin up, staring intently down his nose at Gil. Dark hair sprang thickly from a wide forehead, a square jaw jutted. Robert Montgomery, nephew of that turbulent baron Hugh, Lord Montgomery who was at odds with all Cunninghams.

'Of course,' said Gil after a moment's genealogical reckoning, 'your uncle's lady is a Campbell. She must be first cousin to Lady Stewart, that's the connection. But why here –?'

'Is it any of your business?' demanded the young man.

'I suppose it isny,' agreed Gil. 'Good day to you, Robert. Is Sir Duncan in his house? Can I get a word wi him?'

'No,' said Robert baldly. He glanced over his shoulder. 'He's sleeping the now. He's no had a good day, I'll not disturb him.' Not for you, suggested his tone.

'I'm after a bit of local history,' Gil said. 'Would you say he could manage that some time? How bad is he?'

'Mortal,' said Robert. He looked over his shoulder again, and stepped out into the sunshine. 'He's got a week or so, maybe, but he's on his way out. He's all too like my grandsire in his last days.' He considered briefly. 'You'd get more sense out of him on a morning. If you can get him on to a subject he likes, he's clear enough yet, and the history of the parish would do that.'

'Is he not even managing the Office?' said Gil, dismayed.

'No,' said Robert again. He had a way of saying the word which conveyed volumes, something which Gil recalled from his first encounter with the young man, more than a year since in very difficult circumstances. 'Martainn Clerk and I can deal wi the Office,' he expanded, 'seeing I'm in Minor Orders, but there's no been a Mass said in St Angus' Kirk for weeks.' His face softened. 'He lies in his bed reciting Matins and Lauds over and over again, jumbling all the words and losing the place, certain he's offering up what's right.'

'It is an offering, then,' Gil observed. Robert looked at him sharply, and then away again. 'And you have charge of him and his house, do you?'

'I do.' And do you want to make anything of it? said the tone of voice.

'Not easy. Cooking and keeping him clean, as well as taking care of the Office – it's a lot to do on your own.'

'That was the point,' said Robert, with a sour laugh 'Anyway, it's not as if there was anything else to do out here.'

Gil carefully refrained from looking around at the hills full of game, the river leaping with fish, the meadows full of wildfowl. A young man reared like this one must be tempted almost hourly to go out with bow or spear or line, to fetch home meat for the pot or for salting down for winter. Fighting the temptation would almost be worse than the menial tasks heaped on him by his servitude to the dying man.

'I suppose you're here,' said Robert abruptly, 'about this tale of the fellow come back from Elfhame?'

'I am,' agreed Gil, raising one eyebrow. 'What tellt you that?'

'Aye, well. It's the only thing in the parish for the last hundred years that might attract Blacader's quaestor.'

'How much have you heard about it?' Gil asked. 'You scrieved the letter to Andrew Drummond at Dunblane, they tell me.'

'I did. Two letters, in fact. The old woman asked me to write, told me exactly what she wanted said, made her mark at the foot o the paper.' He shrugged. 'If she's had an answer, I've heard nothing. I've no been asked to scrieve a reply, any road.'

'The second letter you wrote,' said Gil slowly. 'It promised a valuable gift to the Cathedral if they take the boy back at the sang-schule.' Robert nodded curtly. 'Tell me, do you think she had talked it over wi her family?'

'I've no a notion. I never set an eye on any o them, save only the fellow himself when he cam to walk her back to her pony.' He grinned without humour. 'Looked ordinar enough to me, a likely fellow in a blue doublet, in sore need o a barber. I don't think much o the way they clip their hair in Elfhame. Why?'

'So he never heard her talk about the letter?' Gil said.

'No in my presence.' Another sour laugh. 'What, you mean she's made all these plans for him and never consulted him? That'd be right, I suppose.'

'I don't know,' said Gil. 'As for whether the family kens she's planning to give away that much land – or what they'll say when they find out – I wouldny care to guess.'

'Well, I never asked her. I scrieved the note for her, and I took the coin she gied me for it,' Robert said bitterly, 'and learned all the history o the matter from my maister, and that was that.' He tilted his head. 'Is that him stirring? No, maybe no. Still and all, I'd best forgo the pleasure o your company, Cunningham, and go back in. If I'm no there when he wakes he'll take fright, and get up to search for me, and last time he near fell in the peat fire. And if you want a word wi him, come by some morning and see if he's fit for't.'

'I'll do that.' Gil studied the young man, noting the dark rings round his eyes, the way the square jaw was pared to the bone. 'How long have you been here, Robert?'

'A year, six weeks and two days,' said Robert Montgomery succinctly, and ducked back into the priest's house.

* * *

'Penance?' said Alys.

'It must be,' agreed Gil. He picked a sprig of mint growing in a tub by the arbour, and crushed it in his fingers. Socrates came to sniff at his hand, and sneezed. 'I hardly liked to ask how long he has left to serve, but he's obviously keeping a tally.'

'Poor boy,' said Alys thoughtfully, staring across the loch at the Kirkton in its haze of smoke. 'I have wondered what became of him. After all, he never intended – and now he is body-servant to a dying man, and I suppose he cannot leave however bad it gets.'

'If the old man is dying, it must end some time,' said Gil.

She nodded, and leaned against his shoulder. 'I wonder if he is allowed company? I suppose Lady Stewart must know more about him than she said. I can ask her.'

'He might not welcome your company either,' said Gil. 'He keeps his low opinion of Cunninghams. Unless it's his manner,' he added. 'Like Death, perhaps, he *shewith to all rudesse*.'

'Hmm,' she said. 'Tell me again what you learned these two days.'

He drew her comfortably closer and began the account from the beginning. As always, he had already found that setting it in order had helped, and her penetrating questions shed a different light on the several interviews. By the time he had finished, the dog was asleep.

'Someone came for the songman,' she said. 'I suppose the boy heard the arrangements being made. I wonder what he really saw, and where *Hell* is. If he had already decided he had seen the Devil, then he might mishear some other word.'

'Wherever it is,' said Gil, 'it's somewhere with a kirk rich enough to draw away a singer from Dunblane.'

'Dunkeld?' wondered Alys. 'No, surely the songman would have been traced to there by now. Wherever it is, it need not be so big a place itself, even if its kirk is well endowed. You know Scotland far better than I, Gil. Can you think of a likely name?'

'No,' admitted Gil, 'and I've never met such a one in a document either. But I've never travelled north of here myself. I'll ask about when I'm at Perth.'

'And I wonder why the secrecy?' Alys pursued.

'To avoid the donation to the Cathedral for freeing him?'

'Or because the – the agent, whoever he is, prefers to act in secrecy,' she speculated. 'I wonder – how reliable a witness is the boy Walter, do you think?'

'Not very,' said Gil, pulling a face. 'His brother called him a daft laddie, and I'd agree.'

'Hmm,' she said again. 'And the Drummond matter – the brother is fallen into a melancholy, you are saying.'

'So it seems,' agreed Gil. 'Sighing and moping, talking endlessly about his guilt. Lost in the *Forest of Noyous Hevynes.*'

'So it seems,' she repeated, and tilted her head to look up at him. 'Yes. And this strange creature at the farm over the pass – what do you think of his tale?'

'Clear enough, so far as it goes. Someone lifted young David Drummond that morning, before he met the Murray boy, bound him and bore him off southwards. He does seem to have been an outstanding singer, so I suppose he could have been stolen away for the same reason as John Rattray and the others. But why he was lifted there rather than at Dunblane I don't understand.'

'It must have been someone who knew the boy's movements.' Alys considered this for a moment. 'He would be guarded, I suppose, at Dunblane, or at least he would have company and a song-master who would take responsibility for the boys. Easier to steal him away out here on the journey, where he wouldn't be missed for days. And Euan had seen Davie Drummond returning, you said? And spoken to him?'

'Aye, and David knew him.'

'That's no surprise,' she said seriously. 'Davie stood by the track yesterday and named all the hills and farms round about to me. He knows the family song about Dalriach. Whoever he is, Gil, and I'm as certain as Lady

Stewart that he's close kin to the Drummonds, he has been well taught. He has even mentioned having crossed the pass thirty years ago, before he was lifted, but he says he saw nothing when it happened.'

'Clever,' said Gil. She nodded agreement. 'I suppose Euan might have mentioned having seen him stolen away when he spoke to him this time. But why is he here? And where has he come from?' He looked down at the velvet-covered crown of her head. 'Who could have taught him? Questions, questions, and precious few answers that I can see.'

'I would say,' said Alys, 'he has been taught by someone who knows Dalriach and all the land and people round about. So it has to be one of the family, or I suppose one of their tenants at Dalriach. Will you go away again tomorrow, Gil?' She turned to look up at him, and made a face when he nodded. 'I am invited to the harvest celebration in a day or two, and to sleep there afterwards. They called it a *ceilidh* – an evening's merriment. I will keep a close eye on everyone, and perhaps I will see who it might have been.'

'But he wasn't taught locally,' said Gil. 'In a neighbourhood like this, you could never do such a thing in secret. People gossip. We need to find out whether the sister, the one that is married along the glen, has been out of Balquhidder recently.'

'I can ask Seonaid. She will likely know.'

He nodded. 'And I should have asked in Dunblane whether Andrew Drummond or his mistress had had a visitor in recent weeks.'

'She would never have had a guest so close to her time, poor woman,' said Alys firmly, and crossed herself, 'least of all a young man, and the Canon could hardly have kept a kinsman at his manse in the town without it being noticed. I may not know about country life, Gil, but I have lived in towns all my days. Did you say you had spoken to the servant?'

'Drummond's man? Yes – I asked him about the children. A boy and a girl, eight and four years old. Drummond stirred himself enough to take them to their other grandmother in Perth, two weeks since, the man told me. She's remarried to a tanner there, it seems.'

'The poor poppets,' said Alys in sympathy. She waved a hand across her face. 'I think those biting creatures are coming out, and the supper will be ready soon.'

'Yes, we should go in.' He rose, and gave her his hand. The dog woke, and scrambled to his feet, shaking himself. 'I still don't see why Blacader sent me into this thicket. Nobody is murdered, no crime has been committed.'

'Someone may yet be murdered,' Alys said seriously. They began to stroll down the garden, arm in arm. 'Davie told me the same tale as Murdo Dubh. There have been several accidents, which might be attempts at murder, and at least two of them might have injured the old woman instead, if Ailidh or Davie had not detected them.' She paused where the grass paths crossed, and counted on her fingers. 'There was the ladder and the pitchfork that Murdo told us about, there was a pair of shears hidden point up in a basket of fleece –'

'How would that injure David Drummond?'

'He was combing the locks for Mistress Drummond to spin them. Either could have been the next to reach into the basket, and the shears had been sharpened to a vicious point. Ailidh showed me them. Then there was a basket of mushrooms brought in for cooking, that the third grand-daughter Elizabeth had gathered one morning. Davie saw the bad one himself. Elizabeth said she never picked it, and Ailidh says she believes her, for they use mushrooms for all sorts of things, for dyeing and physicking cattle, and their mother has taught them well.'

'All circumstantial,' said Gil slowly, 'but they add up badly, don't they?'

'They do,' she agreed seriously. 'Mistress Drummond will say only that someone has ill-wished them, so they told me, but both Davie and Ailidh think it is more serious than that.'

'Alys, have a care. And Murdo? What does he think?'

Her quick smile flickered.

'If that relationship prospers,' she pronounced, 'it will do well. Murdo thinks just as Ailidh does.'

He laughed aloud, and caught up her hand again.

'Well, I think we should go in to supper,' he said, 'so I hope you do too!'

Chapter Five

George Brown, Bishop of Dunkeld, folded his hands on the stacked papers on his reading-desk and gazed out of the window across the river Tay.

'I caused a search to be made, a course,' he said. 'Jaikie's a good man, a discreet man, writes a fine hand. A witty companion, though his tongue can be sharp. I've aye trusted him well beyond the reach o my arm. He's a valued member of my household, Maister Cunningham, as well as being a good secretary.'

Gil nodded, aware of what was not being said. The Bishop was anxious. He was concealing it well, helped by his natural expression of round-faced good humour, but Gil lived and worked with men of law, and the small signs, the tension at the temples, the stiffness round the eyes, told him a clear tale. Seated now in the quiet study of the episcopal house in Perth, with its painted panelling, its view of the busy waterfront and the green land across the Tay in the noonday sun, he said:

'My lord, what can you tell me about the man? Did you say his name is Stirling?'

'Aye, James Stirling. Forty year old, I suppose, priested, an able fellow.'

'Forty. Was he at the sang-schule at Dunblane, my lord?'

'He was and all,' agreed the Bishop, startled. 'Is that aught to do wi it?'

'I don't know,' admitted Gil. 'But I think he was a friend of this lad that vanished thirty year since and it's said has returned from wherever he's been hid.'

'Aye, aye, Perthshire's buzzing wi the tale, though Jaikie never let on that he might have known him, that I heard. What, are you saying he's been stolen away by the same folk?'

'I don't know,' Gil said again. 'It seems unlikely. Is he a good singer?'

'No bad. A strong tenor, good enough for the Office and well trained at Dunblane, a course, though by something he once said his voice was finer before it broke.'

'Whereas the two men that's left St John's Kirk here are right good singers,' said Gil thoughtfully. 'What more can you tell me about the man himself, sir?'

'Tell you about him?' A small smile crossed the Bishop's face. 'A good secretary. Able, as I said. I've offered him more than once to find him a place in Edinburgh or about the King, but he's aye said he likes it at my side, the mix of pastoral and diplomatic appeals to him.'

'Diplomatic,' Gil repeated, recalling the confidence Archbishop Blacader placed in William Dunbar. 'Was he with you during the negotiations with England?'

'He was.' The Bishop looked directly at Gil. 'He was close involved. It was him and his English counterpart dealt wi some of the preliminaries, agreeing what terms the embassage would sign to.'

'No wonder he's been happy here, if he had that level of freedom to act.'

'Oh, aye, he's happy, maister,' agreed Brown. 'And shown himsel worthy o trust so long's I've had him in my employ. Which is why it's so –' He stopped, and looked away.

'Does he have enemies?'

'We've all got enemies, maister,' said the Bishop, 'starting wi the Deil hissel. I've no notion that Jaikie had more than any other.'

'Is he civil? Friendly in his bearing?'

'He deports himself well in my presence.'

That's no answer, Gil thought. 'And what about his disappearance? Did you see him that day?'

'I did.' Brown's gaze transferred itself to the woodland beyond the river. After a moment he went on, 'I'd had occasion to find fault wi him.' Gil waited. 'He and Rob Gregor my chaplain had had a disagreement, and Jaikie referred to it a time or two through the day, in terms I felt wereny becoming to a clerk.'

'How did he take that?' Gil asked.

'Well enough, I thought at the time, but a course if it angered him he'd a concealed it from me.'

'And then?'

'He went out into Perth to enquire about the rents, seeing it was coming near to Lammastide. I'd expected him back at my side afore Vespers, so we could deal wi the last of the day's papers as soon as Vespers and Compline were done, and he never showed, nor came in for supper though it was late. And he never came back the next morn either. And since he was never liable to stay out, since I might ha need of him at any time, I had them send after him.'

'And what did the search find out?'

The Bishop shook his head. 'They tracked him away through the town, from one property to another, and then lost the scent. Then they asked at all the town ports, and the haven and all, and none had seen a clerk o his description pass through. Wat Currie my steward, that oversaw the search, says it's as if he's vanished into the air.'

'Maybe I should get a word wi Maister Currie.' Gil looked directly at the other man. 'And yourself? What do you think has happened to him, my lord?'

'I dinna ken,' said Brown, his Dundee accent suddenly very broad. 'I dinna ken, Maister Cunningham, but I fear the worst. Jaikie wouldna up and leave me for a wee scolding.'

There were footsteps in the outer chamber, and an agitated squeaking. Bishop Brown turned his head, smiling through his anxiety, as a well-built man in the decent gown of a steward entered the study, followed by a liveried servant carrying a small brown and white dog.

'Ah! Here's Wat the now,' he said, holding out his arms, 'and my wee pet. See him here, Noll. Aye, aye, he's taken well to you. Mitchel will ha his work cut out, when he comes back fro Dunkeld, to get him to mind him.'

The dog was handed over, wriggling and yelping, and the steward dismissed the man Noll with a gesture. The animal was no more than a puppy, perhaps five months old, Gil estimated, and seemed to be some kind of little spaniel, with floppy ears, a soft coat and the beginnings of a plume on its assiduous tail. It was plainly much attached to the Bishop.

'That's a fine pup,' he offered. 'Where did you get him? Is there a breeder hereabouts?'

'It's a woman that settled outside the burgh,' said the steward, smiling at the creature's antics, 'maybe a year since, wi a great kennel-full of dogs, and set hersel up breeding them. She'd come from Glasgow, so she said,' he added, 'maybe you'd ken her yoursel, Maister Cunningham.'

'A dog-breeder?' said Gil thoughtfully. 'From Glasgow. Would that be a woman called Doig?'

'Aye, that's the name,' agreed the Bishop, still petting the dog. 'There, now, Jerome, my wee mannie, that's enough. Right bonnie dogs she has, sound and well-natured, so when my poor Polycarp dee'd last Februar, we negotiated for one of her first litter of spaniels, and got the wee fellow as soon as he was old enough, didn't we no, Jerome?' The pup yipped at him and scrambled up his breast to lick his face. Gil, recalling Socrates as a youngster, somehow doubted that this creature would have the chance to develop his good manners. 'Well, Maister Cunningham, if that's all I can tell you for now, I need to get on wi these papers. Away you wi Wat and he'll let you ha the details you're wanting.'

'Might I ask about another thing first?' Gil looked from one man to the other. 'It's another Kirk matter, though not Dunkeld's.'

'Ask away,' said Brown.

'Canon Drummond of Dunblane was here in Perth two weeks since, I'm told.'

'Drummond,' repeated the Bishop. 'Oh, aye, Andrew Drummond. That's a sad business,' he went on, crossing himself. 'It's a sound lesson, Maister Cunningham, in why a clerk should have naught to do wi women. The vows apart, they're no more than a distraction to a churchman, whether they live or whether they dee.'

Gil, familiar with this attitude, smiled politely.

'Did he lodge here?' he asked. Brown looked at his steward, who shook his head.

'No, never here,' he said firmly. 'I'd mind o that, and so would you, my lord, for he'd be entitled to eat at your own table, and you'd never permit it. Two week syne we had,' he paused, staring at the wall above Gil's head for a moment, then counted off on his fingers, 'Maister Myln that's Rural Dean northward, two fellows from Whithorn travelling to Brechin, a party of Erschemen from Lorne –'

'Ask at the friars, maister,' suggested Brown. 'He could ha lodged wi any of them, save maybe the Whitefriars, for the house there's no fit for guests the now.' He reached round the pup to shuffle at the papers on his desk. 'Jaikie was to ha dealt wi getting their roof seen to, just that week. Here's the docket,' he said, holding it out of Jerome's reach. 'Aye, aye, I'll need to get Rob Gregor to deal wi't now, and it'll never be done.'

'I've a notion Maister Stirling never has took the rent-roll wi him,' said Wat Currie. He nodded dismissal to Noll again and poured ale for both of them, handing Gil his beaker. He was a well-upholstered man some ten years older than Gil, with a round satisfied face and a comfortable manner. Fairish hair hung round his ears below a handsome velvet bonnet, and his long gown of grey-blue worsted was turned back with murrey-coloured taffeta, a superior form of the murrey-and-plunkett livery the servants wore. 'He just made a list in his tablets. He'd not want to take the roll out into the town.'

'I can see that,' agreed Gil, unrolling it cautiously. It was a fragile object, its inner layers clearly of great age, successive strips of parchment glued on the end as the earlier portions filled up. 'Why not simply start a new one?'

Currie shrugged, and pointed to the end nearest him. 'Anyways, there's all your names, and I can gie you the directions to find them.'

'You're sure these are all of them?' Gil counted the entries current in the neat columns. 'Five, six, eight properties.'

'That's right.'

'Just I was thinking that if you lost the trail, maybe he had another place to call.'

'We've searched the burgh,' said Currie flatly, and buried his face in his beaker.

'Fair enough.' Gil began copying down the names. 'Tell me about Maister Stirling. My lord has a good opinion of him, that's clear. Is he liked by the rest of the household?'

Currie shrugged again. 'Well enough, I'd say. He's never been one for idle giff-gaff, you ken, never talks about his own business or what he's doing.' So I'd expect of a confidential secretary, thought Gil. 'He's a bit sharp wi his tongue, just the same. The kind of remark that makes folk laugh, all except the one it's aimed at.'

'Does he make enemies that way?'

'Not so you'd notice. He's as like to strike at one as another, a bit like a fool, there'd be little point in taking offence.'

'Where does he sleep when he's here in Perth? Does he have his own bed?'

'Aye, him and Rob Gregor that's my lord's chaplain has the chamber just off my lord's own.'

'Do they get on, the two of them?'

'Well enough.' Currie smiled. 'I'd defy anyone no to get on wi Rob, the gentle soul he is. Hardly close, but they managed fine.'

'Have you any idea where he might have gone?'

'None. We wondered if he'd maybe been called home,' said Currie reluctantly, 'but we sent to where his family dwells, that's nigh to Dunblane you ken, and to Dunkeld and all, and no word. And he's no private business that any of us knows on, to draw him away so sudden.'

'Is his gear still here?'

'It's all packed up and lying yonder,' said the steward, nodding at a small carved kist set under the window of his tidy chamber. 'Rob was worried,' he expanded, 'after two-three days and he wasny back, about light-fingered laddies, so he stowed it all and brought it to me for safe keeping. I'd vouch for all my household, maister, but a man can aye be mistook in that, and there's no knowing how some will react if they're tempted.'

'Very wise,' agreed Gil. 'Stirling has no servant of his own, then?'

'No, no, managed for himself mostly. He'd ask me for one of the men to carry out the odd task for him. Rob's the same.'

'Did you take an inventory of his goods? Could I see it?'

'It's in the kist, so Rob said.' Currie set down his beaker and moved to unstrap the lid of the little box. The piece of paper on top of the contents had a list on it in careful writing, but Gil had no need to study it to recognize that James Stirling had left behind a very different category of possessions from those abandoned by John Rattray in Dunblane, or by the two songmen here in Perth whose house had also been stripped of all small items. Just under the paper was a sturdy leather case whose shape was familiar to any grown man.

'His razors,' he said.

'Never say so!' said Currie, lifting the case and opening it. 'Our Lady protect him, you're right, maister. They're all in here. Two good razors and the strop, his wee knife to his nails, his box of soap and all.' He looked at Gil, concern slowly deepening in his face. 'Christ aid us, he's no left willingly at all, has he, maister?'

'No,' said Gil rather grimly. 'I'd say he hadn't. And I'm surprised the chaplain never thought of it when he packed the gear.'

'Och, no, that's Rob for you,' said Currie. 'He's some age, maister, he's nearsighted, and he's aye more in the next world than this one.' He shook his head. 'I wish I'd gied him a hand to pack up, as he asked, but I was sore taigled that day.'

He set the shaving-gear in the upturned lid of the box, turned to the table again, and drew the rent-roll towards him, peering at the entries on the free end and blinking hard.

'I had two of the stable-hands ask at all these properties,' he said. 'They all said, Aye he'd been there, and gone on. One of the lads helps me often at the hunt, and had the sense to ask about which way the fellow went each time as he left. He didny get a sensible answer from all, a course, but he worked it out that our man went to,' he leaned closer to the parchment, 'first these three, and then this one, and these two. And then these two in the Skinnergate, though he couldny work out which was the last. And then, he said, they asked about, and found none to say they'd seen him after the Skinnergate, and when I sent another fellow round all the ports none had seen him.'

'Skinnergate,' said Gil thoughtfully. He had the chaplain's inventory in his hand. *Razirs, rol of papirs, crosbo, sanct Jac's*, it read. 'I'd like a look at this *Rol of papirs*, if we can find it, Maister Currie. Papers can aye tell something, if they're worth keeping.'

They unpacked the box, with more care than had gone into packing it. Currie clicked his tongue disapprovingly as he refolded crumpled garments, but said nothing. The roll of papers was near the bottom, under the crossbow in its linen bag, tucked into one of Stirling's riding-boots along with a carved St James whose paint was wearing off his scrip and broad-brimmed hat, and a pair of unwashed hose. Gil untied the tape which bound the documents, and flattened the curling sheets out on the table.

93

'Is it maybe letters?' asked Currie. He shook out the hose, releasing a waft of stale sweat into the room, and peered round Gil's arm.

'There are letters,' agreed Gil, 'but the first ones go back a few years. They don't tell me much.' He turned the sheets, scanning the different scripts. There were several letters from the man's family, with brief accounts of the harvest and the well-being of his kin, and requests for prayers. Under those were two different contracts, which he studied closely, detailing sums which Stirling had borrowed from merchants of Perth. Each was duly signed off by both parties, so the money had all been repaid.

'He's never lacked for coin?' he said casually.

'Never since I've known him,' agreed Currie. 'Which is what you'd expect, seeing how he's placed wi my lord. Weel ben, weel beneficed, as they say.'

'So I wonder what he did with this that he borrowed?' Gil flattened one of the contracts for the steward to see. 'This one a year since, and another two years before that, good sums both times. Have you any knowledge of this?'

'Oh, he wouldny let on about sic a thing,' said Currie, shaking his head. 'Nor any of the household wouldny need to know, seeing he's often about Perth on my lord's business.' His finger fell unerringly on the note of the sum of money. 'Fifty merks! Saints preserve us, what would he want that for?'

'That's what I'd like to know.' Gil leafed further through the bundle. 'He's borrowed and repaid it within the contract, each time, which suggests something gey profitable to me. What have we here? More letters, a docket from my lord – he seems to keep them in order by the date, so you'd think whatever he did with the money the evidence would be with the contracts.'

'Maybe his man of law would tell you,' suggested Currie, indicating the elaborate penwork with which the notary had blazoned his mark on the finished contract.

The loops and curls depicted a conventional mercat cross surmounted by some kind of bird of prey. 'That's Andro Gledstane's mark, you ken.'

'No need to disturb him,' Gil said. He had reached the outermost sheet of the roll of papers. 'Here it is. Our man's bought a pair of properties on the Skinnergate, and paid back the loans out of the rents.' He whistled, running a finger down the page. 'As well he might. Look at this, Maister Currie. He's collecting seven – no, eight merks a quarter on this one alone.'

The steward peered at the writing, and nodded.

'Those are both the far end of the Skinnergate, next the Red Brig Port,' he said. 'That accounts for it, I'd say. The lads wouldny ha thought to ask for him so far along, seeing my lord's properties are this end, and the fellow I sent round the ports would never ha spoke to the houses.'

'What question did your man ask at the ports?' Gil asked.

Currie straightened up, frowning, and after a moment said, 'I bade him ask if Maister Stirling had been by the port. And if they didny know Maister Stirling, I bade him describe him as a clerk, tall and well-made, in a good gown of tawny wool, wi dark hair and a wine-coloured hat stuck all round wi pilgrim badges, and going about his lone.' He smiled wryly. 'I suppose you'd call it his one weakness. He collects the things wherever he goes wi my lord, the good silver ones not the pewter sort, and pins them on that hat. He's got another hat for his best,' he jerked his head at the box, 'I've just saw it in there, but he aye wears – wore – wears the one wi the badges.'

Gil swallowed hard. Somehow this detail brought the man before him as if he was present in the chamber. Currie looked at his expression, and nodded rather grimly.

'I'll send for Peter,' he said, 'and he'll can show you where these properties lie, and the other houses he enquired at forbye. Have you lodging for the night, maister? If you come back here afore Vespers you'll get a bite, and a word wi Rob Chaplain if you're wanting it, and I'll can fit you and your men in somewhere.'

The man Peter, a stocky, long-headed fellow in the Bishop's outdoor livery, led Gil by one vennel and another, talking cheerfully as he went.

'Next the port, Maister Currie tells me, his last place. No wonder we lost him, then,' he pronounced as they emerged into St John's Square, 'though I'm right annoyed at mysel not casting further along the street for him. We'll pick him up this time, maybe. Mind you, the trail's cold by now,' he added.

Gil nodded absently, looking about him. They were next to the high east end of St John's Kirk, a huge, handsome building set in its kirkyard, its tower casting a long shadow over the small houses round about. Folk came and went, the morning's marketing over, the work of the day still to be done. Two women argued shrilly over a basket of washing.

'Which is the baxter's shop?' he asked.

'Where the two men went missing from?' asked Peter intelligently, and pointed. 'That's it there. They had the upper chambers, to the side there, but they're let again long since,' he added. 'They left all seemly, took their boots and their scrips wi them, or so the baxter's man tellt me when I spoke wi him in the Green Man tavern.'

'So I heard,' Gil agreed, studying the building. The chambers Peter had indicated were off a good stone fore-stair; the tenants could have left at any hour without disturbing the rest of the household. He had spoken earlier to the Precentor of St John's Kirk, a long-faced gloomy man, and learned a lot, some of it relevant.

'Brothers,' John Kinnoull the Precentor had said. 'James and Sanders Moncrieff. One tenor, one bass. Probably my best bass, was Sanders, and you ken what it's like finding a tenor of any sort nowadays.'

'The fellow who left Dunblane in February sings high tenor,' said Gil.

'Someone's building himself a choir, then,' said Kinnoull. 'You mark my words, maister, he'll fetch away another mean-tone next to take the second line.' It was not easy to tell whether he was serious.

'Did they take anything with them?' Gil had asked.

Kinnoull, his pink, lugubrious face thoughtful, said, 'Well, now, it's hard to say. By the time the baxter thought to let us ken at the kirk here, their door had likely been standing open all day and neither man to be seen.'

'So everything portable had gone,' Gil suggested.

'Well, I wouldny say that,' admitted Kinnoull. 'But there's no knowing what they took wi them and what was taken after they left.'

'Linen, cooking gear, blankets?' Gil asked, recalling what Rattray had removed from Dunblane. 'Their boots? Music?'

'Oh, aye, music indeed,' said Kinnoull in indignation. 'That was two great bundles of music gone, never to be seen again, and all to be copied fresh afore St John's Day if we were to do justice to the feast.'

It had been difficult to keep the man to the point, but Gil had finally gathered the impression that the brothers Moncrieff had left in good order, much as James Rattray had done, probably by night and taking their portable property with them. After considering the various feasts of May, Kinnoull had given him a date, but seemed to have no more information.

Now, Peter said helpfully, 'Allan Baxter would be in the bakehouse from a couple hours afore dawn, that time of year, and he never heard them go out, so they say. Likely they left just at slack tide.'

'What, you think they went by water?'

Peter shrugged. 'It's the likeliest way to travel out of Perth, maister. No saying where they went beyond Taymouth, a course, but unless they went by Glasgow a ship's the most likely.'

Gil considered this. Landsman that he was, he had not thought of this route.

'Aye, but when would slack tide be?' he wondered. 'Would there be a mariner down at the haven who might recall?'

'Midnight,' said Peter confidently, 'or no so long after.'

'You mind that, do you?' asked Gil in surprise.

The man grinned sidelong at him. 'Aye, I mind it fine. It so happens I'd a night on the Tay wi my cousin that dwells down the river a wee bittie, and we'd some trouble wi the water-bailies, and I was late back.'

Fishing, Gil thought, probably without a permit. 'You're certain it was the same day?'

'Aye, well, Maister Currie had a word to say about my absence,' Peter explained, 'and I had to see to the horses afore I could eat, and by the time I got to the buttery two of the songmen doing a flit was all they could speak of. So I mind it well as being the same day.'

Did the time add up? Gil wondered. He looked at the fore-stair again. It would certainly be easy enough to make one's way down, perhaps by lantern-light, and across the square to one or the other of the vennels which led out between the houses.

'Is it far to the haven?'

'Our Lady love you, maister, it's no but a step. Down this vennel here, see,' Peter beckoned, and dived down the narrow entry like a rabbit, 'and out on to the Northgate, and yon's the haven at the street's end.' He emerged at the vennel's end and pointed. Gil, following him, looked over the heads of the passers-by at the rocking masts, and nodded. 'And yon's the Skinnergate, just across the way,' the man ended.

'And when you had your night on the Tay,' said Gil. Peter gave him a wary look. 'Do you mind if there were any vessels went down the river?'

'Aye, there were.' Peter stepped aside out of the path of two men with a barrel slung on a pole between them. 'Two or three, there was.'

'Who would know who they were?' Gil asked. 'Would your cousin be able to name them?'

'Oh, aye, likely, if he can mind who they were,' said Peter with confidence. 'He kens all the traffic on the Tay, does our Danny. I've no doubt if he can mind them he can name them and who's the skipper. Excepting one,' he added doubtfully, 'I mind he said was a Hollander and he'd no notion who skippered it.'

'Fair enough,' said Gil. 'Now about Maister Stirling.'

With a lot of circumstantial detail, Peter explained how he had tracked James Stirling, from these properties to that one, to this house next to where they stood, and finally into the Skinnergate. He was still annoyed by his failure to follow the man far enough, 'but if even Wat Currie never knew of his having rents of his own to collect, there's none of us would know of it,' he said, more than once. 'I still wonder that he never took any of us wi him, even if he wasny expecting to gather in the money that day.'

'Did he often go about alone?' Gil asked.

'Sometimes aye, sometimes no. This time it was no, I suppose.'

Gil nodded, then clapped the man on the shoulder and said, 'There's more experienced huntsmen than you been caught out the same way. Never mind it now, man, and show me where you were cast at fault.'

The Bishop's Skinnergate properties were the first two houses on the street, a narrow prosperous way lined with leatherworkers' shops, shoemakers, glovers, a bookbinder, several saddlers, all making use of the proceeds of the skinner's trade and the tanyards which made their presence known beyond the town Ditch. In Glasgow the stinking trades were banished east of the burgh, so that the prevailing westerly winds carried the worst of the smell away, but on this side of the country the wind blew as often from the east as from the west. It made sense of a sort, Gil supposed, to put the tanners out to the north. He ducked a set of harness dangling from the overhang of a saddler's house, avoided an apprentice who was trying to sell him a pair of hawking-gloves, and said over his shoulder:

'I'm not surprised nobody saw what way he went along here. Is it always as busy as this?'

'Times it's busier,' said Peter. 'Now that's where I tracked our man last,' he pointed to a sagging wooden building, 'and the wife there said he'd passed the time of day, civil enough, agreed when he'd be back to uplift what was due to my lord, and she shut the door as he got to the foot o the step, so she never saw what way he turned after.' He nodded at the bustling street. 'And if he went on to the Red Brig Port, it's this way.'

The two properties at the end of the street, next to the port, were quite different in aspect. The first they came to was a narrow toft, barely wider than the gable of the low stone house at the street end. A goat's skull complete with horns hung at the corner of the building and a well-trampled path led past the door. There was a number of workshops visible down its length, with smoke and hammering and the various signs of metalworking. From the house itself, a persistent rasping and the pungent smell of burnt horn told Gil what trade the occupant followed, long before Peter said:

'Aye, that's Francis Dewar the horner. Right good combs he makes, and wee boxes and all sorts, maister, you'd get a fairing to take home to your wife if you wanted one.'

'A good thought,' said Gil, looking about him. No wonder Stirling had paid back the loan so prompt; the many small rents from this subdivided property would add up very nicely.

The next toft was much wider and was obviously occupied by a tanner; there was a stretched hide in a frame slung from the eaves of the well-built house and the long yard behind it was full of stacks of half-cured skins. Next to the house was the Red Brig Port, a more businesslike affair than those Glasgow found adequate. The massive leaves of the gate stood open at this time of day, and its custodian was sitting in the sunshine, his back against one of the two great posts. He opened his eyes as they passed him, but did not move. A laden cart rumbled ponderously towards them, on to the wooden bridge, and Gil stopped at the near end of the creaking structure to wait for it, looking down into the Town Ditch. It was both wide and deep, full of greenish murky water and streaming weeds. There seemed to be a strong current.

'The town's well defended,' he commented.

'Oh, aye,' agreed Peter. 'That's why my lord spends the most o his time here. The wild Ersche come down raiding at Dunkeld, three weeks out o four, but they'll no bother coming this far just for a wetting.'

'How wide is the Ditch?'

'Four fathom? It began as the leat for the town mills,' Peter offered, 'and then Edward Longshanks had it dug to this size when he fortified Perth, or so they say. Had all the able men o Perth working at it for weeks, and oversaw them hissel in case they ran away or laid a trap.'

Gil looked at the Ditch again. That would account for its size, he thought. Beyond it was a typical suburb, the usual mix of hovels and larger houses along with the working yards of tanner and skinner, a dyer over yonder, all the stinking trades, as he had surmised. The sound of barking floated over the noises of industry.

'The Bishop got his wee dog out here somewhere?' he recalled.

'Aye, that's right,' agreed Peter. 'It's a woman, a cousin o Mitchel MacGregor that's Maister Currie's own man, which would likely be how my lord heard o her. She's got a place over yonder, at the back o the dyeyard. The most o her dogs is no bad,' he added thoughtfully. 'Were ye wishing a word wi her, or will it be Andy Cornton the tanner's house?'

'I'll see her after,' Gil decided. 'Is she on her own? No sign of her man?'

'I've never set eyes on him,' said Peter, following him back towards the gate. 'He's a mimmerkin, they say. A duarch.' He held his hand out, waist high, to demonstrate. 'They've no bairns, but.'

Maister Cornton was evidently doing well. The house was well maintained, the fore-stair swept clean and a tub of flowers set by the door. When Gil rattled at the tirling-pin the maidservant who leaned out above them to answer took one look at Peter's livery and vanished, reappearing at the door a moment later.

'Come in, maister, come in,' she said, bobbing to Gil. 'Hae a seat, whiles I find my mistress, or was it the maister ye wanted?'

'Either of them, lass,' Gil assured her. She bobbed again, and whisked off, her wooden-soled shoes clattering on the flagged floor. After a moment she could be heard outside, calling to her mistress. Gil moved to the far window, and found himself looking at the yard with its stacked skins, heaped oak-bark chips, two handcarts. Movement in one of the sheds drew his attention, and proved to be two small children playing on another little cart, which they had overturned; they seemed to be competing for which could spin one of the wheels faster. The nearer was a boy, of perhaps eight, and the other child was in petticoats. What had caught his eye was their light hair, standing out in a halo of fine curls on the two little heads.

A stout woman hurried up the yard behind the maid-servant, pulling off a sacking apron as she went. This must be Mistress Cornton. She paused to wave to the children, then hurried on into the house. After a moment she appeared in the hall, puffing slightly, exclaiming.

'Effie, did you never offer the gentleman a refreshment? Away and fetch something, lass, and take his man ben wi you and gie him some of the new ale. Hae a seat, maister, and we'll get this sorted. It's about the rent, no? Maister Stirling's never come back for it, though he was to be here two days after Lammas, so my man said.'

She paused, staring anxiously at Gil. She was a hand-some woman in her forties, he estimated, wearing a grey everyday gown of good wool, its sleeves and hem turned back over a striped kirtle whose margins showed a sprinkling of oak-bark flakes.

'Not so much about the rent,' he said, taking the seat she indicated, 'as about Maister Stirling himself. He called here to arrange about uplifting the rent, then?'

'Aye, that's what I'm saying,' she agreed, nodding vigorously. The little brass pins which secured her kerchief caught the light from the windows. 'He was here on the,' she shut her eyes and counted on her fingers, 'six days afore Lammas, so that would be the twenty-fifth day of July, and got a word wi my man, and they arranged what suited both for him to come back and fetch it away. Only he's never came.'

'He seems to have left Perth,' said Gil. 'I'm trying to find out where he might have gone.' Or been taken, he thought.

'Oh.' Mistress Cornton stared at him blankly. 'He tellt my man he'd be here.'

'Had you a word wi him yourself, mistress?'

'No what you'd call a word.' She shook her head and the pins glinted again. 'I'd gone away into the town, maister, wi the bairns.' Her glance went involuntarily to the window, and Gil said:

'Those are Canon Drummond's bairns, am I right? Their mother must have been your daughter.'

Her mouth twisted. She nodded, and bent her head, dabbing at her eyes with the end of her kerchief.

'My poor lassie,' she whispered. 'Christ and his blessed mother bring her to rest. Aye, he brought them here to their grandam. Cornton's no best pleased at the imposition, but they're my kin, I'll not turn them from me, and their father will pay for their keep.'

'I'm right sorry for your loss,' said Gil gently. 'It must be hard for you. When did he bring the bairns here?'

'Two weeks since, or thereabout,' she said, still wiping her eyes. 'They'd been here no more than a day or two when Maister Stirling was here, I'd gone out to buy them shoes and a bat and ball, for their father never thought to bring their toys. So I never spoke wi Maister Stirling, only

I saw him in the street coming from Frankie the horner's house as I passed by, and gave him the time o day, and the bairns made their obedience and had his blessing. He tellt them he was at the sang-schule wi their father,' she added. 'I'd never kent that.'

Effie came clattering through from the room beyond the hall with a tray, saying in some excitement, 'The man Peter says your landlord's vanished into the air, mistress! Carried off by the Good Folk, most like, he says, never seen again after he was here about the rent! Our Lady save us, were we the last to see him in Perth?'

'Don't be daft, lassie!' responded Mistress Cornton automatically. 'Pour the ale for our guest and be off wi your nonsense. Carried off by the Good Folk, indeed!'

Gil, wishing the Good Folk would fly off with Peter, accepted the refreshment Effie offered him. The girl withdrew, presumably to hear more of Peter's speculations, and Gil drank politely to Mistress Cornton's good health. She raised her beaker in reply, but said:

'Is that right, he's vanished? Has he not just left on a journey?'

'I don't think he's travelled,' said Gil. 'But it does seem your man or the horner next door likely were the last to see him in Perth, as the girl says. Did Maister Cornton say where Stirling went after he left here?'

She stared at him, and he could see her mind working. After a moment she said, 'No, he never. He tellt me when he was to get the rent together, and he's seen to that, maister, it's lying ready in his strongbox. Maybe you should ask him yoursel about that. He's out at the yard, just over the Ditch.'

'Maybe I should,' agreed Gil. 'So you saw Maister Stirling in the street that day, and not since then. Tell me, has he been a good landlord? Is he friendly? Does he see to the repairs?'

'Oh, aye, the best,' she said with enthusiasm. 'We took this place three year since, when Cornton and me was wed, and it was him and Cornton thegither saw to putting in new windows, and built me a good charcoal range in the kitchen, and the like. He's aye been friendly, and been easy about the rent within a day or two, none of your *Twelve noon on quarter-day* demands.'

Gil, with his own experience of collecting rents, nodded at that. It could be difficult for a tradesman to collect the coin needed for the exact date the rent was due; a relaxed landlord could make life much easier for his tenant, but not all were relaxed.

'Was Mistress Nan your only bairn?' he asked, as the name of the children's mother finally surfaced in his head. Mistress Cornton dabbed at her eyes again.

'I've two sons,' she said, 'both at sea. Nan was the only lass I raised.'

Chapter Six

When Gil stepped through the tanyard gate, Maister Cornton was supervising two sturdy journeymen at the task of topping up a pit full of thick brown liquid and seething skins with bucketfuls of something equally brown which stank richly. He had cast off his gown, which hung over a trestle near him, but was readily identified by his decisive gestures and competent directions.

'Yon's the maister,' said Peter unnecessarily. Gil nodded, and stood waiting, on the other side of the gate from a row of reeking buckets, looking about him and trying not to breathe deeply. The yard was busy; two more journeymen were unloading a cart full of goat-hides, unwinding the stiffened, hairy bundles and tossing them into a pit of water, an older man was scraping with a two-handled blade at a skin draped over another trestle, and three apprentices were discussing a game of football and stirring a steaming vat which smelled nearly as strong as the stuff the journeymen were using. One of them noticed Gil, abandoned his long paddle with obvious relief and came forward.

'And how can I help you, maister?' He grinned hopefully. 'If it's hides you're after, you've come to the right place. We've some good red-dyed the now, make a bonnie doublet for yoursel, and some white-tawed kidskin to make gloves for a lady, fine as silk it is, fit for the Queen herself.'

'I need a word with Maister Cornton,' said Gil. 'I might look at skins after it.'

'Right, then, Martin,' said his master, leaving the journeymen to their task. 'A word, was it, maister?' He assessed Gil with quick sharp eyes, taking in Peter's livery and Gil's own dress and bearing. 'Is it about Maister Stirling, then? Come away in the counting-house and get a seat, if you will.'

'You're anxious about him, are you?' Gil prompted, following the tanner into the counting-house, which proved to be merely a weather-tight chamber at one end of the drying-loft. It was evidently the heart of Cornton's domain; there was a green reckoning-cloth spread on a desk in one corner, a rack of shelves in another, and papers and scraps of leather everywhere.

'I am. He's been a good landlord to me, the three years I've dwelt here by the port, and if there's something come amiss to him I'd as soon hear o't and make my preparations to deal wi whoever inherits his property. No to mention amassing the heriot fee.' Cornton cleared a bundle of dockets off a stool and gestured to it, then sat down on his own polished seat by the desk. He was a short fair man with a quick manner, rather younger than his wife, Gil thought. Presumably she had brought good money to the match. And when had she come by it, he wondered, recalling that her daughter had lacked a dowry.

'I'd a word with Mistress Cornton at the house just now,' he said. 'I think you saw Maister Stirling ten or twelve days since.'

'July twenty-fifth,' said Cornton promptly, and turned to the board which hung by his head, its tapes securing more bills and accounts, along with a brightly coloured wood-cut of St Andrew and a child's drawing of a woman in a striped gown. He picked out a slip with a brief note scrawled on it. 'I've a note o't here. And we reckoned up when would suit us both for him to uplift my rent, and between him being at the Bishop's call and me having accounts to collect on we cam down on August third. But he's never been back, though in general he's prompt to the very hour of what we've agreed, and the word in Perth is that the Bishop's seeking him, and no knowing where he's got to.'

'What time of day was it when he left you?'

'Three-four hours after noon?' said Cornton. 'No later, I'd say.'

'As early as that? Do you know where he went?'

Cornton shook his head. 'I saw him to the gate, maister, but other than that he walked off along the Blackfriars path I couldny say.'

'What, you mean he was here?' Gil asked, startled. 'I'd thought he called at the house.'

'Oh, aye, but Effie sent him out here, since here's where I was. We'd a load of goat fells to take out of the first soak that day, and the men hates the task, you have to keep them at it.'

'The men the Bishop's steward sent out,' Gil said carefully, 'asked at all the ports, but nobody had seen Maister Stirling pass.'

Cornton grunted. 'That's no surprise. If a party of wild Ersche cam in across the brig here Attie might notice them, but I wouldny warrant it.'

Now why did the Bishop's men not know that? Gil wondered.

'And did you speak of aught else?' he asked. 'Anything that might tell me what the man was thinking that day?' The tanner looked hard at him 'I'm charged wi finding him, as you obviously worked out for yourself, so anything you can tell me that would be a help, I'd be grateful for.'

'Aye, I see that.' Cornton paused a moment, arranging his thoughts. 'Did Mistress Cornton say he'd met her in the street?'

'Aye, and spoke to the children,' Gil agreed.

Cornton's face twisted. 'Right. So what I got was one of his clever remarks about cuckoo chicks. Mind you, then he said it must be a comfort to herself to have the bairns wi her, and to tell her he'd pray for her lass. The man's like that, maister,' he said earnestly, 'full of jokes at someone else's expense, and then turns round and offers a kindness you'd not look for.'

'How did he know the bairns?' Gil asked.

'Seems he kent their father, and you've only to look at the brats to see whose get they are. Asked me was Drummond still wi us. I was glad to tell him,' said Cornton with restraint, 'that the man was never under my roof save to leave his bastards. He lay at the Blackfriars the whole time he was at Perth.'

'You don't like Canon Drummond?'

'I do not. Nor does he like me.' The tanner grinned wryly. 'And that's exactly what Maister Stirling asked me, and I said to him. Whereupon he said, *You're one of a mighty company, Maister Cornton*, and then asked me if I'd heard the tale of the laddie returned from Elfhame. Which I had, a course, as who in Perthshire hasny, but I'd no notion it was Drummond's brother. Mind you, since I took care no to exchange a needless word wi the man, he could hardly ha tellt me hissel. So it seems Maister Stirling was a friend o this laddie at the sang-schule, and hoped to hear more of him.' He eyed Gil warily. 'I wonder if he went along to the Blackfriars when he left me? The path he took would lead him that way, for certain.'

'I'll ask there,' said Gil. 'You've been a lot of help, Maister Cornton.' He rose to take his leave, and as the other man rose likewise said, 'Tell me, was Drummond in his normal state when you saw him?'

Cornton shrugged.

'Near enough. He's never been more than civil to Nan – to Mistress Cornton, for all he made a hoor of her one daughter.' He paused. 'See, my wife's first man, Jimmy Chalmers, had a few reverses to his business in his time. Dealt in fells and skins, he did, and lost a couple shiploads, oh, twelve year syne it would be, had to sell up. His two sons – Nan's laddies – went to sea, and done well, but the lass took service with a kinswoman in Dunblane, and met Drummond.' He scowled. 'And then when Chalmers' business recovered and he could dower his lass, Drummond wouldny release her from the agreement they'd made.'

Gil pulled a face.

'He was within his rights, I suppose,' he said. 'And the lass herself? How did she feel about it?'

'She'd the laddie, a bairn at the breast by then,' said Cornton, 'and I'd wager he threatened to keep the boy. Whatever the way o't, she stayed.' He grunted. 'Any road, he was much as usual when we saw him, full of orders about how the boy was to be reared and schooled, never a word about the wee lass. I bade him be civil to my wife under her own roof, and he'd to swallow the rebuke, seeing he wanted a favour of us, but he was ill pleased.' He looked about him. 'I'd best put all secure in here and then get the men to start locking down. Nobody's like to thieve a pit-full of half-cured skins,' he said, grinning again, 'but the finished hides needs to be stowed safe for the night.'

Leaving the man shuffling papers, Gil paused in the yard, where Peter was gossiping with the journeymen by the cart, and took the time to bargain for some of the white kidskins, which were indeed unusually soft and fine and would make excellent gloves for Alys. The apprentice Martin folded the leathers and tied them with a length of cord, and said with interest:

'Is that right, what your man says, maister, that that priest has vanished away?'

'I'm trying to find him,' said Gil.

'What priest is it?' asked the youngest apprentice, a small lad in an out-at-elbows doublet and wrinkled hose, still prodding glumly at the stinking vat. They had put the fire out beneath it, but the smell seemed even more powerful.

'How d'you mean, what priest?' said the third one.

'Well, there was two,' said the smaller boy.

'There was just the one, Malky,' said Martin kindly. 'Him wi the badges on his hat. He cam in here and spoke wi the maister, as he's done before.'

'There was two,' said Malky. 'I saw them on the bank when I went home to my supper.'

'Did you?' said Gil. 'Who was the other one?'

'Och, the other one,' said Malky vaguely. 'Him that brought the bairns to the maister's house. Wi the hair, you ken.' He gestured, describing fluffy hair below a hat.

'When was that?' Gil asked.

'When I went home to my supper,' the boy repeated. 'After the badge one was here. So which one is it that's vanished away, maister?'

'The badge one,' said Gil.

'I thought so,' said Malky. 'See, he left his hat. My, he's passed on a many pilgrimages to collect those badges. I wonder what he's doing penance for, and him a priest too?'

Across the yard, Maister Cornton checked in the doorway of the counting-house, met Gil's eye for a moment, and deliberately stepped out of sight. And just in time, thought Gil as Malky looked over his shoulder for his master.

'Left his hat?'

'I found it,' said Malky, nodding.

'Tell me about it,' Gil invited.

Reading between the awkward statements, he ascertained that Malky, going home for his supper on the twenty-fifth of July, had spied the man in the hat with many badges and the man with the fluffy hair, walking together near the Blackfriars wall. Curious to know what priests discussed at their leisure, he had slipped up behind them.

'But they were talking sermons,' he said in disappointment.

'Don't be daft,' said the third apprentice. 'What else would priests talk of, you gowk?'

'Many things,' said Gil. 'What made you think it was sermons, Malky?'

'Well, it was all about forgiving,' explained the boy. 'And maybe confession, and all long words like that.'

Gil nodded. 'And then what did you do?'

'Gaed hame to my supper, for it was late. Later than today, maybe.'

'And what about the hat?'

Malky had found it lying on the bank the next morning, damp with dew but undamaged, when he came by on his way to the yard.

'I brought it in here,' he said. 'I thought when the man cam back to see my maister I could gie it back to him.'

Looking at the innocent expression, Gil reserved judgement. It might well be true.

'Where is it?' he asked.

It was in the boy's kist in the long shed. He ran off to fetch it, and Martin said anxiously, 'He'll get himsel took up for theft, maister, if he goes on like that. Will you warn him, maybe?'

'He's daft,' said the third apprentice. 'Keeping it that way. Now I'd ha sellt it, and got money for ale.'

'And that is theft, Ally Johnston,' said Martin roundly. The boy Malky came back, bearing the hat. It was a fairly ordinary round bonnet with a flat top and a brim which turned up all the way round, of wine-coloured felt as Wat the steward had said, rendered unusual by the many badges pinned or stitched to the brim, silver and pewter, each one different.

'See, it's no hurt, maister,' he said in triumph. 'I took good care of it.' He thrust it at Gil. 'Would you maybe take it, maister, if the man's no coming back to our yard? You could give it back to him?'

'I'll take it, Malky,' agreed Gil, 'and thank you for looking after it so carefully.' He glanced over the boy's head to where the tanner had emerged from the counting-house again. 'Now if your maister will give you leave, I want you to show me where you found it.'

Out on the track that ran by the Ditch he looked about him again. There were two tanyards cheek by jowl, with a skinner to one side of them and a dyer to the other. A path led off between the two in the general direction of the barking dogs. Cornton's was the smaller in extent, but seemed to specialize in the luxury end of the trade, with the stacks of small hides dyed in bright colours which he had already admired arranged on pallets and carts where the passer-by could see them over the shoulder-high fence of stout planks.

Malky led him past the other tanyard and the skinner, to pick up a well-trodden path which worked its way westward along the outer bank of the Ditch. The Black-friars' wall stood high and forbidding, perhaps a hundred paces to the right, and on the open ground between path and wall the evening sunshine was bright on yellow broom and wildflowers.

'They were walking about and talking there,' said Malky, gesturing, 'the two men. I like to go home this way,' he confided, 'acos there's all wee birds in the broom. I like wee birds, see, maister, my granda that's a forester taught me all their names. Last week there was two gowdspinks eating the thistles there, all red and yellow, right bonnie they were.'

'Can you remember anything the men said?' Gil asked, looking at the thistles rather than the boy. There were no goldfinches today, though many small birds chirped and whirred in the bushes. Malky paused a moment in thought.

'No really,' he said awkwardly. 'Just what I said, about forgiving. One of them said, *Even Judas was forgiven,*' he recalled, brightening. 'How would he know that, maister? I thought Judas was burning in Hell. And the other one said, *Aye, but he hangit himsel.*' The intonation said, *Rather than hanging someone else.*

'Which one said that?' Gil asked, trying hard to sound casual.

'The one that brought the bairns to my maister's house. He's got a voice like a corncrake in the long grass, so he has.'

That was clear enough, though whether Drummond had referred to himself, to Stirling, or to some other he would have to work out later. He coaxed the boy a little, but could extract no more information; finally he said, 'And where did you find the man's hat? Can you mind that?'

'Oh, aye,' Malky assured him, 'for there was a throstle's nest just near it. Come and I'll show you.'

The place he picked out was further along the bank, where a clump of hazel and ash provided shade. The grass was well trampled, and a young couple in intent conversation within the grove turned to stare at them when Malky stopped.

'It was yonder,' he said firmly, 'just lying on the grass there, like if it had been dropped. I wondered at it,' he confided, 'for a priest doesny like to go bareheaded for the sun burning his shaved bit, does he?'

Gil, with a sudden recollection of Andrew Drummond's servant putting his master's hat back on his head, nodded at this and cast about, looking at the ground. There was no likelihood of picking up any tracks here after two weeks, the path was too well used and the pair of lovers under the trees were hardly the first to choose this spot. The bank of the Ditch, a few yards away, showed no useful sign at all. He stood looking at the dark water sliding past, the weeds waving in the current and the ducks paddling about under the other bank where the gardens of the biggest properties on the Northgate came down to the water. The occupiers of those must be questioned, anyone else using the path must be asked if they saw the two priests –

'It's getting near my supper,' said Malky diffidently.

'It is,' he agreed, glancing at the sky. The sun was round beyond the west. It must be close to Vespers now, little point in disturbing the Blackfriars who would also be about to sit down to their frugal supper and then go to sing the Office. Moreover it had been a long day. Giving the boy a coin, he dismissed him, and after establishing that the couple lurking in the shadows had not been there at any time when two priests were walking on the path, something which they seemed to think deserved congratulation, he turned towards the Red Brig and the Bishop's house.

'Found on the path?' repeated Bishop Brown, staring.

At his elbow his elderly chaplain bleated in distress. He had a long gentle face and straggling white hair, and wore a felt cap with a rolled brim which somehow suggested the curving horns of the small sheep Gil had seen on the ride down from Balquhidder. His voice reinforced the impression.

'Is it truly Jaikie's hat?' he asked, peering short-sightedly at it and crossing himself. 'Our Lady save us! Why would he leave his hat on the path?'

'Aye, it's Jaikie's own hat.' The Bishop pushed Jerome's enquiring muzzle down and turned the hat round, fingering the sequence of silver images. 'Indeed, I mind when he bought the half of these badges. I've joked wi him about the things many a time.'

'And so have we all, my lord,' agreed the chaplain. 'But why would he leave his hat? He'd miss it, surely.'

Ignoring this, Bishop Brown set the hat on his desk and wiped at his eyes. The dog scrambled up to lick his chin, and he patted the creature. 'Maister Cunningham, what's come to the poor fellow? It looks bad, I'm fearing me.'

'It looks bad,' Gil agreed. 'I suppose he could have gone into the Town Ditch, though I don't see why that should have happened. The path where the boy found the hat is yards from the waterside. He could have met with some other misadventure, I suppose, but why he –' He stopped, reluctant to express his thoughts at this stage.

'Into the Ditch?' repeated Rob Gregor the chaplain. 'Fallen in? Oh, our blessed Lady preserve him! You think he's – And I packed up his gear and never thought,' he said in distress.

'The houses opposite,' said the Bishop with decision. Gil nodded, recognizing how a good-humoured man like this could become a bishop. 'We'll have Wat send in the morning to ask did they see or hear aught that day, and put a couple fellows wi boats on the Ditch, to drag that stretch. Maybe get the Blackfriars to send their lay brothers out and cover the meadow-land, in case he's lying under a gorse bush. Do you think the laddie was telling you the truth?'

'I think so,' Gil said. 'He's guileless, I'd say, and the tanner called him a good laddie.'

'I'll get a word wi him myself, just the same. I should have taken this into my own hands days ago,' said Brown fretfully, stroking his dog's ears. 'Here's you turned up all this in just an hour or two, and my men got nowhere in two weeks. If we'd just known of his interests by the port!'

'I think it might not have saved him,' said Gil deliberately. 'I think he may have been dead by the time he was missed.'

'Aye, but where is he?' demanded the Bishop, over another distressed bleat from his chaplain. 'What came to him? What did Andrew Drummond want wi him?' He lifted the hat again, and turned it in his hands. Jerome sniffed at it with interest. 'If this could tell us, eh, Maister Cunningham?'

Gil answered something conventional, but Brown was not listening. He had tilted the hat to the evening light from the window and was studying it intently, counting and telling off the images.

'Had Jaikie rearranged his badges lately, Rob?' he asked.

'No, no, my lord,' the chaplain shook his head. 'He was quite particular in that. They'd each their own place, he'd spend an hour putting them back if ever the bonnet had to be brushed. And the time the seagull blessed him, d'you recall, sir –'

'What have you seen, sir?' Gil asked.

'They've been moved lately,' said the Bishop. 'Look at this.' He held the item where both Gil and the chaplain could see it, and pointed. 'There's been one there. You can see the mark where the felt held its colour, and the holes for the pin, and there's another there, and another –'

116

'There is,' agreed Gil, annoyed with himself. 'You've a sharp eye, sir.' He bent closer, looking at the traces Brown had identified, and picked at the turned-up brim to look behind it. 'I'd say that's been done very recently. The colour hasn't faded any further. It looks as if one has gone, maybe two, and the rest that are pinned not sewn have been moved about to hide the gap.' He pulled a face. 'I could be wrong about the boy Malky, I suppose, but I'd not have said he'd interfered with the hat. Did Stirling ever mention losing one?'

'No, no, never!' protested the chaplain.

'No that I heard him,' said the Bishop, looking hard at Gil. 'Do you think it has some bearing on his disappearance?'

'It might,' said Gil, 'but it's a thing untoward in any case. Can you tell which are missing, my lord?'

'Let me see.' The Bishop turned the object again. 'Ninian, Kentigern, Andrew, Giles. There's Tain, there's Haddington, Dunblane, Elgin ... All the Scots ones are here. It must be one of the foreign ones, and those I'm less sure of. Rob, see if you can tell us what's gone.' He suddenly thrust the hat at Rob Gregor and covered his eyes with one stubby-fingered hand. 'Ah, my poor Jaikie! What came to you, then?'

'I can't right say,' said Maister Gregor, peering closely at the badges. 'There's St William of Perth from Rochester, that he visited that time we were at London, and there's St Cuthbert a course, and,' he turned the hat round, 'there's St Paul from the great kirk at London, and the sepulchre of the Kings from Cologne, yes, yes,' he murmured, 'they're all there, but there's one, no two missing. What ones is it, now? Our Lady of – no, no, there she is.' He looked up at Gil, with an anxious expression. 'I canny call them to mind, maister. Let me think on it, and tell them over again, whiles I pray for my poor friend. Ah, Our Lady save him, to think he's maybe been dead all this time!'

* * *

Having had a word with his own men and made certain that they were securely lodged alongside the Bishop's men-at-arms, and that Peter had returned with the packet of white kidskins, Gil found a bench in a quiet corner in the garden and sat down with a platter of bread and cold meats which Wat the steward had found for him. It had been a very long day, starting in the early August dawn with a forty-mile ride, and he was tired, but the facts and speculations he had collected were dancing round in his head and he needed to put them in order.

The songmen from St John's Kirk he felt he could dismiss. It looked as if they had departed willingly, and quite possible that they had left Scotland, taking ship from the harbour which he could almost see from where he sat. There were plenty of places in the Low Countries or even further afield where good singers would be welcomed; certainly in Paris the accuracy and purity of tone of Scots and particularly of Ersche voices had been much admired. It might even be that the Precentor at St John's Kirk was right and someone was building himself a choir of Scots singers, but there was probably no way to find out from here.

Which left the question of what had happened to James Stirling. He stretched his legs out, regretting the absence of Socrates who would have had his chin on his knee by now, and missing Alys and her quick understanding and penetrating insight. Was it this evening she was invited to the harvest celebration in Glenbuckie, or was it tomorrow?

Stirling, he told himself firmly, James Stirling had gone to speak to Andrew Drummond, had been seen speaking to him. He had not returned to his post after the conversation, and his hat had been found the next morning, its badges apparently interfered with. That much was solid fact. What were the possibilities?

He might have gone into the Ditch, but it seemed unlikely. There were no traces. We can try dragging the channel, he thought, but I suspect we'll raise nothing that way.

The man might have made a sudden decision to follow the two songmen, wherever they had gone, but what would make someone with such a congenial post do such a thing? Could it have been something in the conversation with Drummond? I need to speak to Drummond again, though I doubt if I'll get any more out of him. That tantalizing snatch of conversation the boy heard was no real help; did it refer to Drummond's long-distant accident, or to his guilt about his mistress's death, or to something else? *Even Judas was forgiven. —Aye, but he hangit himself.* Who had hanged, or killed, or betrayed another, in the present case?

And the question of the missing badge. Someone had removed it from the hat, or found it missing, and taken some pains to hide its absence. A thief, surely, would have taken all the badges and the hat as well. Why remove one badge only? Perhaps someone shared Stirling's devotion to whichever saint or shrine it represented. He wondered if the chaplain would identify the badge. Let's not pin our hopes on that either, he thought, and grimaced at the inadvertent pun.

What else? There was the matter of where Stirling was in the two hours between leaving the tanyard and being seen talking to Andrew Drummond. He might have been waiting at the Blackfriars for Drummond, of course, I can ask them that when I call there, he thought. And we could send a few of the Bishop's men to ask at the various yards and dwellings between the bridge and the Blackfriars, perhaps pick up the trail.

And there is the dog-breeder, he recalled, and recognized the unease which was nagging at him. When he had encountered Mistress Doig more than a year since, it had been her husband who claimed to be the dog-breeder, but his chief occupation seemed to be gathering and selling information. The pair had left Glasgow hurriedly on the same day as Gil had last seen Robert Montgomery, for reasons which were part of the same set of difficult circumstances. He could visualize William Doig now, a squat figure like a chess-piece, no taller than an ell-stick, with powerful arms and shoulders and an ability to conceal his thoughts which a man of law might envy. Could Doig be mixed up in this? Could he have spirited Stirling away on behalf of some other who needed the information he possessed? I'll speak to Mistress Doig myself, first thing tomorrow, he decided.

He was recalled to his whereabouts by a hesitant bleating. Looking round, he discovered that the evening was beginning to darken, and Maister Gregor was stooped beside him, trying to draw his attention.

'Er –' he said again, more than ever like an old sheep. 'I'm sorry to disturb you, Maister Cunningham. Maybe you're deep in your thoughts?'

'No, no,' said Gil, rising politely. 'Come and sit down, sir.'

'I'll not sit down, thank you,' said Maister Gregor, waving the idea away as if it would sting him. 'It's a bit damp for my bones. But I'm sorry to disturb you,' he said again.

'Was it something you wanted? Can I do something for you?'

'Well, no,' the chaplain peered at him in the fading light, 'it's just that I thought on what badges it was that's gone from poor Jaikie's hat.'

'Badges? More than one?' said Gil, and realized that the old man was murmuring one of the prayers for the dead. He waited, and Maister Gregor crossed himself and continued:

'Aye, indeed, maister, it's two badges.'

'And what ones is it?' said Gil encouragingly,

'Well, one of them's St Eloi's horse from Noyon, unusual it is, and the other's the only one that was from a female saint's shrine. Save for Our Lady, and she's aye a different matter,' he added as an aside. 'I mind joking him about it more than once. But the thing is I canny right mind her name.'

'That's a pity,' said Gil in disappointment.

'Aye, for it's an unusual kind of name. I never heard of anybody given it.' The old man leaned forward to peer into Gil's face, and a bony hand came out to clasp his arm. 'See, her shrine's somewhere in the Low Countries, but she's not a Flemish saint, she's Irish.'

'Irish?' repeated Gil.

Maister Gregor nodded. 'Irish, maister. An Irish princess, so Jaikie told me one time. She fled from Ireland with her confessor, and fetched up at this shrine in the Low Countries, where she heals madmen and women. I don't recall the rest of the tale, though I think her father came into it somewhere, and I can't call her name to mind, but I know she's a healer of the mad.'

'Right,' said Gil. 'Maister Gregor, thank you for telling me this.'

'Is it any help?' The sheep-like expression had returned. 'I think it began with a D. Her name, I mean.'

'It's a help,' said Gil. 'It's a lot of help, Maister Gregor.' It means I can probably dismiss the problem, he was thinking. I don't see how there can be any connection.

'I'm glad,' said the old man. 'We want to know what's come to him.' He peered round in the dusk. 'I'd best go indoors, maister. The night air's no a good thing. Are you coming too?'

'I am.' Gil lifted the empty platter and turned towards the house. 'I'm surprised I'm not being bitten here. You can't sit out like this in Balquhidder.'

'It's the smoke,' explained Maister Gregor. 'They stay away from all the smoke.'

'I think you packed away all Maister Stirling's property,' Gil said, gesturing for the old priest to go in front of him.

'I did that,' agreed Maister Gregor in a distressed bleat. 'Never thinking but that he'd come back for it. Poor Jaikie!'

'Was it all in good order? Nothing seemed out of the ordinary about it?' Gil saw that for a foolish question as he spoke. This gentle old soul would hardly recognise trouble if it bit him on the hand.

'No, no, nothing by-ordinar. Save for the crossbow.' Maister Gregor stopped still and nodded, the movement dimly visible in the twilight. 'Save for the crossbow.'

'What was wrong with that?'

'Oh, nothing wrong wi't, it works well, I ascertained that, if you could but draw it. Only I never kent Jaikie had a bow, you see. He'd aye to borrow mine when we went out to the butts.'

Stifling his response to the image of Maister Gregor with a crossbow in his hands, Gil said, 'You and Maister Stirling have been good friends, then, if you'd lend him your bow.'

'Oh, yes, indeed. He's a – he's a good friend,' said the old man earnestly. 'There's some finds his humour a bit sharp, but he's aye a good laugh, and he'll do you a good turn sooner than an ill.' He chuckled. 'Only the day afore he went off, he'd a good crack at Wat our steward, fair made me laugh. See, Wat had misplaced his tablets, and Jaikie found them at the back o a bench, fallen down behind the cushion. *Oh,* he said, *if I kent where to take it, that would be worth a penny or two, wi all the tally o my lord's household in it.* Wat was no best pleased, but the rest o us laughed.' He peered at Gil in the shadows. 'Maybe you had to be there. But the other was better, wait till I tell you. The very day we last saw him, Wat was on about a new way o cooking mutton he'd got off Robert Elphinstone's steward when we was last in Edinburgh, that he'd tried to teach my lord's cook and the man couldny get the rights o't, and Jaikie said, *You should write it down, Wat, and sell it in the Low Countries.* Wat was right put out.'

'I think you and Maister Stirling had a disagreement, too,' Gil said, with faint malice.

'We did,' said Maister Gregor sadly. 'We'd a word in the morning. Sic a small matter, it was, to fall out over a misplaced shoe, and thanks be to Our Lady we were friends again by noon.'

'A shoe?'

'Aye, is it no daft? Jaikie was hunting it all through the chamber, and found it down my side o the bed, and would have it I'd kicked it there in the night. But as I said,' offered the old man earnestly, 'he'd as likely thrown it there hissel while he searched for it. So we got a bit sharp wi one another, and disturbed my lord, who wasny well pleased. But we shared a jug of ale wi the noon bite, and he'd that crack about Wat and the Low Countries, and all was just as usual again.' He sighed, and crossed himself. 'And now he's dead, my poor friend, and him as much younger than me. What are we doing standing out here in the night air, Maister Cunningham? Come away in, afore you take a chill.'

Gil followed the old man along the path and helped him up a set of steps by the house door, running these things through his mind. Just before he set his hand on the latch, he said, 'Where was the bow when you found it, then?'

'In his kist,' said Maister Gregor. 'In his kist.'

Mistress Doig's house and yard were in the midst of the northern suburb, their gateway further from the port than Gil had thought from the sound of the barking. Following the man Peter again past the low turf-walled houses and middens in the morning light, he avoided chickens, goats and a marauding pig and wondered what the Blackfriars thought of the addition to their neighbourhood. The continuous noise from the dogs must affect the singing of the Office. Then again, he reflected, the Blackfriars' convent in Glasgow was right in the centre of the burgh, with full benefit of the sounds of market and traffic.

Mistress Doig herself was at work in the yard, sweeping out an empty pen. When they stepped in all the dogs began barking again, and she straightened up from her task with a swift glance at Peter's livery, then turned from him to survey Gil with displeasure but no surprise. She was a gaunt raw-boned woman wrapped in a sacking apron, sleeves of gown and shift rolled well up above her elbows, the grubby ends of her white linen headdress knotted at the back of her neck. Some of the dogs began scrabbling at the fencing of their pens, eager to get at the visitor.

'Quiet!' yelled Mistress Doig. A silence fell, in which she said, 'It's you, is it? If it's Doig you're after, he's no here.'

'You remember me?' said Gil, raising his hat politely.

She unbent slightly at this, but her tone was still resentful as she said, 'Aye, I mind you. We'd never ha had to move if you'd kept away from Doig. That was a good place we had at Glasgow. Better by far than this.'

He looked about him, and had to agree. The yard here was smaller and the house far less well-constructed than the one he recalled, although the wooden fencing of the pens was new and solid. Peter had wandered off to admire some of the dogs.

'What brought you here?' Gil asked curiously. 'Why not Stirling or Edinburgh?'

She shrugged one bony shoulder, and scraped at something with her brush. 'I've kin here, it was as good as anywhere else. You kept that wolfhound pup,' she remembered. 'How is he?'

'He's well, and growing,' Gil said, aware of smiling as he thought of his dog. 'The handsomest wolfhound in Scotland. A rare beast.'

She unbent further at this.

'I thought that myself. Is it Doig you're wanting?' she demanded, her tone almost friendly.

'Yes, but maybe you could help me if he's not here.'

'I've no idea where he is,' she said hastily. 'He never tellt me where he was off to.'

'No, I'm not looking for him,' Gil reassured her. 'I'm trying to find this man that's gone missing, the Bishop's secretary, a fellow called James Stirling.'

'Him.' She came out of the pen, leaned the besom against the fence, and skilfully extracted one small dog from the next pen without letting the other escape. Pushing it into the newly swept space she shut the gate and twirled the two turnbuttons, then turned to Gil. 'He was here, aye.'

124

'You know him, then?'

'He was here about the Bishop's wee spaniel. My cousin Mitchel brought him here first, and he cam back a time or two wi word from my lord.' Her grim expression cracked as she smiled. 'A rare litter, that was. Off this bitch here,' she pointed to the next gate along. 'Right good wee pups she throws.' The inmate of the pen stood up, scrabbling at the fence and squeaking exactly like her son, and Mistress Doig leaned in and caressed her soft ears. 'Aye, Blossom, that's my bonnie girl.'

'And what about the time when he vanished,' said Gil. 'Had he been here then?'

'That's what I meant. He was here.' She glanced at the sky. 'Doig was home that week, and the man – Stirling, you cried him? – came around looking for him.'

'Did he say why?'

'He did not. Nor did I ask. Doig was in the town, so Maister Secretary said he'd wait, and hung about my yard getting under my feet,' she said pointedly, lifting the besom again, 'and getting my dogs excited wi too much attention.'

'What time was this?' Gil asked.

She shrugged. 'About the time I make their evening –' She broke off significantly, and Gil recalled all the dogs in the yard in Glasgow barking at the word *dinner*. He grinned, and nodded.

'So an hour or two afore Vespers, maybe?'

'About that or sooner. He hung about for a while, and then another fellow cam in seeking Doig, and the two of them knew one another.' She made a sour face. 'If they'd been dogs, there would ha been blood shed. Walking round one another stiff-legged wi their fangs showing, they were, though since they were both priests it was all done very civil.'

'Both priests?' said Gil quickly. 'Do you know the name of the other man?'

'A Canon Andrew Drummond, so he said. From Dunblane.'

'Well, well,' said Gil. 'And he knows Maister Doig as well?'

'So it seemed,' she said, 'but no need to ask me how or why, for I've no notion.'

'So then what happened? Did they speak to your husband? Did they stay here?'

She propped the besom resignedly against the fence, extracted another dog, dropped it neatly in beside its neighbour, and began to sweep the empty pen.

'They stayed here,' she said, 'the half of an hour or so, talking about nothing, very civil as I said. Then they saw Doig would no be back any time soon, and went off thegither the pair of them. Which I was glad to see,' she admitted, pausing to look round for the shovel, 'since if there was to be blood shed I'd as soon it wasny on my yard.'

'What were they talking about?'

'Nothing.' She lifted the shovel. 'A lot of havers. They looked at Blossom, and spoke of the Bishop's wee pup, and Maister Secretary said he'd ha had another of her litter, but that two brothers in the one place are often jealous, which is daft. Maybe it's true of folk, but not of dogs if they're handled right. Then the other said, a dog'll not forget an ill turn done to him as a pup. Now that's true I'll admit, but what was it to the point?'

Well, well, thought Gil.

'And then they left here,' he said.

'They did.' She emptied her shovel into a reeking bucket by the gate of the pen. 'Drummond was back later on his own, no even his man wi him, looking for Doig, and I tellt him where he'd likely get him, but I haveny seen him since, for whenever it was he caught up wi Doig it wasny here. Maybe it was in the town.'

'Did you see Stirling again?'

'Aye, later on.'

'Where?' he asked eagerly. She straightened up and stared at him.

'When I was walking the dogs,' she said. 'I take them out yonder,' she gestured northwards, 'along by the river, and when I cam back I saw him away down this track ahead of me, making for the Red Brig, just his lone, his head and shoulders showing over the rise in the track. You couldny mistake him, wi the last o the sun shining on the badges on his hat. Never saw so many badges on a hat,' she added.

'You're sure of that?' Gil asked.

'Sure of what? I saw the sun catch on the badges, I ken what the time was. They were just ringing St John's bell to shut the gates.' She cast a glance round the pen, stepped out, and retrieved its occupant from behind the neighbouring gate. 'Now, maister, if there's naught else I can help you with, I'd as soon get on wi this task. It's never-ending, you'll believe.'

'I'll believe it,' Gil said. 'Many thanks, mistress.' He reached for his purse. 'Maybe you'd buy the dogs a treat for me.'

Chapter Seven

The Blackfriars' accommodation for guests was spacious and well appointed. It was hardly surprising, Gil reflected, admiring the brocade cushions and rich hangings of the chamber where he had been asked to wait for Brother Cellarer. The court had not used the place for fifty-odd years, not since James First was assassinated here, but it had certainly been founded, long before that, to provide somewhere suitable for the King and his entourage to lie when they came to Perth. Alys would like the detail of the stonework, he thought, studying the carved foliage on the capital of the pillar between two window-openings.

'Can I help you, Maister Cunningham?' asked a soft voice in the doorway. He turned, to find a small fair-haired Dominican watching him with faint amusement.

'It's a fine building,' he said.

'We are blessed,' agreed the friar. He came forward into the chamber. 'They were craftsmen that built it to God's glory. Did you see this?' He stepped into the window-space beside Gil and pointed upwards. Gil followed his gaze and found a tiny head carved in the angle of wall and roof, grimacing at him. He laughed, and Brother Cellarer smiled, then raised his hand and delivered the friars' conventional blessing.

'I am Edward Gilchrist. I oversee the smooth running of this guesthouse. And how can I help you?' he asked.

'I'm looking into this matter of James Stirling,' Gil explained. 'Secretary to Bishop Brown,' he prompted, as the other man frowned.

'Yes, of course.' Gilchrist's face cleared. 'The Bishop sent this morning, and the lay brothers are out just now, searching the Ditchlands.' He nodded at the window, through which several black-habited men were visible on the open ground, peering under gorse bushes. 'I'm sorry to disappoint you, maister, but I –'

'Almost the last action of Stirling's we know of,' Gil pursued, 'was to speak to Andrew Drummond, Canon of Dunblane, who was lodged here at the time. I'll have to go back to Dunblane and speak to the Canon, but in the meantime I hoped, if you can tell me anything about his movements that day, it might shed some light on what Stirling did next.'

'Ah.' Gilchrist studied Gil for a moment, then nodded. 'I'll fetch the record book. Take a seat, sir. I'll no be long.'

In fact he was nearly a quarter of an hour, slipping back into the chamber with a big leather-bound volume clasped against his white scapular.

'Forgive me, maister,' he said, drawing another stool up to the small table by the window. 'I'd to deal wi another matter. The laundry seems to have lost three of the good linen sheets. Now, when was Canon Drummond here? About two week since, am I right?' He leafed backward through the book. Its pages were filled with columns of neat tiny writing and figures, a total at the foot of each in red ink. 'Aye, here we are. Andrew Drummond from Dunblane, stayed three nights with four, no, five men, and what's this? Oh, I mind. He'd a woman wi his company, which was awkward as the women's guest-hall was empty at the time. It's unusual, but it happens.'

'A woman?' said Gil blankly. 'Oh – he was bringing his bairns to their grandmother. Maybe he brought one of the maidservants along to see to them on the journey.'

'I'd say she was more than a serving-lass,' demurred Gilchrist. 'She was maybe his – some woman's companion. I set eyes on her myself, Mistress Ross she was cried, a decent enough woman past forty I'd say, but we'd to put her in a lodging out-by, and Maister Canon insisted we send her food out to her. So hardly a maidservant.'

'That must have been inconvenient. Was she far away?'

'No, no, just at Duncan Niven's house by the dyer's yard. He's kin to one of our lay brothers, we've lodged other folk there afore now, though we don't usually carry their food. The kitchen-folk swears we never got all the dishes back.'

'Irritating,' said Gil. 'So what have you recorded here?'

'It's a note of all the dole offered,' Gilchrist turned the book so that Gil could see the pages, 'the provisions made use of, who ate what and where it was served up. Here's Canon Drummond, see, two messes of food, one manchet loaf and two of maslin, ale and clean water, brought here to the guest hall from the kitchens, and the woman's portion carried forth on a platter from here.'

'You're meticulous.' Gil studied the orderly columns. 'You even record the amount of the broken meats?'

'We're the stewards of what's given over to us for charity,' Gilchrist pointed out. 'It's no more than our duty to make certain it's used well. The broken meats goes for feeding the poor at the gates the next day, and since the poor never get any less in number, Brother Almoner needs to have an idea how much broth he'll need to make up the amount.'

Gil nodded, a finger on the date he wanted.

'Did Drummond's company leave in ones and twos?'

'No that I recall,' said Gilchrist, staring. 'Why d'you ask?'

'They've eaten well, though not inordinately.' Gil paused, calculating. 'Two messes of food served to six people, there would be enough left most days to feed another two mouths at least. Yes, here on the twenty-fourth you've noted exactly that. But on the twenty-fifth, you served up one mess of food only, and there was still some left over.'

'I see what you're saying,' said Gilchrist, tilting his head. 'Salmon in wine with onions and mustard, and they've barely picked at it.' He lifted the corner of the page and peered at the verso. 'Ah – here we are. Drummond left the next day. I recall that one of his men went ahead to order up the fresh horses and that, so he'd have been away before supper on the twenty-fifth.'

'That's only one down.'

'Aye, but Canon Drummond ate his supper at the Bishop's table that day.'

It was Gil's turn to stare.

'Did he so? The Bishop never told me that.'

'Well, so Drummond's man told my sub-Cellarer,' qualified Gilchrist. 'I know he came back late, for he'd to make quite a noise to waken Brother Porter and we all heard him as we came from Compline.'

'Was he alone? When did he go out?'

The Cellarer shook his head.

'Sometime after Nones. It would have been when we were all at our studies, I suppose. Brother Porter might remember – or James my Sub-Cellarer. Certainly he was on his own when he returned, for his man had to be woken to see him to bed.'

Gil looked at the columns of neat writing. If Drummond had eaten with Bishop Brown, it altered matters a lot, but if he had, why had he not taken his man with him? If he had not, then why had he said he was doing so? Was it the delusion of a man in the grip of melancholy? No, surely, his servant had said it was after they returned to Dunblane, after the second letter came from Balquhidder, that the melancholy settled on him. But could it have been starting already?

'How was Canon Drummond in himself?' he asked. 'Did you have any words with him while he was here?' Gilchrist raised his eyebrows. 'The man had just lost his mistress,' Gil expanded. 'I wondered how he seemed to be taking it.'

'So his servants told us,' agreed the Cellarer. 'I wondered at it, a bittie, for you'd never have thought it from his demeanour. Serious, yes, as befits a clerk, but not inordinately so, and not – not irrational, I'd have said.'

* * *

131

'He did not,' said Wat Currie. 'We'd ha tellt you if he had done, Maister Cunningham. My lord's reputation's well known – he would never invite a churchman to his table who'd openly kept a mistress, particularly when it was a Perth lassie. Different if he'd already set her aside, or if we'd had to deal wi him on Holy Kirk's business, a course.'

'Yes, I see that,' said Gil. 'I wonder where he went? The Blackfriars' sub-Cellarer said he went out about five of the clock, and his servant came back later saying the Canon would dine with Bishop Brown. He returned after Compline. Where has he been? And unattended at that.' He glanced at the steward. 'That reminds me, Peter thought Maister Stirling was unattended the day he vanished away. Is that right?'

'Well, there's none under this roof admitted to being wi him,' said Wat. 'More to the point, we've not found where he went. No sign of him on the Ditchlands by the Blackfriars, no sign in the Ditch, and the households opposite saw nothing.'

'He was seen,' said Gil, suddenly recalling Mistress Doig's statement. 'In the last of the sunlight, making for the Red Brig as if he was coming back into Perth.'

'Was he, now?' said Wat, frowning. 'After nine that would be. He'd a been gey late for his supper by then.' He smacked a fist into the other palm. 'Where has he got to? St Peter's bones, how can a man just disappear like that, unattended or no?'

Easier than you'd believe, thought Gil. Aloud he said, 'Did he go drinking? Did he have friends in the town? Maybe the alehouses along the Skinnergate could tell us something. And where do you suppose Canon Drummond ate his dinner, if it wasn't here?'

'No a notion.' Wat pulled at his lower lip, scowling. 'I'd say it wasny on the Skinnergate, for the Blackfriars likes to drink there when they're in the town, they're aye in one alehouse or another.' He thought a little further. 'If he went to a friend, we've little chance of finding out, but I suppose he could ha been wi a woman. Why d'you want to know?'

'He's still the last person we know of that spoke to James Stirling,' Gil said. 'If I know where he was, I might find where Stirling was.'

'Aye.' Wat reached for his tablets. 'I'll send the men out again after they've had their noon bite. They can ask at the taverns, and maybe at the various kirks in the place, supposing he was wi a colleague after all. And maybe we could get the crier to it and all. For the both of them. He's already crying those two badges off Jaikie's hat, and Rob Chaplain and I've been turning away folk wi lead St Jameses all morning.'

Fortified by a slab of bread and cold meat and a handful of raisins, Gil went back out across the Red Brig. Some enquiry took him to Duncan Niven's house by the dyer's yard; it proved to be a neat timber cottage down a vennel, where hens picked around the midden and a stout woman in a crisp white headdress and huge dye-splashed linen apron was sweeping the flagstones before the door. She glanced up at him curiously and bobbed a curtsy as he came down the vennel.

'Good day, mistress,' he said, raising his hat. 'I'm seeking Duncan Niven's house.'

'And you've found it, sir,' she said civilly, taking a closer look at him under well-groomed eyebrows. 'What can we do for you, then? Was it a lodging you was wanting?'

'No, I'm suited, thanks, but I'm hoping to find someone that did lodge here. A Mistress Ross, from Dunblane.'

Her intent look persisted. 'What might you be wanting wi her?' she asked, propping the broom against the house wall.

'I've some questions for her, about Canon Drummond that brought her here.'

He waited, while a sequence of expressions chased across her face: surprise, interest, irritation at the mention

133

of the Canon. Finally, confirming his growing suspicions, she said, 'Well, ask away, maister. I'm Kate Ross, that was waiting-woman to Nan Chalmers, Christ assoil her. You're lucky to find me – I've stayed on here, where I'm suited and Mistress Niven too, to lend a wee hand wi the house for a while, but I'll go the morn's morn to a new situation.' She lifted the besom, and turned to the house door. 'Will you come within, sir, and take a seat, and we can talk in comfort.'

Seated by the house door, her apron discarded to reveal a good gown of checked wool, she served him Mistress Niven's ale and answered his questions. It quickly became clear that she needed to talk, as several years' observation of Drummond's treatment of her mistress spilled over and swamped him in a wash of rising resentment. He listened carefully, trying to retain as much as possible to share with Alys later; he was aware that she was much better at this sort of conversation than he was. Nevertheless, with two married sisters and five years' practice at law, he had some grasp of the reality of human relationships. That shared by Andrew Drummond and his mistress had not been uniformly sweet, but he suspected it had not been as sour as Mistress Ross conveyed.

'He would have no singing in the house,' she was saying. 'Not even a servant lassie singing at her work. It's a strange thing, maister, how you never notice them singing until you've to prevent them doing it.'

'No music at all?' said Gil.

'Oh, he'd to hear my mistress harping whenever he visited. Right fond of listening to the harp, he was. I've no notion where it went, either, that harp,' she added, frowning. 'By rights it should ha gone to wee Annie. But he'd have never a note of singing. She aye said it was the cost o her good life, but I'm no so certain it was a good life.'

'Tell me more about Canon Drummond,' he invited.

She snorted. 'Canon, he calls himsel! No much of a priest, that one. Forbye his having my mistress in his keeping, and getting three bairns on her, may Our Lady receive her into grace,' she paused to dab her eyes with the long ends of the fine linen kerchief on her head, 'he was well acquaint wi the rest o the seven sins.' Gil cocked an eyebrow at her across his empty beaker, and she wiped her eyes again and elaborated. 'I never kent such a man for envying his fellow mortals. All his conversation was how this or that one about the Cathedral had been honoured above him, or the vote had gone against him at Chapter, or Bishop Chisholm had snubbed him. My poor mistress had her work to do keeping him sweet-tempered, and times it defeated even her to turn his thoughts to a Christian frame of mind.'

'Lust, envy, pride,' said Gil, counting off the sins she had identified.

'Anger,' she agreed, nodding so that the damp ends of her kerchief swung. 'If he disliked aught you'd done or thought he'd been disobeyed he'd go all quiet, wi a voice like ice down your back, and nothing for it but to undo what had angered him and apologize.'

'That's four out of the seven,' said Gil.

'Aye, and him a priest.' She shook her head. 'And the way he treats those bairns – see, wee James would make a bonnie singer if he's ever taught right, and the lassie, Annie, would aye sing at her play the way a bairn will, and if he heard them he'd call them afore him in a rage and though he'd never lay a finger on them, just talk at them wi that same voice like ice, they were both feart of his temper. I saw the laddie wet himsel one time his father was chastising him.'

Gil frowned, trying to reconcile this image of Andrew Drummond with the others he had received. It did not seem to fit.

'When I saw him in Dunblane the other day –' he began.

'And that's another thing,' Mistress Ross pursued. 'He brought the bairns here, would have me accompany them, then paid me off, and he's away back to Dunblane and left me here. He never asked if it would suit me to be set down in Perth wi no employment, nor gave me the gown and velvet headdress my mistress left me in her will.'

Could this be the crux of her resentment? Gil wondered.

'He seems to have slipped into a great melancholy since he was here in Perth,' he continued. 'Is that like him, would you say?'

She gazed at him, arrested for a moment, then leaned forward and poured more ale for both of them while she thought about this.

'I'd never ha said so,' she pronounced. 'I'd ha thought it more like him to fly in one of those quiet rages and take it out on those round him. But there's no saying how a man will react to a great loss, and when all's said he was right fond o my mistress, however ill he treated her. None of your great romantic passions like in the ballads,' she qualified, 'but you'd only to see him smile at her, and the way he wept the night she –' She broke off, and turned her head away. It was clear she had loved her mistress too.

'Did he speak to you before he left the Blackfriars?' Gil asked.

'Aye, he was here that evening. He came to let me know he'd be away and leaving me here, and that they'd cease to carry my food here after that night's supper.' She faced him again, a sour smile on her lips. 'We'd plainer fare to eat after that, I can tell you, maister. The friars keep a high diet, poverty or no poverty. And Jennet – Mistress Niven – swears they went off wi two of her good dishes instead of their own when they collected the last ones.'

'What time would that be, that the Canon was here that evening?'

'About the time Niven came home from the dyer's yard,' she said promptly, 'for he passed him in the vennel there.'

'And what time would that be?' he persisted. She paused to consider.

'Niven was late that evening,' she said at length. 'Jennet was home afore him, on account of wishing to see to his supper and her tasks was finished. She works at the dyeyard and all,' she explained. 'She was in at maybe her usual time, and she'd got the stewpot on the fire and simmering, for the Canon made mention of how good the smell was. She was right gratified, till he turned round and gave me my place wi no notice.'

'So that was an hour or so after she got home?' Gil hazarded, with a glance at the peat fire in the centre of the room.

'Aye, likely,' she agreed, in a tone which left him disinclined to rely on the fact. 'What's your interest in Drummond, maister? What's it to you when I last set eyes on him?'

'I'm tracking this man that's missing,' he explained, 'the Bishop's secretary, and it seems as if Canon Drummond was the last to speak wi him. He was alone when he came here?'

'Oh, aye.' She hesitated, then went on, 'Maybe that would account for his mood, if he spoke to a man that's disappeared.' Gil made an encouraging noise, and she gave him a reluctant glance. 'I've no liking for clypes, maister, but –' She closed her mouth tightly, stared at the two pewter dishes on the plate-cupboard for a moment, then began again. 'There was one of the songmen at Dunblane that just up and vanished one day a month or so back, they've never got to the bottom of it and folk were saying it was the Deil flew off wi him, though why – I'd spoken wi the man mysel a time or two, and one of my cousins is in Bishop Chisholm's household and knew him to be a decent body, you'd never take him for a man the Deil would – though they tell us any of us is wicked sinner enough –' She broke off this muddled utterance and drew a breath. 'The Canon was right satisfied about it.'

'Satisfied?' Gil repeated, puzzled.

'Oh, aye. As if he'd had a nice wee gift. All lit up and gratified he was, out at our house the next day, telling my mistress all the tale, which she'd heard already for I'd spoke to the soutar's wife that cooked his food to the songman, the very day it happened. *Vanished*, he said to her, *and none kens where he's gone, and that's one singer the less in Dunblane. A judgement on him,* he said, but when my mistress wished to hear more he would have her harp for him instead.'

'A judgement on him?'

'That's what he said. And why I'm minded o this, maister, is he was in much the same mood when he cam here to turn me off. Lit up, as if he'd been gied some great benefit, or seen someone else cast down, I thought, but if another man had vanished – was he a singer?'

'No, he was the Bishop's secretary, though he was a singer when he was young, and knew Canon Drummond then as well. But this was before the man vanished away, for he was seen down by the Ditch later that evening,' said Gil. 'I suppose it might have been something they said when they were speaking together.'

'Maybe the Canon got the better of an argument wi him,' she agreed, accepting this. 'That would please him and all.'

'And that was the last time you saw Canon Drummond?'

'Well, it's the last I spoke wi him,' she qualified, 'and no loss to me that is, save for my mistress's gown and velvet headdress.'

'Do you mean you saw him again?'

'We all three saw him.' She gestured round the quiet house. 'We'd gone in across the Red Brig after our supper, Jennet and her man and me, for a stoup or two at the Horn tavern on the Skinnergate, seeing I was kind of cast down about losing my place at no notice, and we set eye on the Canon both coming and going. It was Jennet pointed him out to me, and –'

'Where was he?' Gil asked hopefully. 'Was anyone with him?'

'Just in the Skinnergate, away at the far end. He'd be going into the town to his supper, likely. If you've met him, sir, you'll ken he's a big man, easy to be seen in a crowd. I just caught a glimp of him among all the heads, but I

thought maybe he'd wee James wi him, the way he was
looking down and talking as he went, though it was ower
late for the laddie to be out. And then when we cam out
the tavern and across the brig again, there he was ahead
of us on the path his lone. I mind it well for Jennet said,
You'll not get away from the man! and we all laughed.'

It had been a good evening in the tavern, Gil decided.

'Was he coming or going on the path?' he asked.

'He was just taking the road back to Blackfriars. I suppose he'd new come from the town, or maybe been a walk
along by the waterside. It's a pleasant walk of an evening,
there's aye one or two folk on the path.'

'And that was late on?'

'Oh, aye. The sun was not long down – we was near the
last out through the gate afore they barred it. There was
light enough in the sky to go by, it was a clear night, and
no mistaking the man given I'd been ten year in my mistress's household. The way his hair looks when he needs
barbered, you'd ken him a mile off.'

Gil looked reflectively into his beaker. Misreading his
intent, Mistress Ross leaned forward to pour more ale.

'Did you see any others on the path?' he asked. 'Or coming into the town across the Red Brig?'

She thought briefly, but shook her head. 'There's aye one
or two folks stirring, it's no like Dunblane. I wouldny
mind one evening better than another, sir.'

'The man I'm looking for had a hat like no other,' he
said, and described Stirling's collection of badges. This got
a more definite shake of the head.

'No, no, sir, I've not seen sic a thing.' She laughed tolerantly. 'There's aye something folk likes to collect, but I'll
wager that cost him plenty in shoe leather and candles, to
win that mony badges.'

The boy Malky had said much the same thing, Gil
reflected.

'Did you take the bairns direct to their grandam?' he
asked.

She snorted. 'You're right to ask me, sir, for I did not. He bore them off while Niven's brother that's a lay-brother walked me out here, and I'd never a chance to say farewell, poor wee souls.'

'Have you seen them since? Spoken to Mistress Cornton?'

'I have not,' she admitted. 'I never liked – I was feart she'd think I was after a place, and it would never suit. I've a good prospect now, and –'

'I'd think Mistress Cornton would be glad to see you,' he said. 'Your mistress was her only daughter, she'd likely welcome hearing of her life in Dunblane.'

'That's a true word,' she said. 'And I'd like fine to see the bairns. It's a good thought, maister.'

He walked back towards the Red Brig, thinking hard, then turned aside along the path by the Ditch and sat down with his back against an alder tree to consider this information. It was now certain that he should return to Dunblane and interview Canon Drummond; at the very least the man must have been the last to see James Stirling alive but also, he thought grimly, he might have been the first to see him dead as well. Did that add up? What do I know? he asked himself, and took out his tablets.

Stirling had left the tanyard about four of the clock, by Cornton's account. He had fetched up at the dog-breeder's yard, where he had encountered Drummond. That tallied with what the Blackfriars had said of Drummond's movements. By six of the clock Stirling and Drummond together were walking out here on the Ditchlands, talking about Judas and forgiveness. The next few hours held several sightings of Drummond alone, but none of Stirling until Mistress Doig recognized him at sunset on the track going into Perth. Going towards the town, he corrected himself. Where was he all that time? Where did he find his supper? Meanwhile Drummond had not eaten with the Bishop, and was finally seen on this path by the Ditch, no more than half an hour after sunset, alone.

He looked at the list he had made. That space between sunset and darkness seemed to be the important slot. Was it long enough for two men to meet and quarrel somewhere along here, for one to be slain and hidden so securely that he had not yet been found, his hat left by the path where the boy found it in the morning? I suppose it is, he answered himself, if the quarrel was carried over from their earlier talk together. Would the path be deserted? Perhaps not, but it would hardly be busy. No more than three persons had passed while he sat here thinking, in late afternoon. And where would the body go? The Ditch was the obvious place, and with a current like that, and the depth of water it contained, it would take some dragging to find a corpse, even one two weeks old which should have floated by now.

But what was their quarrel about? What did the reference to Judas imply? Judas the traitor hanged himself, not another. Whose death had one of these men brought about? Or had Drummond accused Stirling of treason? Questions, questions, he thought impatiently, but that one might lead me on a sound trail. Doig had been trafficking in information when he lived in Glasgow, he might well be doing the same here, and James Stirling was at the Bishop's elbow when he negotiated the last truce with England. There were princes overseas who would pay to learn the precise terms of the truce, not to mention Margaret of Burgundy. Suppose either Doig or Stirling was involved in that, could Drummond have learned of it? And how did Drummond know Doig anyway?

And then there was the matter of the badges missing from the hat. Did it have any bearing on Stirling's disappearance, or not? I need to speak to Andrew Drummond, and that soon, he told himself. How early can we be off in the morning?

He got to his feet, tucking his tablets back into their pouch. As he stepped on to the path a small figure twenty or thirty yards off waved wildly and shouted his name. He paused, and Maister Cornton's boy Malky ran up, saying in excited tones:

'I kent I'd seen you gang this way, maister. My maister's begging a word wi you. He's found a strange thing at the back o the yard, he'd like you to take a look at.'

'What kind of a strange thing?' Gil asked. The boy shook his head.

'I never seen it,' he said regretfully. 'Just my maister and Rob and Simon, that's the journeymen,' he explained, 'was up that end the yard and came down and sent me and Martin and Ally out to find you. And they've both went into the town, but I thought I'd seen you gang along here by the Ditch.' He turned hopefully, obviously expecting Gil to follow him, and looking exactly like a puppy waiting for a stick to be thrown. Gil grinned, gave him a penny, and obligingly set off towards the tanyard.

Maister Cornton was in his counting-house, seated by his desk and gazing thoughtfully at a small bright object on the green baize. He looked up as Gil tapped at the open door, and nodded.

'They found you,' he said. 'What d'you make of this?'

Gil stepped over beside him and discovered the object of his contemplation to be a pilgrim badge, probably of silver, in the shape of a horse. On its saddle were an anvil and hammer big enough to have brought the creature to its knees. Tiny letters incised on the anvil read S ELIGIVS.

'St Eloi's horse from Noyon,' he said.

'So it would seem,' agreed Cornton, 'though it's far better quality than other Eloi badges I've seen. Is it familiar to you, maister?'

'It could be one of the two we're looking for,' he admitted. 'Where did you find it?'

'Put it safe, and I'll show you.' Cornton set off out through the drying-loft and into the yard, saying over his shoulder, 'The bellman was crying two missing pilgrim badges, as well as the question of where my landlord ate his supper the day I saw him last, and who saw some fellow of Dunblane, so when my man Rob found this I reckoned I'd best send for you.'

He picked his way into the further reaches of his domain, past open sheds containing trestles and racks of skins, vats of strong-smelling liquors, reeking stacks of raw skins, the two small carts Gil had seen earlier. Beyond the sheds were a series of pits like the one near the gate, but these were covered by weighted planks. It was easier to breathe out here, Gil found.

'That's the tanpits,' said Cornton, waving at them. 'See, we do the first soaking and bating down the front of the yard, where it's under my eye, because the skins needs turned or shifted daily. Right?' Gil nodded. 'But once they're in the tanpits they lie for months – up to a year for your stoutest leathers – and we shift the bark maybe every couple of months, no oftener. So the tanpits is all up here out the road and though I take a look round afore I lock up in the evening, we're not working in this bit that often. Which means the Deil alone kens how long that badge has been lying here, though I suppose it canny be more than two weeks. Right?' Gil nodded again, and Cornton led him to the far end of the yard, where one of his journeymen stood by a pit morosely watching the bubbles rise and burst in the scum between the wet planks. 'Show him where you found it, Robin.'

At the sound of his voice, several dogs broke out in a fanfare of barking, quite near. Gil looked round, startled to realize how close they were to the Doigs' yard.

'Is there a reward?' asked the man, ignoring this. Cornton raised his arm to him, but he said hardily, 'The bellman said there was a reward. I found it, I should get the reward for it.'

'We'll ask at the Bishop's steward,' Gil said. 'Now show me where it was lying.'

'Just by that stick there.' Rob nodded at a stick driven into the earth nearby. 'I marked it, like the maister tellt me.'

143

They were near the boundary with the dye yard next door; it was marked by a fence perhaps four feet high, of tightly woven wattle hurdles rather than planks like that at the front of the yard. The ground was well trampled here, with small likelihood of picking out any footprints. The marker stake was midway between the fence and the tanpit where the bubbles were rising.

'It might have been thrown over the fence from the dye yard,' he said thoughtfully. 'But if so, why not cast further, and aim for the pit itself? It would never be found if it went in there.'

'Maybe no,' agreed Rob, 'but maybe aye. I'm thinking one o these oxhides is on the turn, maister, there's ower many bubbles and they stink something rotten. We'll ha to fetch them up, and yir badge might ha come up along wi them. Maybe the ither's in there yet,' he added, brightening slightly.

'They do stink,' agreed Cornton, sniffing. 'I don't like the smell of that. We ought to fetch them up afore the whole lot turns.'

'No reason why you shouldn't get on and deal with it,' said Gil, pacing along the fence. 'I'll keep out of your way.' He bent to peer behind some stained planks which were propped against the fence, but found nothing significant. 'Is there a gate this end of the yard, maister?'

'Fetch Simon and the laddies,' said Cornton to his man, 'bid them bring the long poles and all. A gate, Maister Cunningham?' He turned to fix Gil with a sharp stare. 'No, there's only the one way in unless you sclim the fence. Which I'm aware bad laddies do from time to time,' he added, 'though I'd say we've had no damage or mischief in the yard since Hunt-the-Gowk time. Are you thinking someone's been in here? I took it, like you, the badge had been thrown from over the fence.'

'It could have been,' agreed Gil cautiously. 'Does your neighbour lock up at night too?'

'He does.'

Gil looked about them. The yard was perhaps twenty good paces across, although much longer, and from where he stood the fencing appeared sound all round; the structure of woven hurdles lashed to hazelwood stakes beside him turned the corner to extend across the narrow end of the property, then changed to sturdy planks at the opposite side. The path to the Blackfriars must be on the other side of the planks, but his view of it was cut off by a small open shed containing another tall rack of skins. Just over the fence beside him a complex system of cords and poles in the dyer's yard supported bright webs of cloth and hanks of thread. The dyer's plot was shorter than the tanyard, and in the angle of the two – yes, that was Doig's yard, just next to him though it was near ten minutes' walk by the track. As he stood frowning, working out the twists and turns, Mistress Doig emerged from the house and shouted at the dogs. Silence fell, she glared over the fence at them, and Cornton said:

'They're neighbours I could do without, you'll see.' Gil grunted, and leaned over the stakes nearest him to look into the dyer's property. The ground there was as well trampled as that in the tanyard, and the grass and dandelions at the base of the fence showed nothing untoward.

'If it was two weeks since,' said Cornton, echoing his thoughts, 'there'll be little trace left by now.'

'How would bad laddies get in here without someone seeing and hunting them out?'

'Same as I said, over the fence. There's plenty hidey-holes once you're in the yard. I'm aye feart one will get hissel drowned,' Cornton confessed, 'that's why we've as many planks on the tanpits, it doesny need that many to hold it all down.'

Looking along the fence, scanning the woven withies and the vegetation at their feet, Gil was half aware of the men returning, carrying the poles Cornton had ordered and rolling two rumbling half-barrels. The apprentices set to work with buckets, baling out the liquid in the pit and slopping it into the tubs with much splashing, despite the remonstrations of their seniors, who meanwhile dragged the netted stones off the planks and began to raise them. More bubbles rose and broke at this, and the other journeyman, downwind, fell back with an exclamation of disgust.

'Maister, that's foul! What's come to they hides? I never smelled anything like it at this stage!'

'Eeugh!' agreed the middle-sized apprentice dramatically. A lively youngster, Gil thought, bending to look at a black mark on the fence. It sprouted legs and hurried off into the hollow of the weaving as he approached: one of those finger-long beetles that only seemed to appear at this time of year.

'Call yoursels tanners?' said their master jeeringly. 'My, you're delicate the day, the lot of you –' He broke off and coughed, and then said with more sympathy, 'Aye, well, I'll admit that's strong. Away and fetch a cloth to your nose, any of you, if you wish.'

Nobody took up this permission. Gil crossed the short end of the yard, scanning the hurdles, which were firmly laced to the upright stobs from the other side, none of them sagging as he would have expected if they had been recently climbed. The fence was obviously the neighbour's responsibility here; the plot was a small one, with a sagging house surrounded by a quantity of short lengths of wood and little heaps of shavings, but there was no sign of the occupier or of anything which might be related to the St Eloi badge. He moved on to the corner by the track where wattle gave way to planks, finding some surprising things in the tufts of grass and willow-herb but still no trace of any recent illicit entry to the tanner's policies. Wondering how a single horn spoon came to be wedged under one plank, the leg of a wooden horse under another, he looked back round his shoulder and found he could see only the apprentices moving to and fro with their buckets, his view cut off by the same drying-shed. Judging by the directions Cornton was issuing, the journeymen had begun the task of raising the stacked hides one at a time, brushing the oak-bark chips between them off into the surrounding liquor as they went.

He leaned over the fence, but found the track as uninformative as the dyer's yard had been. At least, he corrected himself, it tells me nobody entered the yard this way. No marks on the fencing, no trampled patch at the foot of the planks, no sign of any recent attempt to climb in. Could he be sure *recent* included the whole of the last two weeks? he wondered.

There was a horrified yell from the tanpit. The dogs began to bark in answer as he jerked upright and round, staring. There was another yell, but he was already running.

'What is it, man?' demanded Cornton's voice as he rounded the shed. 'What gart ye skirl like that? Simon?'

Simon was clinging to his long pole as if he was drowning, his face a mask of horror as he stared into the pit. Rob and the older journeyman were gaping at him, but the boy Ally was on his knees by one of the half-barrels, trawling through its contents with his bucket.

'I seen it,' he said in excitement, 'I seen something go in here.'

'It was a ratton drowned in the pit,' said the older man. 'No need for –'

'It was a hand,' said Simon, his voice shrill. 'It – a hand, I tell you!'

'Aye, and there's the other one,' said his master grimly, hauling another layer of partly cured hide towards their feet. 'Look yonder, under the surface. Hand, arm –'

'You mean it's a whole corp?' said Ally, round-eyed.

'Is he all in there? Watch, or he'll come apart!' said Rob. 'Who is it, anyway? St Peter's bones, how he stinks. How long's he been down there?'

'I think we can guess who,' said Gil. Cornton caught his eye across the pit, and nodded. 'And if so, then we know how long. Is that the head?'

'Aye, it is.' Rob reached in with his long pole and prodded the floating mat of hair. It swirled and clung to the hook on the end of the pole, and the head rolled slackly in the water and fell back again. 'He's face down, I'd say.'

'Andro?' said a voice from among the forest of bright hangings over the fence. 'Is all well? What was that great skelloch about?' A lanky fair-haired man emerged between two strips of indigo linen, and set multicoloured hands on the fence. 'St Nicholas' balls, man, what a stink! What have you found there?'

'Aye, we're all sound, William, and glad of your concern,' said Cornton. 'It's naught but something unlooked-for in this pit of cowhides.'

'What would that be, then?' asked William hopefully. 'Is it a drowned pig, or what?'

'It's a deid man!' burst out Ally. 'He's all drowned in the tanpit and turned to leather!'

'I'm no certain yet,' said Cornton, and clapped a firm hand on the boy's shoulder. 'William, would you do me a kindness?'

'Anything, anything!' said William avidly, stretching his neck. 'Can we help you lift him, whatever you've found?'

'No, no, we've enough hands here. If you'd send one of your lads for the constable, we can get on wi this task.'

'For the constable? What need of him, for a drowned pig? Is the laddie right, and it's a man, then? Who could it be?'

'We'll maybe ken what it is,' said Cornton firmly, 'by the time he gets here. I'd be right glad of the favour, William.'

The dyer retreated, with reluctance. Cornton glared at his back as it vanished between the linen webs, but said only, 'There's no saying he drowned here, Ally, you ill-schooled laddie, and no saying who it is yet.'

'But it's a man rather than a woman,' Gil said, 'by the length of the hair. Now we have to work out how to get him out.'

'A bonny task for a hot August day,' said the elder journeyman, 'wi all his fingers dropping off him.'

'Will he no be half-tanned?' suggested Ally. The other two apprentices seemed to have vanished. 'I'd a thought he'd hold together, no fall apart.'

'Aye, but the bark's only lying one side o his hide,' said his master. 'There's still all the flesh and the fat within –' He stopped, and aimed an angry cuff at the boy, who ducked expertly. 'What am I saying? You don't tan a Christian soul, you heathen laddie. Maister Cunningham, what do we do here? This is beyond my experience.'

Beyond mine, too, thought Gil. Aloud he said, 'You'll need to get all the hides off him, for a start. Then maybe we can get him on to a hurdle or the like, and lift him out of there.'

'Or send to Archie McNab the joiner and see if he's a coffin by him,' suggested Rob. 'Simon, man, are you well?'

Simon shook his head. He was still clinging to the pole, and had turned an unpleasant green colour.

'It was the way it beckoned,' he said faintly, 'like it was calling me. The hand. When it went into the tub, ye ken. It seemed like it was calling me.'

'It's here,' said Ally with some pride. 'I fished it back out.' He peered into his bucket and swirled the dark brown liquid it held. 'See, it's in here under the tan.'

Even with Gil lending a hand under Cornton's decisive directions, it was a good hour before they got the corpse out of the pit. There had been only two cowhides remaining on top of it, but the need to remove these with care slowed matters down, and the state of the corpse itself made getting it on to a hurdle a ticklish business, even though the woollen garments held the thing together to a great extent. In the end they lifted it complete with the part-cured hide beneath it, and transferred the lot to the waiting hurdle, with the interested advice of most of the workers in the dyer's yard, who hung over the fence slightly to one side to avoid the direct breeze.

'And where's wee Malky?' asked his master in quiet concern. 'He'll ha bad dreams if he sets an eye on this.'

'I left him in the counting-house, maister,' said the oldest apprentice, who had rejoined the working party in time to help with the final move. 'He'd had a sair fright.'

'I think we'll all ha bad dreams,' muttered Rob. 'I'll never get the stink of him out my nostrils, I can tell you.'

'Och, no, it's worse a burning,' said the elder man, whose name seemed to be Bartol. 'The stink o that lasts you for weeks.'

'Where's your respect?' demanded Cornton. 'We'll ha less of that talk in the presence of Death.' He crossed himself, said formally to the corpse, 'May Christ Jesus and all His saints receive you into Paradise, Maister Stirling,' then turned to Gil and said, 'I'm near certain it's him, the clothes is right, but I'll need a look at his face afore I swear to it.'

'What I'm wondering,' said Rob, staring gloomily at the hurdle, 'is how he got into that pit o cowhides. He never tucked hissel up like that, let alone putting the stones back on the planks, I'd say.'

'No, he never.' Cornton looked at his stricken journeyman, who had refused to leave but was still leaning greenly against the fence, unable to help with the grisly work. 'Simon, lad, away down the yard and bring me back a bucket of clean water and a cloth, if you will.'

'I'll go!' Ally sprang to his feet.

'Simon will go. You break me a stalk off that grass. No, one of the stout ones.' Cornton watched his man out of sight. 'Maister Cunningham, see this.' He took the grass-stem from Ally, bent and and used it to part the corpse's wet hair, lifting the locks aside until the nape of the neck was exposed. 'Look here. He never died by accident.'

'Is he hunting wee louses?' enquired one of the watchers at the fence.

'There'll be nothing running by now, surely,' offered another. 'They'll all be drowned in the tan for certain.'

'I never thought it,' said Gil slowly, staring at the cross-bow bolt lodged in the base of James Stirling's skull. 'But that makes it certain. And he wasny drowned in the tan,' he added, 'for he'd be dead when he went in. That would slay him on the instant.' And what of the hat he was wearing? he wondered. Were the two badges removed because they were damaged? Not by the shot, surely, the bolt would have struck below the brim. But why not throw the hat in with him? Why take it away at all?

'Let's hope it did,' said Cornton. 'But why? What was he doing to be shot in my yard? Why's he in my tanpit anyway? Did he –' He paused, open-mouthed, and Gil saw him realize for the first time that he might be under suspicion himself. 'No. I never. I swear I never.'

'Do you have a bow?' Gil asked.

'Aye, I do. A'body does, crossbow or longbow, to take to the butts on a Sunday. You've one yoursel, maister, I dare say.'

'Did you leave here at the usual time that day?' Gil went on, nodding to this.

'So far's I mind, aye, we all left as usual, and I was last wi the keys and locked the padlock on the gate as I aye do.'

'And where were you the rest of the evening?' Gil asked.

'Home wi my wife and household, helping her decide on where Drummond's bairns would sleep and who would nurse them.' He laughed sourly. 'After two nights wi the wee lass pissing our bed, if I was to slay any man in secret murder it would ha been Andrew Drummond, no my good landlord.'

Gil nodded again, accepting the force of the argument, and looked down at the flaccid corpse. This made less sense than ever, he thought, but it also made it less urgent to find Andrew Drummond. There was simply not time after they had both been seen last for him to have killed this man, got the corpse back here and into the tanpit, and then reached Blackfriars at the end of Compline.

'Here's Willie Reid now,' announced Ally importantly. The journeyman Simon appeared from further down the yard, carrying a bucket and cloth and followed by a tall lean-faced fellow in the burgh livery, his official staff over his shoulder.

'Well, now,' said the constable, and grimaced as he caught the first waft from the corpse. 'What have we here, then?'

Chapter Eight

Mistress Drummond, in her own chair by the peat fire at the centre of the room, turned to Alys where she sat across the hearth on a kist dragged forward from the wall.

'Will you be starting us off, Mistress Mason?' she asked. 'You must have songs we would not be hearing before.'

There were more people crammed into the house of Tigh-an-Teine than Alys would have believed possible. They were seated on the floor, on benches, on chairs and milking-stools and kists, with children and dogs sprawled among the feet. The atmosphere was already thick. The entire Drummond family was present, but there were also several families who seemed to be their tenants, including old Mairead and her husband Tormod, and a group from further up the glen, their women draped in striped plaids which reached from head to foot and had to be carried on the arms to keep the ends out of the dust. And of course Murdo Dubh and Steenie had ridden up from Stronvar with her in the early afternoon, bringing a great cake with plums in it, with Lady Stewart's compliments, as a further contribution to the feast. Everyone was dressed in holiday clothes, a smart doublet, a bright plaid, a bunch of ribbons pinned at the breast of a good shirt. Alys was glad she had worn the blue gown, even though it meant riding pillion and the box for the headdress had been hard to manage on the short journey. And she finally had the two younger granddaughters, Agnes and Elizabeth, straight in her mind.

To begin, there had been dancing in the yard before the houses, in long sets to a strange sung music provided by the onlookers, rhythmic singing in nonsense-syllables to a catchy tune which made one's toes tap. The changeling boy, sitting in a nest of blankets on the ground, had screeched and beaten his twisted hands together in time with the dancers' feet, but when Alys spoke to him he had stared at her in alarm and screamed his peacock scream again. She had been invited to stand up for every set, pushed and pulled laughing through the complex figures by friendly hands, wishing Gil was with her, Socrates trying to stay at her heels and having to be dismissed to the margins at intervals. To everyone's amusement Davie Drummond was nearly as lost in the dance as she was, protesting when he was teased about it that he had not joined in as a boy, so did not know the steps.

Nor had he taken part when the men danced one by one to the same kind of mouth-music, a wild fierce barefoot leaping with the arms held high, in some sort of competition which Murdo seemed to have carried. There had been more dancing, and then as twilight fell and the biting insects emerged, the company moved indoors bringing the seating with them. Some had spinning or a bundle of grass to braid into rope, others sat and talked. The changeling boy had been strapped into his cradle and was asleep for now. Murdo was seated on a bench near the door, his plaid wrapped round Ailidh Drummond, her head on his shoulder; Steenie seemed to be in a dark corner, from which came occasional giggles.

The sky beyond the open door was still greenish, but a few stars were already pricking through, and the yard was half in darkness. Inside the house there were rushlights and peat-glow, and the refreshments were going round, a jug of usquebae, a jug of ale, slices of the plum cake and oatcakes with green cheese, offered by Agnes and her cousin Elizabeth. Coached on the way up the glen by Murdo, Alys was well prepared for this next stage of the *ceilidh*.

'They will be asking you to begin,' he had said seriously. 'If you wish it, you can be telling a tale or singing, but there is some who would rather be waiting to see what others offer to the company.'

Recognizing good advice, she wished even more that Gil was with her. Most of the music she knew was for several voices. Now she smiled and parried Mistress Drummond's invitation politely.

'No, no, for I have no idea what the company would enjoy. Later, perhaps. Will you not begin, mistress?'

'Aye, Mammy,' said Patrick Drummond in his deep solemn voice. 'Tell us a tale for the bairns, will you not?'

'A tale,' she said doubtfully. 'What tale could I be telling that you have not heard before many times?'

'All the better for that,' said Davie Drummond, at the other side of her chair.

'And our guest has not the Gaelic, and I have no tales in Scots.'

Finally she was persuaded, and launched into a story in Ersche which seemed to be about a cheese, a bannock and a little old woman. The children obviously knew it, and laughed at every sentence; Alys could follow enough of the narrative to smile when the other adults did, but was more interested in studying the faces around her.

The younger Drummonds were all near the door, Ailidh seated on the bench with her lover, the two younger girls now at their feet, Jamie Beag standing by the door-frame. Their likeness to one another was almost eerie, although it could also be seen clearly that Elizabeth was Caterin's daughter, while the other three were Mòr's children. The four were obviously close; the tilt of shoulders, the angle of heads, made that clear to the onlooker, though they might not know it themselves.

The older generation was closer to the fire. Patrick Drummond, seated at his mother's right hand as befitted the eldest surviving son, was a big man nearing fifty, the frizzy family hair receding from his brow, his face and neck and brawny arms burnt red by the weather. He spoke slowly and gravely, his voice deep, and had received his guests with great pleasure. He and his nephew seemed to be in good accord about the work on the farm; Alys had overheard them talking together in Ersche in a pause in the dancing, gesturing at different corners of the infield, nodding seriously from time to time.

The tale ended, with the little old woman catching the bannock and the cheese and eating them both up. The children laughed, the adults chuckled, one or two people offered suggestions as to how the bannock could have been caught sooner, and another volunteer was selected, a man from up the glen who began tale about a calf and a dog.

Next to Patrick, his wife sat twirling a spindle, glancing anxiously from time to time at her son in his long cradle. The boy was a poor creature, with his small twisted figure and sour, whey-coloured face, but he had obviously enjoyed the dancing and the music. Alys looked at him with pity, tracing the family likeness now he was relaxed in sleep, wondering if there was any remedy which would help him.

Glancing up, she met Caterin's gaze, and suddenly quailed. The woman's expression was hostile, defensive, bitter. She put a possessive hand out over the cradle; the shadow of her headdress hid her small face, but it seemed as if she still glared at Alys. I only looked at the boy, thought Alys, why should that trouble her so much?

Mòr, the widow of the eldest son, was at Mistress Drummond's left hand. She sat upright and still, hands folded in her lap; Alys had the feeling this was a rare opportunity for her to do nothing. Between her feet and her good-mother's, Davie sat cross-legged on his folded plaid, leaning back against the old woman's knees, her hand on his hair. The folds of his shirt were drawn decorously over his bent legs; it occurred to Alys that despite the strictures of her Glasgow friends about Highland dress these bare-legged people were far more modest than Lowland men with their tight hose and ostentatious codpieces.

After the debate between the dog and the calf ended, the children from up the glen were persuaded to sing, which they did with aplomb, the sweet young voices bridging the great leaps of the tune with precision, the words clear. There was no direct praise for them afterwards, but several people commented on the tune, on how old it was and how appropriate it was for the season. The children seemed to see this as praise, for they wriggled and giggled among the feet.

'There is music everywhere,' said Alys, as the refreshment went round again. 'Everyone sings, and you all sing well.'

'It is pleasing to God and His saints,' said Mistress Drummond seriously.

'A true word, Mammy,' said Mòr beside her. 'There is no harm coming to a body or to the work, if you should be singing a hymn to Mary mild, or Brìde, or to Angus.'

'There is a hymn to St Angus?' Alys asked.

'More than one,' she was assured. One of the children near her began a list, and was cuffed silent by his father.

'Will you tell me about St Angus?' she prompted. 'He is your own saint here in Balquhidder, is that right?'

'He was a holy man of Dunblane,' said Mòr, 'and was walking to Columba's isle. And he came over the ridge and saw the glen of Balquhidder lying before him in the sunshine, and he was falling on his knees to bless the place, and it is still called Beannachd Aonghais where he kneeled.'

'And he never left us again,' said someone else with satisfaction.

There seemed to be many tales of the saint, one or two of them the same as tales she had heard told of Columba or Kentigern. Someone produced a tiny harp with nine wire strings, and a young woman sang to its shining music about the blessing which Angus had left on the glen. He was buried in the Eagleis Beag, the little kirk down in Balquhidder glen, with his image on the stone laid over him, and if you stood on the stone to be wedded it was as if the saint himself conducted the wedding.

'But you would not be standing on his face,' said someone.

'No, no, that would not be respectful,' agreed another.

'And will Davie be singing for us too?' asked a bold voice from the shadows. 'He could be singing the Oran Mor Aonghais just now, maybe. The lady would be happy to hear it, and so would the rest of us.'

'Och, not tonight,' said Davie awkwardly. 'My throat's dry from the reaping.'

'So are we all dry,' said Patrick.

'Maybe you will not mind it?' asked Mòr, with a challenging note in her voice. 'It will be a few years since you sang it, I suppose, since those ones will not be praising our Angus.'

'Oh, I mind it well enough.'

'Then take some more ale, and sing up, good-brother.' She beckoned, and her daughter Agnes came forward with the ale-jug. Alys, aware of sudden tension in the circle round the fire, watched intently.

'There are others who should be singing before me,' protested Davie. This was argued down by several people.

'Let him alone,' said Caterin kindly. 'He's shy, maybe.'

'Och, yes,' said Mistress Drummond. 'You were always the shy one, David *mo chridh*.'

'He was none so shy last month,' objected Mòr, 'when he sang all evening before my kin.'

'It would be good to hear it,' remarked Patrick, 'though it were thirty year delayed.'

Davie took a pull at the ale-jug, and gave it back to Agnes.

'It's a while since I sang it,' he said, 'as my good-sister is saying, though maybe not thirty year to me.'

'Will we begin it with you, then?' offered Ailidh from her seat by the door. She looked round in the shadows at the other young Drummonds, drew a breath, and began to sing. They joined in immediately, a slow, measured melody which Davie picked up, first in accord with them and then with odd variations, each time delivered with confidence. Alys was still watching the group by the door, and saw their surprise at the first of these, and the second. Then they reached what seemed to be the end of a verse, and fell silent, leaving Davie singing alone, leaning back against the old woman's knee, his eyes shut.

The Great Song of Angus was very long, but as when she had heard this voice before, Alys felt she could have sat listening for ever. The delivery was professional and accomplished, the range of the voice surprising, the low notes warm and creamy, the higher ones golden. Such of the hymn as she understood concerned the saint's miracles and the way he watched over his parish, keeping the calf from straying, the child safe in the cradle, the cattle in the fold and the maiden at the spinning. It seemed to be very old, for the words were oddly pronounced even when she recognized them, and the tune was simple, repetitive, varied by shifting an octave up or down, strangely satisfying. The music seemed almost to float into the house by no human agency, winding into the shadows, spinning a timeless web that linked the hearers with the saint himself. In its midst, Alys's eye fell on the cradle again, and she saw that even the changeling boy was listening quietly, contented, entranced. But over his head his mother had turned that bitter gaze on the singer. Her expression was like a discord in the Great Song; Alys looked away, and when she looked back the child's eyes were closed and his mother's head bent over her spinning.

When it finally ended there was an extended silence, into which Mistress Drummond said happily, 'My, but it is good to hear it sung proper.'

'I never heard it sung like that before,' said one of the younger men from up the glen in doubtful tones. 'Are you sure you mind it right, Davie Drummond?'

'On the contrary,' said old Mairead. 'He has it exactly right. That is the old way of singing it, just as I mind it in his father's mouth thirty year since.'

'Just as I mind it too,' said Patrick in his grave voice. He leaned forward and put his hand on Davie's curly head. 'My doubts are gone. Wherever you have been, if you can sing like that, you can only be my brother returned to us.'

Mòr's face, lit by the nearest rushlight, twisted into a sour smile as she watched. Caterin leaned down to her spindle, whose thread had snapped, and Davie reached up to grip Patrick's wrist and said, 'I was well taught.'

Yes, thought Alys, and who by? And was the hand that gripped Patrick's trembling, or not?

The discussion went into Ersche, and seemed to be a detailed dissection of parts of the song, a consideration of what some of the old words meant. Davie joined in occasionally, with a diffident comment preceded each time by, *My father said*.

There was a touch on her elbow. She looked round, and found Agnes smiling shyly at her in the glow of the nearest rushlight.

'We are going outside, we young ones,' she said softly. 'Will the lady come with us?'

'Gladly,' she said, suddenly aware of being over-warm, and rose to follow the girl. Socrates scrambled up from behind the kist she sat on and followed, provoking warning growls from some of the other dogs lying among the feet, and there was a further disturbance as Steenie extricated himself from his corner.

Out in the moonlit yard the air was cool and fresh. The hills around the farm loomed black against the stars, and the occasional call of a nightbird prompted the Drummond girls to cross themselves and mutter a charm Alys could not catch. The dog paced about, checking the scents, cocking his leg against the fulling-tub and other corners; Steenie took up a watchful stance by the house wall, and Murdo said:

'Are you liking the *ceilidh*, mistress?'

'Yes, indeed,' she said. 'I was never at such an evening before.'

160

'That great song was bonnie,' said Elizabeth softly. 'It never sounded like that when they sang it down in the Kirkton.'

'Maybe he could be singing it next week at the *Feis*,' said Agnes.

'Maybe no,' said Ailidh. 'Murdo,' she prompted. Her lover nodded, and braced himself to speak.

'There has been another accident, just this day,' said Jamie Beag before he got the words out. 'Would the lady be wishing to know more about it?'

'I would indeed,' said Alys, as levelly as she might.

'It was worse than before,' said Agnes. 'For Jamie and my uncle Padraig might have been hurt in earnest.'

'Hush, Nannie,'said her sister. 'Let Jamie tell it.'

Jamie explained. They had gathered in all the barley, and since the stooked straw was dry they had begun to bring it in as well. The far end of the outfield was a good half mile from the stackyard, so the bundles must be laid on a wooden sled, which the pony brought down with reluctance.

'He has never liked the sled,' said Jamie seriously, his voice very like his uncle's. 'Nor he has not taken well to let Davie work him, though he is fine with my uncle and me.'

'He bites,' said Elizabeth. The other girls nodded, the moonlight shining on their clouds of fair hair.

'You should be selling him at the *Feis*,' said Ailidh. 'There is no use of a pony that only two folk on the place can work.'

'You would get a good price maybe if you sold him to the monks,' said Agnes.

'Maybe,' said Jamie Beag. 'Am I to tell this or no? So we had the pony up the field, and the sled loaded, and hitched Lachdann up, and Davie had the rope at his head, and my uncle and me were pushing to start the sled.' He paused, and Alys murmured understanding. 'And then Lachie began snorting, and he shied away, and he was for biting Davie, only Davie got him on the nose with the rope. So I took Davie's place, and he was to push instead, and when

161

I tried to lead Lachie forward he tried to bite me and all, and then he reared up and struck out with his feet, and squealed, and reared again. I thought he would split my head open, even though he is not shod.'

'I saw it from here,' said Agnes. 'I thought the Devil was at the beast.'

'So did I,' said Jamie frankly, 'but my uncle came, and he checked all the harness, and when he looked inside the breastplate he found a needle.'

'A *needle*?' repeated Alys incredulously.

'A broken one,' said Murdo. 'Wedged in the lining of the breastplate, so it would stick in the beast when he leaned into it. They have showed it to me.'

'And those ones,' broke in Elizabeth, 'would not be touching a needle, because it is iron, you know, so it makes it certain it is –'

'Husha!' said Jamie. 'You see how it is, mistress. This time it was no accident.'

Alys nodded.

'Has any of you lost a needle, or broken one, lately?' she asked. A needle was not cheap; even in Glasgow, with merchants and metalworkers to hand, she guarded her own carefully in a little wooden case, and here where the nearest replacement was probably in Perth or Dunblane, it would be wise to keep a close watch on such things. Jamie looked at his kinswomen, and after a moment Agnes said reluctantly:

'I lost my good needle a while ago. Maybe two weeks since.'

'Mammy broke one the other day,' admitted Elizabeth. 'She put it safe, out of Iain's reach. He crawls about the floor, times,' she explained to Alys.

'I never found mine,' said Agnes. Alys nodded. No help there.

'What does Davie plan to do, do you know?' she asked.

'About the needle?' asked Ailidh.

'No, no. Does he mean to settle here, or go back to Dunblane, or go for a priest, or –?'

162

'Oh.' Ailidh turned to her kinsfolk. 'Well, he – we've not –'

'I'll be staying here –' said Davie at Alys's elbow. She jumped convulsively, and he put out a hand to her. 'My sorrow, I never meant –'

'You with the soft feet,' said Jamie, half smiling. 'He goes like a cat, isn't it, mistress.'

'So you will stay here at Dalriach?' she said, her heart still hammering.

'I will, while the old woman dwells here. As sure as my name's Davie Drummond,' he said, on a faint note of challenge.

'But is it?' she said quietly. He looked steadily at her in the moonlight.

'It is,' he said. 'I swear it, mistress.' One of the girls giggled nervously.

'By what will you swear?' she asked.

'Mary mild and Michael and Angus be my witnesses,' he said formally, and crossed himself with each name, 'that I swear I am Davie Drummond.'

Jamie clapped Davie briefly on the shoulder.

'Another pair of hands about the place is a good thing,' he said, 'and the more so when it's kin. I'm right glad to hear that you'll stay.'

'But what will the mammies be saying?' said Agnes pertly, linking arms with Davie. Her cousin Elizabeth moved to his other side, looking up at him, her face shadowed. 'They were arguing again today, about whether there is enough here to be dividing three ways.'

'Husha!' said Jamie again. 'No concern of theirs it is, but only of the old woman's.'

'You can go away up the field and never be listening to them,' Agnes pointed out, 'it's me that has to sit here and wind bobbins and –'

'Mind your tongue, Nannie. What will our guest think of you,' said Ailidh, and pinched her elbow to stop her.

'Did you know,' said Alys deliberately in a soft voice, 'that Mistress Drummond wrote twice to her son who is in

163

Dunblane, and the second time she said that if David went back to his place in the sang-schule she would gift land of twelve merks per annum –'

'*What?*' Davie exclaimed. The noise from inside the house paused briefly, but the silence in the courtyard lasted longer. All the Drummonds stared at Alys, open-mouthed, and Murdo looked from her to Jamie and then his sweetheart. After a moment Davie said more quietly, 'No. She will not be persuading me.'

'Is there twelve merks of land to spare?' asked Murdo.

Jamie shrugged. 'I'd say not, unless it was the whole of the land up by Garachra, and then what would we do for the summer grazing?'

'Do the mammies know that?' wondered Agnes. 'Do you think your father knows?'

'I've not heard them say it,' said Elizabeth cautiously.

'No matter,' said Davie. 'There is no reason I would be going there.'

'Fat Uncle Andrew would never be wanting you back anyway,'observed Agnes.

'He's not so bad as that,' said Jamie.

'Och, he is. Last time he was home, afore Pentecost, and the *cailleach* was lamenting Davie again, he could hardly hear her for jealousy.'

'Andrew was aye jealous,' said Davie rather tentatively.

'He was,' said Ailidh. 'Do you mind, Jamie, when he heard you would have our father's portion entire? He has given up his portion, seeing he is well forward in the great kirk at Dunblane,' she added to Murdo, 'but he could not bear to know that Jamie would get a half-share of the tack.'

A voice rose from the house door, speaking in Ersche. Alys looked round, and saw Mòr standing there. Catching sight of her, the woman switched to Scots.

'Will you be coming away in, the whole of you, and you too, mistress. You will be missing the best of the singing. And we were hoping our guest might have a song or a tale for us,' she added as Alys passed her in the doorway, into the lighted room.

So the moment was on her. She caught her breath, smiled and nodded, seated herself again, while her mind whirled and Steenie clambered over legs and bodies, back to his corner. A song or a tale, a song or a tale? She tried to recall Annec's amusements for a small girl, and could only see her nurse's face and the white linen on her head. None of the tales she had heard in her years in Glasgow would come to mind either.

'A song, maybe,' suggested Mistress Drummond, her hand curving round Davie's jaw as he leaned against her knee again. 'We would like to be hearing what songs they sing in Glasgow or France.'

'A song,' said Alys. That was easier. She thought briefly, opened her mouth, and found she was singing Machaut, one of his endless hymns to his Peronelle. Sweet and demanding, the music took concentration, but she was aware of interest, of careful listening, of a rewarding audience. As had happened for the children, there was no direct praise when she finished, but instead a lengthy discussion of the song itself, which she had to translate into Scots, and then a point-blank request from Caterin.

'Would you be singing more, mistress? I would like fine to hear another like that.'

'Another one?' she said. 'Yes, of course.' She paused, and the evening a few weeks since when she had last sung the Machaut came clearly to mind. They had had some new music from Edinburgh, and she and Gil and her father had explored it happily, but they had finished with some songs they all knew. Gil had played the monocords, and she had sung Ockeghem to the spidery notes. She found her pitch, and began.

Halfway through the first line, she was aware of recognition from somewhere in the room. Somewhere close to her. She looked round in the shadows. Not Murdo, who was engrossed in a wordless communion with his Ailidh again. Not Steenie, surely? No, closer than that – someone at the hearth knew Ockeghem, knew this song. She continued to enumerate the charms of the nameless beloved while looking from face to face, at Patrick listening politely, Caterin gazing at her son still asleep in the cradle, Mistress Drummond nodding gently in time with the tune. Mòr sat with that sour, faintly triumphant smile; her eyes were on the lad who swore his name was Davie Drummond, who was staring at the glow of the peat fire, small movements of mouth and fingers betraying to the watchers how well he knew words and music. He had both played and sung the same piece, Alys judged, many times.

Once her bedfellows finally fell into sleep, she was able to think.

When the gathering ended, the other folk at the *ceilidh* set out with lanterns to pick their way back to one settlement or the other, and the family began the process of readying houses and people for sleep. Alys had tried to lend a hand in the carrying of kists and benches out of Mistress Drummond's house, but it had been firmly refused. Now Mòr's house was quiet, the dogs in the yard and byre had settled down and Ailidh and Agnes, one on either side of her, were warm and somnolent. The *ceilidh* had been an extraordinary experience, one she was eager to discuss with Gil, and the ritual of the night, the smooring of the fire, the washing of feet and covering of dishes, had been fascinating to watch, but she needed to examine what she had learned and observed. She lay staring into the dark interior of the box bed, turning things over in her mind.

Whoever had taught David had taught him well. If he could swear to the name he used, he must be blood kin of the family here at Dalriach, either a legitimate son or an acknowledged bastard. Old Mistress Drummond said that her man was the only child her English mother-in-law had raised. Since the thistledown hair came from the Englishwoman, we need not consider descent from any further back, she thought, counting off the family, but could

Mistress Drummond's man have had a child elsewhere without her knowing? It would need to be a son, to pass on the name. Something to ask down the valley, she thought, rather than up here. And in the next generation – well, whatever their mother said, her sons might have issue elsewhere. Indeed we know that Andrew has children, she realized. The two sons left on the farm would have less opportunity, perhaps, and less chance to acknowledge the result without her knowing. Word spreads fast in the glens, she recalled. I wonder if either of them went as far as Stirling, like their father. Seonaid the tiring-maid had assured her that the daughter, Bethag Drummond, wife to Angus MacLaren, had been no further than the Kirkton these three years, nor had she had any strangers to stay at her house, so it was not her teaching which made Davie so confident.

And that left David. Not this young man calling himself Davie Drummond, but the boy who vanished thirty years ago. Where is he now? she wondered. Could he be alive, and this one his son, and all the impressive knowledge of the place and its music learned from him?

And what had he come back to? Why had he come back? Very different questions, she reflected. The welcome he had met varied greatly in tone. It seemed to her that the young Drummonds had accepted the stranger on other terms than their elders. Patrick now seemed as convinced as his mother that this was his brother returned; what Caterin and Mòr thought was still unclear, but their children had a different attitude. The girls were almost protective, she thought, recalling the way they had gathered round Davie when he appeared in the yard, and Jamie treats him as an equal. I wonder what they know? No hope that they will tell me.

Beside her in the darkness Ailidh and Agnes slept, their breath even and innocent. In the wider space of the house, beyond the bed-curtains, something stirred. She lay listening to tiny movements, sounds so faint they were drowned by the rustle of the bedclothes when Ailidh sighed. Mice?

she wondered. Or rats? Then there was a click, and a thin creak. The door. Mòr or her son, she thought, going out to the yard. Nothing to fear.

The daughters-in-law were both hostile, in very different ways. Hardly surprising, she thought, if it means the land must be further divided. I must check that with Lady Stewart. She considered the two women, Mòr tall and sardonic and simply, politely, hostile, with her prodding remarks designed to trip Davie into giving himself away as an impostor, none of which had yet succeeded; Caterin, oddly ambivalent, jealous perhaps of Davie's effect on her son, and yet valuing his ability to soothe the boy, as well as wary of his claim on the estate. She thought again of the searing bitterness in the woman's face as she watched Davie singing.

The door creaked thinly again, the latch clicked, those small movements reached her. Whoever it was, returning.

Turning all this over in her head, she must have drifted into sleep, because she dreamed about the shouting before she realized she was hearing it. Then there were dogs barking, and she was awake in a muddle of arms and legs. The girls were exclaiming in Ersche, and Socrates spoke urgently by the bed-curtains in the soft, embarrassed bark he used indoors.

'What is it?' she asked, and realized that some of the shouting was Steenie's voice.

'Fire! Fire! Rouse the ferm! Fire!'

'Our Lady protect us!' she said, and tumbled out of the bed after Ailidh, in time to see Mòr kindling a light which showed Jamie struggling into his huge sark. He pulled it down round his knees and seized his belt, fumbling with the buckle as he hurried out of the door. Alys identified her own kirtle by touch and dived into it, stepped into her shoes, and followed the other women out into the noise of the yard, the dog anxious against her knee.

It was the thatch of Mistress Drummond's house which was burning, and it was well alight already. Bright flames leapt from the bundled bracken, smoke towered in their

168

light, a red glow showed at the house door. Alys stood frozen in horror for a moment beside Mòr's house, the ends of her kirtle laces in her hands, then collected herself, knotted the laces, tugged at the arm nearest her.

'Buckets!' she said. 'Water – where is the water?'

'The burn,' said Ailidh, pointing. 'Jamie is there now.'

The men were already running back and forth, but the water they threw made little impression. First Steenie, then Murdo, appeared with pitchforks and began tugging at the eaves with it, scattering burning bracken on to the cobbles, the wooden forks beginning to smoulder almost immediately. Ailidh ran to join them, and Alys went to help handle buckets, aware of Socrates still at her knee and of the tethered horses squealing on the grazing land, the cattle bawling in the fold by the byre. Hens squawked, the changeling boy screamed somewhere, once and not again, the farm dogs were barking madly in the leaping shadows. Caterin came stumbling up the yard into the fire-light, and behind her two of the tenants arrived to help, joining the bucket chain. The water seemed to come from beyond the stackyard.

Agnes raised her voice with a shrill demand in Ersche. Something about the *cailleach*, and then Davie's name. Alys realized she had seen neither since she stepped into the yard. Were they still within, below the burning thatch? she wondered in horror.

At that moment Davie appeared at the door of the house, coughing, gesturing, pointing back inside. Murdo, nearest to him, thrust the pitchfork into Ailidh's hands and ran to join him, and they both plunged into the red glow of the interior. Ailidh screamed, several people shouted, but almost immediately they reappeared, carrying the old woman as an awkward bundle between them. Patrick reached them as they staggered, received his mother's limp form, dragged her away from the flying sparks and flakes of burning thatch to the other side of the yard. One of the younger girls followed, patting ineffectually at the burning spots on the old woman's striped kirtle.

Under Jamie's direction, the bucket chain was now concentrating on bringing water to the roof of Patrick's own house, where the drifting fragments had already started one or two small blazes. Someone freed the beasts from the cattle-fold at the end of the house, and they galloped off into the night, stumbling and bawling in their rush to get away, several goats bleating shrilly among them.

Mistress Drummond had been laid down on someone's plaid, and Patrick and Davie were both kneeling over her in the firelight, more shadowy figures beyond them. Why not take her into the house? Alys thought, and answered herself: If the house roof caught, they would have to move her again. Standing in the middle of the yard she passed empty buckets, tubs, bowls one way, full ones the other way, water slopping on her feet and skirts, the heavy wooden vessels tugging at her arms and back, while she tried to see what was happening. Behind her Steenie was arguing with Murdo, *I tell you I saw it!* What had he seen? she wondered, peering anxiously through the leaping firelight. Caterin and Mòr were by Mistress Drummond, conferring anxiously with Patrick, and Davie was holding the old woman's hands, talking urgently to her.

Patrick looked up, stared around. Elizabeth ran over and seized the next bucket.

'She is asking for you, mistress,' she said breathlessly. 'Will you go to her?' She dashed at her eyes with a hand momentarily free. 'I think she will be leaving us.'

'Leaving you?' Alys hurried across to the anxious group, and Davie looked up as she arrived, tears glittering on his face in the leaping light.

'She is not good,' he said. 'The smoke, and the fright. I did what I could, but –'

'Usquebae?' Alys suggested.

'We tried that,' said Caterin in the shadows. 'Will you be listening to her, mistress? She has a word for you.'

Puzzled, Alys knelt obediently on the hard stones. The old woman did indeed look deathly, her face fallen in, her white hair tangled and sticking to her brow. Her kirtle was ill settled and unlaced, as if she had collapsed in the midst of dressing herself. From the smoke? Alys wondered. The hand which groped for Alys's was cold, and so was the usquebae-laden breath that reached her cheek.

'Lassie? Lassie, will you tell your man?'

'I will,' she promised. Tell him what? she wondered.

'This is – truly my bairn,' said the laboured whisper. 'Tell him. Davie is my bairn.'

'I'll tell him,' said Alys. At the foot of the folded plaid Caterin, kneeling, was intoning prayers in Ersche on a strange low humming note. Quite irrelevantly, it occurred to Alys that the boy Iain had fallen silent some time ago.

'Just as Patrick,' Mistress Drummond's gaze travelled to the man kneeling by her shoulder, 'and Jamie, and Ailidh.' She paused to draw breath. 'Agnes. Elizabeth. Andrew, Bethag, David. All my bonnie bairns. My son James, and Caterin's James, and Iain. Mòr, Caterin, my dear good-daughters.'

'Mammy!' said Davie in anguish. She opened her eyes again and smiled at him, and he leaned forward, made the sign of the Cross over her lips with his thumb, swallowed hard and began to sing. An expression of great peace came over the old woman at the first notes. It was a slow gentle song with a tune as ancient as the hymn to Angus, almost like another lullaby, but the only familiar word Alys could make out was *anam*, soul. It must be a prayer for the departing soul. Caterin ceased her chanting and stared, but Patrick joined in with *Amen* at the end of the verse. Davie went on, and one by one the family drew near until by the end of the fourth short stanza they were all close enough to sing the amen together, on two long-drawn notes.

There was a silence in the circle, though outside it there was noise. Away down the infield, where the hens had fled from the frantic scenes in the yard, the Dalriach cockerel suddenly lifted up his morning voice. The old woman said something in Ersche, smiled gently at Patrick, at Davie and then looked beyond them, sudden delight in her face. Alys

171

looked up, but saw only the hills black against the first light of dawn.

'Och, Seumas *mo chridh!*' said Mistress Drummond clearly, and did not speak again.

After a moment Patrick reached out and closed his mother's eyes. His daughter and nieces began a heart-broken wailing. And then, to Alys's amazement, Patrick too began to sing, another painful, ancient melody. This time Caterin joined in, and those around them took up the song, and still singing turned back to the urgent work, handing buckets and tugging at the burning thatch. Flames still leapt and crackled, but they did not reach so high into the tower of smoke, and the broadcast blossoms of fire on Patrick's house had withered under the drench-ing from the bucket chain. The song rose solemnly above the noise, a weary lament punctuated by the hissing and splashing of water in the flames, and the cries of the animals. Alys watched and listened, the hair standing up on the back of her neck, and beside the dead woman Davie knelt, his face buried in his hands.

The burning thatch fell in with a crash. Sparks and fly-ing scraps of bracken rose up, drifting on the light wind, but the other houses were safe, and the stackyard was upwind of the flames. The song ended, and Patrick touched Davie's shoulder.

'There is work to do, brother,' he said in Scots. 'The House of Fire is burning.'

'I ken that,' said Davie, raising his head. 'That was why I cam home.'

Patrick hardly seemed to hear the words. He bent to gather up one end of the plaid on which his mother lay.

'Come,' he said, 'we will take her indoors, out of harm's way.'

Chapter Nine

'I'd ha thought, Maister Gil,' said Tam, spurring his horse alongside his master's, 'you'd want to bide at Perth while they called the quest on the man you found, same as you aye do at Glasgow. Will they not need you to swear to the facts?'

'I've no remit in Perth,' Gil said, without looking round. The desperate feeling was much less now than when it had woken him before dawn, but he was still pulled onward, away from Perth, on towards Balquhidder, as if by a strong cord. 'I gave the Bishop my report last night, he can order the quest and hear the facts from those that were there. I'll go back when I get the chance.'

'So what's this about?' demanded Tam. 'Is it something up wi the mistress?'

'I must get back to Balquhidder.' He could not put the feeling into speech. He had found himself, in the dead of night, suddenly awake from a dream full of flames, his throat tight with the utter conviction that Alys needed him, that he must go to her. He had prayed for her safety, though it helped him little, and wrestled with the feeling till the first grey light of morning, then rose and dressed, and as soon as the household began to stir he had found Wat the steward, sent his apologies to the Bishop, ordered his men roused and the horses made ready. They had been on the road before sunrise, had changed horses and seized a bite eaten standing at Crieff, and were already nearing St Fillan's Kirk at the foot of Loch Earn. It was not fast enough for Gil, still silently petitioning St Giles for Alys's protection, but he accepted the need for care on the rough roads. If they lamed a horse it would slow them down still more.

'Aye, but is it the mistress? Or is it about that fellow that's been in Elfland?'

He opened his mouth to speak, hesitated, then admitted, 'I think it's your mistress. I think she needs me.'

'Right,' said Tam, with a flat acceptance which both re-assured and chilled. 'Will you and me ride on, maister, and let Ned and Donal follow wi the baggage?'

'Best we stick thegither,' said Ned from behind them. 'These hills is full of Murrays and Drummonds, and worse. Were you not seeing thon burned farmhouse a mile or two back? That was young Murray of Trewin's work, just a month since.'

'So what's worse than a Drummond or a Murray?' demanded Tam sceptically.

'A MacGregor,' said Ned succinctly. 'They'll slay their granny for a hen's egg.'

'Ride on,' said Gil impatiently, 'and stop the chatter. I want to get to Stronvar.'

It was nearly two hours longer before they reached the mouth of the glen, where the view of Loch Voil opened out and the smoke of the Kirkton and of Stronvar and the other settlements rose blue in the warm air. As they neared the stone that marked St Angus' entry to the glen, Gil became aware that there were riders ahead of them on the track, a party larger than their own to judge by the freshly trampled grasses at the side of the way.

'Aye, they came up Strathyre,' agreed Ned when he commented. 'I think they're peaceful, they've a couple baggage-mules wi them, I saw the traces back down the road a bit. Likely they're bound for Stronvar, if it's no Andrew Drummond come home to see what's what at last.'

Despite their haste the two Stronvar men insisted on halting by the stone, to uncover their heads and recite the saint's blessing. Gil, staring round while he waited, saw nothing to suggest any reason for anxiety, nothing untoward. The glen lay quiet under a smiling sky, birds sang in the bushes, sheep called on the slopes. A goat bleated indignantly somewhere nearby. The barley straw was drying in its stooks, the oats were not quite ripe, a handful of women turned the hay down by the river, their work-song drifting on the light wind. He was still uneasy, but the fear, the feeling that Alys needed his help, had dwindled and faded.

The party of horsemen had halted near the bridge. There were five or six riders on better horses than the hardy stout beasts Sir William kept at Stronvar, a pair of sumpter-mules, and in the midst of the group Canon Andrew Drummond, as Ned had surmised, seated on a pretty bay gelding and glowering under his broad-brimmed straw hat at Robert Montgomery.

'I'll not be thwarted by an ignorant clerk!' the churchman was saying in his harsh voice as Gil approached. 'I'm a Drummond of Dalriach and Canon of –'

'I ken fine who you are, sir,' said Robert, only the sudden high colour on his cheekbones betraying his anger at this description. 'But I tell you, if the Holy Father himsel came from Rome, he wouldny lodge his retinue wi Sir Duncan. My master is dying,' he emphasized, 'and I'll not have him disturbed.'

'Sir Duncan's like to live for ever,' said Drummond scornfully. 'Stop your nonsense and take my men wi you as I bid you.' He looked round and stared as Gil and his escort came down to the bridge. 'Oh, it's you,' he said after a moment. 'What's your name again, Cunningham is it? What are you doing here? I thought you were in Perth.'

'Staying at Stronvar,' said Gil unhelpfully, nodding to Robert. 'What brings you here, Canon Drummond? Is aught amiss at Dalriach?' And if you knew I was in Perth, he thought, how did you not know Sir Duncan is dying?

'You ken well things are amiss,' retorted Drummond. 'I've come – I've come to see what's all this nonsense about my brother David come home.'

Gil opened his mouth to speak, but was interrupted as, with a rattle of hooves, a riderless pony scurried towards them, down the slope from the Kirkton. Several of the horses stamped uneasily; Gil's mount pricked its ears and snorted at the sight, and he tightened his grip on the reins. The row of haymakers paused to stare at the beast.

'That's our Bawsie!' exclaimed Ned. 'Donal, catch him!'

Donal heeled his pony towards the runaway, but it jinked sideways, ears flat, stirrups flying, avoided the grasping hands of several of Drummond's followers, and got past them all, making for the bridge. Several of the standing horses tossed heads and shifted uneasily, eager to run with it.

'Will I follow him?' said Donal, as the sound of the hooves changed to a rumble on the planks.

'We'll see where he's come from,' Gil corrected, and followed Ned up the slope. 'Was it the kirk or the priest's house?'

Robert overtook them running, making for the priest's house. It stood silent, though the old man must be within and smoke rose through its thatch as everywhere else. But ahead of them in the kirkyard several men stood round the door of the little church, hay-forks in hand, staring anxiously at the door itself which was moving, slow as a clock hand; Gil was just dismounting when it thumped shut. Throwing his reins to Tam, he drew his whinger, and went quickly up the path with the two Stronvar men at his back. There was an exchange in Ersche, with gestures which seemed to confirm that someone had run into the little building.

'Davie Drummond, it is,' confirmed Donal. 'They are telling he came up from the bridge at the gallop, just before the Canon's men came into the glen, and left the pony here in the kirkyard. They were trying to catch it, though maybe not very hard,' he admitted, 'and now it's away. I think none of them is liking to go into the kirk.'

Gil nodded, glanced at Ned to see that he was ready, and in one swift movement kicked the door open and slipped in and to one side, ready for any attack from behind the heavy planks. Both Stronvar men followed him, equally wary.

There was a horrified gasp from the shadowed chancel, and a voice said, 'No! I claim sanctuary! I'll not – I won't –'

'Who is it claims sanctuary?' Gil demanded, peering into the dimness. The church was small and bare, its chancel even smaller, and the narrow windows admitted very little light. He could just see a low insubstantial form near the altar.

'It's Davie Drummond, right enough,' said Donal.

'I'd never ha thought,' said Ned, sheathing his blade, 'a Drummond would take refuge in a kirk, after Monzievaird.'

'Maybe he would not be hearing of Monzievaird,' suggested Donal. Gil stepped forward, and there was another shuddering gasp from within the chancel. As his eyes adjusted, he made out a huddled figure clinging to one leg of the altar table, a shock of light Drummond hair surrounding a pale face in which huge dark eyes stared at him.

'I'm unarmed,' said the panicky voice. 'I claim sanctuary.'

'I'll not hurt you,' said Gil, putting up his own blade, 'but it's not for me to grant sanctuary or deny it. Why are you here? Has something happened at – at Dalriach?' he asked urgently. 'Is my wife safe?'

'Mistress Alys? Last I saw she was well.'

The church seemed to whirl round him, and darken briefly, though that might have been because Andrew Drummond stepped in at the door.

'What's happening?' he demanded in his harsh voice. 'Who is it claims sanctuary?' he went on, striding forward to stand beside Gil at the chancel arch. 'Who is it, Cunningham? Why should he want sanctuary?'

'It's your brother David,' said Gil, and saw the man jerk

177

backwards as if the words had run him through. 'As to why, I've no notion yet. Maybe you should ask him.'

'Andrew?' said the kneeling figure. 'Is that you? My, but you're like my father.'

There was a tense pause, in which Gil was aware of the two Stronvar men watching with interest. Then Andrew Drummond seemed to relax, and stepped forward into the small chancel.

'You're no David,' he said. 'You're mighty like him, and the voice is good, but you're no David.'

The pale figure by the altar sat back on its heels, looking up at Andrew's face.

'Patrick thinks I am.'

'Patrick was aye a fool. What's brought you here – here to the kirk, at this time? Why would you need sanctuary, if you're who you claim to be?'

'Ca – Caterin,' said Davie, his voice breaking on the name.

'What about her?' said Andrew swiftly.

'She – she – she accused –' Davie whispered, and gulped as if suppressing tears. 'Andrew,' he said more clearly, 'I have to tell you. The *cailleach* is dead.'

Andrew crossed himself, muttered something, and said, 'When?'

An interesting response, thought Gil.

'Last night. This morning.' Davie swallowed again. 'Just about dawn, it was. I was – I was singing for her, the soulsong, and then we all sang her home, everyone that was in the yard.'

There was a pause. Then Andrew said, as if the words were dragged from him, 'Whoever you are, I am glad you were doing that.'

'So am I,' said Davie. 'Though I would rather not have had the need.'

'But what came to her?' Andrew shook his head in bafflement. 'In the yard, you said? What was she doing in the yard? And Caterin, what was she – do you say she accused you of the *cailleach*'s death?'

178

'Not that.' Davie scrambled closer to the leg of the altar. 'No, it – it – the Tigh-an-Teine is burned –'

'Burned?' said Gil sharply. They both jumped, as if they had forgotten he was there. 'Is anyone else hurt? You said my wife was safe!'

'Aye, she's safe,' began Davie.

'What's your wife to do with it?' demanded Andrew. 'What came to my mother? Did she burn wi the house? But she was unharmed when she came –' He checked, and Davie said:

'No, no, we got her out, Murdo Dubh and I got her out. I think it was the fright. Her heart, maybe.'

'Aye, I've wondered about that. And she was full old. But my good-sister Caterin,' persisted Andrew. 'What has she to do with it? What has she accused you of? They're saying out-by you came down here at the gallop on a Stronvar pony. Is that why, then?'

'Yes,' said Davie uncertainly. 'Yes, she was accusing me of setting the fire, and – and causing the *cailleach*'s death. And I never would.'

Gil moved forward. 'David, give us the short tale, will you, from the start, and then I think we must leave you to whoever is in charge of this kirk for now, to make the decision about your sanctuary. Canon Drummond needs to ride up Glenbuckie, and I'd as soon go wi him and find out what's ado.'

'But who's in charge?' said Drummond, staring round as if a rural dean might emerge from the damp stonework. 'If old Sir Duncan is finally on his road out, is it that impertinent clerk that's minding the place?'

'Sorry to say it,' said Robert Montgomery, stepping past the two Stronvar men where they still stood gaping under the chancel arch, 'but you're right at that.' He peered at the pale figure of Davie Drummond still clinging to the leg of the altar table. 'It is you, then? Sir Duncan said it would be, and bid me promise you shelter here, at least till Sir William gets his nose into the business. What are you feart

for, any road?' he went on, over Davie's grateful exclamation. 'What are you accused of?'

'Arson and death,' said Gil. 'Mistress Drummond is
dead.'

'Two deaths,' said Davie. 'There is two are dead, up at
Dalriach.'

'Canon Drummond, I must speak wi you,' said Gil.

'Must you?' returned Andrew Drummond.

They were working their way up the steep side of the
glen towards the hanging mouth of Glenbuckie, in the
midst of a party of men from Stronvar led by Sir William
himself, who was now deep in consultation with his steward about what aid they were able to offer Dalriach.
Encountering them at the fork in the road, the Bailie of
Balquhidder had demanded what they knew about the
riderless pony, extracted the kernel from the explanations
which reached his ears, and offered Gil one of the beasts
with him. Its rider, Gil's weary men, Drummond's retinue,
had all been despatched to Stronvar, and Sir William had
observed:

'Well, if it's no your bonnie lass or Murdo's boy lying wi
a broken limb, the saints be praised, it's still a trouble, and
I've no doubt they'll welcome a bit help at Dalriach. Let
me ha the tale again, maisters, and get it clear in my mind.'

He listened acutely while Gil recounted the news Davie
Drummond had stammered in the dim chancel, and
frowned and shook his head at the news of Mistress
Drummond's death.

'This is all at second-hand,' Gil said apologetically, 'and
if you'd sooner go over to the Kirkton and hear it from
David, I can ride on alone.'

'No, no, I'll trust you for a messenger,' said Sir William.
'This is no good, maister. Arson and murder are the
Crown's business, and I'll not ha folk accused of them on
my land and sit by on my backside watching the play. I'm
right sorry to hear of old Bessie Drummond's death,

Andrew, she's been a good tenant and a good woman.' Andrew bowed over his saddle-bow and crossed himself at this. 'And this second death – and the laddie accused of it – I canny tell what to think. Maybe when we find your wife, maister, we'll get a clearer tale.'

'If Alys observed it,' said Gil, 'we will.'

He was still anxious for Alys, though the cord which had drawn him here so relentlessly seemed to have slackened, but he was also aware that he should make the most of the chance which had thrown Drummond into his hands, and had made certain he rode beside the man as the party moved off.

'I'm sorry for this new loss,' he went on now. 'It must ha been a great shock to you when David gave you the word.'

'No,' said Drummond, 'for I kent it already.'

The man was by far less fey than he had been at that first meeting in his own garden, but this remark was startling. Then, with sudden insight, Gil said, 'Was it a dream fetched you here? Or a – a feeling that –'

'Aye.' Drummond nudged his horse round a boulder. 'I dreamed the dead summoned me. She stood at my bedside in this day's dawn, in her good red gown, and the brat Iain at her side, and bid me come home to Dalriach and untangle matters.'

'Did she so?' Gil said without inflection. Drummond shot him a wary look. 'What is there to untangle? This business of your brother reappeared?'

'Aye, likely.'

'You don't accept that fellow in the kirk as your brother, do you?'

'David,' said Andrew Drummond, reining in to look at Gil, 'was three year younger than me. He's a – if he lives,' he corrected himself, 'he's a man grown, no a laddie wi an alto voice.'

The man behind them pushed his horse past, and Gil checked his own beast as it threatened to kick.

'You don't believe he was lifted away by the fairies, then?'

'You're a man of learning,' Drummond stated harshly. 'Do you?'

'So what did happen to him?'

'A better question is, Who's that yonder in St Angus' Kirk? I'd accept him as kin, now I've set my een on him,' admitted Drummond, spurring his horse on, 'but he's no my brother Davie.'

'If he's not your brother, who might he be?' Gil asked levelly.

'I've never a notion,' said the other man. 'Unless my father had bastards we were not knowing of, you understand, and my mother never gave him the opportunity for that.'

'I'm told he knows the glen and the farm as if he was born there.'

'That can be taught,' said Drummond grimly.

'And the songs your father made? How would he learn those?'

This got a frowning look. 'Do you say so? That's harder to guess, but I suppose he could be taught those as well.'

'But what benefit is there?' Gil asked. 'Suppose that laddie has been sent by someone who taught him that way, what would they gain by it?'

'That's what's eating at me!' burst out Drummond. One or two of the group ahead of them turned at his words. 'Why is he here? There's naught to gain but the tenancy o the land, that the *cailleach* still held, and David had – has little claim on that, as the youngest. It depends on Sir William, I suppose, but most like it will go to Jamie Beag as tenant in chief now, seeing his father is dead that was the oldest of us, and likely Patrick as occupier.'

'Did Mistress Drummond have any savings?' Gil asked. 'Any valuables to leave?'

Drummond snorted.

'Why do you think I went for the kirk?' he said. 'We're over the Highland line here, maister. Folk eat well enough, in a good year, and dress well enough in their own web and spinning, but goods and furnishings costs siller, and siller's gey scarce in this country, scarcer than elsewhere in Scotland.'

'What, barely forty mile from Perth?'

'It could as well be four hundred. My mother would have little enough to leave. Her gowns to her daughter and good-daughters, likely, her linen to the granddaughters, maybe her spindle and the beams of her own loom, my grandsire's St James badge to one of us –'

'St James? If your grandsire went so far as Spain could the laddie be his get?'

'No,' said Drummond briefly, then expanded, 'We all take our hair, that marks us as Drummonds of Dalriach, from my grandam that was an Englishwoman. My grandsire looked like any other fellow in Balquhidder. I mind him well enough.'

Alys had said that, Gil recalled.

'What did happen to David, thirty year ago?' he asked a second time. Drummond's horse stumbled, pecked, nearly dislodged him, and he spent the length of a Paternoster steadying the beast and settling himself in the saddle again. Finally he looked at Gil.

'How would I ken better than those that were here?' he retorted. 'I was at Dunblane. All I kent was that he never turned up when he was expected.'

'Did you miss him?'

'No at the time,' said Drummond oddly.

'But later you did?'

'Aye.' Drummond looked at the rest of the party, which was some way in front of them, and urged his horse forward. 'We will be left behind.'

They rode on in silence for a short space; then Gil said, 'When you were in Perth two weeks since, you spoke with James Stirling.'

Drummond turned to stare at him again.

'I did,' he agreed.

'What was it you learned from him?'

Another silence.

'I canny be telling you,' said Drummond at length. 'It was confession.'

The priest's escape clause, thought Gil, and I can hardly press him on it.

'That's unfortunate,' he said. 'Have you heard the man is dead?'

Drummond's head came round sharply at that. 'Dead? Last I heard they were asking at Chapter had anyone word o him. Georgie Brown seemed to think he'd gone off somewhere. What's come to him?'

So he took that much in at Chapter, thought Gil.

'It looks very much as if you were the last to speak wi him,' he said carefully.

'I was? He was hale when I left him.'

'And when was that? How much can you tell me?'

Drummond halted his steed and stared up through the trees at the rest of the group nearing the skyline; his face was shadowed under his straw hat.

'I met him by chance,' he said, 'the last day I was in Perth. To begin, he was offering sympathy for the death – the death of my friend –' Gil made an understanding noise. 'And then he was talking of another matter, and then he asked if I would hear his confession.'

'But when did you leave him? Where was he?'

Drummond glanced sideways, and pursed his lips.

'Not as late as seven of the clock,' he said at length. 'We had walked and talked on the open ground by the Blackfriars' convent, maybe you know it if you've been in Perth, and I left him there. I had an errand to see to in the suburb near the tanyards.'

'Was that with William Doig?'

'Doig?' repeated Drummond sharply. 'No, not – I had a servant to dismiss, that was all. Nothing to do wi Doig.'

'Did you see Stirling again? What did you do after your errand by the tanyards?'

'I did not,' said Drummond firmly. 'I went on into the

town to my supper. I returned to the Blackfriars just as they came from Compline.'

'Where did you eat your supper?'

'In the town. But tell me what came to him, man? How can he be dead, and so soon after I saw him hale?'

'That's what I'm trying to find out,' said Gil grimly. 'The more you can tell me, maister, the sooner I'll find his killer.'

'His *killer*?' repeated Drummond. 'I took it he'd fallen ill, or – or – Who can have killed him? Why would –' He broke off, and crossed himself. 'Christ be praised that we –' He stopped again, and shook his head.

'What did you discuss?'

'A matter relating to what we – to his confession.'

That trail was blocked, it was obvious. Gil thought for a space, and then said, 'Did you see anyone else while you were with Stirling?'

'Och, yes indeed.' The man's Ersche accent seemed to be strengthening with every word he spoke. 'Let me see,' he said slowly, 'there was the woman who breeds dogs. Mistress Doig. It was in her yard we met. There was passers-by on the road to the Blackfriars' meadow. There was folk on the path by the Ditch. And of course there was my man and his.'

'Your men?' repeated Gil, startled. 'I had thought he was alone!'

'No,' said Drummond.

'Who was it with him?'

Drummond shrugged. 'It was just an indoor servant in Georgie Brown's livery. I was never speaking with the man. You could ask at my Benet, the two of them was sitting under a tree the whole time we was talking on the meadow.'

'I will,' said Gil, trying to fit this to the information he already had. It did not seem to connect well. 'Canon, how much are you able to tell me without breaking the seal of confession? Is there anything else he said that might help?' Drummond turned an unreadable stare on him. 'James

Stirling was killed, and his death hidden,' he pointed out. 'I'm charged wi finding his killer, and any wee sign that might point me to him would be of value.'

'Aye, well, I'll consider of it,' said the other after a moment. 'If I mind he said anything not connected with his confession, I'll write it down. But at this time, maister, my chiefest concern is to come to my home and offer prayers over my mother's body.'

'Then we ride on,' said Gil. 'We –'

There was sudden shouting ahead. One of Sir William's men came crashing back through the woodland, calling to Gil, pointing up the slope. Heart hammering, he urged his stout pony onward, and as he came level with him the man exclaimed:

'Is your lady, sir. She safe!'

His heart leapt, but went on hammering. He could scarcely breathe. The pony, having decided to run, thundered on up the hill and out from under the trees, into the open green space of Glenbuckie, though he did not see that nor Murdo feeling his son all over as if he was another pony, because twenty yards away Alys was at the centre of a knot of riders, sitting on a weary beast, clad in a ruined kirtle, her hair loose down her back. She saw him at the same moment, and broke free of the group to ride towards him, Socrates bounding forward at her side.

In front of such an audience they neither kissed nor embraced. Instead, as their ponies halted nose to tail, they reached out in silence and gripped one another's hands as tightly as if drowning. And he could almost have drowned in her eyes, he thought, seeing his relief reflected in her face as she absorbed the fact of his presence. The dog danced round them, pawing at his knee, and his mount tossed its head uneasily, but he ignored them.

'I'm safe,' she said in French after a while, answering what he had no need to say. 'Are you? What – why are you –'

'I'm safe,' he agreed. 'Nothing touched me. But you –' He took in her dishevelment, and groped for something to lighten the moment. *'Goying in a queynt array With wind blowing upon hir tresse* – If you're going to make a habit of riding about Scotland in your kirtle, wife, you'll be a deal cheaper to gown than I feared.'

She giggled, though tears sprang to her eyes.

'Steenie is hurt, he has a burn to his ear and face. But Gil – there is so much I need to tell you, so much to – Davie has fled to the kirk, he –'

'We spoke to him.'

'So you know –' Her mouth trembled.

'We know.' He finally broke his grasp of one of her hands, to pat his importunate dog. She reached across with the freed hand to caress the animal's ears, saying shakily:

'And Socrates has been a very good dog.'

'Best to get these folk home to Stronvar,' said Sir William briskly beside them. 'Your wife needs her bed, Cunningham, and your man needs something for that burn. As for young Murdo here –' He clapped the steward's son on the shoulder. 'He's earned your favour the day, I can tell you.'

'Indeed, Gil, he has,' agreed Alys earnestly.

'It was no more than my duty,' said Murdo Dubh, the dark lashes sweeping his cheek as he looked down, his father beside him trying to look impassive at the compliments.

'Will you come wi us, Cunningham, or see your wife down the road?'

Her hand clung to his, but her eyes had a different message.

'I must talk to you,' she said in French, 'but later. You need to see what –' She looked hard at him. 'Talk to Jamie Beag, Gil, and try to get a sight of the dead.' She put up her other hand and ran it around the back of her head, fingers against her skull. Gil understood the gesture. One of the deaths at least was suspect; she wished him to inspect the bodies closely.

Chapter Ten

The smell of the burnt thatch met them fully a mile down-wind of the farm. Drummond's face darkened at the first tang, and he spurred his bay gelding forward more urgently.

'Is it just my mother's house that has burned,' he demanded, 'or is it the whole farm?'

'Just the house, my son was saying,' said Murdo the steward.

'I don't like this business of accusing the laddie of arson,' said Sir William. 'Bad enough the woman making the accusation, folk make mistakes in the heat of the moment, but to uphold it against your man's evidence, that's a worry. Either she's right sure or it's a malicious charge, and I'd as soon not get mixed up in either. How trustworthy is the man?'

'Steenie? He's a good fellow, and I've aye known him truthful.' Gil called up what Alys had reported while the dazed groom was helped on to a horse fit to carry two. 'He said he had seen someone set the flame and run away across the yard, and when he hammered on the house door to raise the alarm, Davie Drummond answered him from within.'

'Aye, that's it,' agreed Sir William. 'And here's Caterin Campbell saying she saw the laddie set the fire himself.'

'He swears he has done no such thing,' said Gil. 'Kneeling by the altar as he said it.'

'Aye,' said Sir William sceptically.

They came over the flank of the hill to see the township

laid out below them, the blackened rafters and walls of the burnt house nearest to them and beyond that the yard busy with neighbours, peat-smoke rising blue from the two stone-built houses at either side, more people coming and going from the smaller habitations further down the slope.

'Christ aid!' said Sir William. 'It's going like a bees' byke!'

'We're expected,' observed one of his men.

This was clearly true. Gil, armed with all Alys had told him of her first visit, identified the little group waiting in the centre of the yard to receive them readily enough. The foremost must be Patrick, big and broad-shouldered, his fair skin reddened by outside work; next to him stood his nephew. Both wore velvet bonnets and their clean shirts were half-hidden by layers of carefully pleated wool, Patrick with a silver-mounted belt and pouch restraining the chequered folds. Behind them was a much older man in a mended plaid and blue woollen bonnet, whom Gil could not place, and off to one side were the women, plaids drawn modestly over their faces, the two weaving sisters-in-law and the oldest granddaughter distinguishable nevertheless.

As their landlord entered the yard the two Drummond men swept off their bonnets and bowed with a grace one might barely see equalled in Edinburgh. The oldest granddaughter stepped forward with a lugged bowl in her hands, to offer refreshment to the guests, and amid Sir William's bluntly expressed sympathies and the general dismounting, Gil thought he was the only person to notice Andrew Drummond's expression as he stared at the black ribcage of his mother's house. He moved to the man's side and said quietly:

'She got out of it, man. She breathed clean air afore she died.'

Drummond nodded, without looking round, and turned away to greet his brother with a curt nod and a word in Ersche. Gil went closer to the ruin, gazing in at the doorway. The thatch, he supposed, would have burned most completely at the point where it first caught fire. If the fire had been set, presumably that would be at the eaves somewhere, within reach of the person responsible, whereas if it had begun from a spark flying up from the peat fire the higher parts of the roof would have burned first. Or would a firesetter have thrown a burning brand up on to the roof? No, Steenie had talked as if the eaves caught first. The collapsed layer of ash and bracken leaves draped over the internal structures of the house told him nothing useful, and the smell of damp ashes was overwhelming. He stepped back, and found the younger Drummond at his elbow, velvet bonnet in hand.

'I am thinking,' said the young man, 'you are Maister Cunningham, that is Mistress Alys's man.' Gil admitted this. 'I tell you, maister, she is our heart-friend so long as she lives for last night's work. She and your man Steenie carried water the night long and she helped to dress burns and wash the dead.' He turned his face away briefly, then went on, 'Can you tell me where is – where is Davie?' he ended in a rush, going scarlet.

'He's in St Angus' Kirk,' said Gil. Jamie sighed in relief, and crossed himself, the bright colour fading already. 'Sir Duncan sent his clerk to say he can stay there.'

'Then there is things we would like to tell you.'

'My wife bade me talk to you,' Gil said, nodding.

The dead, it seemed, were laid out in Patrick's house, on the southern side of the yard, and the most of the visitors were there or in the yard itself. Seated by the hearth in the other longhouse, his back to the tall loom with its half-worked web of bright checks, Gil listened to Jamie's account of the fire and the death of his grandmother while one of the younger granddaughters offered him usquebae and oatcakes, and the other watched at the door.

'But it was the fire itself killed her,' he said as the tale ended, 'not a direct injury?'

'That is so,' agreed Jamie. 'The *cailleach* had no injury, thanks be to Mary mild and Angus.' Gil waited. 'My cousin Iain,' Jamie said at last. 'He is dead, poor laddie, when the beasts ran over him out of the fold.' He pointed, out and across the yard, at the lower end of the other house. 'He was a changeling, poor bairn, he neither walked nor spoke, it's a mystery how he got there when his mother says she was putting him safe by the wall away from the flames.'

'Could he crawl?' Gil asked.

'He might have crawled so far,' admitted the prettier of the girls.

'What are his injuries?'

'Dreadful to see,' said the other girl, who seemed a little younger. 'There is bruises all over him, and a great gash here,' she drew a hand across below her ribs, 'and not a mark on his face. I was there when they washed him.' Her cousin made a small distressed sound, and she put her arm round her, murmuring in Ersche.

'Do you know where he was found?' Gil asked.

'It was his mother picked him up,' said Jamie, 'and bore him up into the yard. Will I be asking her?'

'Not yet,' said Gil. 'May I see him? I'd want to look close.'

'Aye, you would,' said Jamie darkly.

The younger girl left her cousin and slipped out, to return in a moment saying, 'There is nobody there just now but Ailidh. If the gentleman were to be quick it would be good.'

Across the busy yard with its subdued conversations, the other house was similar in size and shape to the weaver's, as if the two had been built at the same time, but it was furnished differently, and the chill smell of death overlaid that of the dried plants hung in the roof and the brews in the row of dyepots by the wall. Directly before the door Mistress Drummond was laid out in her shroud on several planks set across two barrels; at the foot of the makeshift bier stood a cradle, draped in clean linen, with the dead child reposing in it as if he slept. The oldest granddaughter was kneeling by his head, her beads in her

191

hand, but her lips were still, her eyes distant. She looked up as they entered. The two younger girls stayed outside.

'Maister Cunningham wishes to see the harm that came to the boy,' said Jamie quietly.

'Harm enough,' said the girl, rising. She bobbed to Gil, and bent to draw back the linen. 'But it was only the beasts, surely? No blame to them, poor creatures, they were terrified. Or else the – Those Ones, that took him home again. No blame in either case.'

'No blame,' agreed Gil, kneeling in his turn.

'Then why must you be disturbing him?'

Why indeed? Gil wondered. 'Because,' he said, feeling carefully along the spindly limbs, 'Davie Drummond is accused of this death as well as the fire, and –'

'Och, her!' said Ailidh. Her brother spoke sharply in Ersche, and she made an equally sharp retort and went on in Scots, 'She was outside herself, with the fire and my grandmother's death already, and then Iain, the poor soul. No need to pay her any mind, surely?'

'I think Sir William will want to ask questions,' said Gil absently. The wound on the belly might have caused the child's death, but none of the others seemed severe enough. He touched the little pale face gently, ran his palm behind the curve of the head, fingers pressing gently at the scalp under the pale frizz of hair, and stopped.

'What is it?' demanded Jamie. 'What have you found?'

'Jamie!' said one of the girls urgently from the yard.

'I think,' Gil began, 'his skull –'

'What are you doing?' demanded a shrill voice in the doorway. 'Leave my boy alone, whoever you are, have you no notion of respect for the dead? Under his own roof, at that?'

Gil and Jamie tried to speak at once, both stopped to let the other continue, and Caterin took full advantage of the hesitation and stormed into the house, pulling at her nephew's arm, haranguing him in Ersche. Gil might not understand the words, but her meaning was clear. He apologized, drew the linen back over the small corpse and withdrew in good order to the yard, where several of the neighbours were coming to see what the trouble was, exclaiming and shaking their heads with shocked murmurs as Caterin explained in a rising torrent of Ersche. The two younger girls had vanished.

'Ailidh is right,' said Jamie in some embarrassment, drawing Gil down the slope from the door. 'She is outside herself still. What had you found? Is his skull broke?'

'I think so,' said Gil. 'Skull and scalp both, I believe, though I'd want longer to make certain of it.'

'Will I get my uncle to make her allow it?'

'Show me the fold and the gate first.'

The fold below the byre, at the lower end of the longhouse, was a substantial walled structure of field stones, with a hurdle gate standing open, the bar which would hold it in place lying at the wall's foot. The enclosure was trampled and spattered with animal dung, as was the gateway. The younger girls had taken refuge down here, out of sight from the door of the house.

Gil studied the area carefully. Now he had seen the corpse it was not hard to pick out the place where the child's body had lain, the imprint of thin shoulders and legs, the marks of his mother's bare feet where she had bent to lift him.

'Who penned the beasts last night?' he asked. The cousins looked at one another.

'My father, it would be,' said the pretty girl.

'Does he go shod?'

'*Brogainn*,' said Jamie, 'like mine.' He held out one foot in its soft deerskin shoe, laced up his ankle with scarlet braid.

'Only his is laced with leather,' said the plainer girl.

'Husha, Nannie! Why do you ask it, maister?'

Gil bent to look closer at the prints which interested him.

'See this,' he said, pointing. 'There is a bare foot there, and another, and the cattle have gone over the top of it. Someone was down by this gate before the beasts were let out.'

'Maybe it was whoever left them out,' suggested the girl addressed as Nannie. That must be Agnes, Gil, recalled, and her cousin must be Elizabeth, sister of the dead boy.

'No, for that was old Tormod,' said Jamie. 'I called to him, and he went – aye, here is his print.' He bent to a spot by the wooden bar at the wall's foot. 'See, maister, he goes shod, but his feet is twisted with the joint-ill, his track is easy known.'

'We was all down here,' said Agnes. 'We came down to find buckets and the like, for the water.'

'Not here,' said the other girl. 'We went that way, to the stackyard and the burn beyond it. No need to go by the wall here.'

'Someone did,' said Jamie. He returned to stare down at the marks Gil had pointed out, then at the prints close by the marks of the body, where the boy's mother had lifted him. His mouth tightened.

'But there was no need,' objected Elizabeth again. 'Why come by here, into the shadows, when the stackyard is yonder, and the path lit up bright as day by the – the flames from the house –' Her face crumpled again, and she turned away. Jamie, who had wandered off along the wall, looked up and spoke to his sister in Ersche. As Ailidh had done, she argued in the same language, but led her cousin off towards the house where they had sat before. Jamie watched them out of sight, and said quietly to Gil:

'See this, maister.'

'What have you found?' Gil went to his side, and found him looking at one of the dark grey field stones.

'That is skin,' said Jamie. He lifted the stone, and turned it to the light. It was small in his big hand, but big enough for its purpose. It might have fallen off the top of the dyke, though if so it was not lying immediately below its place of origin, for the grass where it had lain was green rather than white. On one ragged corner of the stone something was clinging. 'Skin, a little blood, white hair.'

'Likely one of the beasts hurted itself on the stones,' said another voice. Gil turned, and found the other daughter-in-law, the widowed Mòr, standing by the corner of the fold watching them. 'Jamie, what are you doing down here, upsetting your cousin, poor lass?'

'Is any of the beasts lame?' Jamie challenged her. She shrugged, and moved forward with an uneven step. 'Mammy, it's not the hair of a beast. Look here – it's as fine as any of ours, and curls the way Iain's does.'

'Or yours, or your sisters'.'

'My sisters and I do not have a broken head. Is this what broke Iain's skull, do you think, Maister Cunningham?'

'Yes,' said Gil deliberately. 'I think it could be.'

'Is the bairn's skull broke?' said Mòr with a show of indifference. 'That would be when Those Ones were taking him back. Leave it, Jamie, we'll not be meddling with their business.'

'Mammy, look!' Jamie held it out to her, pointing out the stains along its sharp edge. She took it in her hand, turned it over, looking impassively at the marks, and suddenly sent it spinning off into the rough ground between them and the nearest of the cottages. Jamie exclaimed, but she repeated, with emphasis, 'No need to be meddling in that. Maister Cunningham, Sir William is asking for you, and my good-brother Patrick would be glad of a word before you are leaving.'

'That will be a speak for the whole of Balquhidder,' said Gil's guide chattily. 'The more so if the Tigh-an-Teine has burned after all, and the *cailleach* dead in the flames, and the changeling stolen away back under the hill in exchange for Davie Drummond. Is it the kirk we're for just now, so you can be seeing young Davie again, or no?'

'No, I'll speak with him later,' Gil said. He stepped on to the bridge and whistled to the dog. 'I'm for the priest's house. I could do with a word with Sir Duncan, if he's equal to it, and certainly with young Robert.'

'I was hearing Sir Duncan is good today,' offered the guide. He was a stocky, fair-haired fellow with a broad, open, guileless face. Murdo had referred to him as Alasdair nan Clach, whatever that might mean. 'He has good days and bad days, you understand. It's no more than you'd be expecting, the age he is.'

'I understand,' agreed Gil. 'What age is he?'

Alasdair nan Clach shrugged.

'Maybe ninety?' he said. 'Maybe one hundred? Old as these hills, you would say.'

Discounting this, Gil strode on up the slope from the river, past the watchful haymakers and quietly ripening oats. A bite to eat, a word with Steenie, and the assurance of Lady Stewart and the girl Seonaid that Alys was unhurt and was now asleep had helped a lot, but he was still slightly shaky with relief, and his head was whirling with the information he had gathered this noontime. He would infinitely rather have stayed to talk it through with Alys when she woke, and hear the full tale of her adventures in Glenbuckie, but if his suspicions were correct he had already put off more time than he should before making this visit. He hoped his third quarry might not realize yet that he was pursued.

He passed the circle of tall stones, where Socrates pricked his ears at the children playing among them, and turned along the little path to the priest's snug stone house, aware of eyes on his back from the other cottages of the Kirkton. Rattling at the tirling-pin, he pushed the door wider without waiting for an answer, saying, 'Robert? Are you within?'

There was a startled movement, a deep-voiced exclamation. Not Robert Montgomery's voice, not the priest's. Socrates pricked his ears again, then rushed forward, his tail wagging wildly. Gil stepped after him under the lintel.

'Maister Doig,' he said. 'It's good to see you here.'

The place was sparsely furnished, and smelled of damp earth and illness. A three-legged stool and a great chair of solid local work stood by the hearth in the centre of the house, where a pot simmered on the peats. There was a bench against the wall by the door; beyond the fire a meal-kist stood on top of a bigger, painted kist, and two books and a silver crucifix were propped on a shelf. In the partition between the lodging of human and animal yawned two dark shut-beds, and there Socrates had rolled on to his back, yammering like a pup and waving his paws before a squat bulky shape, no higher than an ell-stick, which stood beside one of them.

'I'll no say the same o you, Maister Cunningham,' returned the deep voice, and the outline changed as if the short figure bent, extending a big hand to rub the dog's narrow ribcage. 'What brings you and your dog to the Kirkton? You're no here to distress the auld yin, I hope?'

'I've no intention of distressing him,' said Gil. 'How is he? I'd hoped for a word.'

'He's asleep for now. Maybe once he wakes he'll be up to talking.' The dark shape moved forward into the light from the door, and became the figure Gil remembered, like someone from his nurse's tales: short legs, broad shoulders, powerful hairy arms, a big head. Unlike his wife William Doig presented a much sprucer persona than the last time they had met, clad as he was in a red velvet jerkin and blue hose, the sleeves of his good linen shirt rolled back. Socrates scrambled to his feet and followed Doig, head level with his, nosing at the angle of his neck, tail wagging again. There was no doubt he remembered him.

'You've given up the dog breeding?' Gil asked. Doig shrugged, a seismic movement of the broad shoulders, and flung an arm round the wolfhound's neck.

'Herself has care of the dogs for now. She's a good eye for it. I miss it,' he admitted.

'Leaves you free for other business,' suggested Gil. Doig eyed him resentfully, much as his wife had done in Perth, but said nothing. 'I've a thing or two to ask you as well. Shall we sit out at the door, no to disturb Sir Duncan?'

'No,' said Doig bluntly. 'We'll sit here. I'm no welcome in the Kirkton, I'll no remind them I'm here, if it's all one to you.' He hoisted himself on to the bench next the wall, glowering through the open door at Alasdair nan Clach who was quite openly making the horns against the evil eye at the sight of him. 'Ask if you must,' he said grudgingly, patting Socrates, whose chin was on his knees.

Gil sat down beside him and thought briefly.

'When were you last in Dunblane?' he asked. Doig's head snapped round; whatever questions he had been expecting, it was not this one.

'Dunblane? Never been near the place,' he returned, almost automatically.

'That won't do,' said Gil, allowing amusement to show. 'You were seen at John Rattray's window.'

'Who's he?'

'Where did you take him to?' Gil countered. 'I'm guessing it was nowhere in Scotland, or we'd ha heard of him, seeing how word gets about. The Low Countries? France?'

'I've no notion what you're talking about,' said Doig steadfastly. The dog looked from one man to the other, and wagged his tail uneasily.

'Rattray's servant took you for the Deil himsel, with your wings down your back.'

Doig's wide mouth twitched, but he said nothing.

'But you know Canon Drummond,' Gil stated. 'Andrew Drummond of Dunblane.'

'Do I?' said Doig. 'No that I can think of.'

'That's a pity, for he speaks well of you,' said Gil mendaciously.

'Beats me where he gets the knowledge.'

'And then in Perth,' Gil went on. The sturdy figure beside him seemed to brace itself. 'The two brothers from St John's Kirk.'

'Oh, them,' said Doig, and then, 'What two brothers?'

'So that's three tenors, is it?' Gil said, still deliberately inaccurate. 'Men their choirs can ill spare, seeing how scarce good tenors are. Who is it that's collecting singers?'

'It's quite a puzzle,' agreed Doig.

'And are you shifting words as well as voices? Information about the English treaty, maybe –' Had Doig's expression flickered at that? '– or letters from the great and good of the Low Countries?'

'How would the likes of me be acquaint wi sic folk?' parried Doig.

'How long have you been here with Robert?'

The small man blinked at the change of direction, but shrugged again and said, 'Too long for him and me both.'

'Why not leave, then?'

'I can lend him a hand about the place.'

'And Montgomery hasny sent word for you to move on,' Gil suggested. This got him a sharp look from the dark eyes, but still no answer. 'Does he know you're working for someone overseas as well?'

'Ask all you want,' said Doig, his deep voice even. 'I never said I'd gie you answers.'

'No,' agreed Gil, 'but it tells me near as much when you don't answer.'

There was a short silence while Doig considered this. Then he wriggled off the bench.

'I've more to do than sit here listening to you,' he said, straightening his jerkin. Gil grinned at him.

'I'd agree. You've been seen about here,' he said. 'There's talk of the *bodach* over at Gartnafueran, and up in Glenbuckie. You fairly get about, Maister Doig.'

'Where's Gartnafueran?' asked Doig. 'Never been near the place.'

'So you've been in Glenbuckie, then? Did you go there to check on young Davie Drummond? I know you set him down the other side of the pass, to climb over into the top of the glen. I suppose you went up from here to make sure he got safe to Dalriach. You were seen the same day he came home.'

Doig glowered, and crossed the room, watched carefully by the dog, to peer up into the open box-bed. After a moment Gil heard him speaking quietly, in a much gentler tone. Shortly he turned, to say sourly, 'Sir Duncan's awake, and glad of a wee bit company. But you're no to tire him.'

The priest of Balquhidder was very old, and it was clear that Robert was right and he was very near death, lying bonelessly in the shut-bed, the flesh on his face almost transparent. But his eyes were alert in the dim light from the doorway, and his speech was clear, though faint. He gave Gil a blessing, raising his hand briefly from the checked coverlet, and said slowly, 'William tells me you've a question, my son.'

'I have, sir.' Gil fetched the stool from the hearth and sat down, to bring his head nearer the old man's. 'And forgive me for disturbing you when you've better matters to think on.'

'I've done all my thinking,' said Sir Duncan in his thread of a voice. 'Ask.'

'I wondered what you'd recall of the time when young David Drummond vanished away. Do you mind that?'

'A course I mind that.' There was humour in the faint voice. 'I've no notion what day this is, but I mind that well. All the women in the glen grat for the boy. Well liked, he was.'

'I thought you would. He went away up Glenbuckie, didn't he?'

'He did. And down the other side of the pass, so Euan nan Tobar said. I spoke with Euan the year after, at the fair here. He told me how he saw the boy borne away.'

'Did you credit that?'

'Euan's a simple soul. He doesny lie. He doesny aye understand what he sees.'

Gil nodded. 'And can you mind, sir, had there been strangers in the glen afore that happened?'

The fleshless mouth drew into an O of surprise at the question.

'Strangers, now.' The old man fell silent, considering this. 'I don't recall. I need to consider of that one, my son. We don't see so many strangers, you'll ken. Just William here and yourself since Robert came to me. And now Davie,' the thin voice added. 'The dear child.'

'No hurry,' said Gil, but Sir Duncan looked at him with those bright eyes. Even in this light, it was hard to meet the direct gaze; the old man seemed already to see the world from a different standpoint.

'Not true, my son,' he said. 'You need an answer, and I've little time, praise to Mary mild and Angus, before I go to what waits me.' Gil thought he smiled in the dim light. 'Away and let me think. I'll send William to you if I mind anything.'

'My thanks, Sir Duncan.' Gil slipped from the stool to kneel before the old priest. The hand rose from the coverlet and dropped back again, and the faint voice said:

'You'll see those bairns right, my son?'

'Bairns?' Gil looked up, and found that blazing, direct gaze on him. 'Davie, you mean, sir?'

'Or whoever he is. And Robert, poor lad.'

Gil nodded. 'I'll see them both safe if I can. I swear it.'

Accompanying him to the door, Maister Doig divulged with reluctance that Robert Montgomery was gone over to the kirk again to see about this matter of the claim of sanctuary.

'He's been gone a good while,' he said irritably, having admitted it, and patted Socrates, who was trying to lick his ear. 'Get away, you daft dog.'

'You know that's Davie Drummond in the kirk? You can give him his scrip back now,' said Gil. Doig stared up at him, face studiously blank. 'Maister Doig, do you know anything about the accidents up at Dalriach?'

'Accidents?' said Doig, his dark eyebrows drawing together. 'No. I hope none's been hurt?' His concern sounded genuine.

'Wee things to begin wi',' said Gil. 'A ladder, a pitchfork, a needle in the wool. Things a *bodach* might do.'

'Who are they aimed at?'

'Who knows?' said Gil. 'Other than the body that's causing them. But it turned serious last night. The farmhouse is burned out, and two dead.'

'Is that –' said Doig, and broke off. Nobody seems capable of finishing a sentence today, thought Gil in irritation. 'Who died? No young Davie, I take it, if that's who's in the kirk.'

'No. The old woman, and the changeling boy.'

'A changeling,' said Doig flatly. 'Is this another one? I thought it was Davie was the changeling, or was returned by the Good Neighbours, or something.'

'Maybe you should talk to Davie about that.'

Doig grunted, and opened the door wider. 'If you see Robert, tell him he needs to fetch water. The house is about dry.'

Alasdair nan Clach unfolded himself from the opposite bank where he had been squatting and followed Gil towards the little kirk in its round walled kirkyard, saying, 'That's an ill sign, a *bodach* like that to be dwelling in Sir Duncan's own house. It will be carrying him off one night, for certain, and him such a good man.'

'Why would he do that?' Gil asked.

The man shrugged. 'That is its nature. Mary and Michael and Angus protect him, but when the *bodach* is dwelling in his own house they will find it hard.'

Gil decided to ignore this. Reaching the kirk, aware once more of eyes on his back and cautious movement among the houses, he pushed open the door, more gently than he had done earlier, and stepped in, removing his hat and identifying himself aloud.

The two youngsters were seated with their heads together, side by side on the same flat stone before the altar where Davie Drummond had been kneeling earlier. As the light from the door reached them, Robert Montgomery sprang up.

'What are you after, Cunningham?' he demanded, standing warily in front of his companion. At Gil's knee the dog growled faintly, head down, hackles up, his stance remarkably like Robert's.

'A word with your friend here,' Gil said, making his way to the chancel arch. 'I'm no threat to him,' he added directly, 'as I told him this morning.' He dropped his hat on the earthen floor and sat down on it; after a moment Robert sat down likewise, saying:

'I'm surprised they're not down from Glenbuckie already, wi swords drawn and roaring for Davie's blood. They're wild folk here, Cunningham. Sir Duncan's told me some orra tales.'

'So did my father,' said Davie, and bit his lip.

Gil opened his mouth to speak, hesitated, and changed his mind. He was not quite ready for that one. Instead he put an arm across his dog, who had also sat down and was leaning against him, and said, 'Sir William bade me tell you he'll be here to speak wi you the morn's morn.'

'I'll not be from home,' said Davie wryly. 'But I'd be glad if Mistress Alys was present and all.'

'My wife?' said Gil, startled. 'I'll tell her that.'

'Maister, were you up Glenbuckie just now?' Davie went on. 'What – Are they all hale? Is Caterin still crying out against me?'

'She is,' admitted Gil, 'but the rest of them are hale enough. The lassies seemed sore afflicted by the two deaths, which I suppose is natural. The place was overrun wi neighbours and guests, but I had a word with James Drummond the younger, and a sight of the two corps.'

'What would that tell you that you hadny heard already?' demanded Robert. 'Better, surely, to find whoever set light to the thatch!'

'It's all part of the same tale,' said Davie.

'The boy Iain's skull was broken,' Gil said. 'Deliberately, I'd say.'

Davie drew a shivering breath, and bent his head into his hands. Robert reached out and touched his wrist, and after a moment he straightened up, turned his hand to grip Robert's, and said painfully, 'I feared it. The poor laddie. He was so – he had so much pleasure of my singing, of any music he was hearing, but he was such a burden on his mother, to be fed and kept clean and amused. When she carried him into the yard, all bruised and bloody, I feared it was no accident.'

'Who broke it for him?' asked Robert.

'That I don't know yet, though I suspect,' said Gil. 'And I don't suppose anyone would notice who was down by the end of the fold, between the dark and the flames and the commotion in the yard.'

Davie shook his head. 'They were bringing water up from the stackyard that way. Everyone on the clachan was past there at some point in the night.'

'That's no good,' said Robert, 'a helpless bairn to be struck down like that. Who would do sic a thing?'

'Young James's mother was quite clear it was the fairies,' said Gil. 'She ordered him not to meddle in their business.'

Robert snorted. 'That's one explanation, I suppose.'

'It would be one the folk of Dalriach would accept,' said Davie slowly.

'Aye, but it's nonsense,' objected Robert. 'You'd think we were in a ballad or an old tale, to hear it!'

'Sooner that than accuse one of their own,' said Davie, and shivered.

And of course, Gil thought, to some of them you are not one of their own. But who?

'Who do you think killed the boy?' he asked.

'I don't know,' Davie said firmly. 'And I've no more reason to suspect any than you have, and maybe less. His – no, his mother loved him beyond reason!'

Gil paused a moment, arranging his thoughts.

'Tell me, Davie.' The young man turned his face towards him. In the dim light he seemed to brace himself. 'Had there been any word before now from Dunblane? From Canon Drummond?'

'From Andrew? None that I ken,' said Davie. 'I know the *cailleach* sent to him, twice so your wife told me, sir, and Robert has let me know now what she sent. But there's been no answer yet that I've heard. Maybe that was what brought him home today.'

'You'd be the last to know,' said Robert rather bitterly.

'No,' said Gil deliberately, 'he's told me he came home in haste because his mother summoned him, this morning in the dawn.'

'Och, that's havers!' said Robert.

'No,' said Davie quietly. 'I'm believing him. It's what brought myself, a month since.'

'Is it, now?' said Gil. Davie's chin came up, but he said nothing. 'Were they concerned, up at Dalriach, about having no answer?'

'I'd not say so. Andrew was never one for sending home every week, even as a boy.' The voice was light, confident, but not wholly convincing.

'Let alone coming home for the Lammastide holiday,' Gil suggested. There was a pregnant pause. 'Had he come home in other years, before you were lifted away?'

After another pause Davie said, 'I don't recall. Is that not strange?'

'It was thirty year syne,' Robert protested, looking from one to the other. 'At least –'

'Not for Davie,' said Gil. 'How long has it been, Davie?'

Pale in the shadows, Davie shrugged one linen-clad shoulder.

'Who can say? Time passes differently under the hill. Andrew was aye glad to get away from Dalriach,' he added. 'He never felt he had what was due to him there.' Gil made a questioning noise. 'Och, with there being two brothers older, he was never hearkened to, for all he was a clerk and could read the Psalter.'

'That's how it is,' muttered Robert, 'whatever your place in the family.' Davie broke the clasp of their hands and laid his own rather diffidently on the other young man's shoulder, and Robert looked sideways and nodded brief acknowledgement.

'And last month,' said Gil. Both faces turned to him. 'When you were set down at the foot of the path over the hill did you see anyone?'

'I did,' he answered readily. 'A poor misshapen wretch from Stronyre township they cry Euan Beag nan Tobar.

205

Wee Euan of the Well,' he translated for Robert, who nodded again rather impatiently. 'He spoke to me, gave me my name. It seems he – saw me taken up, all those years since. We talked about my friends Billy Murray and Jaikie Stirling, and he gave me news of Billy, who was born at Stronyre. He'd no knowledge of Jaikie, and I never expected it.'

'Jaikie Stirling's dead,' said Gil, more abruptly than he had intended.

'Dead? I'm grieved to hear it. When? What came to him?'

'Two weeks since,' said Gil. 'I'm seeking his murderer.'

'Murdered,' Davie repeated in a whisper, and crossed himself. 'And since I came – the poor man. Poor Jaikie.' He bent his head, murmuring the same prayer for the dead as Rob the chaplain had used in the Bishop's garden.

'Stirling?' said Robert. 'Is that –?' He broke off, and after a moment Gil said:

'He was secretary to Bishop Brown.'

'Oh, at Dunkeld,' said Robert dismissively.

'He died in Perth.'

Robert crossed himself, muttered a perfunctory prayer, and said with determination, 'If you've naught more to ask us, Cunningham, we should get on and make that loft fit to dwell in. Davie won't want to leave the kirk, and it's over a year since we moved Sir Duncan into his house out of here, it's likely damp and full of cobwebs.'

'And I was to tell you,' said Gil, 'that the house is near dry. Doig said you should fetch in water.'

At his feet Davie Drummond jerked as if he had been stabbed. Robert said sharply, 'You've spoken wi Doig? What was he saying?'

'Nothing,' said Gil. 'Quite determinedly, nothing. But as I told him, it's near as useful when he won't speak as when he does.'

'Aye,' said Robert sourly. 'My uncle tellt me no to get into conversation wi you.'

* * *

206

'Did he really?' said Alys in amusement, turning her head against his shoulder. 'I'd have thought he would see what he was giving away.'

'I suppose he didn't consider it,' Gil said lazily. 'He seemed mostly concerned about young Drummond.'

They were lying against the pillows within the linen-hung bed in their chamber, close and reassuring. He had returned from the Kirkton to be informed by Lady Stewart that Alys still needed to rest and directed to make sure she did so. Rest was not what either of them needed most, but he had accepted the order with pleasure. Now, sated and comfortable, each certain the other was safe and hale, they were discussing what they had learned.

'So he reports to Lord Montgomery, and gets word back,' she said now, still speaking French. 'And that since we got here. I suppose Lady Stewart corresponds with her cousin.'

'It's the likeliest route,' he agreed. 'And Davie knew Doig's name. He also confirmed meeting Euan nan Tobar, poor creature, and seems to be making friends with Robert. Myself, I'd as soon befriend an adder on a rock, but I suppose the lad has his merits.'

'You're hardly impartial.' She rubbed her cheek on his bare chest. 'We must take care how we speak of this – Lady Stewart could be involved in whatever Robert is doing. And do you suppose she and Sir William know Doig is here?'

'I don't know that, but they're well aware of him in the village. I wish you had been in Perth with me – I've missed talking things over like this. I missed you.'

'And I have missed you. What brought you back here so prompt, Gil?'

'I don't know,' he confessed. 'I woke before the dawn, and knew you needed me. We set out as soon as it was light. Not as vivid a summons as Andrew Drummond's, but one I couldn't ignore.'

'I did need you,' she said wonderingly, 'and just at that time. I was so frightened, and the fire – and the old woman dying like that – and then the boy – it was such a night, Gil.'

'It's over, and you are safe, St Giles be thanked.' He kissed the crown of her head. Her hair was silky under his lips; it smelled of an unfamiliar hairwash and, faintly, of smoke. 'I owe him several candles.'

'But how did you know? You were so far away – forty miles, Lady Stewart said.'

'I don't think the distance matters. Tell me about it again, sweetheart.'

She recounted the events of the night, shivering a little as she described the two deaths, steadfastly repeating the wild accusations the dead boy's mother had flung at Davie Drummond.

'The woman was in much the same state when she found me examining the boy,' he said. 'That wild flyting is very hard to withstand. But I suppose if they believed her, they'd have been down here before now burning the thatch off the kirk to get him out.'

'I don't think the family did. Believe her, I mean. Davie took fright, for that or – or some other reason, and ran.' She was winding her fingers through the hairs on his chest. 'But you found the boy's skull was broken. Could that be what killed him? I thought none of the other injuries was mortal, or not instantly perhaps, but his mother insisted only she would wash his head, I could not examine it.'

'I think the blow on the head and the damage from the beasts would be enough together, and I think he was deliberately set where I found the imprint of his body. He was certainly murdered by someone, poor little fellow, but the other daughter-in-law, Mòr is it? would hear nothing of the idea. She is fixed on the notion that the fairy folk have taken him back.'

'Lady Stewart thought Sir William would question them all.'

'He did,' Gil said, recalling Sir William's baffled expression as he crossed the yard to meet him, 'but he got no more than we have between us, and less in some ways.'

'She thought also Caterin might accuse Davie again when they all come down for the burial.'

'Mm,' he said. They lay in silence for a while; Gil was thinking deeply, and eventually realized from her level breathing that Alys had fallen asleep. He looked down at her face, feeling the familiar sensation as if some giant fist squeezed his entrails at the sight of her relaxed and secure in his embrace.

There were things he must do. Easing his arm reluctantly from under her shoulders he drew the covers up round her, slid off the bed and reached for his shirt. Sir William must be somewhere about the place.

Chapter Eleven

The Bailie of Balquhidder was seeing to his hawks, in a reprehensible leather doublet and stained hose which it was likely his lady did not know he was wearing. While he made much of a peregrine tiercel and inspected the bird's barred feathers Gil sat on the falconer's workbench at the end of the mews, amid the familiar smell of raw meat and bird-droppings, wax and leather, and gave him an account of his findings, first in Dunblane and then in Perth. Sir William listened carefully, and stood for some time after Gil finished, feeding the hawk with morsels of rabbit.

'It seems to me,' he said at length, 'you've raised three separate quarries.'

'I think so too,' agreed Gil, 'but one of them's gone beyond my range.'

'The three songmen?' Sir William stroked the peregrine's breast. 'Aye, if we learn where those have got to, it's a grace. But it does look as if Maister Secretary's matter has naught to do wi them. Found in a tanpit, poor devil! What an end! Who is it that's stealing voices, then? Will he take any more?'

'I don't know that,' said Gil blandly, 'but I've dropped a hint that I'm aware of it. I hope that might put an end to the business.'

'Hmf,' said Sir William. 'And the secretary? A crossbow bolt through the neck, you said. Who shot him, have you worked that out?'

'Not yet,' said Gil. 'I need to speak to Drummond's lad,

who's here somewhere, and to this man of the Bishop's household that was wi Stirling.'

'Ask at Murdo for Drummond's lad,' said Sir William. 'Likely he's still about the place.'

'I'll do that,' said Gil. 'Once I know how Stirling got into the tanpit I might be closer to finding out who put him there. I've still to give a full reckoning to Bishop Brown, and it's possible he'll have some news for me. They were crying a couple of questions round the town of Perth these two or three days, so I'll go back as soon as I may. And I must go to Dunkeld.'

'Dunkeld?' Sir William turned to look at him, and the peregrine opened its wings and reared back, hissing at him. 'Peace, peace, Mercury. What's at Dunkeld?'

'The third of the three friends is Precentor there.'

'Hmf.' Sir William soothed the bird, and it hunched itself indignantly. 'Best take a couple more men wi you, in that case.' He eased the hawk back on to its perch, transferred the leash, and moved on to another bird. 'This is Eleanor. I gentled her myself, did I no, my bonnie girl,' he stroked the gold-brown feathers, and Eleanor bent to nibble delicately at his finger, 'from the egg. Why was Stirling killed, do you suppose? Is it connected wi the English treaty, or no?'

'I've no notion yet. Maybe when we find who killed him we'll find out why.'

'Aye. Well, I suppose you've no had a week's work on the business so far.' Sir William looked down his long Stewart nose at Gil. 'And what did you discern up at Dalriach? Did Andrew Drummond tell you anything worthwhile on the road up there?'

'He told me a little,' said Gil cautiously. 'He claims Stirling made his confession to him.' Sir William snorted. 'I agree, it seems unlikely, but it prevents questions.'

'Clerks!' muttered Sir William.

'And I found the injury that killed the boy Iain. His skull is broke.'

'Aye, I heard about that. The bairn's mother came raging to Patrick while we drank to the memory of the dead.'

'I've no doubt of it,' said Gil drily. He summarized what he had learned, at Dalriach and from Alys. When he had finished there was another long silence, broken by the occasional clink of a chain and ruffle of feathers.

'Bad,' said Sir William at last, sucking his teeth. 'I've no stomach to execute a woman.'

'And it's not right clear yet,' said Gil, 'which of them it might be.'

Sir William nodded, and set Eleanor back on her perch. Having fastened her leash and tugged it to check it was secure, he led the way out into the yard, where Socrates rose and padded over to thrust his nose into Gil's hand. 'How much d'you need to do about secretary Stirling? How close to his killer are you?'

'Not close enough,' said Gil, grimacing. 'I should return to Perth tomorrow, as I said.'

'Hmf,' said Sir William again. Behind him his falconer slipped into the mews to continue his work. 'Cunningham, I'm told that information about the English treaty got where it should never ha been, and a bit more besides. Even if you think he's been dead these two weeks, it might still have been Stirling's doing.'

'It could,' agreed Gil cautiously.

'And I'll need to act in the other business the morn's morn, speak to David and send up Glenbuckie for more answers. The laddie can hardly stay prisoned in the kirk while we bury the folk he's accused of slaying, even if Andrew will conduct the burials.'

Why not? Gil wondered. 'Sir Duncan has no more than a day or two to live,' he said. 'Robert and his – assistant have their hands full, but while the other fellow's there Robert can leave Sir Duncan long enough that he could at least commit the dead, even if he's not able to say a Mass for them.'

'That's true,' said Sir William, making for the house. 'I

212

aye forget the boy's clerked. My lord Montgomery plans Holy Kirk for him, when all's over and paid for.'

Sweet St Giles, you'd as well cage the lad, thought Gil, aware yet again of the strange feeling of sympathy for a Montgomery. Does that explain his bitterness today?

Andrew Drummond's man remembered Gil clearly.

'And I've called a many blessings down on you these last days, maister,' he said earnestly.

'Have you, indeed?' said Gil, closing the garden gate behind them, and opening it again to allow Socrates through.

'Aye, many and many. See, it was after you called on him that my maister rose up out of his melancholy. I'd no notion what to do for him, the way he'd sat and stared at nothing ever since –' He paused, staring out across the loch in the early evening sun. 'Ever since the second letter came from his mother,' he reckoned finally. 'Two weeks since, that would be, a day or two after we got back from Perth.'

'After you got back from Perth,' Gil repeated. 'What state was he in before that? Just after you got back?'

'Oh, he was eased in his mind,' asserted Benet. 'That was why it was sic a painful thing to see him so cast down again, for we'd ridden back from Perth much easier than we'd been on the road there. Calmer, if you take my meaning, and more able for making decisions.'

'His stay in Perth had helped him, then,' Gil suggested.

'Aye.' Benet nodded firmly, and looked about him at the low hedges and plots of bright flowers. 'It's a bonnie garden, this. What was it my maister said I should tell you about?'

'About Perth.' Gil strolled along the path towards the seat at the far end. Socrates set off to patrol the maze of box hedges, his nose to the ground. 'Do you mind, the last day you were there, Canon Drummond spent a while talking wi someone.'

Benet nodded again.

'I wondered at it,' he admitted, 'for he'd not been seeking out company, and he and this fellow never seemed like friends when they met, but they must ha spent a couple of hours walking on the meadows by the town Ditch, talking of all sorts.'

'Who was the other man?' Gil asked. 'Did you learn that? Do you mind anything about him?'

'Oh, aye. Well, his man tellt me who he was. At least, he wasny his man, he was another of the household. Fellow cried Mitchel, good company he was and all, the two of us sat down by the Ditch and had a right good crack while our maisters were talking.'

'Mitchel,' repeated Gil. 'And his maister?'

'Well, his maister was the Bishop o Dunkeld,' explained Benet scrupulously, 'but he was waiting on this man my own maister was talking wi, that was the Bishop's secretary so he tellt me. Name o Stirling, he said. Tall fellow, well set up, wi his hat all ower badges.'

'Benet, have you heard that Stirling was murdered that evening?'

He had judged his audience right. Benet's eyes opened wide, with a gleam of pleasurable amazement.

'You don't say! Murdered! And my maister walking and talking wi him just that day!'

Gil nodded corroboration to this, and went on, 'I'm charged wi finding out who killed him. So anything you can mind about the afternoon might be a help to me.'

'The afternoon,' repeated Benet doubtfully. 'Murdered! But I never spoke wi him.'

'No reason you should,' agreed Gil. 'But you're a good servant, and take note of aught that affects your own maister, I've no doubt.' The man made no comment, but looked gratified at this. 'Start when the two of them met. How did that chance?'

'Oh, we went to the dog-breeder's yard and there he was, and they was talking over the dog-pens a wee while.' Benet grinned. 'I was thinking the dog-breeder wasny

214

best pleased at that, for they were right in her way, but it seems the man Mitchel was some kind o kin, and he talked her out of her strunt and gave her a bit hand wi the tasks she had.'

'What did you go there for?'

Benet shook his head.

'My maister never said. I wondered at it mysel,' he admitted, 'for he's no one for dogs in the house.'

'So you never got a word with Mitchel while you were in the yard?' Benet agreed to this. 'What was Stirling talking to the Canon about?'

'Dogs, mostly,' said the man, 'seeing they were all about them I suppose. How they get on wi one another, and the like. Training them. The fellow Stirling said how it's amazing what a dog'll fetch and carry if you reward it well. And that's a true word,' he added, 'my uncle's got a sheepdog, it'll fetch him anything he names in the house and set it in his hand.'

'And then they left.'

'Aye, and went out on to the meadow land. I did wonder,' said Benet, 'if all would be well, for they marched along the track wi never a word, till they got out on to the open ground, and then they directed Mitchel and me to wait under a hazel-bush, and went off into the midst of the meadow. But they were quite civil wi one another after that.'

'So you never heard what they spoke of,' said Gil. Socrates, his tour of inspection completed, came and sat down by his feet. 'It's a good way to be private, to go out where you can see anyone else approaching.'

'Aye, but I think they forgot about being private,' said Benet, grinning. 'Once they got well into their talk, they were walking back and forth and came often within earshot. No that we listened, a course,' he said virtuously.

'No, of course not,' agreed Gil. 'So what did you and Mitchel talk of? Were you there a while?'

'Oh, aye, the best part o two hour. Beats me what they had to talk over that took as long. We'd tellt one another our lifes and run out o riddles by the time they called us.'

'And then you went your separate ways,' Gil prompted.

'Aye, all in different directions, too,' Benet said, laughing. 'My maister sent me back to the Blackfriars, saying he'd dine in Perth, but he'd an errand that side the Ditch first. The other fellow sent Mitchel in to Perth, bade him say he'd be in to his supper but he'd stroll a while on the meadow first. So none o us went the same way.' He held his hand out for Socrates to sniff.

'Was the Canon to dine wi Bishop Brown?' Gil asked casually.

'No, no, never wi the Bishop.' Benet pulled a face. 'That Bishop's ower nice to be dining wi a man that keeps a mistress, no like our Bishop at Dunblane. But to tell truth,' he slid an embarrassed glance sideways at Gil, 'I tellt them he would. To raise him up a wee bit, you see,' he said earnestly, 'for they were no best pleased wi him about his staying, and who he had wi him, and all.'

Gil nodded slowly. Parts of this fitted well; parts of it did not.

'What can you recall about Mitchel?' he asked. 'Tell me what you spoke of.'

'Why d'you want to know that?' asked Benet warily. 'I'd no want to get the fellow into trouble, I've nothing against him.'

'No, no,' said Gil reassuringly. 'I'd hoped he might ha said something about Maister Stirling. Anything that would tell me what the man was doing and why he was killed. Did he mention him at all?'

'Oh, aye, he did,' agreed Benet, obviously turning this over in his mind. 'Though it was only to tell me he wasny his right maister, that he mostly attended on the Bishop's steward, that seems to be a right good maister and free wi money.'

'He said that, did he?'

'Aye, so I tellt him a thing or two about attending on a priest, and we'd a good laugh about some of the cantrips

I've seen about my maister's employ.' Benet recalled who he was speaking to and added quickly, 'Not at my maister, you understand, sir.'

'Of course not.' Gil prodded a clump of box with his foot, and Socrates leaned down to snuffle into the rustling leaves. 'And Maister Stirling was less generous, was he?'

'Oh, he never said that. Just that the steward was mighty free. And this man Stirling was heedful o poor folk, he said, look the way he'd sent us to sit in the shade while they talked.'

'What were they talking about, for so long?'

'Beats me,' said Benet. 'I never got more than a snatch of it. When they left us under the hazel-bush they were talking about my maister's brother, had he heard from him, I suppose meaning this brother that's returned from Elfhame. Are we to see him, do you suppose, sir? Is that right he's shut up in the kirk across yonder?' He pointed across the loch at the Kirkton, its smoke rising quietly in the sunshine.

'He's asked for sanctuary in the kirk,' said Gil. 'Of course your maister said he'd not heard, I suppose.'

'Aye, that's the truth,' agreed Benet. 'And I heard him mention his family. But I've no notion after that, save that they were both of them weeping at one stage.'

'Weeping?' Gil repeated in astonishment. 'Sweet St Giles, whatever caused that?'

'I've no notion,' repeated the man. 'Mitchel saw it too. The Canon's done his share o weeping since Mistress Nan dee'd, poor lady, Our Lady bring her to Paradise, but why the other fellow – and Mitchel said he'd no idea neither.'

Gil looked out at the hills around him, without seeing them. What lay between the two men to prompt such a long, intense discussion, tears and talk of forgiveness? Andrew Drummond had taken benefit of clergy; it would not be easy to find out from him, and Stirling was not telling.

'Did they part on good terms?' he asked.

'Oh, aye, the best,' agreed Benet. 'They embraced like brothers, so they did, and my maister showed me a siller badge the other fellow had gied him, and tellt me the tale of it and bade me stitch it to his hat first chance I had.'

'A badge! What like was it?' Gil demanded.

'Oh, right strange. A lassie, a saint I suppose wi a sword, but it's never St Catherine. It's some strange tale about a princess out of Ireland, but her shrine's in the Low Countries. Seems this fellow Stirling had been there.'

Gil stared at the man. That was the hat Andrew Drummond had been wearing the first time he saw him, he realized. With the missing badge stitched to its brim.

'It's a right shame the man being murdered,' said Benet, looking uneasy. 'I wish I'd a known afore we went to Dunkeld –'

'Dunkeld?'

'Aye, that was what I was saying, sir, after you called on him my maister rose up and came out of his melancholy, and set out for Dunkeld that same day to speak wi the Precentor there, that he was at the sang-schule wi, and parted wi him next day on the like terms, all tears and embracing on the doorsill. And if I'd a known of Maister Stirling's being dead,' persisted Benet, 'I'd a tellt Mitchel when I saw him in Dunkeld.'

By the time supper was over and they had retired to their chamber and dismissed Seonaid the day seemed to have been very long already, but neither Gil nor Alys was sleepy. Sitting on embroidered cushions, he sipped Rhenish wine from the dole-cupboard and watched her comb down her hair by the window while he described the interview with Andrew Drummond's servant.

'They talked about David,' she summarized thoughtfully, the honey-coloured locks slipping through her fingers. 'And about forgiveness, and Judas. They wept, both of them. Stirling gave Andrew the badge off his hat, and they parted on good terms, or so it seems.'

'The woman Ross said Andrew was *elevated* when she saw him. It must have been something important they had out between them.'

She nodded at that, and went on plying the comb, moving her arms cautiously as if she was stiff, and gazing out at the summer twilight gathering blue over loch and hills.

'Then that evening Stirling was shot with a crossbow and put in the tanpit. I wonder if it was a consequence of that? Who else might have put him there?'

'More than one might have reason to, I'd have said,' said Gil.

'Andrew Drummond,' said Alys. 'The old priest. The man Mitchel. The tanner, do you think?'

'We have to include him,' Gil agreed, 'though I think it unlikely.'

'Can you think of anyone else?'

'Mistress Doig, I suppose, though I don't know that she could use a crossbow. It was a neat shot, right in the lethal spot at the base of the skull.'

She shivered, and crossed the room to put her comb back in its case.

'So any of those four could have killed the man, but when? How? How did they have the chance? You told me the tanyard is in the midst of the suburb, surely there must have been people about!'

'Nobody had come forward before I left Perth to say they had seen anything.' Gil poured wine for her, and drew her down beside him. 'One thing about a crossbow, it means the murderer need not have been close to Stirling when he struck.'

'Yes, but he still had to dispose of the body.' She sipped at her wine. 'But why, whoever it was – what reason? And why the tanpit?'

'It must have been convenient. Presumably he couldn't be left wherever he was killed, and the tanpit presented a way of concealing his death, for a while at least.'

'How long?' she wondered. 'If the tanner's man had not found that badge, and so chanced to see the bubbles rising in the pit, how long before they found Stirling?'

'Long enough for him to be unrecognizable, I would think,' said Gil. 'He was well on his way already. The – the skin is well preserved, but the flesh within has gone, and the weight of the skins and planks over him has –' She grimaced, and he left that and went on, 'Cornton knew his clothes. Once they rotted there would be little to go on, particularly since whoever put him there took his hat away with them.'

'Whoever put him there,' she repeated.

'Whoever it was,' he agreed.

'Consider them one by one. Why should Andrew Drummond kill James Stirling? What linked them? I suppose it might have been what they were discussing on the meadow.'

'David,' offered Gil. 'The sang-schule. The past.'

'To which we have no real access. That would mean David is a part of the tale – so the two matters are linked.'

'They're linked by Andrew Drummond anyway.'

'True.' She tipped her head back, gazing up at the panelled ceiling. 'If Andrew slew the man, was it for guilt, or revenge, or because either he or Stirling knew too much?'

'Any of those, I should think,' he said ruefully. 'If Andrew disposed of David, for instance, and Stirling finally showed him that he guessed he had done it, that might provoke Andrew into getting rid of him.'

'And you said Stirling was prone to making jokes at people. Perhaps he made the wrong joke about it. Or if he had disposed of David himself –'

'I never thought of that!'

'Or perhaps he was given a part Andrew had wanted to sing, after his accident.'

'Ancient envy, you mean.' Gil poured himself more wine. 'You see, there are so many possibilities. But if it was

Andrew who killed him, why now? Why not any time the last thirty years? I think if we consider that, it might tell us more. What had Stirling seen or done in his –'

'Or said.'

'True, or said in his last hours that provoked someone to kill him and hide the body?'

'Which takes us back to this conversation on the meadow again. I wish Benet had heard more. It's obviously important. And what about the others? The old chaplain, for instance.'

'The chaplain? He has a crossbow, so he says, but if he could hit a barn from inside it I'd be much amazed.'

'He had quarrelled with Stirling in the morning. Did anyone see them together at the noon bite? Did they really make up their difference?'

'I suppose even if they seemed to, he could still have wanted revenge.'

'Could he get the body into the tanyard?'

'Not alone, I'd have thought. He must be past sixty, and looks frail, I'd not have said he had the strength.'

'If he practises archery,' Alys observed, 'he may be stronger than he appears.'

'True. Then there's the steward's servant, the man that's now in Dunkeld. I need to send Tam for him tomorrow, with a couple of men, to fetch him to Perth for me.'

'Yes,' she said thoughtfully. 'Why is he in Dunkeld, I wonder?'

'I wondered that too. As for why he would kill Stirling, we know no more than for any of the others, maybe less. He told Benet that Stirling was considerate. That's no reason for murder.'

'And the tanner. You know, Gil, the tanner would find it easiest of all of them. He could arrange to meet his landlord at the yard, shoot him there, put him in the tanpit –'

'But why? He seemed to have no quarrel with the man either, he said Stirling was a good landlord –'

'One of those sharp remarks? A sudden quarrel?'

'I suppose it's possible. But he also said he was at home all evening, which I must check, and we know Stirling was still alive at sunset.'

'Do we?' said Alys. 'Do we?' She turned to face him. 'Mistress Doig recognized the hat, not the man! Gil, do you suppose –?'

He stared at her, turning this over in his mind.

'Sweet St Giles,' he said. 'That leaves it wide open, doesn't it?'

'How does the time work? The man in the hat went towards the town, and then Andrew Drummond was seen going away from it. Could Andrew have worn the hat?'

'I think Mistress Doig would have recognized the Drummond hair, the way it sticks out below his hat, even at that distance.'

'I suppose so,' she agreed. 'So does that mean we can strike him off the list?'

'No,' he said, 'for I think there must have been more than one person involved. Getting him into the tanpit and covering him up would be done easier and quieter by two than by one.' He thought of the planks and their nets of stones which covered the soaking hides. 'Near impossible for one, in fact.'

'When was he last seen?' Alys asked. 'Before Mistress Doig thought she recognized him, I mean.'

'I suppose when Drummond parted from him,' said Gil, thinking it through. 'Benet said they all separated about the same time, and Stirling said he would stay and walk on the meadow for a while. I wonder if anyone saw him there later? Drummond, perhaps, or Mistress Ross and her friends when they went into Perth?'

'They parted about seven o'clock, by what you said,' Alys recalled. 'And he was probably dead, or at least he no longer had his hat, by sunset. Perhaps two hours.'

'But what happened?' Gil slapped his knee in frustration. 'Where was he killed, and who killed him? The most

222

of Perth seems to have been at supper during that time, but surely somebody saw him?'

'You need to ask more questions,' said Alys seriously.

'I do. I must speak to Andrew Drummond before I leave for Perth tomorrow, and then the other three – if Tam can fetch the man Mitchel from Dunkeld, it will help.'

She was silent for a little, while he sipped at his wine, turning the questions he must ask over in his mind. Then she said, 'Does Andrew believe that Davie really is his brother?'

'No. Nor do I.'

'Nor I,' she agreed. 'But who is it? And who taught him? Oh – the sister has not been out of the glen for three years.'

'She has small children, I suppose,' Gil said.

'I expect so. But Mistress Drummond –' she bit her lip. 'When she was dying, Gil, she gave me a message for you. *Tell your man*, she said, *Davie is truly my bairn.*'

'That's the crux of the whole problem,' he pointed out.

'No, but then she said, *Just as Patrick*, and then she named all of her children and grandchildren and called them her bonnie bairns too, and then the two good-daughters. Though not her good-son,' she added thoughtfully. 'And – oh!' She clapped a hand to her mouth. 'She named the boy Iain after she named his brother and his uncle who are dead, and he was dead by then, though none of us knew it.'

'An accident? Forgetfulness? The woman was dying, Alys.'

'She was clear in her mind,' she protested. 'I think she – she would have known. The dying sometimes know things we can't know, Gil, so close to the next world as they are. My mother –' She bit that off. He waited, but when she did not speak he said:

'Drummond dreamed she summoned him home, standing in his chamber with the boy Iain at her side.'

She nodded at that, but returned to the main point: 'I think Davie is close kin to the family.'

'So if he's not some bastard of her husband's, and he hasn't been taught by the daughter, we're only left with one real possibility. He must be the son of David himself.'

She turned her head to look at him, held his gaze for a moment, then looked away.

'Yes,' she said. 'It seems the most likely solution.'

'It's the only one I can see,' said Gil. She nodded, still looking away. 'Who else could he be, sweetheart?'

'But where is David?' she asked, not answering his question.

'What do we know?' Gil set down his glass, and began to count points on his fingers. 'He – this David, if that's his name –'

'He swore that he is Davie Drummond,' she said. 'He always calls himself Davie.'

'Yes. Well, firstly, he was set down by a group of horsemen, the other side of the pass from Dalriach, and secondly Billy Doig was one of the party if we can believe Euan Beag. Doig certainly seems to feel responsible for Davie. But where had he come from before that? What did you think of his clothes, Alys?'

'Not Scots made, I would say,' she pronounced. 'The linen was good quality, but the cut of the shirt was not the same as yours. Not French either,' she added, 'the sleeveband was set on differently from the shirts my father had when we came to Glasgow. But the plaid he was wearing was certainly old Mistress Drummond's weaving, they all recognized that, even Caterin.'

'You mentioned something he said about where he lived. Was it about food?'

'Oh – yes! Where he was, he said, they have no great love for kale, and they eat bread of wheat and rye. And less meat than they do here, which would not be difficult,' she added thoughtfully.

'Rye bread. The Low Countries,' he said. 'High Germany, the Baltic lands.'

224

She nodded. 'The Low Countries would be nearest, and the most convenient to find a ship, wouldn't it? So do we assume that David, the older David I mean, is there now?'

'If he still lives, it seems likely.' Gil moved on to another finger. 'You know, it fits. If it was Doig enticed the singer in Dunblane away, rather than the Devil himself, it seems most likely he called away the two in Perth as well, and if he then took them to the Low Countries he could well bring young Davie back with him.'

'I wonder if brother Andrew knew about Doig,' said Alys.

'He certainly knows him. He went to the yard at Perth looking for him.'

'It's all supposition,' she said, 'we've no firm evidence, but you're right, it does fit. It makes a structure.'

'But why?' he asked. 'Andrew said the same thing. What gain is there in pretending to be his own father? Why not just –'

'It might have begun as a joke,' she said doubtfully, 'or a game. Or even –' She turned her head to look at him. 'Old Mistress Drummond told me the first thing he said to her was, *Are you my grandmother?*'

'Oh!'

'And then *she* said, *No, it's your own mother*. So he can't have intended the pretence when he arrived.'

'That makes better sense,' he said. 'He said Euan Beag *gave me my name*, assumed he was David. He didn't correct that either, but it wouldn't be easy to disabuse Euan of an idea he'd settled his mind on, I'd think. And having let Mistress Drummond assume he was David, it could be very hard to confess that he wasn't.'

He sat turning these conjectures over in his mind. As Alys had said, it was all supposition, there could be a separate explanation for each of the points they had considered, but placed together they did offer a coherent story.

'I don't imagine it was Doig who took the older David away,' she said suddenly.

225

'It might have been, you know,' said Gil. 'I've no idea how old Doig is. Past forty, I suppose, but how far is another matter.'

'And Andrew knows him.' She sat up straight, turning to stare at him. 'Gil!'

'Andrew knows him,' he repeated. 'Well, well.'

'No,' said Andrew Drummond. 'William Murray confessed nothing to me.'

'Or you to him?' Gil asked carefully.

'Nor I to him.'

'In that case,' Gil observed, 'you'll be able to tell me what you spoke about.'

'Why would I be doing that?' Drummond looked hard at Gil, his expression giving little away. 'That is surely my own business and Billy's.'

'I think it may be mine as well,' said Gil, 'as Archbishop Blacader's quaestor.'

'Is that right?' said Drummond.

They were standing a little aside from the great door at Stronvar, waiting for a long procession to set off for the Kirkton. Before the door horses stamped, grooms shouted, Sir William on the fore-stair bawled contradictory orders and pointed in several directions at once, but where they were it was reasonably quiet.

Drummond had arrived at the house early in search of his servant and the rest of his baggage, and was now wearing the felt hat with the silver badge on its brim, set off nicely by a gown of dark green broadcloth faced with crimson taffeta. Alys, eyeing this, had said nothing, but slipped up to their apartment and returned with Gil's better gown, the blue brocade he had worn at their wedding, and persuaded him into it despite his protests. As he had feared, he was already much too warm.

'Canon Drummond,' he said, going on the attack, 'when you were at Dunkeld did you have any words with a man of the Bishop's household, by name of Mitchel?'

226

'No,' said Drummond blankly. 'Who is that? Should I have spoken with him?'

'He attended James Stirling the day you walked with him in Blackfriars Meadow.'

'Oh,' said Drummond, in a changed tone. Then, 'When I was at Dunkeld, I'd no notion Jaikie Stirling was dead. I'd have no reason to speak wi the man even if I set eyes on him.'

'True,' agreed Gil. And how far on the road to Dunkeld was Tam by now? Was Mitchel still there? 'So what did you speak to Murray about? A Drummond and a Murray embracing in the streets of Dunkeld? There must be a strong reason.'

'Aye, and all the more private for that.'

Murdo the steward strode past them, feathered bonnet askew, issuing brisk instructions in Ersche. One of the ponies broke free and was pursued through the mêlée.

'When you left Stirling on the meadow, what was he going to do?'

Drummond blinked. 'He said he'd walk there and muse a while. We'd both a deal to think on. He sent his man, Mitchel did you call him? He sent him back into Perth.'

'Did you see him there on the meadow later, when you went into Perth yourself?'

'No,' admitted Drummond. 'I was not looking, you'll understand, but he's – he was a tall man, near as tall as me, he would be easy seen if he was still walking there. Not if he was sitting under a whin-bush, mind you.'

'No, I suppose not,' agreed Gil. Nor if he was lying under one with a crossbow bolt in his neck, he thought. 'Returning to the point about William Murray, Canon, you realize I can easy ride to Dunkeld and get the tale from him. You might as well tell me what you spoke of.'

This did not appear to have occurred to Drummond. He scowled at an inoffensive clump of foxgloves for the space of a *Gloria*, and finally sighed deeply and said, 'We spoke of the past. Of events which – we'd much to forgive one another for, maister, and it took a long evening's talking to

227

get to the root of it, but we found forgiveness. Is that enough to your purpose?'

'Why now?' Gil asked. 'What brought the past to mind?'

Drummond gave him a goaded look.

'My brother's return,' he said. 'Is that no enough?'

'Yesterday you said he wasn't your brother,' Gil objected.

'I spent last night in talk with my brother Patrick,' said Drummond. 'He gave me good reasons to think that the young man is our brother David, and it was my mother's stated belief and all. I'll not go against that, maister.'

That feeling of wrestling with salmon came over Gil again. Unable to answer civilly, he swung away from Drummond and located Alys, standing aside with Lady Stewart watching the commotion.

'I won't wear this,' he said firmly, pulling off the brocade gown and thrusting it at her in a bundle. 'I'm by far too warm already.'

She met his eye and took the garment reluctantly, but only said, 'Have you looked at the badge on the Canon's hat?'

'Not yet,' he admitted.

'It's a fine one,' said Lady Stewart. 'I was admiring it earlier. From the Low Countries, he tells me, though I had no notion he had passed overseas on pilgrimage.'

'What saint's shrine is it from?' asked Alys casually, without glancing at Gil.

'One I've not heard of. A princess, with a sword and a lamp. Some Irish woman, who cures the mad, so he said. Doris, or Daphne, or something of the sort.'

So Marion Campbell reads the classical authors, thought Gil, and recalled the sheep-like Maister Gregor. *It began with D*, he had said. It seemed as if nobody could recall the name easily.

'They're mounting up,' said Lady Stewart. 'Best go and take your places, both of you. Give me the gown, my dear, and I'll put it safe.'

* * *

'I took refuge,' said Davie Drummond, 'because I was wrongly accused, and I was afraid.'

He was standing braced in front of the altar in the chancel of the little church, behind a row of five of the village men, who had left their work in the fields when they saw the string of riders clattering along the causeway. By the time Sir William and his entourage had dismounted and entered the kirkyard there were ten or twelve men and a handful of women round the door of the Eagleis Beag. They had been invited, with great courtesy, to leave their weapons outside; when Sir William identified Gil, Andrew Drummond and two of his own men to accompany him their numbers were scrupulously equalled. There was no doubt, Gil thought, where the sympathies of the Kirkton lay. He looked down at Alys, watching intently at his elbow, and wondered whose side the villagers had placed her on.

'Right,' said Sir William. He had halted at the chancel arch, his escort ranged on either side of him, facing Davie and his bodyguard. Nobody was openly hostile; everyone was alert; even in this light Davie was visibly trembling. *Men seiden, I loked as a wilde steer,* Gil thought. 'Now,' the Bailie continued, 'I've spoke wi those that were present at the time, and I've heard what the woman that accuses you had to say.' He did not sound as though he had enjoyed it. 'And I've spoke wi your man Steenie, Maister Cunningham,' he added formally, 'and heard his tale and all. So now I'll hear yours, Davie Drummond.'

'I have no tale to tell,' said Davie, spreading his hands. 'I was asleep within the house, and woken by shouting of Fire! By the time I had my shirt on and tried to waken the old woman, the roof was well alight. She rose in her shift, and would dress herself, and though – though I tried to help her she – she fell down, and could not rise up again. Murdo Dubh MacGregor came into the house to help me lift her and we carried her,' he looked down for a moment, his voice cracking, 'we carried her out and laid her down across the yard, and after a wee while she died. And then I was helping to carry water and put the fire out, only we had no success and the Tigh-an-Teine is burned.'

'Is that in accord wi what you saw, madam?' Sir William turned to Alys, still very formal. She nodded, and he faced Davie again. 'Aye, and the man Steenie says he heard you within when he hammered on the door and shouted Fire. It seems like a piece of foolishness to me,' he stated bluntly. 'If the thatch was lit from outside, and you were inside, it doesny seem to me you could ha set the fire.'

'Then who did?' demanded Andrew Drummond from Sir William's other side. 'Someone set the fire, and brought about my mother's death. Who was it?'

'Steenie never saw who it was,' said Sir William. 'Nor nobody else, so far as I can jalouse.'

Alys stirred beside Gil, but said nothing. He looked down at her again and saw her biting her lip anxiously.

'I'll agree it wasny David,' persisted Andrew, 'but it must ha been someone.'

The men standing in front of Davie Drummond were looking sideways at one another, in a kind of wordless communion. Finally one of them said quietly, 'It was maybe Those Ones set the fire. There has been bad luck enough at Dalriach, so they are saying. Maybe this will be part of it.'

Sir William produced an incoherent gobbling sound, like a blackcock in spring, and finally burst out with, 'Havers, man, how would the fairy-folk do that? I've never heard such nonsense!'

'They would not be using flint and steel,' observed one of the Stronvar men, 'how could they set a fire without flint and steel?'

'Maybe Sir William would not be talking of them so loud,' said another of the Kirkton men in diffident tones, 'even here in St Angus' own place.'

Sir William growled, and Andrew Drummond said, 'So we've still to seek for whoever set the fire. And what about this matter of the boy Iain? Patrick tells me you sang to him, Davie. Why does his mother think you killed him?'

This was not the way Gil would have wished to handle the matter. This confrontation in the shadowy kirk seemed likely to elicit nothing they had not heard already.

'She said I killed them both,' said Davie, his voice suddenly thin and lost. 'She blamed me for all of it, for the fire and all that followed, and I never –'

'She said more than that,' said Sir William. 'She told me you had moved the bairn into the track of the beasts as they left the fold, so he would be trod to death.'

Davie looked down and shook his head.

'Likely he crawled into the gateway, poor laddie,' offered one of the Kirkton men. 'I was hearing he could crawl a bittie, like maybe a bairn of one year old.'

'No,' said Gil. 'It wasn't the beasts killed the bairn.' Sir William turned to glower at him. 'I saw his body yestreen. His skull was broken, by a blow to the back of the head with a stone, which we found. And he'd been set down in the gateway of the fold, on his back, by someone going barefoot.'

There was a pause, in which several people's eyes travelled to Davie's bare feet, planted firmly on the tomb slab before the altar.

'No,' said Alys suddenly. 'Davie had not left the yard when the beasts were let out of the fold. I'll swear to it.'

'Will you, madam?' Sir William swung round to look at her closely. She nodded, and he turned back to Davie.

'Right,' he said. 'All we need now is to know whether your good-sister, or whatever she is to you, will persist in accusing you of arson, for I see no purpose in charging you with the bairn's death. Far too little to go on, we have –'

'Sir William!' It was Murdo the steward, at the door of the kirk. Sir William turned to glare at the man. 'Sir William, there is folk coming over the causeway. I am thinking it is a party from Glenbuckie, maybe the young folk all in a body.'

'From Glenbuckie?' said the Bailie in surprise, and a faint echo at his side seemed to be Andrew Drummond saying the same thing. 'I'd best come out into the daylight, I suppose.'

Chapter Twelve

It was indeed the young people from Glenbuckie, and it seemed to be a formal deputation. Jamie Beag at their head, dressed once again in the elaborately folded plaid, the yellow-dyed shirt and velvet bonnet he had worn the previous day to greet the mourners, bowed deeply to Sir William, and behind him his sisters and cousin curtsied and stood silent, faces hidden. Jamie cast one quick glance at the door of the kirk, his colour rising, and said in Scots:

'I have a word for Sir William from me and my uncle, as the tenants of Dalriach.'

'Have you now?' said Sir William, glowering at him under his eyebrows. 'And what might that be? Do I need to hear it now, or can I get on wi this matter of your uncle Davie or whoever he is?'

'It concerns D – Davie,' said Jamie, very upright, quite expressionless. At the hesitation Ailidh turned her head to look at him, but did not speak. Why is he so embarrassed? Gil wondered.

'Go on, man,' said the Bailie.

'We have been talking it through, all the matter of the fire and the death of my grandmother and the death of Iain mac Padraig,' Jamie said, still without expression, 'and we are concluding that it was the Good Folk that caused all of it.'

'What?' exclaimed Sir William.

Jamie nodded, but Andrew said, 'I've decided no such thing, nephew, and you know that!'

232

'It was us on the farm that decided it this morning,' said Jamie steadily. 'So you will see there is no need for Sir William to be concerning himself with it at all.'

'Right,' said Sir William. 'So you tell me it was nobody set the fire, and nobody caused the bairn's death –'

'Excepting the Good Folk,' agreed Jamie.

'No such thing!' said Andrew again, but Ailidh drew her plaid away from her face and said quietly, speaking to him direct:

'My uncle's wife is agreed to that, in particular.'

'Caterin?' said Andrew, arrested. 'She agrees?'

'She does,' said Ailidh.

The two younger girls nodded silently. One of them was Caterin's daughter, Gil recalled. He looked from one fair-skinned Drummond face to another, and then down at Alys in dismay. Her hand tightened in his, and she nodded, as silent as the Drummond girls; she also had recognized the nature of the bargain which had been struck. So had Sir William, it appeared, and what astonished Gil was that he seemed to accept the matter. The woman will get away with it, he thought, only so that Davie can go free. Is that justice? And who set the fire in any case?

'Well,' said Sir William. 'In that case, you might as well ha your kinsman out of the kirk here. But afore he goes, I want the truth from him.'

He flung round and strode back into the little kirk, taking those around him by surprise. There was a minor scuffle at the door, as Gil tried to give way to the younger Drummonds, whom he felt to have the best claim to be next after Sir William, and first Andrew and then the Stronvar men-at-arms tried to push past. In the disturbance Andrew Drummond's hat fell off. Gil moved towards it, but Alys got there first and snatched it up.

'Your hat, Canon,' she said, brushing it with her cuff, and turned it to make sure it had suffered no damage.

'My thanks,' he said in his harsh voice, hand out. She paused, admiring the bright badge.

'Whatever saint is that?' she asked innocently. 'It's a pretty image, with the sword and the lamp like that. I can't read the name – is that D-I –?'

'DIMPNA. It's St Dymphna,' he said, hand still extended. She apologized and gave him the hat. 'My thanks,' he said again, and turned away before she could ask him anything else.

'Well done,' said Gil softly. She gave him a quick smile, and preceded him into the kirk.

By the time he got to the low arch, the Bailie was within the small chancel saying, 'Right, my laddie. You've sworn to your innocence of the charges. And your kin here, if that's what they are, have decided there's no charge to bring in any case, so come out of the shadows, will you, and tell me who you are.'

Davie stared at him, eyes and mouth wide and dark in the dim light.

'No charge?' he repeated.

'The woman's changed her mind,' said Sir William.

'Caterin has said it was all done by the Good Folk,' said Alys, beside Gil. Davie caught his breath on a little sob, and put the back of one hand to his mouth. Ailidh, right by the pillar at one side of the arch, looked at him and then round the rest of the company, and slipped in to stand close to him.

'Did you hear me, laddie?' said Sir William, raising his voice a little. 'I bade you tell me who you are.'

Davie laughed unsteadily, and took his hand down.

'I told you that already,' he said, 'but I'll swear it again. Here on St Angus' own grave, I swear to you that I am Davie Drummond.'

'Aye, but which Davie Drummond?' demanded Sir William. That's the right question, thought Gil. 'Are you the one that vanished away thirty year syne, or are you another? Tell me that, now, while you're standing on St Angus' grave!'

'Who could I be if I wasny that Davie?'

'Don't play games wi me, laddie.' Sir William was becoming angry. 'Andrew, what do you say? Jamie? You lassies? Is he your kin, the one that vanished away, or is he another?'

Outside, a bell rang, once, twice. It left a humming silence, which seemed to last for ever. Then the door of the little kirk creaked open, and a dark figure appeared against the light.

'Sir William?' Robert Montgomery's voice. 'Are you here? I've a word for you from Sir Duncan, and it'll not wait.'

Sir Duncan had very little time left. He lay propped on a stack of cushions, sheepskins, folded plaids, to raise him a little on the hurdle on which they had carried him out of his house. Below the kirk the slope of the land made a half-bowl, and the old man had been set down at the centre of this, another very elderly man who must be the clerk kneeling at his feet and weeping. By his side Robert stood, holding the bell; from time to time he rang it twice and then stilled it. Gil would have liked a closer look at it, for it was clearly very old, a box-shaped thing with an extraordinary sweet, carrying sound.

The inhabitants of the Kirkton, leaving whatever occupied them, leaving the hay unturned and the beasts to mind themselves, were gathering in silence on the slopes of the bowl. The sound of the bell must be audible clear along the glen; people could be seen in the distance, making their way in knots of two and three and five, hastening to its summons. Occasionally Sir Duncan raised a hand in blessing; his flesh was so transparent that Gil was surprised when it cut off the sparkles of the sun on the river beyond.

He was uneasily aware that he should set out for Perth as he had planned. There was much to find out there before he could come to any conclusion about James Stirling's death. He had said as much to Alys, but she said seriously, 'You may learn more here before you go, Gil. Wait a little longer.'

He had already learned a little. Following Sir William along the path through the kirkyard, he had found Robert Montgomery at his elbow.

'They're saying Davie's safe now, Maister Cunningham,' he had said abruptly. 'Is that right?'

'The woman has withdrawn her charge of arson,' Gil agreed.

Robert sighed faintly in relief, and crossed himself.

'St Angus be praised,' he said. 'And I've a word from the old man for you.' Gil raised his eyebrows. 'I was to tell you, he minds no stranger the same week you asked about, but he had spied a *bodach* in the glen himself the week afore it.'

'Well, well,' said Gil. 'My thanks to Sir Duncan.' He put his hand briefly on the young man's shoulder. 'You're doing him good service, Robert.'

Robert looked at the hand and then at Gil, gave him a swift startled smile, and slipped off round the people in front of them with his head down, leaving Gil himself to recognize yet again that extraordinary feeling of sympathy for a Montgomery.

He had lost sight of Alys now; she might be with the Drummond girls. Sir William, abrogating responsibility for the scene before them, was sitting on the kirkyard wall, watching the parish gathering and chewing his lip. He had got no answer from Davie Drummond, and it clearly rankled. And where was Davie? Gil wondered. Come to that, where was Doig?

He moved quietly away among the gathering crowd, and made for the priest's own house. He could hear voices as he approached it, but Doig was seated just inside the door as he had been before, and the conversation ceased before he came close enough to catch words. He rattled politely at the pin nevertheless, and said:

'I hoped I'd find you, Maister Doig. And is Davie here too?'

236

'I am,' admitted Davie reluctantly as he pushed the door wider.

'It's you again,' said Doig in hostile tones. 'I suppose you'd better come in. At least you'll no disturb the auld yin. Did you ever hear o sic a thing as that?' He jerked his head in the direction of the gathering parish.

'I have,' said Davie. He was sitting on one of the painted kists across the room, swinging his bare feet against the wood with regular soft thumps. 'When St Angus himself died, the whole parish came to say farewell to him, and he sat out there in his preaching-place, that he made by a miracle –'

'Oh, like St Mungo,' said Gil, appreciating this.

'I wouldn't be knowing,' admitted Davie.

'Aye, well, I suppose this one's near enough being a saint,' said Doig sourly.

Gil looked from one to the other. They were clearly acquainted, and Davie was comfortable in the older man's presence, though just now both were watching him closely. And now he knew that there had been a *bodach* before the young David vanished, and one when he returned. Robert had clearly not recognized the significance of the message; his mind was probably occupied by his concern for the dying man.

'Davie,' he said. 'Is your father still alive?'

'James Drummond died years ago,' said Davie.

'Not your grandfather. Your father.'

The two of them stared at him, Doig impassive, Davie apprehensive.

'What I think happened,' Gil said slowly, 'was that thirty years ago someone was paid to snatch David Drummond away, on his way back to Dunblane just at this time of year, and take him to the Low Countries and sell him to some kirk or other as a singer.' Davie's gaze slid sideways to Doig, but Doig's eyes were unwaveringly fixed on Gil. 'I think David prospered where he ended up, maybe even married, had a son anyway. Then this summer the son came back, was dropped off in the same place where his father was snatched, climbed over the pass and was taken for his own father by old Mistress Drummond, who was near blind at close quarters though she could count the sheep on the hillside.'

'That's a good tale,' said Doig approvingly. 'You should get a harper to set it to music.'

'What year were you born, Maister Doig?' Gil asked.

'Forty-seven,' said Doig, without thought.

'So you were sixteen when you lifted David Drummond.'

'I never said I –'

'Sir Duncan saw the *bodach* the previous week. Was it your own business at that time, ferrying information and singers abroad, or were you the junior partner?'

'You're talking nonsense,' said Doig. 'What would the likes of me do that for? How would I do it?'

'I've met you before, Maister Doig,' Gil pointed out. 'So did you bring Davie in by Perth, or by Leith and Dunblane?'

'Why would I do either?'

Abandoning that for the moment, Gil looked at Davie.

'Where is St Dymphna's shrine?' he asked. 'This Irish saint that cures the mad.'

He could see, even in the poor light within the house, how Davie considered the question and found the answer harmless.

'Gheel,' he replied. 'So they say.'

'Gheel,' repeated Gil, sounding the guttural at the beginning of the word. 'Where good singers are always wanted, Maister Doig? No wonder that laddie took you for the Devil himself, wi your leather cloak down your back like wings, talking about Hell at the window.'

'Where?' said Doig. 'What window would that be?'

'Did he so?' said Davie, laughing rather madly. 'Billy, you'll need to keep that quiet, or the Bishop's men'll no come calling.'

'What Bishop was that?' Doig said, with that monitory stare.

238

'Och, maybe I dreamed it,' said Davie, suddenly deflated. Gil made no comment, but got to his feet.

'Davie, I'd like to know what you'll do next. Robert Blacader put me in here to find out who you are, and now I've discerned that my task's done, but if I can assure him you'll not pursue a place in the choir at Dunblane he'll be happier.'

'Was that what fetched you here?' said Doig in amazement. 'One old woman's daft notion?'

'I've no notion to sing in the choir at Dunblane, maister, and I'll swear it by any saint you care to name.'

Gil studied him for a moment.

'Will you talk to my wife?' he suggested. Davie nodded. 'Good. She can likely help you, she's an ingenious lassie. Now I've to get to Perth afore supper, so I'll leave you.'

'And, by the Rood, I'll be glad to see you go,' said Doig.

'It's quite a tangle,' said Bishop Brown. He leaned back from his desk and stroked his dog's soft head. 'But are the two matters connected other than by the man Drummond?'

Gil hesitated, staring out of the study window at the evening sunlight on the fields across the Tay and trying to put his thoughts into words.

'There's a pattern,' he said at length, 'and it seems to me it involves both matters. All three, indeed,' he added, 'though I'm certain the three singers are safe enough in Gheel.'

Getting the explanation and apology for his sudden departure accepted had not been easy. The Bishop was inclined to be affronted by what he saw as desertion, and Gil had had to invoke Blacader's original commission and stress its priority. He had still not been offered any refreshment, though he had missed supper, and he had only achieved this private interview by insisting on it.

'So what will you do now?' asked Brown. 'Where will you hunt next?'

'I'll need a word wi your steward,' Gil said, 'to learn if there's been any answer to those questions we were having cried through the town. Then I'll have to ask more questions.'

'Aye questions,' said the Bishop. 'I need answers, maister. You'll ha heard, maybe, that there are folk in the Low Countries know more than they should about the English treaty?' Gil nodded. 'I want to learn whether my secretary was Judas or Sebastian, and I want it afore we bury him.'

'I'll be out first thing,' Gil promised, appreciating the reference, 'and I'll keep you informed, sir.'

'Aye, do that,' said the Bishop. 'But my carpenter tells me he'll no keep long, tanpit or no tanpit, lead coffin or no lead coffin, so I'd be glad if you brattle on wi't, maister.'

Jerome suddenly jumped down from his knee and bustled over to inspect Gil's boots, tail going. Gil bent to make much of the pup, and Brown's expression softened.

'Whether he's traitor or martyr, that's one thing Jaikie did for me,' he said, 'fetched me my wee dog.'

'He's a bonnie pup,' Gil said. 'A good memorial, sir.'

'Maybe,' said the Bishop. 'Well, if that's all you're wanting to let me know the now, you'd best go and get a bite to eat and shift your clothes. Wat will see to all for you. And he'll tell you,' he added, 'the constable has took up the tanner for Jaikie's death. I'm no convinced, but the Shirra gave his approval.'

'Andy Cornton the tanner?' said Currie, pouring ale for Gil. 'The constable lifted him, oh, about noon yesterday, and one o his journeymen and all. Quite a scene it was, so they say, his men wereny for letting him go quietly and the constable had to break two o their heads. He denies any connection wi Stirling's death, a course, but what I say is, Willie Reid must ha had something to go on, whatever my lord thinks.'

'Have they been put to the question?' Gil asked. 'This is an uncommon good pie,' he added, and cut himself

240

another wedge. The steward, when applied to, had taken him to his own chamber and sent a man for a tray of food; Gil hoped the two men at arms who had ridden in with him were as well looked after.

'We keep a good kitchen,' said Currie, nodding at the compliment. 'Question? No, by what I hear, they're waiting for you to come back afore they proceed.'

Gil chewed on the mouthful of meat and pastry, thinking guiltily that if he had not gone to Balquhidder he might have prevented the arrest.

'I learned a few things, these two days, just the same,' he said aloud. 'I've found the second badge, for a start.'

'So I can send the bellman round, can I, to tell folks no to bring me any more lead St Jameses?' said Currie with a rueful grin. 'What's it doing at Balquhidder, then?'

'Andrew Drummond has it. He says Stirling gave it to him.'

'St Peter's bones, why'd he do that?'

'He didn't tell me,' said Gil evasively.

'That's no like Maister Stirling,' said Currie, 'he set great store by those badges, I'd never ha thought he'd part wi one. Oh – speaking o the bellman, the Precentor at St John's Kirk, what's his name? Kinnoull, that's it, he sent to say he'd a word for you about something the bellman was crying.'

'Did he say what? There were several things we sent to the bellman about.'

'Never a word. That was all the message, sent wi one of the laddies in his choir.'

'I'll go by the kirk tomorrow,' Gil said, glancing at the window of the chamber where they sat. 'It's near sunset now.'

'Your man Tam's late,' said Currie anxiously. 'He'll maybe no get into the town if he's much longer.'

'I'm not looking for him till the morn,' Gil said.

'You're no? Just the lads you had wi you thought he'd come ahead, they were right confounded when they didny find him here already wi his boots off.'

'No, no, I sent him an errand, and two more men wi him.' Gil selected a plum from the dish of fruit and bit into it. 'They should be here by the morn's noon. Where are Cornton and his man held?'

'They're in the Tolbooth, in chains by what I hear, and they're saying his wife's in a rare taking, poor woman.'

'I'm not surprised,' said Gil.

Maister Gregor, accosted in the hall before Prime next morning, was disinclined to chat. It took Gil a little work over his bowl of porridge to persuade the old man to think about the evening his friend had vanished.

'It's none so easy,' he said glumly, 'for a course I didny realize then that he'd vanished, so I took no note of the evening, any more than I did the previous one.'

'I can see that,' Gil said. 'It was that day you had the argument about the shoe, did you tell me?'

'Aye, it was.' Maister Gregor rubbed his eyes with the sleeve of his old-fashioned buttoned gown. 'To think it was near the last words we spoke, it fair makes me greet.'

'But you were friends again by noon?' Gil prompted.

'Aye, we were, you're right. Jaikie cam to sit by me here at the board, see, and we shared a mess of boiled mutton wi two Erschemen from Lorne and spoke Latin wi them. Their Latin wasny very good,' the old man recalled, 'they couldny understand the most o what I said to them. And Wat was on about a new way to cook mutton, wait till I tell you this.' He recounted his friend's witticism again, obviously forgetting that he had already told it to Gil.

'What happened after that?' Gil asked.

'Why, Jaikie went out about my lord's errands, about the rents, and I went to copying the diocesan returns for my lord. They go to Rome, you'll understand, maister, so they've to be in a good clear hand, and my lord's aye commended mine.'

'A dull task,' said Gil, pulling a sympathetic face. 'How long did that last you?'

'Aye, but a needful. I stayed at that till Vespers, and then seeing the supper was a wee thing late I walked in the garden for a bittie. My lord was there and all, wi his wee dog, and he asked me where was Jaikie,' he rubbed at his eyes again, 'and a course Jaikie never cam here again.'

'I think my lord had a great trust in Maister Stirling,' said Gil. Maister Gregor nodded. 'Did he tell you anything about the English negotiations while he was caught up in them?'

'Me? No, no, I kept away from that,' said Maister Gregor virtuously. 'I think my lord was feart I'd let something slip at the wrong time,' he added. Surprised by this show of self-awareness, Gil nodded. 'And a course Jaikie was maist discreet. Never a word till all was signed and sealed, and then it was only a bit gossip about the ambassadors,' he said with regret, and sighed heavily. 'Aye me, it's hard to think I'll not see him again in this life.'

St John's Kirk was busy with folk making their morning observations. Several priests were saying Mass at different altars, their bright vestments catching the light, the incense rising up into the high roof past the gleam of the huge silver chandelier on its chain, and another two appeared to be showing some relics to a group of pilgrims. Enquiring for Kinnoull led Gil to the choir itself. It was empty and quiet just now, between Prime and Terce, except for the Precentor poring over the great choir-book on its stand while the clerks of the choir refreshed themselves with a jug of ale in the vestry.

'Oh, it's you,' he said as Gil made his way through the curtained doorway in the choirscreen. 'I sent you word, did I no?'

'You did,' agreed Gil.

'I think we'll use this one the day.' Kinnoull spread the great pages flat, and drew the bar down on its hinge to keep the book open. 'I'm still short o basses since the Moncrieff lads left us, maister, and it limits which settings of the Mass we can use, it limits them. You've no idea where they've gone, I suppose?'

'The Low Countries, I suspect,' said Gil.

'Aye, I feared as much,' said Kinnoull, nodding gloomily. 'They've more wealth than us, maister, we'll never get our singers back now. Where in the Low Countries?'

'A place called Gheel.'

'Never heard of it. Well, maister, I'll ha to get on, we've Terce to sing, but just afore you go, was it you was looking for where Andrew Drummond o Dunblane ate his supper one night?'

'It was,' agreed Gil, without much hope.

'I thought it was. Well, I canny help you there, maister, but I can tell you where he was after it. He was in here.'

'In here?' repeated Gil, startled. 'You know him, do you?'

'Oh, I know him well. I'm fro Dunblane mysel, maister. So when I saw him here in St Andrew's chapel, I said to mysel, You're not wanting disturbed, man, I'll just leave you be.'

'He was at prayer?'

'That's what I'm telling you. He spent the most of an hour or maybe more on his knees afore St Andrew. I was in here, looking through the choir-book just as you find me now, maister, and when I'd finished I should ha gone out and locked the place, but I didny want to chase Andrew Drummond away. Times you can tell when a man needs a quiet word.'

'So you weren't close enough to tell whether he'd been drinking.'

'Drinking? No, I smelled no drink. Frying, maybe, I'd say he'd had fried bread to his supper, but no drink. Anyway I just sat here till he left.'

'And what time would that be?' Gil asked hopefully.

'Near curfew,' said Kinnoull confidently, 'for I'd to hurry mysel to get a jug of ale afore they rang the bell. And now I'll have to hurry mysel to lead the choir in for Terce.' He gave the great book one last glance, and moved away from the stand. 'But when I heard the bellman asking where Andrew ate his supper, I thought to mysel, that might be what the man needs to hear.'

'It is,' said Gil. 'My thanks, maister. It's something I needed, right enough.'

'I can ask,' said Brother Dickon. 'But it was two weeks afore we sought him, maister, and I'd ha thought if any o my lads – my brethren,' he corrected himself, 'had found aught like that, they'd ha said so at the time.'

'I agree,' said Gil, 'it's a long shot, but I have to check.'

'So you want to know,' said the senior lay brother, a wiry grizzled fellow with a scar across one eye, 'if there was any sign o a struggle, or a patch of blood.'

'Any sign of where the man died,' Gil agreed, wishing he had brought Socrates. But even the dog might have difficulty after two weeks, he thought, supposing the man did die out on the Ditchlands.

Brother Dickon jerked his head at the open doorway.

'We're just come from Terce,' he said, 'so you've catched us all thegither. Come and wait while I ask them.'

Gil rose and followed him out of the snug porter's lodge into the first courtyard of the convent, where half a dozen lay brothers, bearded men in the black Dominican habit with the black scapular instead of white, were clattering across the outer courtyard in their sturdy boots, making for the gate. Brother Dickon summoned them with a piercing whistle and a wave of his arm, and all six came to stand obediently before him, hands tucked into their wide sleeves, heads bent, faces half hidden by their hoods. Dickon glared at them, and they looked sideways and shuffled into a straighter line.

'Aye,' he said at length. 'You'll do. Listen, lads. Er, brethren. You mind the other day when we had to hunt for that clerk that got hissel missing?'

He propounded Gil's question accurately, and glared along the line of black hoods. There was silence for the space of an *Ave*, then one of the hoods rose and its wearer said diffidently, 'Permission to speak, sa – er – Brother Dickon?'

'Speak up, Brother Archie.'

'I don't think any of us seen anything like that.'

Heads were shaken all along the row.

'Damage to any of the bushes?' Gil said hopefully. 'Signs of a struggle?'

'Christ love you, maister,' said Brother Dickon toler- antly, 'there's struggles to damage the bushes any evening a lad walks his lass across the meadow.'

'Aye, and it's never –' began a mutter from under one of the hoods.

'That'll do, Brother Dod,' said Brother Dickon.

'Does that happen most evenings?' Gil asked. 'Would there have been youngsters there the night Maister Stirling vanished?'

'Likely enough,' said Brother Dickon, and heads nodded along the row. 'But as for minding whether or no, two weeks after it, it's more than I can do. Any of you lads?'

Clearly, none of his troop remembered either. Gil looked from them to the spare, upright figure of their superior, and said, 'I've another question, if I may. Was any of you along the Skinnergate that evening? I realize,' he said men- daciously, 'you'd not be in the alehouses, but I wonder if anyone saw Andrew Drummond there in the street.'

Brother Dickon's expression was wonderfully ambigu- ous. After another, longer, pause, the same man as before spoke up.

'I was on the Skinnergate after our supper,' he admitted. 'I'd to fetch a harness to the white-faced mare, that Will Lorimer was mending for us.'

'And did you see the Canon, Brother Archie?' demanded his superior sharply. Brother Archie nodded.

'I did and all,' he said. 'He was just going into the Northgate as I cam out of Lorimer's shop. He never saw me, but. He'd the duarch wi him, the mimmerkin that dwells at the dog-breeder's yard.'

'And what time would that be?' Gil asked.

Archie shrugged. 'After supper. I'd gone into the town, I'd spoke wi Lorimer, I'd shown him why he should do the work as a gift. Eight o' the clock, maybe?'

'You'd swear to that?' Gil said. Archie looked at Brother Dickon.

'Aye, lad, brother, you can swear to it,' Brother Dickon informed him.

'I'll swear to it, maister,' said Brother Archie.

'That's excellent,' said Gil. 'My thanks, brother.'

'Is that all you're wanting?' demanded Brother Dickon. 'For they've to get on wi stacking the great barn afore the tithes come in.' When Gil nodded, he jerked his head at the row of men. 'Right, lads, get on wi't.'

They bowed, in unison, the black hoods falling forward over their brows. Then they turned and clattered towards the gate, rather self-consciously not walking in step.

'What did you do before you took the habit, brother?' Gil asked curiously, watching them go.

'Serjeant-at-arms to the old King,' said Brother Dickon.

Mistress Doig was not at home. Several of the dogs he had seen on his first visit were absent as well, so it seemed likely she was exercising them out on the common land to the north of the suburb, as she had described. Most of the remaining dogs barked at him when he entered the yard, but he stood quietly, and after a while they settled down again, though one liver-and-white bitch pressed her muzzle into the corner of her pen and snarled steadily. He ignored her, and took the opportunity to examine the premises with more attention than before.

Out here beyond the burgh walls – no, the Ditch, he corrected himself – the ground was not laid out in the long narrow even-sized tofts which were usual inside a town. The Doigs' premises consisted of the house set at the further end of the ground with the yard in front of it and a long shed to one side. The yard was perhaps twenty-five or thirty paces long, and the same width as the dyer's yard, fenced all round with woven hurdles lashed securely to solid posts. Within this space the pens had been constructed of solid timber, the lowest planks half-buried to prevent enthusiastic inmates tunnelling out, the higher ones separated enough for the occupant to see something of the world. None of them was against the boundary, so that a lean person such as Mistress Doig or Gil himself could walk right round the fence.

The liver-and-white bitch, getting no reaction, had given up her harangue to lie down within her kennel, but when he moved to explore the layout of the yard, she leapt out with a savage snarl, provoking the other dogs as well. He recognized why Mistress Doig had no hesitation in leaving the premises unattended; two of her neighbours had already looked out to see what was going on, alerted by the noise. Waving politely to them, he picked his way round the double row of pens, peered into and then behind the shed, studied the hurdles which composed the fence, leaned over to see into the tanyard.

'She's out wi the dogs,' said a voice over the barking. He looked up, and saw one of the neighbours still watching suspiciously from the property that lay between him and the Blackfriars' track. 'She'll no be long.'

'I can see that,' he agreed. 'I'll wait for her. Likely she knows I'm here by now, wi the dogs barking like this.'

'Aye, likely.' The man stood watching him. He was clad in a worn leather jerkin and blue workman's bonnet, and held a knife in one hand and a slat of wood in the other; probably he was one of the many manufacturers of smallwares, little boxes and wooden combs, needle-cases and tablet covers, who could be found scraping a living in the suburbs of any burgh. That would explain the litter of timber and shavings lying all about the yard, Gil realized.

'Is trade good?' he asked casually, picking his way over to the fence.

'It keeps us.'

'There's a lot of buying and selling in Perth, I think, what wi the overseas merchants and the like.'

'They're no wanting Ally Paterson's wares,' said the man resentfully. 'It's all sheep fells and salt salmon they take out o Perth, and they bring in stuff to compete wi decent craftsmen and take the bread out our mouths.'

Recognizing his duty, Gil enquired further, and found himself bargaining over the fence for a handful of wooden combs and several tiny boxes which might hold a needle. The things were well made; he was sure Alys would not want them, but they might make gifts for someone.

'You keep an eye out for one another in these yards,' he commented, counting out the sum agreed.

'I'm sorry if I was a bit sharp,' said Paterson obliquely, and handed the goods over bundled in an oddment of striped woollen cloth. 'You'll ha heard, maybe, Andy Cornton the tanner's in trouble the now wi a dead man in his tanpit, and there was a wee bother in Mistress Doig's place the other week and all.'

'I'm sorry to hear that. Was there any harm to her? Or the dogs?'

'No, I'd say not,' said Paterson drily, 'for I heard her complaining to her man about it after. No, just something set the dogs barking and her man was shouting, right angry he was, about folk coming into his yard and misbehaving theirsels, and right enough there was a couple men there earlier though I never learned what they'd done, for I was at my supper at the time,' he admitted with regret. 'So when I seen a stranger, and I ken she's out –'

'Very wise,' said Gil, 'and I'm sure Mistress Doig would do the same for you.' A fresh outbreak of barking made him look over his shoulder, in time to see the dog-breeder herself approaching her gate, towed by a mixed leash of half a dozen excited animals. 'Good day, mistress,' he offered, and raised his hat to her.

'You again,' she said.

'Oh, aye,' agreed Paterson. 'And you'll mind Ally Paterson next time you're needing a comb, maister.'

By the time Gil extricated himself from the conversation, Mistress Doig had returned the dogs to their various pens, screamed at the others for silence and obtained it, glowered at her neighbour and at Gil, and was waiting in the midst of the yard, arms folded, to learn his business.

'I'd a good word wi himself in Balquhidder,' he began, making his way past the liver-and-white bitch again.

'Is that where he is?' she retorted, in unwelcoming tones.

'He was saying he misses the dogs.'

She snorted at that. 'Aye, well, he kens what he can do about it.'

'You were to show me the fence.'

Her eyes widened, but she said without moving, 'What about the fence, then?'

'The new mended spot,' he prompted.

She studied him, glanced briefly at Paterson still standing in his doorway watching them, and said sourly, 'Come in the house.'

The house was a single room, though it had a fireplace with a chimney in one gable. Mistress Doig stalked in ahead of him, tossed her plaid on to the bed, pointed to a stool and said, 'You can as well be seated. Now what's this about? I'll not discuss my business or Doig's afore the neighbours.'

'The new mended spot on the fence,' he repeated. She hooked a second stool away from the wall with one foot and sat down, giving him another hostile stare.

'I've no notion how that came about. I heard him shouting when I was out wi the dogs, maybe it was about that. He'd mended it by the time I cam back, he was just putting the tools past in the shed. Same evening you were asking me about afore,' she added, 'after I'd had the two priests in the yard. I'd enough to do wi the dogs when I came in, the ones I'd left here were in a right tirravee wi him shouting and all, I never heard what came to the

250

fence. Maybe Doig and our Mitchel had a fight,' she speculated, without much conviction.

'Not round by the fence, surely?' said Gil. 'It's a tight squeeze for a burly fellow like Doig, I'd have said, let alone starting a fight in the space.'

She shrugged. 'He never said.'

'Mind you, the damage is none so bad,' he pursued. 'Did he just have to cut a new cord and tie the hurdle to the stobs again? Or was there more to it than that?'

'I've no notion,' she said again. 'Doig never said. You've been round and looked at it yoursel, then?'

'I have. It's well trampled, for such a simple repair, I wondered if you'd had a bit trouble.'

'I keep telling you,' she said impatiently, 'I wasny here and Doig never let on.'

'Did your cousin not tell you what happened?'

'I've not seen him since. Likely he's away a message for his maister.'

'He's away, is he? Who carries the word instead of him, then?'

'That daft fellow that was wi you the other day. Peter.' She snorted again. 'No more sense than turn up here asking for Doig so all the neighbours can hear.'

'What's Maister Doig doing now that he'd as soon keep quiet?' Gil asked casually.

'Why ask me? If you've spoke wi him in Balquhidder, you ought to know,' she retorted. 'You're mighty full o questions every time I see you, maister, and answering them's never done me any good. I think I'd as soon you left my yard.' She rose and shook out her striped homespun skirts, and stood glaring at him. 'And I'll no look for you –'

'Mistress Doig!' shouted a voice outside. 'Mistress Doig, are you there? You're socht!'

She snatched up her plaid and hurried out to the yard, Gil following. Paterson was out at his door again, shouting; another two or three neighbours were hastening down their gardens with excited cries.

'What's amiss? Who wants me?' she demanded.

'It's the Blackfriars!' called another neighbour. 'See, there he comes yonder! It's your man, I doubt!'

'Doig!' she said, on a breathless little gasp, and froze on the spot.

'No, it's not her man,' said someone else, 'it's her cousin. He's carried in dead, and asking for her.'

Chapter Thirteen

'I'm that sorry, Maister Gil,' said Tam yet again, over the head of the man bandaging him.

'You did your best, man,' said Gil. 'None of us was expecting an attack.'

'That's it,' agreed Ned, his hands round a pot of hot spiced ale. 'We never expected sic a thing that close to Perth.'

They were in the guest hall of the Blackfriars' convent, a high light chamber with painted walls and a long table down its centre, where the injured men had been carried when they reached the gatehouse. By the time Gil arrived at the run, with Mistress Doig on his heels, Brother Infirmarer had made his decisions, told off two of his lay brothers to see to Tam and Ned, and was just following Donal as he was borne to the Infirmary. His assistant, crucifix in hand, was kneeling over a fourth man who lay groaning on the bloodstained flagstones.

Mistress Doig had dropped to her knees beside him in silence, seizing the injured man's hand. Gil stood by, staring in horror, while the sub-Infirmarer recited words all too familiar to everyone in the room and Tam said urgently in his ear:

'They came down on us no a mile fro the town, Maister Gil. There was six o them, we was lucky to get away, and it was Mitchel there they was after, they were out to kill him!'

'Looks as if they've succeeded,' said Ned beside him.

Gil stepped forward as the sub-Infirmarer reached the blessing, and hunkered down beside the dying man. The narrow, dark-browed face was glistening with sweat, blood bubbled on the bluish lips, and he whimpered as another spasm of pain jerked through his body. The two deep wounds to chest and belly would see him off within a few minutes, to judge by the sub-Infirmarer's manner.

'Mitchel,' he said quietly, 'who killed Jaikie Stirling?'

Mitchel groaned again, and Mistress Doig threw him an angry look.

'Leave him at peace!' she said. 'He's more to think on than that! Brother Euan, can you gie him nothing for his pain? I'd not –' She choked on the words. 'I'd not leave a dog to suffer this way.'

'I can,' admitted the sub-Infirmarer in his deep gentle voice, 'though whether he'll get the good o't is another matter.' He turned away to receive a small bottle from his servant, unstopping it with big deft hands. Gil leaned forward, looking into Mitchel's eyes.

'Who killed Maister Stirling?' he asked again. The man drew a shuddering breath, twisted away from his gaze, and gasped, faint and high-pitched:

'Wha –? Wha?'

'He doesny ken what you mean,' said Mistress Doig. 'Here, my laddie, drink this.' She almost snatched the little cup from the Infirmarer, lifted Mitchel's head, eased water between his bloody lips. He swallowed once; she tilted the cup again, but this time the water ran out at the sides of his mouth.

'I feared as much,' said the Infirmarer. 'No, daughter, no use giving him the rest.'

Gil sat back and crossed himself, muttering a prayer. He was almost stunned with anger. Someone had taken advantage of his own action, had made him partly responsible for this man's death, and by it had snatched the information Mitchel carried out of reach, out of Gil's own grasp. He rose and stepped back from the little group, Mistress Doig in her knotted headdress and striped gown,

Brother Euan and his servant with their tonsured heads bent, and Mitchel with his face already relaxing into the painless depths of the next world. He looked younger than Gil had expected, not much past thirty perhaps. Biting back his anger, he joined Tam and Ned where they were seated at the long table, their helmets discarded beside them. The other Infirmary lay brother was still smearing salve into the long slash on Tam's knee.

'The horses have taen no hurt,' said Ned now, 'and they're saying young Donal will be well enough, wi God's help, and get a scar to fright the lassies wi.'

'I'm glad to hear it,' said Gil. 'I wish none of you had been hurt. Who was it? Did you get a look at them?'

Ned shrugged, and winced as the movement shifted his bandaged arm.

'I took it they was Murrays,' he admitted. 'They're no likely to be MacGregors, this close to Perth, and besides he,' he jerked his head at the dead man, 'he was a MacGregor, though I suppose –'

'Aye, it means nothing,' agreed Gil. 'Tam? Did you jalouse anything?'

'They were after him,' said Tam, 'like I tellt you, Maister Gil. The first two made for Donal and me, the next two got past us and went straight for him, and I'd say they wereny looking to take him prisoner. Him and Ned took them on, and Donal and me struck one of ours down and took the last two from behind, and then –' He swallowed, and winced as the man at his side tightened the bandage. 'Then we ran for the town, and them after us, such as could still sit a horse, and when we cam by the barn the lay brothers cam charging out, right handy wi brooms and pitchforks they are, and we turned there, and then we saw how Mitchel –' He swallowed again. 'I'm right sorry, Maister Gil, I never –'

'Leave it, Tam,' said Gil, reaching out to grip the man's hand. 'And thank God you came out alive. Ned, is that how you saw it and all?'

'Close enough,' agreed Ned.

255

'It's the lay brothers that gets me,' said Tam, with a slightly hysterical laugh. 'They come down to the roadside at the charge, wi their brooms and pitchforks levelled like they was pikes. You'd ha thought they was a regiment.'

'Likely the Murrays did think they were a regiment,' observed Ned, 'the way they cut and ran.' He took another swallow of his spiced ale.

'That's Brother Dickon's doing,' said the man who was bandaging Tam. 'He's got the outdoor men well trained. The hounds of the Lord need a stout collar, he aye says.'

'They're that, all right,' said Ned. 'Saved our skins, they did, and I'd like to shake them all by the hand and buy them a stoup of ale for it.'

'I'll pass on your thanks,' said the Dominican, gathering up his materials, 'if you'll thank God and His Mother for it first.'

'Oh, aye!' said Ned, shocked.

When Gil stepped out of the hall Mistress Doig was seated on the porter's bench in the courtyard, her expression grim. She looked up as he approached, impaling him with a hot dry stare. There was blood on her cheek; she must have kissed the dead man.

'What's he got tangled up in?' she demanded. 'Was it you sent for him? Why you and no his own maister?'

'You were close?' Gil said gently, sitting down beside her. She turned her face away.

'First cousins,' she said. 'My mother wouldny let me wed him.'

Revising his estimate of her age sharply downwards, Gil said, 'I'll pray for him. He died confessed and shriven, that must be a comfort.'

'Aye,' she said bleakly, 'and why? What for? Your man said those Murrays, or whatever they were, went for him a purpose.'

'That's what I'd like to know,' he answered. 'What can you tell me about it?'

'Me?' She stared at him again. 'What would I ken? Him and Doig never let on.'

'So he was in something with Doig,' he prompted. She nodded at that, looking down. 'What did you see? Did he come to the house with word for him? Bring messages?'

She nodded again.

'He'd turn up once in a while, saying he'd the evening free,' she said. 'I was aye glad to see him. Then one time I saw him slip Doig a letter o some kind.'

'Can your man read?'

'Oh, aye. Read and write and cipher.'

'Did you ask them what it was about?'

She looked at him.

'You've questioned Doig, maister,' she said bluntly. 'How would I get any more out of him than you?'

'I'm not wedded to him,' Gil pointed out. Her trap of a mouth twitched at that, but she said nothing. 'Was the letter for Doig, or for him to carry overseas?'

'He never tellt me.'

He pressed her a little, but she would not admit to knowing anything more, and he was unhappy about trading on her obvious grief. This was probably not the best time, either, to question Tam and Ned about Mitchel's reaction to his summons, he realized, and it was probably the only way he would find out anything now about the man's involvement in Stirling's death. He would have to come back out here later in the day, when the two might have recovered their spirits in the care of the convent Infirmary.

'Will I walk you home, mistress?' he offered. 'Is there a neighbour would sit with you?'

She shook her head, but rose to her feet, wearily, as if she carried a great burden.

'I've the dogs' dinner to see to,' she said. 'That won't wait.'

Making his way towards the Red Brig, Gil turned his next move over in his mind. He was uneasily aware that he needed to speak to the Sheriff or his depute; he knew he would have to carry the word of Mitchel's death to the Bishop's household. On the other hand, he still had a lot to find out, and neither task seemed likely to contribute to that. He paused beside Cornton's yard, looking over the planks of the fence at the silent sheds and drying-racks. If nobody drove his men to work, he thought, the tanner would find no business left when he was released. And that was what he had to do next: he must speak to Mistress Cornton.

The tanner's house was quiet, though when he rattled at the pin he could hear footsteps beyond the sturdy door. After a moment a shutter opened and the girl Eppie popped her head out, saying in a subdued voice:

'My mistress is no weel, maister, can your business wait? Oh,' she went on, recognizing him. 'It's you, is it? Was it you that got my maister thrown in the jail?'

'No,' he said firmly, 'I hope I can get him out. Can I get a word wi your mistress, lass?'

'Wait and I'll speir,' she said, and withdrew, closing the shutter. He waited on the fore-stair, watching the traffic in and out of the port, aware of voices inside the house, one querulous, one persuasive. Eventually Eppie's wooden soles clattered, and the door swung open.

'Just a wee word,' the girl said, and then in a whisper, 'and if you'd persuade her to take a morsel to eat, maister, it would be a kindness. I think she's swallowed nothing since Martin prentice came to the door to tell us. Will you come up, sir?' she added, more loudly. 'My mistress is abed, but she'll receive you.'

He was shocked by the change in the woman. Stepping into the upper chamber from the newel stair he found her lying back against the pillows of a handsome carved tester-bed. Her hair was straggling from under a night-cap tied beneath her chin, her shoulders were wrapped in a quilted garment of some sort, and the bright embroidered counterpane and pillow-bere showed signs of having been spread in haste and made her flushed face look almost

258

purple by contrast. He bowed, concealing his dismay, and said:

'I'm glad you could see me, mistress, but I'm right sorry to find you like this.'

'Can you help him?' she demanded, ignoring this. 'Can you get Cornton out of the jail? I never thought I'd be married on a man that got put in the jail.'

He came forward to sit down, and she reached out a claw-like hand to grasp his. Eppie placed herself by the neatly bagged curtain at the bed-foot, saying, 'Now, mistress, there's none of us believes it was him.'

'His customers will,' she said urgently. 'It's no good for trade, and besides I canny bear it, to think of him in all that dirt and the rats and all –'

'If you can tell me a thing or two,' Gil prompted, 'it might help him.'

'I'll try,' she said, staring at him, her grasp on his hand tightening. 'But I'm that dizzy, my head's going round like a mill, I canny think clearly.'

'That's no wonder,' he said with sympathy, and she managed a weak smile in response. 'What man was it they arrested with your husband?'

'Oh –' she said faintly, groping for the answer.

'That was Robin Hutchie,' supplied Eppie. 'He found the corp, so Martin prentice said, and Willie Reid said he should ha raised the hue and cry instead of just telling our maister, so he must be arrested.'

Gil nodded. The constable was following the proper procedures, but it was hard on the man Rob.

'And then he arrested Maister Cornton,' he said.

'Well, no at first,' said Eppie, 'by what Martin said, for he didny find it easy. But he lifted him away in the end.' She became aware that her mistress was weeping, and said awkwardly, 'We'll make him regret it, mistress, dinna fear.'

'Tell me, mistress,' said Gil, 'The day you last saw Maister Stirling, can you mind if your husband was home that evening?'

'Oh,' she said again through her tears. 'Oh, what evening would that be? I canny mind, maister.'

'It was the third evening the bairns was here,' said Eppie. 'You mind, mistress, the maister said that was two wet beds and he wasny sleeping in a flood again, and –' She bit off the words, looking embarrassed, and Gil pulled a face.

'It's hardly to be wondered at, poor bairns,' he said, 'but you can see his point. Where are they today?'

'I took them to my sister's,' said Eppie a little defiantly. 'She's got two near the same age, she said she'd take them the now till we're a bit –'

'My poor lassie's bairns,' whispered Mistress Cornton.

'That was wise, when the house is as troubled. But that evening,' Gil returned to the point, 'Maister Cornton was wanting to talk about where the bairns would sleep, is that right?' Mistress Cornton nodded. 'Was he home all the evening?'

'Oh, he was,' agreed Eppie, 'for once it was decided we'd to move a couple of kists and a truckle-bed, and me and Rob Hutchie was kept busy all the evening shifting them, and the Maister taking charge and telling Rob he was doing it wrong.'

'Would you swear to that, lass?' Gil asked her. She nodded emphatically. 'That ought to be enough. Tell me another thing, though. Is Maister Cornton a good shot?'

'A shot?' Mistress Cornton stared at him. 'What wi, a shot?'

'Wi an arrow,' said Eppie. 'Aye, he's no bad. He goes to the butts of a Sunday, maister, like the rest o them, though I'll say this,' she gave a subdued giggle, 'he's soberer when he comes home than my last maister.'

'A course he is,' said Mistress Cornton, with dawning indignation.

'Aye, that's better,' said Eppie obscurely.

'Does he have a bow?' Gil asked.

'Oh, aye, he's got a right good one,' Eppie said.

Her mistress nodded. 'From William Pitmedden, that's the armourer along the street, one of a batch he brought in from the Low Countries.' The quilted covering fell away from her arms as her fingers described a long elegant curve. 'It's a right bonnie thing, the way the grain shows in the layers and the different colours of the wood.'

'You mean it's a longbow?' Gil said hopefully.

'Oh. aye. He doesny like a crossbow. He's aye said there's nothing like a longbow.'

'He's aye arguing wi Brother Dickon about it,' said Eppie, with another subdued laugh. 'You'd no think a lay brother would be in favour of a crossbow, would you?'

'Does Brother Dickon shoot at the butts too?' Gil asked, amused by the idea.

'Shoot at them?' said Eppie scornfully. 'He oversees it all, orders who'll shoot next, tells them how to do better. He's in charge, is Brother Dickon.'

The Blackfriars' Infirmary had its own small garden, where Brother Euan the Infirmarer grew his herbs and where his patients might take the air. On a day like this it was warm and peaceful, full of the scents of the herbs and the chirping of a colony of sparrows in the holly tree which stood at one corner. Both of the day's ambulants were sitting there when Gil found the place, Ned dozing and Tam with his injured leg propped on a stool and a stout stick beside him. He looked up when Gil approached, and pushed the fair hair out of his eyes. His face was drawn, and pale under the tan, but he seemed to have no fever.

'I hoped you'd come back, Maister Gil,' he said. 'There's things you ought to hear, I couldny tell you at the time.'

'I thought that,' said Gil. 'How's the leg, first?'

'None so bad,' the man claimed.

'Poor way to get a day off,' Gil said. 'Tell me these things I ought to hear, then. Start at the beginning. What happened when you got to Dunkeld? Was it easy to find the man?'

261

'Oh, aye, no problem. He was lodged in the Bishop's palace, one of the household, just as you surmised. So we went there, the three of us, and spoke to the heid-bummer, fellow called Geddes, the depute steward, and showed him your letter.'

'How did he take that?' Gil asked.

Tam grinned crookedly. 'He wasny best pleased, for it seems Mitchel had been helping wi some heavy work needed about the place, shifting bales and sacks of goods and that, and he seemed to think you might wait till he'd finished.' He shifted his foot on the stool, and went on, 'We came to an agreement about that, wi a wee bit persuasion, and he swore to it that the fellow has been in Dunkeld since the date you asked him about in the letter, and then he sent for the man, and after a bit he came to this fellow's chamber.' He hesitated again. 'I'm no glad I did that, maister, for all it was by your command.'

'Tam, I think he killed James Stirling and hid the corp,' Gil said, irritated by this. 'If I'm right, he'd have hung for it. Instead he's had a quick death, and been shriven at that.'

'Aye, but he said he never,' said Tam. 'See, maister, he took one look at us, still in pot and plate,' he gestured to indicate a helmet, 'and the letter in the other fellow's hand, and he goes, *I never done it. I never killed him.*'

'Well, that's a bad conscience speaking!'

'That's what the other fellow said. What's his name, Geddes. And Ned and Donal made certain to be atween Mitchel and the door. But he said it again, no, he never killed him, he just helped put him away. And he's carrying on, and swearing by all sorts and more besides, and he keeps saying he never killed him.'

'Put him away,' repeated Gil.

'That's what he said. So then Ned says, *How did you put him away? Where did you put him?* And he says, *Into the tan-pit where Doig showed me. We cut a hurdle out the fence,* he says, *and carried him into the yard wi't,* and then he tells us they took the planks off a tanpit and tipped him in, and covered him up. Filthy job it was, too, and the dogs barking all the time, but he said it never took them that long, and Doig tied the hurdle back into the fence, and you'd never ha known he was there. He said he'd show you what tanpit it was, and he swore to the whole tale, offered to go up the High Kirk and swear by Columba's relics.'

'He's right,' said Gil, staring at Tam. 'You'd never have known it. So who did kill Stirling? Did you ask him that?'

'Oh, we did. Often and often. He aye said he didny see who shot him, all he saw was the man fall down among the dog-pens and when he got to him he was dead. He said, he didny ken what to do, whether to set up the hue and cry or no, for it seemed to him it could ha been someone on the track or in any of the yards or houses about, he said, but just then Doig cam back to the yard and found him there wi the corp, and created a stushie. Wouldny have a dead man found on his ground. And I think,' said Tam, the crooked grin appearing again, 'Mitchel wasny too keen what Doig's woman would say when she found out. Is she some kind o kin? And that's why he went along wi Doig's plans to hide the corp.'

Gil considered this, gazing at a brown butterfly which was sunning its wings on the bed of marjoram nearest them.

'It's a good story,' he admitted. 'But did the man say why he and Stirling were in the Doigs' yard? What took him there?'

'He said,' said Tam doubtfully, 'it was an order from their lord. From the Bishop.'

'From the *Bishop*?'

'That's what Ned said. And Mitchel said, Aye, he was sent from the house to find Maister Stirling, that was still walking on the meadow by the Blackfriars, and bid him go to the dog-breeder's yard and ask for a bar of her soap against fleas, for the wee dog.'

'Sent? Who by?'

Tam shrugged.

'We tried asking that, but he just said it was the Bishop's errand. He seemed mighty certain it was the Bishop's message and all.'

Gil contemplated the idea. It did not seem to fit into the picture at all. He visualized Stirling, summoned from his meditation by the Ditch. He would have walked round to Mistress Doig's yard taking Mitchel with him, waited in the yard for Mistress Doig herself to return, perhaps talked to some of the dogs again. Did the liver-and-white bitch go for him too? he wondered. Then, almost silent, wholly unexpected, the crossbow bolt struck home, Stirling dropped dead. But who held the crossbow? And by whose order?

'Maybe the Bishop right enough?' Tam suggested. 'Could he ha wanted rid o him?'

'Maybe.' Gil stared at the butterfly again. 'Did Mitchel say anything else at all, Tam? Why was he in Dunkeld? Who sent him there? Did he mention the hat?'

'Oh, that was the mimmerkin's idea, by what he said. Mitchel had to leave it by the Ditch so folk would think he'd fell in. As for who sent him to Dunkeld, he never said, only that he was ordered there as soon as he showed his face the next morning, no even time to let his kinsfolk know he'd be away.'

'And then kept there kicking his heels, with nothing but maintenance work to do, for two weeks,' said Gil. He sprang to his feet and strode up and down, as if that would make his mind work more clearly. He was nearly there, he knew it. Some of the cords that linked this knot to the one in Balquhidder still had to be loosened, but he was fairly sure of why James Stirling had been killed. If he could just establish who it was who had killed him, he could take the whole thing to the Bishop, and account for his summons to Mitchel MacGregor in the same breath.

'Did you say the man was shot, Maister Gil?' said Tam.

'Aye, with a crossbow.' Gil paused in his pacing. 'He was enticed out to the dog-breeder's yard, and someone shot him while he stood waiting there.'

'I was out that way when we were in Perth afore,' said Tam. 'It's right in the midst of other yards and gardens, is it no? How would he get close enough?'

'It must have been a longish shot, but our man could have hidden close to the yard. He could even have stood on the track itself and aimed across several fences. I'm certain he was a good shot, it had struck the base of the skull just where it needed to.'

Tam nodded his understanding of this, but said gloomily, 'And how would you find out who in Perth would be that good a shot? There must be plenty folk can use a bow.'

'Near a'body can use a bow,' concurred Ned, suddenly opening his eyes. 'That's what for they all goes out to the butts on a Sunday.'

'And there's my answer,' said Gil. 'I need to find Brother Dickon.'

Making his way back to the Bishop's house by the busy streets, he thought through all he had learned so far today. It was extraordinary how the two problems had proved to be linked; he wondered briefly if Blacader had suspected that, or if he had simply assumed that his quaestor could handle two sets of questions at once. Either possibility was gratifying, he considered, stepping round a stout burgess who was bargaining with a patten-maker.

Deep in thought he might be, but his senses were alert, and when the man darted out of the crowd, the short blade glinting as it rose, it did not take the stout burgess's cry of 'Ware cutpurse!' in his ear to rouse him to action. Almost before he knew it his whinger was in his hand, his other arm was swinging up across the attacker's throat, his blade was striking the knife aside. He stared, briefly, into a worried, sweaty face under an ordinary blue bonnet, and dimly noticed a leather doublet, hempen shirtsleeves, bare forearms, a smell of horses. The stout burgess was still shouting, and lunging forward to help. His whinger

265

came round again almost of its own volition, caught the weapon hand.

His assailant cried out and ducked sideways, dropping the dagger, and took to his heels through a rising torrent of exclamations and grasping hands. Gil turned and pushed after him, shouting 'Stop thief! Hold him!' through an eddy of noise which built up along the street as people turned to see what was happening, exclaimed, reached for one man or another.

With some trouble, he managed to get as far as the corner of the Northgate, and realized he had lost his quarry. He stood still, heart hammering, breathing deeply and staring over the heads, but there was no disturbance to the cheerful bustle of the street. The man must have ducked down a vennel, or else simply stopped running and lost himself in the crowd. Every other man in the burgh wore a blue bonnet, and in this weather many were in doublet and shirtsleeves, he would never pick him out by his clothes.

'Did you ever!' said a voice in his ear. It was a stout citizen in a blue stuff gown and felt hat, clutching his own purse securely at his belt and puffing slightly. 'I never saw sic boldness! To try for your purse in broad day, and then to get away like that!'

'Was it you that shouted?' said Gil, understanding. 'My thanks, man.'

'It's up to us all to keep an eye to each other's purse,' declared the burgess, 'and Our Lady be thanked he never got your money.'

It wasn't the money he was after, Gil thought, turning towards the Bishop's house again. That blade was going for the heart. Now I know I'm close to the solution.

'Do you say, Maister Cunningham,' said George Brown formally, 'that you have discerned who slew Jaikie?'

'I have, sir,' agreed Gil. At the Bishop's side Rob Gregor bleated in what seemed to be dismay. 'And I think I've learned more than that.'

266

'Well, let me have his name, maister,' requested the Bishop. His dog, curled in the basket by his feet, raised its head to look at Gil.

'First, could we have your steward in, with Maister Stirling's kist?'

'His gear's all in order,' said Maister Gregor. 'I packed it up mysel, my lord, when Wat asked me, and made a list and all.'

'Why do you want Wat present?' asked the Bishop over his chaplain's assurances.

'If he could bring the kist,' Gil said, 'I'll make all clear.'

Brown rang the bell on his desk and gave the order, then sat in brooding silence, his round face shadowed and serious, until Currie arrived with two servants bearing the kist by its rope handles.

'Wat,' the Bishop said. 'Set it down there and wait. Maister Cunningham has something to tell us.'

Currie turned a startled face to Gil, but dismissed one of the servants and muttered in the ear of the other, the man Noll, who looked sharply at his superior then nodded and went out. Jerome bustled across the chamber to inspect the kist, snuffling at the leather strap which held it shut. Currie bent and patted the dog, then stood back against the wall to wait as he was bidden.

'Well, maister?' said the Bishop.

Gil settled himself on the padded backstool, gathering his concentration, wishing Alys was present. If I could explain a head in a barrel to the King, he thought, I can explain a man in a tanpit to a Bishop. But I'd sooner be more certain of the facts.

His audience was waiting.

'We know,' he began, 'that Maister Stirling was party to the negotiations for the English treaty, and we know that some of the terms of the treaty have got to ears or eyes they should never have got to. We also know,' he said carefully, 'that Maister Stirling was at the sang-schule in Dunblane along with Andrew Drummond, and also with

David Drummond, who vanished, and William Murray, who is now Precentor at Dunkeld.'

'He's told me that often,' said Maister Gregor happily. 'At least, no about the laddie that vanished.' He paused, finding his master looking at him, and bleated in faint apology.

'But are the two connected?' asked the Bishop.

'More than you'd think,' said Gil. 'You've described him to me as an able man, my lord, a good secretary, well content with his position here.' Brown nodded. 'I've also heard of his humour, of his trick of making clever remarks at other folk's expense, though he seemed not to make enemies by it.'

'Och, no, he was a right good friend,' protested Maister Gregor, 'you could never take offence at what he said –' He subsided as his master looked at him again.

'Now, the day he vanished, Stirling went out to see about the rents as you bade him, my lord.' Brown nodded, his mouth tightening. 'Then he saw his own tenants, and then he went out to the dog-breeder's yard, looking for Doig himself rather than Mistress Doig. I think you'd given him no errand there, my lord.'

'That's right,' agreed Brown. He bent and scooped up his dog to set it on his knee. 'I sent him out about the rents, he'd no errand to the dog-breeder that day. So what had he to do wi this man Doig?'

'Doig,' said Gil carefully, 'seems to run a regular messenger service to the Low Countries. It was Doig called away the singer that's gone missing from Dunblane, though I've no proof he spoke to the two men here in Perth. He's good at shifting information, and I think now he's shifting people as well.'

'I knew it,' said Currie in deep regret. 'I feared it. So Jaikie was –'

'Hold your peace, Wat,' said the Bishop, still caressing Jerome.

'I thought so too,' said Gil. At his tone Brown looked up from his dog. 'In Mistress Doig's yard, Stirling met Canon

Drummond, who was also looking for Doig. They got into conversation, which the woman described to me as being like two dogs circling one another with their fangs showing. Stirling made some of his clever remarks, and the two of them ended up going off to the Ditchlands to talk the whole afternoon.'

'So was it Drummond?' said Brown. He reached for his tablets. 'I'll send to Dunblane and have them summon him –'

'He's in Balquhidder,' Gil said. 'No, my lord, I think it wasn't Drummond. I'll come to why not in a wee while.'

'So what came to him?' asked Brown. 'Maister Cunningham, I ken you're a busy man, and so am I. I'd be grateful if you'd get on and tell me what I'm needing to know.'

Gil nodded, but continued in the same measured tone.

'I've asked Drummond what they spoke of, and he claims the secrecy of confession – that each of them confessed to the other. I've learned from one or two other sources that they spoke of betrayal and forgiveness.'

'Betrayal!' said Currie. 'Who had he –?' The Bishop glanced at him, but said nothing.

'Drummond,' pursued Gil, 'went on into Perth and likely had a bite to eat, found Doig and had a word wi him, then spent the rest of the evening in St John's Kirk afore St Andrew. I've a good witness for that.'

Bishop Brown nodded his understanding, but Maister Gregor said, 'Oh, no, surely no, if he'd just slew –'

'Hold your tongue, Rob,' said Brown.

'Now,' said Gil carefully, 'Stirling had been accompanied on his errand. One of the household servants had gone with him.'

'Very proper,' said Brown, 'but if that's so, why did the man no come forward after, when Jaikie never returned home? Or is that –?' He turned an appalled gaze on his steward. 'Wat, has one o our men –?'

'I'd vouch for all of them, my lord,' said Currie.

'He's made his confession,' said Gil ambiguously. 'It

seems Stirling sent him back to the house, saying he'd walk on the Ditchlands for a space.'

'You mean you've spoke wi him? Who is it?' demanded Currie.

'A man called Mitchel MacGregor,' Gil replied.

'Mitchel?' exclaimed Currie, with a faint echo which must have been Maister Gregor. 'Christ preserve us, what's he done?'

'I thought he was in Dunkeld,' said Brown.

'He was,' agreed Gil. 'He is now in the care of the Blackfriars.'

'Oh, what a terrible thing! Will Wat send to the Black-friars, my lord,' asked Maister Gregor, 'and get him fetched here? Or will you go out to question him yoursel maybe?'

'Go on, Maister Cunningham,' said the Bishop rather grimly, ignoring this.

'Mitchel returned here,' said Gil, 'and was sent out again with a message for Stirling, bidding him go to the dog-breeder and ask her for some of her soap against fleas.'

'Fleas!' exclaimed Currie. 'The wee dog's never had fleas!'

'And who sent him this errand?' asked Bishop Brown.

'He seemed very clear,' Gil said with care, 'that it was an errand for yourself, my lord.' Brown shook his head. 'So Stirling went to the Doigs' yard, with the man Mitchel, and found Mistress Doig from home walking the dogs.'

'Aye, they'll need to be exercised,' agreed Maister Gregor. 'They get melancholy if they don't get exercised.'

'Rob, hold your tongue,' said Brown again. 'Wat, where are you away to, man?'

'I'll just send a couple men out to the Blackfriars,' suggested Currie from the door, 'the way Maister Gregor says, and they can –'

'We'll hear Maister Cunningham out,' said his master, 'and then I'll determine what's to be done. Stay here and close that door. Come on, Maister Cunningham, let's get this done wi.'

'Mitchel says they waited in the yard,' Gil continued, 'talking to the dogs or the like, for a wee bit, and then Maister Stirling fell down dead.'

Three shocked faces stared at him.

'But he'd been shot wi a crossbow bolt,' said the Bishop, recovering first. 'Was it no Mitchel that shot him?'

'He swore it was not,' Gil said. 'He said he never saw who loosed the bolt.' And that's entirely hearsay, he thought, and would never stand as evidence at law, but it serves my purpose.

'You're fairly taking your time,' said the Bishop irritably. 'I suppose you're making it clear, man, but we've still the two questions. Who killed Jaikie, and how did he get into the tanpit? Was it Andrew Cornton right enough? I'd thought it wasny, but –'

'Maister Cornton spent the entire evening in his own house,' said Gil. 'They were moving furniture. His maidservant will swear to it.'

'Aye, but surely a man's own household will swear for him –' began Maister Gregor.

'There's one of my household done me a very ill turn,' said Brown grimly. 'Go on, maister. Who was it, then, if it wasny Cornton?'

'I want to check something first,' said Gil. He bent and drew the kist towards him, startling Jerome as it rumbled across the floorboards. 'There was a crossbow in this kist when we checked it before, you mind that, Maister Currie?'

'Aye, there was, and a good one,' agreed Currie. 'It's right on the top, next his razors.' He came forward and helped Gil to unfasten the strap and open the lid. 'You see, it's well kept, well oiled –'

Gil pushed the pup away, lifted the crossbow and drew it out of its linen bag. The weapon was, as Currie said, a good one, and well cared for. He turned it over, admiring the finish and shaping of stock and crosspiece. Not an ounce of spare timber, he judged.

'An arbalest!' exclaimed the Bishop. 'I never knew Jaikie had an arbalest.'

'Nor did I, my lord,' said Maister Gregor.

'Our Lady save you, my lord, it's no an arbalest,' said Currie over the old man's remark. 'You'd never get an arbalest into thon wee kist. It's a crossbow, just.'

'It's a crossbow,' agreed Gil. 'Not my weapon, but my brother Edward was skilled with the crossbow.' He held it up, sighting along the stock, then passed it to Currie, whose hands closed on it covetously. 'It's a bonnie thing, but it's unusable.'

'Unusable?' said Currie sharply, staring at him. 'How's it unusable?'

'There's no means of bracing it.' Gil gestured at Maister Gregor's inventory lying in the open lid of the kist. 'There should be a belt-hook, or a goat's foot, or the like.'

'I thought that,' remarked Maister Gregor proudly.

Seeing the Bishop's blank look, Gil explained, 'It's the means of bracing the bow so it can be loosed, my lord. The arblaster sets his foot in yon stirrup at the nose of the bow,' he pointed, and Currie raised the weapon, which he was still cradling. 'Then he attaches something to the cord, and straightens up, and that draws the cord and lodges it there –' He pointed to the nut that held the cord braced till the bow was loosed, and the Bishop peered closer and looked away again, shuddering.

'It's an unchristian weapon,' he declared. 'So you're saying Jaikie couldna loose this?'

'Nobody could loose it,' Gil said, 'because nobody could brace it.'

'I thought that too, you ken,' repeated Maister Gregor. Everyone else turned to him, and he ducked his head and bleated in faint dismay at the attention. 'When I put all Jaikie's gear by,' he said almost pleadingly. 'I saw there was no means to brace the cord, and I saw there was no bolts to it and all.'

'So why is it in his kist, if he couldny use it?' demanded the Bishop.

272

'I think it isn't his. I think someone hid it among his gear,' said Gil. Brown met his eye across the chamber, but was silent. 'Maybe in haste, so that he forgot to lodge the belt-hook and the bolts there too.'

'What use would that be?' wondered Maister Gregor. 'He could never use it, whoever it belongs to, while it was in Jaikie's kist.'

'Maister Gregor,' said Gil. The old man looked at him, still frowning in puzzlement. 'Did you tell me you had walked in the garden that evening, the evening Maister Stirling died?'

'I did, I did that, though a course,' he qualified, 'I never knew Jaikie was dead then.' He crossed himself and murmured something. Gil waited till he finished, then went on:

'I think you said my lord was there too, with Jerome.' The chaplain nodded. 'Do you recall that, my lord?'

'I do,' said Brown. 'Wat, be still. Where are you off to, man?'

'You'll want a couple of the men –' Currie began.

'Be still,' said Brown again, quite mildly, and the steward's feet were rooted to the spot. 'I also recall that the supper was late, and I can see by the way you hold it that you know every inch of that dreadful weapon. Wat, why did you kill Jaikie?'

'No!' Currie fell to his knees, his plump face suddenly glistening with sweat. 'No, I never, I didny! It wasny me!'

'I'm told you're the best shot with a crossbow in Perth,' Gil said, and then with sudden comprehension, 'and Mitchel named you as he died, man.'

'I never – I never did! I had to!'

'Who was it then?' asked the Bishop, looking very solemn, his voice gentle. 'Who killed Jaikie Stirling, Wat, if it wasna you? Or why would you have to? A man never has to kill, Wat, you ken that.'

'Maister Gregor knows why he killed him,' said Gil.

'Oh, aye,' agreed Maister Gregor. 'Er – me? Ken why? Why?'

'Tell me again,' Gil invited, 'the crack Jaikie made at Wat's expense that day at the noon bite. Tell my lord.'

'At the – oh! Aye, it was right comical.' He recounted the tale of the new way to cook mutton yet again, clearly unaware of what he was saying. Gil met the Bishop's eye.

'Write it down,' he repeated, *'and sell it in the Low Countries.* Maister Stirling had realized who was selling information. He had to be killed before he told you.'

'Why did he no tell me first off?'

'I was doing no sic a thing!' protested Currie, scrambling to his feet. 'I never – I would have –'

'The man Mitchel?' said Brown to Gil. Gil shook his head.

'Mitchel is dead,' he said. 'My men were attacked outside the town as they brought him to Perth today. But I've spoken to Doig, I've spoken to his wife, and –'

'Stop him!' exclaimed the Bishop. Gil spun round, in time to see Currie dive out of the door, fling himself across the next room and on to the stair. He plunged after him, followed by an excited Jerome, as shouting and the sounds of a fight broke out below them.

'Let me pass, you fools!' howled Currie. 'I've an errand won't wait! Let me pass!'

'Hold him, lads!' Gil shouted, swung himself down the newel stair after the steward, and leapt on to the battle at its foot. The two Stronvar men he had posted there, Ned's henchmen, were having trouble holding Currie. More of the Bishop's servants were appearing in answer to his cries for help, but with Gil's assistance they were held off and the man was overcome, his arms pinned at his sides, the point of Gil's dagger under his chin, while his master came down the stair at a more dignified pace.

'Take and bind him,' the Bishop said, 'and send to the constable to come for him. Treason is a plea of the Crown,' he said to his servant, 'and by Christ I'll see you tried and hung by the Crown for this, clerk or no clerk, Wat Currie. And bid the constable release the man Cornton now.'

* * *

'I still don't see how Jaikie got into the tanpit,' said Maister Gregor. 'And the badges and all, what had the badges to do wi't?'

'Nor I,' admitted Bishop Brown. 'Can you tell us that, Maister Cunningham?'

After the steward had been removed, still struggling and protesting his innocence, the two churchmen had spent some considerable time at prayer. Gil had occupied himself in searching the man's own chamber, with two of the Bishop's men as witnesses. He had found documents sufficient to condemn Currie out of hand, notes of the content of the English treaty, a half-written letter to a Fleming whose name Brown recognized ('Margaret of Burgundy uses him,' he said cryptically) and other papers which the Bishop immediately confiscated and placed in his own locked kist.

'The badges have nothing to do with it,' Gil said, 'excepting that they led us to find Stirling's body. He'd given his badge of St Dymphna –'

'That was her!' exclaimed Maister Gregor. 'Diffna!'

'To Andrew Drummond, for reasons connected with whatever they confessed to each other that afternoon on the Ditchlands. It was sewn on to the hat, he'd have had to cut it off, and I suppose loosened the Eloi badge at the same time, and that fell off when Doig and the man Mitchel were getting his body into the tanyard.'

'I see,' said the Bishop. 'So it's St Eloi's doing, or perhaps St Dymphna's, that he was found and can be given Christian burial.'

'It is,' agreed Gil, taken with this. 'If – I'll not speculate what they discussed –'

'No, of course not,' the Bishop said quickly.

'– but if it's what I suspect, then it would be agreeable to St Dymphna to have it cleared up and all forgiven. I can see that she might protect him so far.'

It would have been more to the point if she had prevented his death, he thought, but did not say so in this company.

'If either confessed the other,' said Maister Gregor, 'then Jaikie died shriven. Had you thought of that, my lord?'

'That's a true word, Rob,' said the Bishop, much struck. 'And a comforting thought, at that. But the man Mitchel –'

'He was shriven by the Infirmarers,' said Gil quickly.

'Aye, and sore need of it. He was far from blameless,' said the Bishop with disapproval. 'He was Currie's own servant, I suppose he obeyed him without question, but –'

'And Mistress Doig is his kinswoman,' Gil said. 'I suppose that led Currie to Doig, or the other way about.'

'I'll have the woman out of that yard,' said the Bishop. 'She'll not remain on my doorstep. As for her husband, I want him found.'

'He's a slippery character,' Gil said. 'You may find all he's done is carry letters, with no certain knowledge of their content.'

If you can find either one, he thought, recalling the sight of Doig and his wife leaving Glasgow a year since, an hour ahead of the pursuit, with the largest mixed leash of hounds he had ever seen.

'And who is St Dymphna, anyway?' asked George Brown, Bishop of Dunkeld.

Chapter Fourteen

Alys, standing with the Drummond girls on the rough grass of the preaching-field, gazed round her at the people of Sir Duncan's parish. They were still gathering, the stragglers from the far end of the glen, the last few people from Glenbuckie still hurrying over the causeway. They carried crosses, scraps of linen inscribed with ill-spelled prayers, rosaries, anything to protect the sanctity of the occasion. The old man was drowsing now, lying on his bed of sheepskins at the centre of the bowl of ground, but Robert was still tolling that strange sweet bell, and the people watched in a silence broken by the occasional sob, a child's question, a hushed adult answer.

'Sir Duncan is much loved,' Alys said quietly to Ailidh Drummond.

'There is not many can recall the man that was before him,' said Ailidh, equally quietly.

As the last parishioners reached the field, Robert silenced the bell. Sir Duncan opened his eyes. A murmur ran through the gathering, and he raised one hand and delivered a blessing in Latin. Daughter of a master-builder, Alys recognized how it was some trick of the shape of the ground that made his thread of a voice audible to all. People bent their heads, crossed themselves, said *Amen* with that strange Ersche twist to the word. The old priest surveyed them, and began to speak, very slowly, in Ersche.

He spoke for near a quarter of an hour, Alys estimated. After a while, as his voice failed, the aged clerk began to repeat each sentence aloud for him. She had long since lost the thread by then, though the words she recognized told her it was a sermon about love, about duty, about redemption. Instead she watched the people, who were listening to every syllable, many with tears on their cheeks. Most were in the dress of the Highlands, the men in their belted shirts and huge plaids, the women in loose checked gowns, their smaller plaids drawn over their heads; the upper servants from Stronvar and Gartnafueran were conspicuous in their Lowland livery. Next to Alys, Ailidh Drummond gazed intently, chewing a forefinger; Murdo Dubh had appeared beyond her and the younger girls were gathered close. She looked the other way, and found a man in a long homespun gown and faded plaid standing beside her, right at the edge of the crowd, leaning on a long crook and watching the faces in the same way that she was. He was oddly made, tall and broad-shouldered with a small head and greying red hair.

He turned to look at her. She had a momentary impression of a bony face, of an unnaturally high forehead (or was he bald? or shaved?) before she was swamped by a sea-green stare which seemed to look right into her soul. Without having to think about it, she curtsied.

'Davie needs you, daughter,' he said.

'Me?' she said, startled. 'Where is he?'

'Yonder.' He nodded towards the priest's house. 'Go now, daughter. This is nearly done.'

Hurrying up the path towards the stone house, she could hear the voices. They were so intent on their discussion that she reached the door unnoticed.

'I can't go yet, Billy. There's things to sort out. I'll not leave without telling them –'

'I have to go now, you wee daftheid! If yon Cunningham's got so far, he'll have jaloused the rest by Vespers, I need to be out of sight for a bit.'

'Then go, and I'll meet you in Perth, or Leith, or somewhere –'

'Aye, and how will you get to Leith on your own? I'd never look your faither in the ee again if I –'

Alys rattled at the pin and the argument was cut off. She stepped into the house, to find Davie Drummond standing by the glowing peats on the hearth, facing an indignant Doig who scowled at him across the width of the house.

'My husband has left Balquhidder already, Maister Doig,' she said politely. 'Does that affect your decision?'

'Spoke to you and all, has he?' Doig snorted, and turned away, opening one of the kists against the far wall. 'Robert has the rights o't. Best no to get into conversation wi thon one.'

'Mistress Alys,' said Davie. 'What – I thought you –'

'I was told you needed me,' she said.

'No,' he said, puzzled. 'I sent no word. Will you – will you have a seat?'

She took the stool he offered, and looked from one to the other of them.

'It's good to see you, Maister Doig,' she said. 'The wolfhound is doing well.'

'I seen the brute,' said Doig, delving in the kist. 'Heard it was you he wedded,' he added. 'I'll wish you good fortune, mistress.'

'Thank you, maister,' she replied composedly, hoping he referred to Gil and to Socrates separately. 'Are you just leaving Balquhidder? Do you have a horse?' *A dwarf from the cyte of Camelot, on horsbak as moche as he myght,* she thought, relishing the image. This forceful man could equal any of Malory's characters.

'I'll manage, thanks,' said Doig, without looking round.

'Will you have – will you have some refreshment?' Davie offered. 'Ale, or buttermilk, or the like?'

Drinking the buttermilk, enjoying its sharp flavour, she studied Davie and said, 'You're right, there are things that must be said before you leave.' Bright colour washed up over Davie's face. 'How many of them know?'

'Know what?'

'What you have to tell them.' Two could play at this

game. 'Now Mistress Drummond is gone, there is no need to pretend further.'

Davie looked down at the glow of the peats, and nodded reluctantly.

'Maister Cunningham bade me talk to you,' he admitted. 'He has the rights of it, it was my father that was stolen away thirty year since. I never meant – it was one thing Euan Beag taking me for my father, poor soul, but then the *cailleach* did the same, and I was so amazed I didn't contradict her, and then –'

'It would be hard to explain,' Alys agreed, 'and it would get harder.'

'Every time I spoke!'

'And it was Maister Doig fetched you here.'

'No such thing,' said Doig sharply. Davie shook his head, apparently to contradict this denial.

'Billy here was one of the company that lifted my father away, and saw him to the Low Countries.' Doig growled at this and went on stuffing a scrip. 'He came back a few year syne to see how my father got on.'

'I cam back,' corrected Doig, 'when yir Dimpnakerk burnt down, and found yir faither high in the choir, chapel-maister or whatever they cry it, and him widowed.'

'Never one to miss an opportunity, is Billy,' commented Davie. 'We're building a fine new Dimpnakerk, and there'll be a fine new choir to sing in it.'

'And you already have three of the voices,' said Alys, understanding.

'And more,' said Doig. 'Scots singers are weel thought on, but they're no the only ones.' He looked round the house, and crossed with his rolling gait to fetch a pair of heelless shoes from the shadows under one bed. 'Right, that's me. I'll just need to wait for Robert, I'll not go without a word to him.'

'But Sir Duncan –' objected Davie.

'The two o you can sit up wi him, and see you behave yoursels. He'll no last the night, particular after this.' He jerked his head in the direction of the preaching-field.

'Dimpnakerk,' Alys repeated. 'That is the shrine to St Dymphna, am I right? And she heals mad people?'

'The folk o Gheel heal the mad people,' corrected Doig.

'With St Dymphna's help,' said Davie.

'They take them into their own homes,' Doig said to Alys, 'and treat them like family. More than I'd do, for no kin –'

'Billy, we are all kin! We're all God's children, and Our Lady is our mother!'

'Hush,' said Alys. 'What's that?'

'Is that him away?' said Doig, listening.

There were only a few voices at first, singing in Ersche. Then gradually more joined them, some above the note, some below it, rising in the song Alys had heard before, the song for the departing soul. More and more voices, high and low, swooped through the summer noon, till the melody seemed to be braided out of shining ribbons of sound, slow and heartbreaking.

'*Lead this soul on your arm, o Christ,*' Davie translated softly, '*o king of the Kingdom of Heaven. Since it was you that bought this soul, have its peace in your keeping. May Michael, high king of the angels, prepare the path before the soul.*'

'That was what you sang for your grandmother,' Alys said. He nodded, his eyes glittering in the glow from the peat fire.

'They're coming back,' said Doig from the door. 'I doubt he's no deid yet, the way they're carrying him.'

'Mistress Alys,' said Davie, in a sudden rush. 'Would you – will you – if Billy's leaving, will you come back and watch wi Robert and me?'

When she returned some hours later, the house was surrounded. Still clutching their talismans, linen and crosses and rosaries, against the dangers of the night, Sir Duncan's people watched with him, a steady murmur of prayers drifting into the darkening air. Leaving her escort by the little kirk Alys approached through the velvety summer twilight and they made way for her, but she felt like an intruder, a stranger in the house of the dying. As she and Lady Stewart had suspected there was no need of a third person under Sir Duncan's roof; there was a group of people at the door, waiting to take their turn within the house, and Robert and Davie had been relegated to the bench at the gable of the house.

'Martainn clerk is with him just now. I'd be just as glad if you stayed, mistress,' said Davie, when she commented.

'Robert?' she asked.

'You might as well,' he said in his ungracious way.

'Doig got away, did he?'

'He did,' said Robert. 'Thanks to your man that he had to go.'

'We went into all that, Robert,' said Davie. The two were dark shapes against the stonework of the gable, still glowing faintly in the green remnants of the sunset. They seemed to be sitting shoulder to shoulder, as if for comfort. She sat down at Davie's other side.

'He's in no pain,' said Robert after a moment. 'That's a grace. My grandsire – Aye, well.' Davie moved; Alys thought he put a hand over Robert's. 'And he's been confessed, your – your uncle saw to that, and shrived him and all. But it's taking him so long!'

'It's a long road,' said Davie. 'A long road, and a hard one.'

'Tell me about Gheel,' said Alys softly.

After a moment Davie began to describe the town, so vividly she could almost see it, its narrow streets and squares, the tall white kirk growing in its midst with the striped tower beside it, and the poor creatures with their injured minds walking about where they were treated with love and respect rather than being taunted and tormented.

'It's all some of them need,' he said, 'to be treated like ordinary folk, but a lot of them need physicking as well, and there are aye some that are too wild to live out at first, they're tended in the hospital. They go home cured, or they die, or they stay wi us for ever. As St Dymphna chooses.'

'I'd like to do that,' said Robert after a thoughtful silence.

'What, cure the mad?'

'Look after the mad,' Robert corrected. 'It's a service. I could do it.'

'You could,' said Davie, considering it in a way that told Alys he knew why Robert was here. 'It would be a – yes, you could!' he exclaimed.

Would Robert's uncle permit it, Alys wondered.

'No ropes round the neck?' he was asking. 'No chains?'

The two voices murmured on in the shadows. Alys leaned back against the house wall, listening carefully, but she was still very weary and after a time she lost the thread of their conversation.

A sharp movement woke her. She sat up straight, closing her mouth, and discovered that it was full dark, they sat under a field of stars, and her companions were silent, though the hum of prayers still surrounded the house, like bees in clover. Then she became aware of tension beside her, of someone – Davie? – taut as a bowstring and breathing fast, of Robert suddenly sitting at the further end of the bench. What had happened?

'I'm sorry,' whispered someone, almost inaudible. Had there been a sound before the movement? A tiny sound, like a kiss?

The house door opened, shedding lamplight which gleamed on weary faces and prayerful hands in front of it, but cast the three of them into shadow here at the gable. A tall figure strode round the corner, broad shoulders black against the stars, stick in hand.

'It is near ended, my son,' said a voice. The same voice that had spoken to Alys in the preaching-field, the red-haired man's voice. 'Go within now, it is your turn. You have earned the right.'

Robert stood up, hesitated as if he looked back at Davie, or Alys, or the red-haired man; then he moved obediently towards the house door. Beside Alys Davie rose, and she heard him trying to calm his breathing.

'Will I go too?'

'No. Your duty together is not yet.' The dark shape moved, as if to set a hand on his forehead. 'The calumny is avenged, for the woman was swearing falsely, but there is things you must be setting right and all, Davie Drummond.'

'I ken that,' said Davie.

'The blessing of Angus be upon you,' said the man. 'And upon you, my daughter.'

'Amen,' Alys said. Something touched her bent head, lightly. When she looked up the tall figure had gone, though it was too dark to move swiftly.

There was a sudden outbreak of wailing at the house door, and within Robert's voice rose in Latin. The prayer for the dead.

'They'll regret waiting this long,' observed Sir William.

'It's no more than three days,' said his lady.

'Aye, but in this heat?'

Alys kept silent. She was not entirely sure whether she should be present at Mistress Drummond's burying, but she had been determined to attend.

She had already taken a liking to her hostess, but the heroism with which Lady Stewart had refrained from questioning her until she was ready to talk had won her deep respect. They had spent the whole of yesterday afternoon in the solar discussing the events in Glenbuckie and in the Kirkton. The Bailie's wife had taken a pragmatic attitude to the death of the child Iain.

'He was an innocent. He'd likely go straight into Our Lady's arms, for I ken he was baptised, so he's in a better place and his people are better without him and all.'

'But surely –' Alys had protested. The older woman looked pityingly at her across her needlework.

284

'Out here, the way they work the land, they're never more than one bad summer away from famine. It's a thought to feed a bairn that willny work for you in its turn.'

She heard her own voice, talking to Gil. *I may not know about country life, but I have lived in towns all my days.* Quite so, she thought.

'So it was the Good Neighbours,' she said aloud.

'It was. And Dalriach might as well blame the fire on them and all, if it stops Caterin making trouble for young David. What do you think of that matter now? Sìne tells me he has spent the day in the loft in the kirk and won't come down.'

'I think the Good Neighbours may take Davie back soon as well.'

'Do you now?' Lady Stewart's needle was arrested again. 'Even though Patrick has accepted him?'

'Maybe because Patrick has accepted him.'

So now she stood near the edge of the circular kirkyard, too hot in her best black velvet headdress with the gold wire braid and a great black cloak borrowed from her hostess, and watched while Andrew Drummond, in the vestments out of the kist in the priest's house, committed his mother and his nephew to the earth. He was dry-eyed, his harsh voice giving nothing away; round him the men of the family in their best clothes watched solemnly, Jamie Beag and Patrick, Davie with Murdo Dubh beside him. The other men of Dalriach were present, a stranger in plaid and feathered bonnet who must be the son-in-law, and a few men of the Kirkton still in their working shirts, but none of the folk from the glen, and no women at all apart from herself and Lady Stewart, not even the boy's mother.

'They'll bury Sir Duncan tomorrow,' said Lady Stewart. Alys nodded; that much she could understand. St Angus' fair had been postponed till after the priest's burial; the entire parish would wish to see Sir Duncan to his grave and be at the fair as well, and three days in a row away from the harvest was too much.

285

Robert was present in the kirkyard too. He had acted as Andrew's clerk for the Mass. Watching him now, Alys recognized that he had placed himself where he need not see Davie Drummond, though every so often he could not help looking for him. Davie, on the other hand, was conspicuously not looking at Robert.

'I'm glad to see Robert about,' said Lady Stewart. 'Sìne says he never crossed the threshold of Sir Duncan's house yesterday, either, I feared he was going to fall into melancholy. He's done well by the old man, poor laddie. It's been a hard road for him.'

Alys nodded again, thinking of the moments before Sir Duncan died, and then of Lady Stewart's reply when she had asked about the red-haired man.

'Red hair?' she had said. 'No, I don't think so. Most of our people are dark, except the MacGregors, and he doesn't sound like any MacGregor I can think of. And if Sìne's right he was up at Dalriach and all,' she added thoughtfully.

'He was going bald. His hair was back behind his ears.' Alys demonstrated the retracted hairline.

'What was his accent? Ersche or Scots?'

'I don't know,' Alys said in dawning disbelief. 'He just spoke to me. That's strange, I can usually tell the difference.'

The mourners were tossing clods of earth into the grave. Sir William stirred, and muttered a prayer, then strode forward to say something appropriate and accept the invitation to ride back to Dalriach. Lady Stewart crossed herself and said:

'That's over, then. It'll no be the same in Glenbuckie without her.'

'I suppose Mòr will take her place,' said Alys deliberately.

'It will hardly be Caterin,' said the other woman. Alys nodded. The whole of Balquhidder was buzzing with the news the ubiquitous Sìne had brought her mistress yesterday, of how, while the young Drummonds were down at the Eagleis Beag in the twilight, watching the deathbed with the rest of Sir Duncan's parish, a tall, broad-shouldered stranger had walked into Dalriach, summoned Caterin from her house out into the yard, and spoken to her sternly. Curiously, nobody had got a close sight of the man, and there were many different versions of what he had said, overheard from one corner or another. Caterin herself was no help; she had not uttered a word since, and seemed unable to make any sound at all except, so Sìne reported, a wordless singing of one of the hymns to St Angus.

'I'd best visit her, I suppose,' continued Lady Stewart. 'What is it, Murdo?'

Murdo Dubh replaced his feathered bonnet in order to take it off to them both.

'The Drummonds are wondering,' he said obliquely, 'if Mistress Alys could be sparing them a little longer of her time. In the kirk, if you would be able.'

She looked at him, and then eastward, to where the road out of the glen lifted to the Beannachd Angus stone. Three horsemen – only three? – had halted by the stone. She glanced at Lady Stewart, who nodded slightly.

'I'd be honoured,' she said. Who were the riders? she wondered as she picked her way past the open grave. Who was missing? One of them had not uncovered his head, surely that one was Gil?

The interior of the kirk was dark after the sunshine, and full of Drummond men standing about awkwardly in silence. She followed Murdo in, and Andrew's harsh voice said, 'I thought this was a family matter.'

'Mistress Alys is a good friend to the family,' said Patrick, which did not strike Alys as an adequate answer. Andrew appeared to think the same way, for he snorted and flung away into the chancel where he began extinguishing candles.

'I wished her here,' said Davie. Behind Alys the door was still swinging ponderously shut. The daylight flickered as if a branch stirred across the opening. 'I have a thing to say to you all,' he went on, swallowing hard.

'I am thinking we mostly know it,' said Patrick after a moment.

'What, that I'm not –'

'I never thought it,' said the brother-in-law, 'nor herself neither.'

'That you are not our brother David.' Alys's eyes were becoming used to the gloom, and she saw the glance Patrick cast at Andrew, who was still moving about in the chancel.

'David is my father,' said Davie.

'We thought that must be it. Is he well?'

'He has the joint-ill, but otherwise he's well. He sends you his greetings.'

The conversation seemed quite unreal. Alys stood watching, gauging the reactions of the men present. Patrick was solemn; Jamie was still stiff and embarrassed; Murdo was puzzled. Davie was braced like a crossbow.

'Why?' asked Patrick.

'Why did I deceive you?' There was a break in the voice, as if Davie would weep on little more provocation. 'I never planned to, I swear it. But the *cailleach* took me for – and then how could I –'

'Och, no, that's a wee thing,' said Patrick. 'It gave her such pleasure to think you had come home, it's easy enough forgiven. But why did you come?'

'My father dreamed,' Davie swallowed. 'He dreamed of the house in flames. Three times he dreamed it, and he was wishing to come home and – and warn you all, or see what had come to you – but he had so much to do, and he – he sent me instead.'

'But then the – the Good Folk set fire to the Tigh-an-Teine,' said Jamie slowly, 'only because you were here.'

There was a long, long pause. Then Davie Drummond slowly tipped his head back and howled, one deafening syllable of denial. Alys jumped forward and seized him by the arms, and Murdo Dubh grabbed his shoulders.

'No! It canny be!' he wailed, struggling with them.

Alys tightened her grip, breast to breast, and said, 'Davie! All falls out as God wills! The guilt is not yours, it's –' She checked, swallowed her words and concentrated on holding Davie. After a moment he was still, head bent, saying:

'And she was so good to me, so loving, and first I deceived her and then I slew her –'

'No,' said Andrew. 'You caused someone else to do something that led to her death.'

'I betrayed her.'

'She named you as one of her bairns, as she lay dying,' said Alys. 'And your father as well,' she realized.

'David.' Andrew stepped forward, reached past Alys, tilted Davie's head up to look in his eyes. 'Even Judas will find forgiveness. The guilt is not yours.'

Alys looked over Davie's shoulder towards the door. Gil was standing there, as she had been certain. Their eyes met, and he nodded. He had seen the parallel.

'Judas is not in it,' said Murdo Dubh, letting go his grasp of Davie's shoulders. Davie immediately gave at the knees and slid downwards through Alys's grasp, to collapse in heartbroken sobs on the earthen floor.

'I killed her. It's my fault!'

'Come, come, laddie,' said Patrick stiffly, beginning to be embarrassed. 'There is none of us is blaming you for it, and no need to be carrying on like this at the age you are.'

He paused, and his brother said in his harsh voice, 'We don't know what age he is, Patrick, but I agree he is too old for weeping like a lassie. Get up, David.'

'Davie.' Alys knelt beside the sobbing figure. 'Davie, there is still something you have to tell us, isn't there?'

'Is he not telling us enough?' asked Murdo Dubh. In the corner of her eye Alys was aware that Andrew had lit the candles in the chancel again. No, surely Andrew was standing beside Patrick? She moved so that the light fell on Davie Drummond's face. Beside Patrick, Jamie Beag had stepped back, turning away from the group as if he knew what would come next.

'Davie?' she prompted. The sobs ceased, briefly, and then completely. Davie looked at her warily in the light.

'What do I have to tell you?'

She sat back on her heels, still holding one wet hand.

'What is Davie short for?'

There was another long pause.

'Surely,' said Murdo, 'it's only short for David?' Alys shook her head. 'Though he ought to have been called James like his grandfather,' Murdo added with disapproval.

'Should you, Davie?' Alys rubbed her thumb gently on the back of the hand she held. 'Should you have been called for your grandfather?'

Davie used the other wrist to scrub at wet eyes, and whispered, 'No.'

'Don't be daft, laddie,' said Patrick. 'Who else should you ha been called for? If not your grandfather, then your father, that's proper enough.'

Davie laughed unsteadily.

'No, uncle. I was called for my mother.'

'For your *mother*?' repeated Andrew incredulously. 'Your mother?' And then, with sudden comprehension, 'What was her name, then? Was she Dymphna?'

'Nearly.' Davie sat back, still gripping Alys's hand. 'She was from Ireland, she had the Irish form of the name. Demhna. I was aye called Davie – Devi – to make a difference.'

'Devna,' repeated Andrew.

And no wonder, thought Alys, you could swear your name was Davie Drummond. She glanced over to the door, and saw that Gil was still watching, as fascinated by the scene as she was herself.

'Demhna,' said Patrick slowly, and unbelted his great plaid. He shook it out, and held it to his niece. 'Cover yourself, lassie,' he said gently. 'I can see that you would travel safer dressed as a laddie, but it's not decent now.'

There was a movement in the chancel, and Robert

Montgomery came slowly forward into the nave, as if pulled, with the candle-snuffer still in his hand. He stopped on the edge of the group, staring at the kneeling figure in its midst.

'Are you saying,' he asked, in a tone between hope and amazement, 'are you saying Davie Drummond is a lassie?'

There was a taut silence, in which Davie looked up and met Robert's eye.

'Yes,' she said simply.

'Well,' said Robert, 'Our Lord be thanked for that.' The candle-snuffer fell to the floor, and he strode forward into the group and pulled Davie briskly to her feet, gathering up the plaid in his other hand. 'Cover yourself, as you're bid,' he said, swinging the heavy folds round her, 'and then tell me how we're to get to the Low Countries. I'll want to speak to your father.'

The Drummond men looked at each other, open-mouthed, and then at Davie and Robert, still and handfast in their midst, staring at the light blazing in one another's eyes. Alys, trying not to laugh, slipped out of the circle and went to Gil.

'Have you found who killed James Stirling?' she asked.

'I have,' he said, sounding pleased with himself.

'Good. And here I think,' she said with equal satisfaction, 'we've answered all my lord Blacader's questions, and some more besides.'

'Our Lady preserve me from Hugh Montgomery's wrath,' said Lady Stewart, putting her feet up on a low stool. 'He'll no be pleased at this.'

'The boy's near seventeen,' said Gil, after taking a moment to work it out. As was Alys when we were betrothed, he realized. 'He'll certainly believe he's old enough to make his own decisions.'

'I was,' said Alys, 'and I was right.' He tightened his arm about her shoulders, and they smiled at one another.

'Aye, but lassies are different,' said Lady Stewart.

'I don't see why,' said Sir William. 'Would you let your stepdaughters choose a husband, Marion? But never mind that,' he added hastily, perhaps detecting an argument he might lose. 'Let's have the reckoning from Perth, Cunningham. What was going on? Was Andrew Drummond in it?'

'Only by accident.' Gil frowned, arranging his thoughts. 'He was deep in the family's own matter, and that was linked to the Bishop's matter.'

'Go on, and stop speaking in riddles.' Sir William sat back in his great chair.

'It was Andrew Drummond that got David stolen away thirty years ago. I suppose a boy's jealousy was what drove him, and he was repaid for it, because someone arranged an accident for him. It went wrong, and he lost his voice, and might have lost his life. I think,' he said cautiously, 'he blamed one of the cathedral servants for it, and the man died soon after.'

'Ailidh said he was always jealous,' Alys remarked.

'So did David – this David. Davie. Now, what began things this time was when Doig stole away the singer from Dunblane in March. Drummond recognized what happened, asked about, and when he was next in Perth he went to challenge Doig with it. He met James Stirling, who was close friends with David when they were boys. Stirling had heard of Davie's return, and challenged Drummond about his disappearance, speaking very elliptically.'

Lady Stewart was watching him carefully; Sir William was frowning.

'They went out on to the meadow and talked,' he continued, 'and it seems they made confession to each other. I think they both had a lot to forgive. But that's the end of Andrew Drummond's involvement in Stirling's death, for he went into Perth, met Doig and talked wi him, and then spent the evening on his knees in St John's Kirk.'

'Ah.' Sir William sat back again. 'I'm glad to hear he's out of it.'

'So was it the tanner killed Maister Secretary?' asked Lady Stewart.

'No,' said Gil. 'It was Bishop Brown's steward. He was the spy in the household. A good steward can learn more about his maister's business than the maister himself, and he had the contact with Doig to get the information overseas. I think James Stirling had recognized who was responsible, and he made a serious mistake when he found out.'

'He let the man know he knew,' said Alys, nodding.

'He gave it away,' Gil agreed, 'for the sake of one of his jokes. He had to be killed before he told the Bishop. So when the steward learned from his own servant that Stirling was alone and outside Perth, he sent a message to decoy him to the dog-yard, found a place to hide and killed him with his crossbow, and hurried back to the house to serve out the Bishop's supper, which was a little late that evening. He left his servant to dispose of the body, and hid the bow itself in Stirling's own kist. The tan-yard was handy, and Doig saw a way in, so that was where the body went.'

'But if he was known to be a good shot,' said Alys, 'why did he hide the bow?'

'I suppose he must have panicked.' Gil shook his head. 'There are loose ends, I don't expect we'll ever know exactly what Drummond and Stirling discussed, though I can make a guess, I don't know if the Dunblane cathedral servant fell to his death by accident, and I don't know who killed the man Mitchel though I assume Currie had paid them to attack our men. I'm right sorry about Donal's injury,' he added to Sir William. 'The Blackfriars' Infirmarer thinks he'll do well enough, if it doesny fester.'

'I wonder how old the lassie is?' remarked Lady Stewart, who had clearly stopped attending to Gil. 'And should we make them wed afore they set out?'

'That really would anger my lord Montgomery,' said Alys.

'No, Marion,' said Sir William firmly. 'The laddie, or

lassie, or whatever she is, is none of our mind. Let the Drummonds see to her, and if Robert leaves the glen on the same day she does, there's no need to tell your kinsman the boy wasny alone.'

It was several days more before Gil and Alys left the glen in their turn. It had been good to go hunting or laze in the sunshine after the week of hard work and hard riding it had taken him to untangle the death of James Stirling, but Gil was aware that Archbishop Blacader would prefer a report delivered in person rather than the written account he had sent by one of the Stronvar men. When Tam and Ned arrived from Perth with a good account of Donal's progress, and Lady Stewart declared Steenie well enough to travel, they set out, on a morning full of sunshine and wisps of small white cloud.

Their hosts accompanied them on horseback as far as the Beannachd Aonghais. Crossing the causeway to the Kirkton, Sir William remarked to Gil, 'You said your wife was a surprising creature.' Gil, with a slight effort, recalled the occasion and nodded. 'I'd put it stronger than that, man. I'd say she was byous by-ordinar, the most unusual lassie I've met. You're a lucky man, Maister Cunningham.'

'I know that, sir,' Gil assured him.

The byous by-ordinar lassie, his periwinkle of prowess, had turned her horse at the far end of the bridge, and called to him, her face shadowed under her straw riding-hat.

'Gil, I would like to go into the kirk here before we leave.'

'A good thought,' he agreed.

They left the rest of the party at the crossroads, and walked up to the little kirk. Alys paused at the door, looking out at the loch.

'Davie once said to me,' she said, 'that her father, I suppose she meant David, called this a place where you are close to the kingdom of the angels. I can see why.'

'It's beautiful,' Gil said, looking where she did, at the still reflections and the smoke rising up from the nearby houses.

'Not just that,' she said. 'It feels – it feels as if – one might almost see –'

'That too,' he agreed. She flashed him one of her quick smiles, and pushed open the heavy door.

He spent a little while on his knees, ordering his thoughts about the two puzzles they had unravelled, asking for justice and mercy for all who had done wrong. He felt it unlikely that the King's Justiciars would be able to combine the two virtues for Wat Currie, but something of the sort had been achieved in Dalriach, it seemed.

A sudden flare of light distracted him. Rising and looking about him, he found Alys had moved into the chancel, a place usually forbidden to women unless they held a brush or a duster, and must have lit one of the altar candles. When he followed her there, she was standing before the altar, holding the candle in its pewter candlestick, staring down at her feet. He came to stand beside her, and she nodded at the floor.

'The stone,' she said, 'St Angus' stone. I think he must be under it.'

'Very likely,' agreed Gil, taking the candle from her. 'Shall we go out now? It's a long ride to Stirling.'

'Yes, we should go,' said Alys, still looking at the stone. She bent, tracing the outline chiselled in the sandstone. 'It isn't local stone. Do you suppose it's a portrait of St Angus?'

'Tomb slabs usually are, aren't they?' Gil took hold of her elbow, drawing her away. 'Mind you, his head must have been on the small side.'

'Yes,' she said, studying the outline again, the long robe and broad shoulders, the hands cradling the chalice. 'Yes, let's go. It will be good to go home.'

Author's note

Balquhidder is a real place, but it has changed since the fifteenth century. I found a great deal of value about the history and folklore of the glen in Elizabeth Beauchamp's excellent local history, *The Braes o' Balquhidder: a history and guide for the visitor*. The wider folklore and the Gaelic songs quoted are to be found in Alexander Carmichael's great collection, the *Carmina Gadelica*.

St Angus' little church has long gone, even its successor standing in ruins now, but his grave slab is preserved inside the present Victorian building. A service, in Gaelic and English, to celebrate the bringing of Christianity to the glen, takes place in the church every year on the Wednesday after the second Tuesday of August, the Wednesday closest to St Angus' Day.

Ever since it became a kingdom, Scotland has had two native languages, Gaelic (which in the fifteenth century was called Ersche) and Scots, both of which you will find used in the Gil Cunningham books. I have translated the Gaelic where needful, and those who have trouble with the Scots could consult the online Dictionary of the Scots Language, to be found at http://www.dsl.ac.uk/dsl/